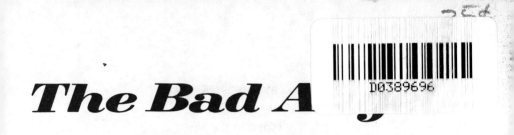

The Bad A

ALSO BY ERNEST K. GANN

Island in the Sky
Blaze of Noon
Benjamin Lawless
Fiddlers Green
The High and the Mighty
Soldier of Fortune
Twilight for the Gods
The Trouble with Lazy Ethel
Fate Is the Hunter
Of Good and Evil
In the Company of Eagles
Song of the Sirens
The Antagonists
Band of Brothers
Flying Circus
Brain 2000
The Aviator
The Magistrate
Gentlemen of Adventure
The Triumph

THE
BAD
ANGEL

Ernest K. Gann

ARBOR HOUSE

New York

0 6 4 1 4 5 6 9

Manufactured in the United States of America

10 9 8 7 6 5 4 3 2 1

Library of Congress Cataloging in Publication Data

Gann, Ernest Kellogg, 1910–
The bad angel.

I. Title.
PS3513.A56B35   1987   813'.54   87-11429
ISBN 0-87795-929-3

Text design by Maggie Cullen

For my dear friend Hank Ketchum,
who goaded me into it

A SPECIAL NOTE FROM THE AUTHOR

This is the story of an international outrage that has escaped the truth, while bathed in notoriety.

We are fed all kinds of claims and statistics by various government agencies—all designed to demonstrate their diligence and alarm us. While most of these polemics are sincere and accurate, the sad facts are that we have merely stepped on the tail of this terrible reptile. So far the body has always wiggled away and stayed in business.

There are times when an author's admixture of facts and fiction has an uncanny way of becoming actual history. Almost incredibly, characters who have been lurking in the imagination for years are discovered in real life. The effect is at first disturbing, and then exciting, and finally puzzling: How can it be that this very real person matches so exactly someone imagined six months ago? Is there some kind of pattern? Does such honest coincidence mean that if you live long enough, you will meet at least one of everyone?

The sequence of international events can be even more perplexing. If, as Napoleon once suggested, imagination rules the world, is outright plagiarism an irresistible bedfellow of history?

The research on this book was begun in early 1984 and intensified all through 1985. The actual writing of the story commenced on October 1 of that year. After some six months of the usual travail involved in the development of any book, the print and video news media seemed to be copying the writing of my pen. Time after time, events written months before became fact, and the similarities were shocking. It was as if my pen had some mysterious influence on events—which, of course, was ridiculous.

As of 1987, real happenings and personages still seem to be mimicking those I have written about. If certain episodes herein seem improbable, think back a year or even six months and you may recognize that they are happening or have happened. I can only assume this strange concurrence will persist.

If what I have written, in some unholy union with real life, will encourage those who are trying valiantly to curtail the flow of drugs to this country and halt the subjugation of our youth, then I will be satisfied.

"That humanity at large will ever be able to dispense with Artificial Paradise seems very unlikely. Most men and women lead lives at the worst so painful, at the best so monotonous, poor, and limited that the urge to escape, the longing to transcend themselves if only for a few moments, is and has always been one of the principal appetites of the soul. Art and religion, carnivals and saturnalia, dancing and listening to oratory—all these have served, in H. G. Wells' phrase, as Doors in the Wall. All the vegetable sedatives and narcotics, all the euphorics that grow on trees, the hallucinogens that ripen in berries or can be squeezed from roots—all, without exception, have been known and systematically used by human beings from time immemorial."

—Aldous Huxley, *The Doors of Perception* (1954)

The Bad Angel

1

So it begins.

Now don't make this some frivolous female's journal, or a middle-aged lady's lament. Your intention is to give with the words so there will be some sort of record of what has befallen the survivors of this little family. No, cross out same. I must not think as a survivor. You there, Lily Rogers, straighten up. Put on your mental corset and be damned grateful for what you have. This record is a catharsis. Good for the soul . . . I guess.

It says everything should be just dandy here in the nation's capital, and it says we should all be enjoying our newfound status, not to mention the luxury of a regular paycheck. It sure beats the cattle business—if ever it could be called a business. But something is kinky somewhere. Whatever is awry, it won't stand up and be recognized. But it certainly is a presence, and it stinks just enough to make me uneasy. Like it had bad breath, and exhales in my direction. And still I can't seem to put my finger on whatever it is.

I'm beginning to wonder if maybe I'm slightly paranoid about my surroundings, not to mention recent events. A few pages back I was just trying to write in this fancy little book as an experiment—something to keep me out of mischief. But ever since we came here to Sin City, it seems to haunt my thoughts. Sometimes I wonder if I'm just making mischief that might do some real harm.

I'm beginning to wonder if I should cease and desist immediately, and get on to more productive . . .

She wrote in an easy flourishing script, which ill matched the green leather notebook she had come to regard as her "first and last ever" journal. She had tinkered with the first page several times, adding curlicues to the graceful sweep of her letters and embellishing the lines here and there with wavelike underlinings and decorative asterisks.

The Journal of LILY ROGERS
Wife to LEE ROGERS
While he is serving as a
Representative from the state of Montana in
The United States Congress

She was tall, blond, quite spare, and fading slightly in the manner of Anglo-Saxons who blossom early and are then driven by some ancient residual impulse to spend as much time as they can challenging the natural forces. Now she was crumbling a trifle about the corners of her mouth and eyes, yet obviously years would pass before major deterioration became evident.

Have an honest look at yourself these days. Are you a dingbat? Could be? But you never think of yourself as one of those women with premonitions or even as especially intuitive. As far as you've ever known, your emotions have never run any mysterious courses, and you've never felt the need of a "shrink" to tickle your libido, or whatever those people do to other troubled human beings. You're no movie star, that's for sure. You're just the daughter of a Montana farm machinery dealer and for the past nineteen years your emotions and fortunes have been alternately inspired and curdled by your husband, Lee; your sons, Jack and Robert; and your daughter, Fay. (Sometimes I think that should be spelled "fey," which she certainly is.) And you should say "our" because Lee is as responsible and devoted to the kids as you are.

I'm so proud of my husband, although his fierce determination almost frightens me . . . sometimes. Still, if you can have love and pride together, then . . .

The black bull resembled a locomotive and he roared of his agonies until he could be heard all over the high pastureland. He pawed at the earth, sending up explosions of dust, and his powerful muscles flexed in a mighty effort to resist the forces against him. Young Rogers had roped him in the middle of a glade, dallied the rope to his saddle horn, and was now trying to haul him toward a tree. If he could make even half a turn around a tree, then some of the pressure on the rope and his horse would be relieved.

He was losing ground because no saddle horse could match the brute power of a full-grown bull.

Young men matured early on a Montana ranch, and Jack Rogers was no exception. At the high school in nearby Clayburn, he was elected outstanding athlete of the year and his scholastic record was the highest in his graduating class. Everyone in this part of Montana knew young Rogers was a winner; most of all his father, who watched the tug-of-war with increasing misgivings.

The father saw how the rope pinned his son's leg against the saddle and how, step by step, his horse was losing ground. Any moment the horse might be pulled over backward, for this bull was the largest in their herd, and every beast on the place, including the other bulls, stayed out of his way.

Except for a Montana porcupine.

Somehow the bull and the porcupine had met face-to-face. A challenge was met with a threat and suddenly a hundred-odd quills stabbed into the bull's snout. Howling his torment, the bull rampaged the pastureland until Jack succeeded in getting a rope on him. Then fifteen hundred pounds of muscle went wild. Insane with pain and anger, the bull had no intention of being dragged anywhere behind a horse. He tugged, dodged from side to side, planted his forelegs firmly, and threatened to charge.

The father thought that an older hand would have released his dally long ago and let the monster suffer. He was also reminded that trying to improve the physical welfare of cattle was rarely appreciated.

"Let him go!" the father shouted.

He was not heard. The son shook his head and set his jaw while he urged his horse to even greater effort.

Jack was like that—all Rogers were like that. Iron-head stubborn. Something had to be done. Immediately.

The father squeezed his legs. His horse, Tango, plunged forward. If he could knock the bull off-balance, Jack might have time to gain a few feet. Hit him again if necessary, until Jack could take his rope around that nearby tree.

Tango was a strong quarterhorse and he seemed to know exactly what his master had in mind. He collided violently with the bull's rump and knocked him aside. Young Rogers almost gained the tree before the bull roared his fury and planted himself again. He tossed his head toward the sky as if to display the quills puncturing his face and he snorted sprays of mucus in every direction. His roaring and howling became continuous and his wild eyes sought everywhere for vengeance.

"Let him go, Jack!"

Either he failed to hear his father above the din, or his natural determination had taken charge. His horse was doing his utmost, but he was no match for his adversary.

Lee Rogers spun Tango around and charged the bull again, hitting the hindquarters so hard the bull's legs went right out from under him. The son seized the moment and managed to drag the bull far enough to take half a turn of the rope around the tree.

Good enough, Lee Rogers thought. With a second rope around his hind legs, they could go to work on the poor fellow. As always, there was a pair of pliers in his small saddlebag.

He had just taken his lariat in hand when he saw his son's rope leap into the air like a striking snake. It had parted at the hondo.

The bull was free.

The father saw the bull turn toward him and lower his head. There was not even an instant of indecision before he charged and struck Tango full bore. Rogers hit the ground so hard he lost consciousness momentarily. Then the light and shadow became recognizable again, and he saw the bull standing like a mountain only a few feet away from him.

He pushed himself to his knees, hoping to escape.

The bull lowered his head. The next charge, Rogers knew, would be final. A total end to things for Lee Rogers, father of three. God Almighty! All over so soon? Not even the first rancher to die this way. His brain saw a flashing image of himself crushed by the huge black bulk.

The bull hesitated and shook his head vigorously. The porcupine quills glistened in the sunlight. Rogers tried to scramble away on his knees, but he seemed to have lost all strength. He moved as in a dream.

Just as the bull set himself for a charge, something dashed between them. Rogers barely had time to identify the object as his son. Now on foot, Jack kicked the bull in the snout and ran to one side. The bull grunted, bellowed in rage, then took after him.

Lee managed to reach his feet and saw his son scramble up a fall of shale. He reached a shelf and leaped out to catch the branch of a sycamore tree.

Beneath him the bull became mired in the loose shale.

"Beat it, Dad! While you have the chance!"

Now, months later, there were patches of snow in the glade, and Lee Rogers thought those words were the last he remembered Jack speaking. Even now, paused in the same location, he could hear the mischief and triumph in his son's voice.

It was only two nights after Jack had saved his life that the terrible thing happened. Not that Jack's quick thinking and courage had been any surprise. Their relationship had never been of the ordinary father-son variety; they had been man-to-man friends; a priceless link existed between them that nothing could destroy.

Or so he had always believed.

He was thinking of Jack again as he stood looking down upon

the rolling sweeps of land he had known ever since he could remember anything at all. His own father had brought him here to this special glade many times—those glorious days when his pony, Buster, was hardly more than a yearling and he was not much more. Once his father had said, "Let what I tell you stay in your brain long after you grow into my boots. Your grandfather Lee, whose name you wear, brought me to this very place—I must have been nine or ten then. I remember his words so well I can almost repeat them verbatim.

"Says he to me, 'Someday this land will be yours. But you really won't own it, nor will the bank own it. God owns it and you're just a caretaker. Be kind to the forest and meadows. It's not a very big outfit, but big enough. It goes from Gibbet Peak over there, down to the valley about to where Ginger Creek cuts through to the rail line. Nobody ever got rich outta ranchin' and I sure haven't. Nor will you. Just figure it's a good life, and defend it with your life because this is the toughest but best state in the U.S.A. Runnin' cattle here is a gamble, and most times makin' a profit is just plumb impossible. But when you see the little calves sashayin' along the grass in the spring, and the replacement heifers chasin' after a bighorn sheep just because they got so much energy and so little sense . . . then, son, you figure this place is neighbor to heaven. And nobody can tell you different.' "

Lee Rogers tried to smile as his father's words came echoing back to him on the November wind. Three generations of Rogerses now on his land, and a fourth who had been coming along just fine. Son Jack had been a natural with cattle. He was able to do just about everything on the ranch—until the sonsabitches got to him. Oh, they knew a leader when they found one, all right. They didn't know that Jack could make a horse do things the beast never thought possible. They didn't care if Jack could bring a prolapsed cow back to health as if her birthing had been normal—magic it was. And they cared even less if he knew just when to pull a calf, how to brand and cut, and how to sense the urgings of a herd's movements so they would drive easily to where they should go, rather than scatter all over the state of Montana.

6

The sonsabitches knew from observation that Jack was a leader in his high school, and if they could hook him, then for sure others would follow suit. They didn't care if he had risked his own life to save his dad's. Without hesitation.

The smile that Lee Rogers attempted collapsed and was replaced by a grimness about his mouth that was never to be seen before the thing happened—before Jack was no more. Sure, Jack had been the apple of his eye. But he had managed to keep it to himself, because it would never do to make daughter Fay feel underestimated, or let Robert, the youngest of the Rogers clan, discover that he wasn't the most important kid in Elk County.

Lee Rogers raised his head from the sagging it seemed to have acquired since the terrible thing happened, and he braced his heavy shoulders. He squinted at the Bear Paw Mountains standing out like the cutting edge of a saw on the distant horizon, and he thought that after all his forty-three years of looking at the state's terrain, there was just no place in the world to compare with right where he stood. Holy cow, you could reach out and touch the cobalt sky. When his eyes were younger, he remembered, his sight was so keen he shot and killed flies on the manure heap down by the barns with his air rifle. Hell, there never had been any smog in Montana, and there still wasn't except in maybe a few places like Billings or Butte, and then rarely. For sure, here were mountains and plateaus, and mighty weather to remind people down to the last woman and man that they were no bigger than insects.

His father had been right. The Rogers tribe lived next door to heaven—at least in the summertime and on rare days like this one.

He thought about the black bull and how Jack had thrown himself directly in its path. He frowned and shook his head vigorously to shake away his melancholy. Heaven? Right now this place was a corner of hell, an empty cesspool still stinking of people who should be dead. In the old days, he thought, they would have been, by God.

The kind of people who got Jack into trouble would have answered for it right away. A rope around their necks or some lead in their heads would have put them out of business forever. Now things were different. Nobody knew who they were or where they had gone. And if they did get caught, they barely got a spanking. In Malaysia they would be hung for the same crime. Right now.

Even in his own father's time, any individual who would exploit school kids the way they did with Jack would have been perforated with thirty-caliber holes before he could clear out of Clayburn. And no one, including the sheriff, would have asked or said anything. "Unidentified man found on road. Suicide." That would have been the end of the problem as well as the man. But these days?

Montana had changed along with the rest of the world. Some mighty crummy people had found their way to fresh pasturage, and they were smart enough to start with the schools because people who had lived in these parts for a few years were old-fashioned enough to believe in family, the church, the American flag—and of course the quality of their cattle. They believed. They ate meat, and they lived a long time. Cholesterol? People needed the protein absorbed from good beef. And the wheatlands? They stretched for hundreds of miles. Enough grain to feed the world? Maybe man couldn't live by bread alone, but he sure could stay healthy with a combination of the two. Only the newcomers ate pasta and frozen fish and voted Democrat.

He hitched up his worn chaps, polished with the oil of thousands of calves and the friction of years in the saddle. He eased down until he squatted on his heels Indian-fashion. He plucked a blade of the good pasture grass, a native fescue his father had said was the best cattle feed in the world. He stuck the blade between his teeth and worked it across his lips and listened to the silence. Sometimes the peace was broken when a jay called, and once a passing transcontinental jet made a sound across the sky that reminded him of a bear he had once encountered. Seven or eight years back it must have been when that old boy was guarding a cave high up on the mountain, obviously figuring the mountain was his and not, as the deed read, Rogers family property. He rose on his hind legs and made the same jet sound, and there was an immediate choice of shooting him or getting the hell out of the neighborhood. The horse, big old Belinda, a wise old mare of independent mind, actually made the choice. She whirled without hesitation and clattered over the shale until she came panting to a halt half a mile away.

Now there was only this vast stillness, the calm before the war. That's what it was going to be, all right. Now, quite suddenly, when his tear ducts had damn well run short of water, he could see it more clearly than he ever had before. Lee Rogers, who some time back had found himself fighting a dismal war in Vietnam, and had a purple heart to prove it, was now about to engage in a more personal war. Maybe he wouldn't get to the same guys who killed Jack, but, by God, he would exterminate all their kind if it could be done.

And it must be done.

The first battle was already won because there just weren't enough people in this particular voting district who would consider that Lee Rogers might not know what the hell he was doing. This was home. He had always been just one of the locals; everybody knew the Rogers family and believed in the same things they did. So if Lee wanted to represent the First District in Congress, why not vote for him? His opposition had been an ex–real estate salesman from Honeywell County named Boniface, who didn't stand a prayer even if he promised free irrigation for all applicants.

The results were downright embarrassing. Boniface gathered a few votes, but Lee Rogers was a shoo-in as representative from the great state of Montana.

It was going to be hard to get used to that kind of political lingo, especially for a guy who had never even seen Washington, D.C., and had always been just a tad suspicious of all politicians, no matter who and what they were. That would include presidents, Democrat or Republican. And now, by God, look who was going to be sitting in the Congress of the United States. And about to start a war.

He rose to stand erect and watched a pair of Hereford bulls in the cut below who were snorting and kicking up ground and butting heads to prove how tough they were. Their behavior reminded him of his own rampant fury when he had tried in vain to get something done about Jack's situation—so it could never happen again to some other local kid.

The sheriff said, "Lee, I'm sure sorry about your boy. He was something special—always. It's a terrible thing, but I can't get a hold on it. These guys come here from nowheres and go back to nowheres after they've made a few sales. Tomorrow they might operate down Billings way, and the next day up by Great Falls. Gettin' a rope on 'em is not easy."

Of course it wasn't easy, and going right up the law-enforcement line had not accomplished much of anything except to educate two brokenhearted parents in the nightmare of narcotics. New York, Boston, Chicago, Los Angeles—yes, it was at least partly understandable in the big cities, where people just existed instead of lived, but it was just plumb incredible that such things could be going on in Montana. Talking to people at the Drug Enforcement Administration was like talking to all bureaucrats. The sympathy faucet was turned on for ten minutes, then referred to higher authority. Out of my territory. We'll work on it even so. My ass is covered.

He heard a soft, rhythmic crunching behind him and knew without turning that his horse was working his way toward him, nose-to-grass. It was going to be hard to desert a good old fellow like Tango. They must have ridden thousands of miles together over the years— maybe more, everything reckoned. Maybe it would set fire to a few Washington asses if he rode ol' Tango right into the House of Representatives. Maybe it would get their attention long enough to say, "Hey! We're being attacked! Are we going to fight with both fists or just lie down and die?"

Very peculiar, he thought, how a person could suddenly get all fired up about flag and country. Just don't forget that patriots with loud mouths are inclined to believe their own bullshit. And they sometimes lead their followers into some ugly ways. Still . . . it would be mighty sad to live in a nation of noodle-heads. Maybe this was Bunker Hill time, or another Gettysburg?

He smiled. And who the hell are you? Paul Revere?

Never mind. People could go right ahead and say Lee Rogers was off his nut. Lots of them would say, "What the hell're you raving about? I don't see any real problems. My kids are doing well in school and so are all my neighbors', at least almost all. I couldn't care less about a handful of junkies. You want to get your sights set on more important things. Like the budget and inflation. Stuff that affects me. I don't even know anybody who takes dope, except maybe my aunt Lois, who takes stuff for arthritis. And anyway, things change. Maybe it will just go away."

Now looka. Looka me and mellow up. Businessman, tha's me. Once I poor Panama boy. Now you don' see that boy and I never see me again. I new man—businessman. I deal. I drive the avenues. I big. People smile. They wave. They know who is me. I don' even need one dolla ta get laid, understan'? A little crack here, a little stick there, a gram here and I take my choice. I gotta beat 'em away from me.

Okay? You wanna be businessman? You gotta know your product. Understan' you ain't gonna fiddle around with, like, Romilar cough syrup, or powdered belladonna, or Ban deodorant, or airplane glue. Same goes for, like, amphetamines, Benzedrine, Methedrine, Dilaudid, Talwin, same for Librium, Valium, Miltown, Seconal, Nembutal. Time wasters, understan'?

You seventeen? Don' tell me no fairy tales 'bout what you hear. You worry? Stop it. You afraid the narcs'll bite you? Shit. They make a big stink an' you smell it, but it all fades away. Think about Frank Matthews. He fades to South America with over a hundred million bucks, where he lives to this day. He wasn't even a poor Panama boy. Just black. You think you stop here? Man, you just begin. Maybe you end up a big boy like Marco Fedles, or some Chinese—like Hsu Shui. They really *big,* man! You, me . . . just little turds compared to them. Fuck 'em. We got plenty a action right here.

Build your business. You got, say, twenty percent a the students now. Okay, say the jocks're smokin' pot on weekends. Give 'em a nibble of free crack now and then—the big guys, the leaders, understan'?

You say, I be the man with the Porsche, and whatta you got? Now you bound to meet assholes. They all the time wanna tell their momma or some cop how you is sellin'. You stop an' think. How do I shut up this jerk? Maybe I hit him, but maybe he hit me back, and he's bigger'n me. You poke your finger in his kidney, which is right here. You show him this knife I give you free of charge, and you say if he opens his mouth again it will not be your finger you gonna poke in his kidney till he's dead. No sound. No nothin'. Just good-bye, asshole. He never trouble you again.

All the time remember, don' believe what come to your ears except from me. I'm your angel, man.

2

The sodden air bubbled up reluctantly from the Colombian jungle, waiting, it seemed, for that precise moment in the day when the adiabatic lapse rate would release the eternal showers of the region. Here amid the great trees of Colombia, the birds lamented, screeched, and persistently squawked their self-importance. The army ants paraded disdainfully past the giant slugs, and the bright blue butterflies fluttered and chandelled through the tangled botanical halls of their habitat. The canaries sang almost continuously, proclaiming this wilderness as their own and seeming to direct their more resentful stanzas only at man's intrusions. If they actually despaired of the neighborhood's recent strange activities, then heavy vengeance was inflicted by the lightest of their compatriots, for nothing so ephemeral could inflict such misery as the malarial mosquito. And in this section of Colombia, there was a multitude.

According to their every-evening compulsion, the mosquitoes rose in swarms from their breeding places and deployed in swift armadas searching for blood. They found it in the imported *pisadores* who had lived with malaria since birth anyway and were more than willing to waste themselves further at wages previously unheard of anywhere in South America.

The *pisadores* were peasants who hailed mostly from Bolivia, Peru, and Ecuador. They were hired because their Colombian supervisors were not given to trusting their own nationals in so clandestine an operation, and their duties were simple. They had only to stomp all day long, barefoot, in a mixture of kerosene and coco leaves. The result brought them pay far beyond their understanding, and they thought it wonderful that anyone would bother to go to so much trouble since the leaves could be sucked or simply chewed to achieve a similar sense of well-being. Sometimes they sang along with the canaries to relieve the monotony. They laughed together and told wild stories of other ways to benefit from the coca leaf. Ancient witches, they said, rubbed their bodies with the stuff or inserted it into their vaginas and were then able to fly with the birds.

The *pisadores* died with almost predictable regularity and no one, least of all their employers, cared. The survivors returned home with funds enough to assure their comforts for years if they minded their own business.

The *pisadores* relieved all the curses laid upon them since the beginning of time by chewing on the supplies of coco leaves, which were also imported. Their lifetime devotion to the habit left them suspended in a blissful and stupid mental haze, and yet they remained capable of elementary tasks. Even the most muddleheaded could be taught his minor functions in the manufacture of the stuff.

Although there were other sources of supply, most of the leaves of the coco plant were brought down to this place from the Huallaga Valley of Peru. After the crushing, the leaves were further moistened with a mixture of sodium carbonate and kerosene, then transferred to a separator. A two-percent solution of hydrochloric acid was added and the whole well shaken. After separation, the liquid was drawn off from below, placed in another separator, and the process repeated three times. The alkaloid remained in the first separator as an acid hydrochlorate.

The final product was joined in ether while more sodium carbonate was added, and the mixture stirred constantly. At last the true cocaine was precipitated and promptly collected by the manager, a fat, slovenly man with tiny eyes and an inexhaustible supply of sweat. Day or night he dripped liters of sweat, and though he wiped at himself constantly, there was always more to come.

Here, where the standards were relatively high, the manager himself saw that the precious product was further purified by recrystallization in a mixture of acetone and benzene. He always examined the final product suspiciously, as if it had somehow betrayed him by becoming a powder, and he often sniffed a pinch to confirm his displeasure.

The manager knew that "Camp FARC" was owned by the Revolutionary Armed Forces of Colombia, the armed wing of the Colombian Communist party. He was justifiably terrified of his superiors and came very close to kissing their tennis-shoed feet on those rare occasions when a few of the leaders arrived by helicopter to make an inspection tour. He was grateful that they were mainly interested in knowing of any interference from the Nineteenth of April movement, a rival insurgent group known as M-19. Both organizations were the result of thirty years of political violence in Colombia, and each blamed the other for any recent atrocities. Both groups depended mainly on the manufacture and distribution of narcotics for their arms and even their very existence. Despite their lack of popular support, they were far from tolerant of the slightest interference with what they considered their ordained mission, and the government of Colombia had not demonstrated any enthusiasm or success in thwarting them.

The chieftain of FARC was Marco Fedles, born in Malta but long since a self-proclaimed citizen of the world. He had surfaced in Colombia after a long career in crime and wit-living in Morocco, Spain, Paraguay, and Brazil. Although he had derived no more than momentary spells of wonder and amusement during his cursory study of Marx and Engels, he had been known to order the instant execution of any colleague who displayed the slightest lack of devotion to the communist cause or to Fedles himself. While he admired the machinations of the Sicilian and the American Mafia, he considered them gone soft with time and bound for extinction since they lacked political drive. There was nothing like the power of naïve people.

Fedles had no intimates. Those few who knew him said he was unquestionably the cruelest and yet the most charming man they had ever met. They also hinted that his lust for money was being replaced by an obsession with power. It was he, they whispered, who had engineered the assassination of the Colombian minister of justice, Rodrigo Lara-Bonilla, and the later gunning down of eight other judges. Fedles had never been seen to carry a weapon, yet he had caused the deaths of hundreds with only a nod of his head. He took pleasure in viewing the remains of those who had displeased him and saying softly, "Now you are nothing." Then, man or woman, he would kick the corpse in the face.

None of these rumors and allegations bothered Oscar Brimmer, once of Tonapah, Nevada, where during nearly forgotten years he had operated a small airport. According to his American license, which he pulled from his wallet on occasion and stared at as if it were a complicated document, he was qualified as an airline transport pilot. It was the highest classification issued by the FAA, but Oscar Brimmer knew it was now meaningless.

"I are one of the Untouchables," he was fond of orating when his lips were loose with whiskey. Yet no matter how much he drank, he never made further disclosure. Few pilots were still alive who remembered why a man of his flying experience should have become so undesired in his profession. And drunk or sober, no amount of cajoling could pry the story out of him; nor would he divulge any detail of his present employment.

Brimmer, a man of extraordinarily frugal speech when sober, did admit that his nose was sixty-four years old and troublesome. It blossomed a funereal purple when he was drinking, and the surface was normally sun-scorched to a flaky pastry, which caused him considerable distress. For in spite of the nearly total disintegration of his once tolerable appearance, he remained surprisingly vain and even carried a small pocket mirror to ease his plucking at the ravaged layers of skin on his beak.

Oscar Brimmer was in exile here and in his own country. Now, it seemed his loneliness came upon him more frequently and supported on great waves of self-condemnation. Once known as the Loch Ness Monster because of his onetime vow to retire to Scotland and drink the land dry, he now remained sober only when he was scheduled to fly. It was a task he performed with consummate skill and it remained his ultimate passion.

It was the waiting for departure that nearly drove Oscar Brimmer mad. After a brief inspection of the ancient DC-3 that would be his night-borne chariot for the next fourteen hours, there was nothing for him to do except lean against its tail, pop quinine pills against the possibility of yet another onslaught of malaria, and wish he were aloft where at least a man had a few stars and clouds for company. He watched while the manager supervised the loading of his cargo. He saw the rivers of sweat irrigate the folds of fat about the man's face and neck and he thought how much he hated him.

The manager was an animal, he thought. He cheated on everything possible, including Brimmer's flight pay, which was adjusted according to the cargo carried. The sonofabitch should be kept in a cage.

Until all was ready, Brimmer would fret at the mosquitoes, waggle the duffel-bag pouches drooping from his chin, and hum old jazz tunes in a sort of monotonous gargle. He knew the flight would be sprinkled with uncommon dangers, and the realization that very few pilots would willingly face similar challenges, regardless of the money involved, pleased him. He had once confessed that he cared little if he died as long as his tomb was an airplane. Meanwhile, if by his remaining skill he survived, there was certainly enough money available to buy the most rambunctious whore in Colombia, and what was left over funded his worldwide love affair with gambling.

Brimmer was seldom required to fly more than twice a month, and his dispatching always followed a similar pattern. A FARC courier would arrive at the camp bearing a worn briefcase for the manager, whose dumpling fingers would tremble badly as he read his instructions. The forms inside would specify the precise weights and packaging of cocaine to be shipped, along with the weight of high-potency marijuana (sinsemilla), packed in a certain number of bales.

Once all was aboard the DC-3, including Brimmer, the manager made a final and most meticulous check of the cargo, locked the door from the outside, and sealed it with heavy plastic tape. He then applied his signature and droplets of perspiration to all of the forms, signing with a flourish that helped only a little to bolster his confidence. He was acutely aware that should there be the slightest discrepancy between form and actual delivery, he would be better off swallowing the barrel of the Luger that always hung from his belt.

Once the tape seal was in place, the manager waddled around to the nose of the DC-3 and looked up at the cockpit. He expressed the wish that Brimmer crash into the sea and walked away without smiling.

Now it was Brimmer's turn to officiate, and he had often thought it a pity that the actual exercise of his talent and skill was invisible to the rest of the world. He knew only that the consignees of his cargo would be waiting at his destination, some seven hours' flying time away. He knew nothing of the weather or the winds en route, nor was he offered any information on the anticipated conditions at the open field in Arkansas where he would land. Regardless, it was his duty to find it, as he often grumbled, "by osmosis."

He had one invaluable aid in the long darkness to come. At the approximate time of his approach to the area, those who awaited his arrival would activate a weak homing signal for one minute, then turn it off again. After five minutes, they would repeat the procedure, and each time the needle of his direction finder would swing automatically toward the signal. The chances of the signal being heard by the wrong people were almost nil. The frequency was discreet, the range no more than thirty miles, and the times of transmission too short for an accurate fix by triangulation. It was, Brimmer thought, a thoroughly professional operation unmarred by the makeshift naïvetés of so many others.

Once he was gone into the twilight sky, no one at the camp wanted to see Oscar Brimmer again—at least until a meeting was unavoidable. Even the imported *pisadores* whose coca-leaf minds were numbed beyond redemption considered the abuse of his body shameful. They thought it very odd that he would never touch the products they manufactured, and yet lost himself in liquids. They called him "the man with six livers," and the sight of such wreckage destroyed their faith in the aging of human flesh.

Brimmer flew the DC-3 alone; no need for a copilot if a man knew every twist of the hydraulic system and the fuel system, which were all the complications the old goat had anyway. The Pratt and Whitney engines would run forever as long as their enormous thirst for lubricating oil was met and the rest of the aircraft just followed along. Best of all were the extra fuel tanks in the cabin, which was one of the reasons Brimmer had chosen a DC-3 over any other aircraft. People in this business got into trouble when they had to land for fuel. The DC-3 could make the round trip and still carry the load. One landing. One exposure. As long as the DC-3 remained airborne, Oscar Brimmer could thumb his sun-mauled nose at the world.

The routing of his flight was bold and uncompromising. Brimmer took off from the strip beside the factory, climbed to a hundred feet above the forest, and remained there until the coastline became visible. Then, in the very last of the light, he descended to a comfortable fifty feet, where he set his course to the northwest and his altimeter to zero. Thus he held a slight margin against collision with the surface of the sea and his only immediate concern was the possibility of a chance encounter with a large vessel. He was convinced the DC-3 would emerge the survivor from any encounter with a yacht or small fishing boat, so let them beware.

What did increasingly concern him were the various technical elements that his own countrymen had recently employed to discover his presence over the southern Caribbean, but so far he had not experienced any trouble. Of course, there was a chance that aircraft with "look down" radar might spot the moving blip of his DC-3, but as yet those wide-eyed instruments did not cover the whole of the Caribbean, nor even the Gulf of Mexico. Furthermore, the time difference between discovery and apprehension was always in his favor. The islands of Jamaica and Cuba offered protection from horizontal radar, and Brimmer reasoned that he would still rather carry out his mission in an airplane of total dependability than in a faster, much smaller craft that might or might not be more difficult to identify. The little Cessnas, Beechcrafts, and God-only-knew-what were flown by more timorous traffickers. They were usually stupid youngsters, Brimmer reminded himself. Time behind bars was not reckoned by the amount smuggled.

As his hands caressed the control wheel of the DC-3, Brimmer chuckled softly to himself. Hell, it wasn't only the money involved in this here operation. Why ride on the back of a mouse when a lion was available?

As Lee Rogers rode down the mountain, he saw his house nestled among the cottonwood trees and the old red barn beyond it. Both, he thought, could use some paint. He tried not to think of what the barn did to him these days. God Almighty, on a day like this, a true chinook day that sometimes made Montana seem like a suburb of Florida, a man just had to throw a saddle on old Tango and have a look around the place—see how those Hereford shorthorn crosses were doing over in the east section. Lots of people who didn't know any better thought eight thousand acres was one hell of a big spread even if it was only a little bitty outfit compared to some like the I-X east of Great Falls, and Box Elder over by Lewiston.

Making a cow-calf outfit pay on only eight thousand acres some-times had nothing to do with reality. It wasn't the best of land, so forty acres per animal unit was about all a person could expect. That was roughly two hundred head of mother cows plus some replacement heifers that had to be carried until they started producing.

The price of calves on the hoof at Billings was about sixty to seventy cents a hundredweight, *if* the stock was good and *if* a lot of buyers happened to be in the mood to bid. That was about the same price offered in the early 1970s—and meanwhile every damn little thing a rancher bought to keep his place alive seemed to have about tripled and often quadrupled. A Ford tractor could be bought then for eight thousand dollars. Now the same damn machine cost eigh-teen thousand. It was no wonder old Cecil down at the bank said, "Lee, something's got to give pretty quick. When in the name of Almighty God are you going to come to your senses and sell the place to some rich easterner, or start a dude outfit or something where you're not wearing yourself to a frazzle trying to make ends meet?"

Lee Rogers's answer was always quick and predictable: "Now come on, you old miser. Share the wealth. I've got kids to think about and we'll make out—somehow. The place is their future."

Both men laughed sourly and agreed they might as well talk bullshit as facts.

There were many times when Rogers wondered how much of a favor he'd be doing his heirs by leaving them a ranch that had teetered on the edge of bankruptcy for the past ten years. Lily sure wouldn't need a chunk of raw real estate hanging around her widow's neck if his ticker went bad or some hot-rodding cowboy with a skinful decided he owned the whole Montana highway.

As he rode down from the hills and approached the old barn, he realized it was still standing more or less erect only because his grandfather had been a stickler for good lumber and solid workmanship. He'd settled for only the best. Today, that wasn't always possible. The substitute was mule stubbornness and a flat refusal to view the ranch from the sharp end of a pencil. It was downright un-American to admit you were going down the drain. It was impossible to believe that if a man worked hard and gave of himself in a basic industry like food, he would not be rewarded with a decent living.

Who the hell would dare to say the Rogers family couldn't make it if they worked hard together? A family like the Rogerses could accomplish anything they put their minds to. Of course the numbers the last few years were discouraging. The calves he had sold just last month went to feedlots, and naturally the man who bought them expected to make some money. Next the packinghouse would buy them from the feeder, and he made out fine, but the fancy restaurants still wouldn't have their tenderloins, and Mcdonald's still wouldn't have their hamburgers. The steers would be butchered and sold to stores that made some money, and the truck drivers who transported the carcasses and cuts from here to there would make very good money. None of those people, except the feedlot variety, were obliged to spend much of their time arguing with the elements. Which was why, he thought, ranchers were ranchers and just naturally drifted a little apart from sensible individuals.

Now a new and unforeseen threat had taken firm hold on the scheme of things and there was no guessing where it would finally lead. It was now unfashionable to eat meat! Doctors and dietitians and various faddists of all descriptions were saying meat was bad for Americans and was responsible for the high measure of heart problems. God Almighty! Meat—good grass-fed meat, built in America! Americans were the strongest people in the world, and anyone who doubted that the availability of meat had anything to do with it was just plumb ill informed. Lee Rogers, grandson of a meat provider, son of a meat provider, was going to stick with the business until Montana was covered with palm trees. The world was just a little crazy right now. People would come back to red meat when they got tired of swimmers and squawkers. Then there would be a decent profit—say ten percent for the people on the first rung of the ladder.

"You always make me think of a Spanish guy who also rode a horse," Cecil down at the bank would laugh. "You some kind of a Don Quixote looking for windmills? You know as well as I do that finding a working windmill in Montana is about like sighting a herd of buffalo. Only rich guys can afford to be stubborn. You got to get with this here new world."

New world? It was an ugly new world that took Jack away. His bay gelding that no one else could handle worth a damn would be waiting in the barn right now, looking wild-eyed, snorting and shaking his head. He was asking where Jack was, or so it seemed. After almost six months, he was still going through the same act and it was a terrible thing to watch. The beast should be put down and let that be the end of it, but Lily wouldn't hear of such a thing. Lily seemed to think Jack would just come sauntering over the horizon someday, moving as always like a mountain cat and flashing that jillion-dollar smile.

Talk about stubborn! Lily Rogers didn't know the meaning of defeat. She'd gone to pieces momentarily at Jack's funeral, but she'd recovered and contained her grief, keeping everyone else from breaking down. Including Jack Rogers's father.

It had been so unexpected. It was like being horned by a bull. One day there was Jack, top of the honor roll in his senior class, and almost the very next day he was gone forever. It was so hard to swallow when a young guy never had his chance at a full life. You wanted to holler out, "Damn you, God! What the hell are you doin' here? You're taking the wrong person! It's all wrong!"

Everybody knew most kids in the school had tried marijuana at least once. But, hell, that was just youth being curious—so everybody thought. It seemed Jack wasn't satisfied, which was quite natural for a champion. So when that bum came along and said he had something a lot more exciting, Jack just had to give it a try.

None of the later stories about the episode made sense, nor matched for that matter. Young Barney Kendall, Jack's best pal, also took some of the stuff, but he said he just felt sleepy. He tried to walk and fell down, and all the kids who were watching laughed their heads off. Even the girls said Barney was smiling in his sleep, so they let him be. Lots of kids fell asleep rather than leave a graduation party too early. This one last June wound up on the school roof, of all places.

According to conflicting stories, Jack also became drowsy, but suddenly his mood changed and he started yelling that there was water all around him and he just had to go for a swim. "Feel it!" he yelled over and over again as he wiggled his fingers in invisible water. "It's cool, man! It's the coolest stuff you ever touched!"

Those were his last words. His audience was still laughing when suddenly he jumped up on the parapet surrounding the school roof, poised with his hands above his head for an instant, and then dived headfirst into the hot June night. The roof of the school was two stories above the ground.

After he had pulled the saddle off Tango and hoisted it onto the empty arm next to the one that still supported Jack's saddle, Lee gave Tango a quick grooming and hung his chaps next to Jack's. Then he opened the gate to the corral and watched Tango slide by him and go into a full afterburner lest one of the other horses get one more seed of grain than he would.

Lee watched the horses for a moment, listening to the sounds of their snoffling and munching in their feed bins, and he wished the sound he found so satisfying were all he had to think about. It was always hard to leave the familiar stable sounds. They must be bred into a man's blood, he thought. The calling of a cow for her calf, owl hoots in the night, the clacking of a baler that was working properly, and the eagles and hawks diving between the windrows for field mice were all part of a guy. From now on, though, it would all be different. This coming year old Vernon Taylor would be putting up the hay with a whole new crew of youngsters stacking for him—if he could find them. These days even the young guys who wanted to make the football team shied away from stacking bales. Maybe they were right. It was tough work, hot and dirty, and the pay was peanuts compared to waiting tables in a fast-food joint.

Never mind. Old Vernon would find a way to get the job done and the ranch would still be in the same place when the time came to return from Washington. God Almighty, imagine sitting right there in the halls of Congress totally surrounded by lawyers. Dangerous territory for damn sure. Worse than an ambush in Nam. It was an even bet almost any one of those law-school graduates could make a fool of a man unless he trod like he was crossing a mine field. Still, since when wasn't the University of Montana just as good as Harvard or Yale? Hell, those eastern hotshots put on their pants one leg at a time just the same as any old Montana cattleman.

For a moment he wondered if this whole thing might be like some poor guy coming out from the East, without knowing one end of a cow from the other, and deciding he would make his fortune ranching because the world sure needed food more than it needed anything else.

It was mighty strange, he thought, how Lily always knew he was bound for the house even before he arrived. He had even tried tiptoeing so his boots wouldn't crunch in the gravel walk, but if she was home at the end of the day, the back door would open and there she'd be with a big smile on her face. Not so much of a smile lately, of course, but the sense of welcome was there. Magic. But then, she was a magic woman.

They argued now and then, for sure, because Lily was very much her own woman. Still, she could be reasoned with, a quality every man he knew complained was completely absent from his own wife.

There was one thing wrong about their relationship—not really wrong, perhaps, but difficult. Lily was right too often for comfort.

She had a way of letting a man go on and on until he hung himself. Then she would chime in with the facts, of which she had a great and accurate supply. Facts were engraved on her computer brain, and once in a while that made it awkward to keep discipline in the family. A guy could look pretty silly saying "stick to your pots and pans, woman" when she could prove that the rate and poundage of gain of black-baldy calves was so much better than the purebred Herefords your grandfather raised.

There were softer things that made it impossible not to stay in love with Lily. She laughed a lot, or used to, and she was as quick to find humor in a rough situation as anyone he had ever known—man or woman. She was a perpetual student, forever storing away in that warehouse brain of hers information that she could pull out years later. Swear to God she had memorized every book in the Clayburn library.

As he kicked the mud off his boots in the vestibule, Lee Rogers tried not to look at Jack's boots, which were still standing behind the door along with the rest of the family's. Why the hell didn't Lily put them away someplace so that pain wouldn't strike like lightning every time he came into the house? By God, if she didn't get rid of those boots, he was going to start using the front door! That would set off some fireworks! Because with all her qualities, Lily was one hell of a long way from being an angel. She had a flash temper that would be less frightening on an Angus bull. Admittedly she had never thrown anything when she was pissed off, but she had picked things up and assumed the pitch position!

For sure it was an impressive act to behold when Lily Rogers decided she had been wronged. If any female in Montana hadn't heard about women's rights by now, Lily would be pleased to inform her. She was hellfire and leather, but she was still willing to do her chores without complaint—as long as it was recognized that she was doing them and was not complaining. So it paid to compliment Lily on her cooking, which was sure no great strain. And it paid to listen to Lily when she decided that her husband and family needed further enlightenment on anything from the political situation in France to the latest medicine for calf scours.

After the terrible thing happened, it took her about a month to get herself back in gear, and the thunderstorms of information were still booming. For sure this very night while he was packing for the flight to Washington, she would offer some last-minute information she considered he absolutely must have at his fingertips. "There was a British admiral named Cockburn who burned down Washington during the War of 1812," she had said yesterday, as if the announcement had just been made on the evening news. "And by golly, you're going to burn it down again if necessary, and I'm going to make sure you have plenty of tinder!"

Foster Harris ran a fine hardware store in Trenton, New Jersey. He was a big man somewhat gone to blubber because of his fondness for his wife Valerie's cooking, and he was known as one of Trenton's more dependable citizens. He was particularly liked for his infectious laughter. Small children adored Foster Harris because he was somehow capable of becoming one of them. He would drop whatever he was doing to solve a problem for a child, whether he knew him or not, and he had a magic way of sending most of them away smiling. Such was his popularity with the neighborhood children that they voluntarily made up a parade celebrating his forty-fifth birthday.

It was said that God had given Foster Harris this special quality because he and his wife had been unsuccessful in conceiving children of their own.

The indomitable little boy in Foster Harris eventually led him into a passion for steam trains. Anything even remotely connected with the era of steam trains inspired his boundless enthusiasm. He collected photos of old locomotives; the more smoke they were making, the better. He built a model railroad in his garage and powered his locomotives by steam. Sometimes when his genial nature was tried, he played records of steam trains whistling and click-clacking along the rails. The effect soothed him marvelously.

Except for a few steam trains in the United States, which were fired up only occasionally, nearly all steam aficionados were obliged to accept their pleasures electrically. The same held true for most of the world; all gone now, Foster Harris lamented. An era of sounds, smells, and customs had vanished forever.

Then one day Harris discovered steam trains were still earning their way in Thailand. Fearful they, too, might disappear before he could view them, he immediately booked a flight to Bangkok, a place his Valerie thought was populated mainly by English governesses and elephants.

They arrived after sixteen hours confined in the nearly unbearable discomfort of economy class, but once they reached the railroad station, Foster hooted with joy.

"Valerie! Do you see what I see?" he cried out.

For there before his very eyes was a steam locomotive huffing and puffing. Then another and another. Foster Harris was beside himself with anticipation as they boarded the train for a place called Chiang Mai—somewhere to the north on the Burmese border.

Now a man who had never had the slightest desire to see Europe, or any other part of the world, was bound for a place where there were said to be many operating steam locomotives with pressure domes of polished brass, whistles, smoke, and all the goodies a train devotee could imagine. All right there, operating and perhaps even to be touched.

Light on luggage, although nearly smothered in cameras, recorders, film packs, lens cases, and exposure meters, Foster and Valerie stood in awe until a conductor ushered them aboard. Their train was itself hauled by a steam locomotive. Despite the cloying heat, Harris was nearly ecstatic as he photographed everything, including the rivets in the door of their compartment and the embarrassed conductor who found such behavior incomprehensible.

Harris enjoyed himself so much during the long haul north to Chiang Mai that every time the train stopped and then pulled away from a station, he would stand up and shout, "My God, Valerie! Isn't this just the ever-lovin' nuts? Wait till the guys back in Trenton hear about this!"

Valerie agreed. She loved her husband devoutly, and if trains were his thing, that was certainly better than golf. Besides, the conventions of railroaders were always so much fun.

Once arrived in Chiang Mai, Valerie had to make a fuss before her husband would leave the railroad station and go to the hotel. "You can come back later—as many times as you want," she promised.

But Harris was like a voluptuary in a harem. The yard was full of what he called "living artifacts." He was profoundly thrilled at the sight of a few old but polished locomotives, several pieces of defunct railroad machinery, and countless cars and their gear to be photographed and examined. "Valerie," he declared, his entire face illuminated with his boyish smile, "you cannot imagine what pleasure this gives me."

Thus for two days and part of one night, Foster Harris wallowed in old-style railroad "memorabilia" and he said, laughing, "By golly, Valerie, you may call this a pilgrimage, but I've seen the genuine thing and now I can die happy."

The third night was the Harrises' last in Chiang Mai and they had chosen to dine in a small open-air restaurant near the hotel. Halfway through their meal, which Valerie said was spicy enough to fuel a blowtorch, a Thai man in a white jacket approached their table and said in passable English that Harris was wanted on the telephone.

"Telephone? I don't know anybody in Thailand."

"Please. Come."

Harris rose. Bewildered, yet accommodating as always, he followed the man to the entrance and then out to the street. He was saying, "I don't think there's any telephone out here" when the man stuck something hard in his back and, despite the difference in their sizes, propelled him toward a large tree on the opposite side of the street.

"Hey! What's this all about?"

Harris started to turn on the man when an explosion ripped through his entrails. He heard the first explosion and gasped with pain, but he did not hear the second and third and fourth, which sent bullets through his heart, his neck, and finally his brain. He fell down in the darkness beneath the tree, collapsing into a mixed pool of blood, flesh, and brains. Although there were many people on the street who gathered around the mess, none thought to look for the assailant.

It was two days before the grief-stricken Valerie was offered any plausible explanation. "He was so sweet," she kept repeating. "He couldn't even bring himself to swat at a fly."

The explanation offered by one of the staff at the American Embassy in Bangkok was delivered by a stone-faced young man fresh out of Georgetown. It had been unfortunate that Foster Harris, proprietor of a hardware store in Trenton, New Jersey, bore an uncanny resemblance to Peter King, an American drug-enforcement agent stationed in Chiang Mai.

Valerie Harris had never heard of the Golden Triangle, the Shan United Army, or even the Drug Enforcement Administration. Nor did she realize that Chiang Mai was the very hub of one of the world's most active narcotics suppliers. The network included Burma and Laos, and the products of the area were dispatched all over the world. The traffickers were utterly ruthless, and agent Peter King had not been content to just accept his pay and look the other way. Thus he was troublesome and his assassination had become a certainty.

Valerie Harris did not understand.

So you wanna be a businessman.

It's easy for a dude like you to own, like, say a Ferrari. In Westport, Connecticut, good, flaky, moist cocaine brings a hundred forty bucks a gram. New York? Right now s'pose you have a little Afghani black hash . . . you can do 'leven hundred to fifteen hundred bucks a pound. Easy. In California "skunk" goes for sixty-five bucks the quarter-ounce—nonsinsemilla, of course. Even in a place like Bloomington, Indiana, real high-grade "skunk" is bringin' a hundred bucks, maybe a hundred fifty the ounce. We talkin' big bucks, man.

If a dude's real dumb, he can always go to acid like Purple Road—two hits, you gone, at four bucks each. Anywhere. But why fuck with such stuff? In Vegas ninety-percent rock coke is takin' sixteen hundred, maybe nineteen hundred bucks the ounce. And crack? Man! That is easy street! Thank you all. Enjoy.

It be the same all over the world, except can you believe the Japanese makin' "synthetic coke" for which they got the fuckin' nerve to ask eighteen hundred bucks an ounce? I say to you, don' be honked into such junk!

29

Still be some dudes think they be runnin' a pharmacy. They waste time on inventory, man. They got speed, downers, uppers, MDA, THC, angel dust, acid, mescaline, peyote, and even DMT. It be safe to say some a them dudes carry airplane glue for the third graders! A serious businessman don' need all that shit, man!

Why, what I gots to sell is a quality product, my man. And you gots to know your product, and your customer. The numbers'll blow you away—so much to be made, and it's so easy! And you be a respectable businessman!

True to Montana tradition, the Rogers family always referred to the evening meal as "supper." They also held faithful to the custom of saying grace prior to actually eating, and that task was normally rotated among the children. This night it was daughter Fay's turn and she was more than usually diligent to her assignment.

She regarded her meat loaf, potatoes, and gravy with the eyes of an anxious glutton sacrificing precious moments to a worthy cause, and she foresook her usual saucy air for one of profound gravity. "Now hear this, dear Lord," she began. "We thank you for our meat and potatoes, and all the other stuff on the table, including the beans, which some people eat and others just can't. But mostly we want to ask you to protect our dear father on his trip to Washington, D.C., tomorrow morning and help him to be a good congressman for the American people. Thank you for trying, and amen."

Fay had her fork in the meat loaf before her father had finished wiping at his eyes. He said, "Just where do you get this 'Now hear this, Lord'? Have you been promoted to some kind of admiral?"

"It's certainly not the proper way to address our Lord," Lily said solemnly.

"What's the matter with it? I wanted to get His attention."

Robert Rogers—known to his comrade ten-year-olds as "R.R." or sometimes as "the Genius"—was not so deep into his potatoes that he would relinquish a chance at his older sister. "She hears that stuff from her new boyfriend, Nelson," he said with a strong suggestion of disgust in his voice. "Nelson is going to join the navy when he's sixteen because he says farming is for dreamers."

"Nelson is not too bad a name for a sailor," Lily said, "but I would imagine Nelson's mother and father would not exactly applaud his opinion since farming is their livelihood."

"Does Nelson say ranchers are jerks?" R.R. demanded. His voice cracked at the top of the question, and his father wondered if some unique physical strain might have brought on an early maturing.

"I do not care to discuss Nelson Hogarth any further," Fay said haughtily. A moment's silence followed and then she asked, "Dad? What do congressmen do all day besides spend money?"

"That's something I intend to find out."

"They pay you money for doing this—like going to the nation's capital and making speeches and all that stuff?"

"Yes."

"How much?"

"Quite a bit."

"Then we won't have to worry about our electric bill no more!" R.R. yelled.

His mother was quick to correct him. "You will repeat that question and in a gentlemanly tone. We won't have to worry about the electric bill *any longer.*" She smiled and added, "Or at least until the next election."

R.R. turned to his father. "What do you do for all that money?"

"He has to kiss babies!" Fay became almost convulsed in appreciation of her own wit.

"I'm supposed to look after the welfare of the people in this district in relation to the United States government."

"You mean you give the people on welfare their money?"

"No, bureaucrats do that. But I might be asked to vote on how much they receive."

"Holy cow! In the whole state of Montana?"

"In the whole United States. All fifty of them."

R.R. said, "So some people will like you and other people won't?"

"Sometimes I wonder why you don't receive better grades in school."

It was a typical Rogers family evening meal, and Lee tried hard not to think what the conversational differences might have been if Jack were still around. He supposed they would all be talking at once as they usually did. There might not have been so many questions or so much involvement with school. Jack liked to talk about cattle and the possibilities of getting more irrigation on the place. There were moments like just now, Lee thought, while Fay and Robert were momentarily absorbed in their eating, when the silences fell upon the table and became almost unbearable. He would seek Lily's eyes and find them, and they would exchange a thousand messages in seconds—all sad and understanding and agonized. Still? God Almighty, would this sense of having lost most of your own life ever go away?

Later, when he was in their bedroom packing, Lily came to him and put her arms around him. They stood locked together for a long time listening to the soft brush of the chinook wind on the window-panes. Finally Lily asked, "Will you call me as soon as you arrive? As soon as it's convenient?"

"Of course."

"I know you'll be very busy at first. I wish you knew more people there. I wish I could go with you and take over finding a place to live, but with the kids in school and all, it just doesn't make sense."

"By summer I'll have found some sort of place . . . and I'll manage to get back here once in a while. I think it's called making a political junket."

"Maybe I can talk Mrs. DeLancey into staying with the kids for a few days and I could come to you."

"Start working on that right away. I'm too old to be a bachelor."

"Ho-ho. At forty-five you're just ripe. A fine stallion on the loose. I must be out of my mind to let you go." She pinched the flesh between her eyebrows with thumb and forefinger to indicate how she was suffering. Then she pressed him more tightly to her.

He said, "They tell me it's one long orgy every night at the Army and Navy Club. Plenty of dancing dowagers."

She said in a husky voice, "I see her now . . . dark brunette, ivory skin, shimmering white teeth . . . and big boobs."

"Probably an international spy."

". . . And rich," she said. "Her name is . . . Celeste. She calls you 'dahling.' "

She held herself against him and he responded immediately. They moved as if in a slow dance toward the bed. He said, "This is the best idea you've had in a long time."

"I guess it really is my idea. I've always had a thing about middle-aged cowboys. You might call it lust."

"Why don't we pretend I'm not going."

"Isn't that what we're doing?"

After a time, she sighed and whispered that she could see the stars right through the ceiling.

Far to the south, between the Gulf of Mexico and the state of Arkansas, Oscar Brimmer dialed the Fayetteville VOR on the aircraft's single radio and checked the bearing along with his DME. The information he needed came to him digitally, the green numbers welcoming him as a wandering stranger. They told him he was on the 243° radial of Fayetteville and nine miles distant.

Very good. His intention was to be on the 245° radial, which was easy enough to achieve after a minute course correction. On the horizon he could see a low glow, which he knew would be the town itself.

He had no need of it. Now he had only to turn away on the 245° radial and hold with it until he was approximately twenty-five miles from the transmitter. By then, since his arrival in the area was within a few minutes of customary rendezvous, his direction finder would respond to what he thought of as his personal homing beacon.

There it was already! He laughed. He thought it was as if the needle were saying, "Hey there, Mr. Magellan. I'm just over this way!"

The signal maintained its power for less than a minute and then the needle swung freely. No mind. The bearing was established and the field would be straight ahead in the night.

It was wise to stay above two thousand feet in this country until an absolute fix was established. There were hills, and people were always stringing high-tension wires across the valleys. The wires sometimes became almost invisible even in daylight.

Although Brimmer had long since disconnected the running lights on the DC-3, there was nothing he could do about blinding the nearest air-traffic center's radar. He reasoned that controllers would be too busy to get overly curious about a relatively dim blip at an unknown altitude. Unless he had been followed all the way, Brimmer assured himself, he would be out of the field and gone merrily back to Colombia before anybody could actually step on his neck.

He slowed the DC-3 to a hundred and twenty knots and eased down fifteen degrees of flaps. Easy now. Patience. Old straight arrow is bringing home the sheaves, right down the slot.

Bingo! He saw a pair of car lights at each end of a large open area. They had heard him coming. Just line up the lights and land.

Okay? Gear down. Hold ninety knots until past the black line of trees and put her down on the wheels. No need for his own landing lights.

The moment Oscar Brimmer felt the wheels touch, the car lights were extinguished. He eased the DC-3's tail down and braked to a stop. He shut down the engines and waited. The only sound was the tinging of metal as the engines cooled.

After ten or fifteen minutes, he knew he would soon have company. Now they would be waiting somewhere in the darkness—just to be sure no uninvited spectators had been attracted by his skillful landing.

It was said that Mort Steiner knew every individual in Washington, which was a wild exaggeration. What was meant by such approbation was his long record of knowing or at least having some sort of access to every individual of influence in the capital. Including the president. Mort Steiner was particularly assiduous in cultivating anyone who might have even the most remote possibility of helping Mort Steiner. It was surprising that he had not gone farther on the national scene, but one of his unique qualities was a deep appreciation of his own limitations. There were times when he refused to regard himself as a local regiment of power. He preferred the role of a sniper possessed of an incredibly accurate aim.

Fortunately for those congressmen he had served—and there had been many—Steiner was selfish enough to want his boss, whoever he might be, to make a success in Washington and thus not only caress the already smooth feathers in Steiner's nest, but allow him no little reflected glory at the same time. In a sense Steiner was Mr. Washington, D.C., and his last employment was no indication whatsoever of his actual influence on the area known as the "Hill." His relatively obscure job was exactly what Steiner wanted; it paid his lunch checks and the rent on his bachelor apartment, which each month ran about the same. Steiner knew his job was not important or influential enough to put the slightest fear in anyone except the office secretaries and his own. Thus he was always privy to countless matters that he would not otherwise have known about, and his friends-of-friends were legion. Like an ambidextrous tennis pro, he played both political parties with equal grace.

During the past five years, Steiner had served as executive assistant to the representative of the First Congressional District of Montana. "That hardly puts me at the helm of the Ship of State" was his laughing quip when anyone expressed surprise that he should be of such relatively low status after so long in public service.

Mort Steiner thought of himself as the ultimate survivor, and in Washington, where self-preservation had become a fine art, his escutcheon remained unblemished. He did not consider himself one of the teeming swarm who marched to work at their federal offices every morning and then marched away again because the clock said they were released at last. He was, he thought, not unique in position but very much so in his attitude and his personality. His job was his life—there was really nothing else—and he never abandoned it until everything he might do that day was done. "I am a labor snob, a food snob, and a social snob," he once confessed to his friend Wilma

Thorne. "In fact," he added, "you would be perfectly justified in saying that I am a snob's snob."

Steiner's manner and his record were as deceiving as his appearance. Although he seemed to wear the cloak of a world-weary Cassius most of the time, no one had ever known him to betray a trust. His large brown eyes snapped with intelligence and his ears were capable of scanning any roomful of people and picking up pieces of conversation that would later serve him well. He was a master of two invaluable Washington stratagems. Not only could he select a whispered confidence from the babble of almost any gathering, when visiting about the capital he could read a memo on his host's desk from a distance of three yards, despite the fact that to his eyes it was upside down.

Steiner was short and somewhat overweight, a condition that inspired his forlorn-and-abused act when he was obliged to share a table with others. He was a devout calorie counter and relished the recital of numbers for everything on the menu. He also seemed to have an adjustable neck, the result, he supposed of his years in Washington. When he sensed danger or unpleasantness, he appeared to retract his head like a turtle's and he would then turn his whole body right and left, as if it were a true protective shell. He was not given to smiling in such a guarded circumstance, but when the threats had vanished or had been obliterated, he suddenly reblossomed into a rather jovial individual.

Steiner was bald, although he took meticulous care of the fringe of hair that flanked his ears and still climbed partway up his skull. He lived alone in a small apartment above a Greek restaurant on Pennsylvania Avenue Northwest, and his neighbors supposed he was either a homosexual or a sexual neuter.

The facts were otherwise. Once a week, with unswerving regularity, Steiner telephoned Wilma Thorne, who came to his apartment, removed her wig, and disrobed with no more than a question or two about his health. Naked on the bed, she assumed the lotus position while she waited for Steiner to join her. They manipulated and copulated for approximately half an hour, and then Wilma departed fifty dollars richer. The routine had been going on for so long that a strange affection had developed between them, and during their birthdays, which happened to be the same week, they spent extra minutes in mutual congratulations and phrases intended to make the other feel especially comfortable.

Even so, they both found their relatively new affection disturbing. Their fear of any sentimental attachment became so powerful, they both made secret resolves to forsake each other. Their efforts were unsuccessful, and now when they joined company it was for "just one more time." Wilma was torn between her pride of profession and the realization that money was money no matter who romped between her legs. And Steiner had contributed more than just the mandatory payments. He had passed on occasional tips, she had invested wisely, and Wilma thought she had enough for her fifties. "After that I'll die anyways."

For his part, Steiner knew instinctively that Wilma would never use her knowledge of his position to embarrass him. They trusted each other, and in an irresistible surrender to mutual dependence, they found their faith in each other refreshing.

Thus Mort Steiner was not so much alone in the world as most people assumed. After the departure of the former congressman from the First District, what was left of the staff noticed that Steiner's head was well retracted into his shoulders on the day Lee Rogers was scheduled to arrive in the capital. Their pending introduction triggered some instinctive sense of survival and left Steiner suspecting that he might be in for some awkward surprises. Of course he would soon have all under control, but the notion of being even temporarily off-balance was so unique to him that he was almost looking forward to watching matters resolve. Still, he thought he detected little warning signals that told him some of his tried and trusted rules would not apply.

He had prepared himself carefully for the arrival of his new boss. The Montana papers had assiduously covered the Rogers campaign (amateurish and clumsy—how did the man ever get elected?) and various friends in the military, plus friends of friends from the boondocks who had migrated to Washington, gave him what he hoped was a reasonably accurate portrait of the new congressman. Rogers was a native of that wild and woolly region that Steiner had always supposed must be somewhat like Siberia in terms of cultural advantages as well as weather. Rogers's service with the marines was, Steiner thought, more or less standard for the area. Why did heroes so seldom come from California, or Florida? As far as he could ascertain, Rogers was financially stable, although he certainly had not lavished money on his campaign. Was he taking the job for the money? Would he prove to be just another bib-overalls bumpkin who couldn't make it outside of politics?

Such personal flavor of his new man as Steiner had been able to gather indicated he was anything but that sort. He was said to be scrupulously honest, forthright in his beliefs, and a tough cookie when anything or anyone stood in his way.

At the moment Steiner could only assure himself that Congressman Lee Rogers's office in the Longworth House building would be waiting for him, along with Alice Morgan, the secretary and scheduler; Connie Marcus, the receptionist-typist; Charles Jackson, an administrative assistant (gofer); and Randy Lewis, another gofer. And then there would be Edward Starbuck, whom Rogers would inherit as press secretary. Dear Edward. The man was altogether too clever for anyone else's good. *Obnoxious* was the word, an oaf in silk shirts. He was, as Steiner reported solely to himself, the most cunning little man he had ever known, a virtual Iago in a meticulously tailored suit, with a revolting habit of stowing his handkerchief in the cuff of his jacket. But Edward knew his business and everyone in it. He also knew how to erase the verbal pratfalls so common to freshman congressmen. It was significant, Steiner thought, that no one ever considered addressing Edward as anything but Edward.

Such was the staff of newly elected Congressman Rogers, and all were commanded by Mort Steiner. They had served as the regulars of previous congressmen from the same district, and Steiner preened himself in believing they knew their jobs well. After all, they had been trained by the master.

Steiner reasoned that he had faced the same transition problems before, and had always managed to hold on to the same basic staff— not to mention his own job. It looked like Rogers would not prove to be one of those less than forthright individuals who took full advantage of their authorization to hire eighteen employees—all, of course, to be paid by the government. It had long since ceased to raise eyebrows when needy relatives appeared on a congressman's payroll, most of whom, in Steiner's opinion, had not the grace to offer a kernel of ability. His telephone conversations with Rogers had indicated that he did not intend to bring any staff with him, which was odd, and he had professed to be thankful that the personnel were already in place. "I guess I'm going to need all the help I can get back there."

What kind of a humble Sam answer was that? Rogers was a freshman congressman, and he would have to spend some time at the Brookings Institution learning the congressional ropes, and after that he would still need someone to lead him around by the nose. But to foresee and admit it? Some just-arrived freshman congressmen couldn't find the men's room without an escort. They became lost right in the Capitol itself—sometimes for critical hours. Without their Mort Steiners, a few might have trouble understanding the difference between a committee meeting and a State of the Union address.

When Steiner asked the new man if he could accomplish any specifics pending Rogers's arrival, the cowboy's reply had been equally indefinite, or was it just naïve? "I won't need much, I guess, to do what I have to do. Just stick around until we have a chance to talk things over. I don't expect to have time for a lot of rigmarole."

Rigmarole? There were certain fixed rules and duties in the daily life of all congressmen, and smart ones rarely stepped out of line. It was men like Steiner who kept new congressmen from disaster. Did Rogers think that Mort Steiners were to be had by the bucketful here? Did he realize that diamonds were not to be found in the streets?

On the way to the airport, Steiner reassembled his Lee Rogers index. Forty-five years old. Graduate of the University of Montana, which must be as far from the Ivy League as any could be. No criminal record. Voted Republican. Owned ranch of respectable size. Newspaper photos revealed a tall, spare man with, dear God, what one might classify as a crew cut. A service photograph (obtained with great effort and some risk by one of Steiner's naval friends in the Pentagon) showed a strong face and piercing eyes, which Steiner remembered had at first glance made him vaguely uncomfortable.

The longer he examined the photograph, which he had promised
with the very breath of his life to return, the more he knew a need
to share his reaction with someone else. He chose Alice Morgan, who
was his longest associate in the office. "What do you think of our new
boss?" he asked as casually as he could manage.

She studied the photograph carefully and sighed. "Wow. I wonder
how old this photo is?"

"What's that got to do with it?"

"He's one hell of a hunk."

"I assume you intend the word *hunk* as a compliment."

"Indeed," she said, still staring at the photo. "But I don't think
I'd want to cross him."

"Funny," Steiner said, retracting his head even further, "I sort of
have the same feeling."

Thank God, Steiner thought later, Rogers's airplane was coming
into Washington National instead of into the Dulles boonies. This
way he could escort Rogers to his office in a relatively few minutes,
and the initial shock might make him pliant. One had to think of
such things. Wait until he had a closer acquaintance with grungy old
Longworth House! Now, before he had time to adjust his sights to
the local scene, he must acquire the habit of looking to Mort Steiner
for his every need. Once let loose in the countryside, a freshman
congressman could wiggle himself into all kinds of trouble. And
rescue was ever so much more difficult than prevention.

Steiner held back from the crowd and watched disdainfully as the
slovenly horde emerged from the boarding gate. What a pity the
American public left all their personal pride behind when they traveled these days—or had they ever had any? Such a collection of
wrinkled, strung-out shirts, frumpy tennis shoes, and torn Levi's
caused him to reflect on how much harm the faddish were doing to
the United States of America. Only the Orientals and blacks seemed
to have troubled with their appearance; the others, Steiner mused,
had been stuffed into one end of a giant refuse truck and spewed out
the other end. For these creatures, these tapioca-eyed castaways,
honest senators and congressmen (not to mention Mort Steiner) were
working at least fifteen hours a day?

As he watched the parade of protruding bellies, stubble beards, barbed-wire hair, sagging tits, and Hawaiian shirts, Steiner found that he was not amused. He had always thought his tolerance for his fellow Americans was limitless, but now on this January afternoon the visions he had held for so long seemed to have all been jumbled recklessly across a single landscape. These were the people who set the pace for the rest of the world? These were the members of the wealthiest club on earth, the inheritors of a huge land so rich in resources no one could calculate the country's true value? These were the blessed people who should be down on their knees giving thanks for the incomparable daily bounties that fell upon their addled heads every morning?

No wonder cynicism was an acquired disease in Washington! Or was it acquired back home when a congressman returned to court his voters?

Steiner's eyes sought reassurance in the few passengers who wore ties—probably lawyers, he thought, and then chastised himself for cynicism in its prime. He was momentarily relieved to observe three ladies wearing skirts that appeared to have been recently cleaned and pressed. Not one was even gray-haired. Pity. The three obviously lived in some distant cocoon and were doubtless yearning for liberation.

Then he saw his man.

There was no mistaking him, for not only did he tower over his fellow passengers, he stood up straight—as if, Steiner thought, he was not like all the others carrying some invisible heavy-water burden between their shoulders. He was wearing cowboy boots and a five-gallon hat. Where was his horse?

Steiner moved quickly through the crowd of squalling infants. Why did every young mother now consider it part of childbirth to take her loathsome, miserable little offspring for an airplane ride as soon as possible after the thing had emerged from her womb? Why was the thing never born in the same community in which the mother lived?

No, his man did not smell of manure. "I would suppose," Steiner said, displaying his most winning smile, "that you, sir, are Congressman Rogers of the great state of Montana." He held out his hand.

"Right. You must be Mort Steiner. It's very kind of you to meet me."

Steiner reached for Rogers's briefcase, but it was pulled away.

"No, no. It's no problem. There's nothing in it but a few papers."

Borne so lightly in Rogers's big hand, the briefcase did indeed look like a toy. Steiner smiled again as they moved away from the gate. "Of course," he said, "we couldn't let you come to Washington without a welcoming committee, even though I'm sure you've been here many times before."

"No. Never."

They were moving rapidly now with the stream of people, looking, Steiner thought, somewhat like the retreat from Moscow, or possibly—with the notable exception of the three ladies, the gentlemen with ties, Rogers, and himself—more like a convoy of hapless Hungarian gypsies bound for a concentration camp.

"Well, then, sir, we shall have a great deal to show you. This is one of the most fascinating cities in the world. The museums and art galleries are unsurpassed, and—"

"I didn't come here to see museums, or galleries."

"Of course not, sir. But one should take advantage of the amenities." Steiner paused in his niceties; he sensed that his listener was not very interested. "And then we do have some fine restaurants. Every ethnic culture is represented, and it will be my pleasure to steer you toward the best."

"I'm pretty much a steak-and-potatoes man."

Shit, Steiner thought. His dreams of delicious meals at places he could not ordinarily afford exploded. The Jockey Club, Madison House, Jacques's? Their menus were so exotic it was questionable if they even knew how to simply broil a steak. Maybe the food at the Army and Navy Club (dear God, how pedestrian!) would eventually pall upon neophyte Rogers so he would listen to gastronomic reason.

"I thought you might like to go straight to the office," Steiner said.

"I would. I've got to get cracking. Time is short."

Cracking? Steiner found the word ominous. Did this Montana cowboy think he was going to clear the national debt in two easy moves or, heaven forbid, did he entertain some crazy notion that there really was a way to reduce taxes and all he had to do was stand up on the House floor and say so?

As they genuflected into a taxi, Steiner knew a moment of compassion for his new charge. He would get in an extra supply of crying towels and take such care as he could to spare Congressman Rogers the deflowering of his innocence on his very first day.

As usual the lobby of the Longworth House office building was alive with people flowing in two steady streams past the officious security guards. Everything in Washington was that way now. A special army of blue-uniformed security people, paid by the government, were supposed to guard the lives of other government people from some unidentified nut who had convinced himself that blowing up an office would ease his resentments. Rogers was taken aback by such arrogant rule in a public building, but at least this place had that peculiar smell of all public buildings, whether in Montana or Saigon.

The lobby of Longworth House looked run-down and unkempt, and Rogers wondered if the fault lay in the lack of interest of federal employees who presumably maintained the place.

The attitude of an elevator operator was not very encouraging. While the incoming streams of visitors waited in line before the bank of elevators, Mort Steiner had guided his charge to an elevator marked "Members Only."

The operator, a black woman with a stentorian voice, announced in forbidding terms, "This here elevator is for members of Congress *only!*" She regarded both Rogers and Steiner with open distaste.

"I hear you," Steiner said unctuously. "Apparently you are new here. At the moment you are about to transport to higher altitudes Congressman Rogers from Montana and his administrative assistant."

"Yeah?" She examined Lee Rogers carefully. "He don' look like no congressman to me."

Rogers chuckled and asked what a real congressman should look like.

"Well, you know, like he wears a real tie—not one of them funny stringy little things, y'know, and, well . . ." She smiled suddenly and added, "Y'all look like some country-music singer, know what I mean? But I guess you can't help it, so I'll take you on up anyway."

"That's most gracious of you," Steiner said sourly.

Senior congressmen had offices in the much newer Cannon Building, or in Rayburn House, both nearby and connected by underground trolley to the Capitol itself. Senators, existing on a different political plateau, were accommodated more luxuriously in the Dirksen, the Russell, or the Hart office buildings. Within this cluster of outwardly imposing edifices, the men and women who had been elected to their station tried, sometimes in vain, to guide and administer a country that had grown much too large and complex for the total comprehension of any individual. They were assisted, hindered, and sometimes spurred in this mighty endeavor by the executive branch of the government, which was centered in the White House and was spread like a beached octopus through the tentacles of countless agencies, some eternal and others at least intended to be temporary.

After a long hike past the offices of other congressmen, they came to what Steiner said would be Rogers's new home. He paused for a moment regarding the Great Seal of Montana on the door. As they entered the outer office, Steiner emitted a soft whistle and a mock "Ten*shun!*" The staff gathered, smiling, and he introduced them.

". . . The invaluable, incomparable Alice Morgan . . . Connie Marcus, who keeps this front office from chaos . . . my assistant, Charles Jackson—poor chap has been on the team with me for years now—and Randy Lewis, our newest staff member, who serves in several capacities according to our immediate needs. And last but far from least, Edward Starbuck, your press representative, or public-affairs officer, if you please."

Rogers marveled at his assistant's easy finesse during the brief and the welcoming formalities. Holy cow! His own memory for names was about one inch long, and he had been known to stutter or entirely forget a name even when introducing old friends.

Steiner led him into his private office in the rear of the complex and persuaded him to sit down in the government-issue leather chair that stood behind the desk. Edward Starbuck slipped silently into the room behind them. He folded his arms, leaned against the wall, and smirked at the ceiling.

"Nothing fancy here," Steiner announced, "but you won't be here as much as you might think."

"Where will I be?"

"Everywhere. Routine things you can leave to me because you'll find that the demands on your time are almost overwhelming. No fear, sir. I shall see to it that you begin gently."

This man, Lee Rogers thought, is pretty damn bossy—and he presumes. I haven't hired him. He's a legacy. It was, Rogers decided, time to set things straight.

For a moment he could not for the life of him think of his assistant's name. Then it came to him. "Now look here, Mr. Steiner—"

"Mort. Please, just let it be Mort. And I trust you won't mind if I address you as Lee? We're just family here."

"No problem. But now look here. I wasn't elected to this job just to shake hands and slap backs. I have a definite purpose in mind and I want to get right at it. I hope I can count on your cooperation long enough to get things launched."

"Launched?" Steiner's head retracted slightly. "I'm afraid I don't follow you, sir. Are we getting ourselves into some kind of shipbuilding campaign? If so, I must warn you that enthusiasm for our Merchant Marines is absolutely zilch around here, and the chances of getting *anyone's* attention on that forlorn subject are zero. Of course, if you're thinking about naval warships, that's quite another bag of weeds, and eventually I suppose we might ease you into some committee—"

"I'm talking about narcotics."

Rogers was surprised at the stunning silence that seemed to have overcome his loquacious assistant. He saw Steiner take a deep breath and also saw that his eyes were troubled. "Well, sir, I'm afraid that the whole problem is something that is being handled farther up the line. Everybody's on the narcotics bandwagon now and the DEA finally has money coming out of their ears. That's the Drug Enforcement Administration, and I suppose they are doing the best they can. Of course they're part of the bureaucracy and they have to fight for survival like all the other agencies, which—"

"Sometimes intrudes on their energies, would you say?"

"Bravo," Edward Starbuck said, still pouting at the ceiling.

Steiner threw him a glance of disapproval. "No, I wouldn't go so far as to say that, but anything to do with narcotics is sort of politically touchy, if you know what I mean?"

"No, I don't know what you mean, Mr. Steiner, but I'll guarantee you that I'm going to get somebody's ass in active gear around here, starting tomorrow morning."

"But, sir, you must realize that bureaucracies are extremely sensitive to criticism and—"

"How do you mean, sensitive?"

"Unsolvable problems are sort of eased to one side. The drill is to make all the necessary noises and then wait until the problem goes away. There's a new administration, or the public forgets about it—whichever comes first. Narcotics are extremely troublesome because so many agencies have to get into the act. Some of our most senior congressmen have tackled it, and found themselves frustrated. The State Department gets to swing its weight, which is always bad news. And the appropriations are always challenged because other problems are easier to understand. Finally, history always intervenes. Today's need does not always become tomorrow's, because something more appealing, or thought to be more vitally in need of attention, comes up. Whether it's the Russians, or Wall Street, or whatever, sir, change is the one sure thing."

"Okay then. We're going to make some history right here. I think it's damn important to recognize that eighty percent of our school kids have at least tried some kind of narcotic and about twenty percent are now hooked on something or other. We spend an awful lot of time and money worrying about the Russians, while our armor is going rotten inside. I don't think the Russians have a damn thing to do with it, but the narcotics situation in this country couldn't be working better for them if they had planned it."

"Noble sentiments, sir. And quite true, I suppose. But I would not, were I you—and I speak from many years' experience—run the risk of becoming identified with a losing cause right after you've arrived. People don't know you, and we certainly don't want to inspire any headshaking during the overture."   .

Edward Starbuck interrupted. "If I may suggest, Mr. Rogers, best you play it mellow for a while. Let things simmer until you're well known and popular enough to rally a few of the more powerful to whatever it is you have in mind."

"I have in mind a declaration of war, Edward. Even if we have to do it on our own." Rogers spoke as flatly as he could.

Steiner cleared his throat delicately, allowed his eyebrows to rise, and said, "Excuse me, sir, I must have missed something. Perhaps I misunderstood you?"

"It's simple, Mort. We have to go to war because we have an internal Vietnam in this country, and we're fighting it just as half-heartedly. We can't allow the same thing to happen again, because if we lose this one, our whole society will fall to pieces. It won't take as many years as you think. We've got to go to war like we mean it. We can't be satisfied with a few busts here and there. Drugs are a trillion-dollar business, run by people who should be hung up by the balls, and I intend to see that they are."

Rogers rose suddenly to his feet and smiled at the two men. "Now, can you guys tell me where's the best place to get a taxi for the Army-Navy Club?"

Rogers watched in fascination as Steiner's head seemed to bury itself in his shoulders. The man seemed to be having difficulty swallowing.

"I'll go down with you," Steiner said nervously. "Washington taxis are very difficult to find at this hour."

Rogers put his hand on Steiner's shoulder and shook him gently. "Don't be so unhappy, Mort. We won't kill anybody—the first week."

A light snow began to fall as Lee Rogers's taxi twisted through the end-of-the-day rush hour. Elsewhere within the city a small group of young federal employees had gathered in a renovated Georgetown house because the word was already out that it would "really be snowing hard tonight." They said all things came from heaven and that the snow inside the house would be much deeper and more satisfying than what could be found outside.

Their names were Agnes and Sam and Harry and June and Dale and Gerry, and a married couple known as Teresa and Max. No one ever bothered with last names in these purely social events because last names were unimportant. What was important was being there. Agnes, who owned the house, had a new lover, a stripling of half her weight from the French Embassy. His name was Guy, and Agnes fawned on him continuously. Agnes was offering her guests some of the best "blow" to be hauled out of Colombia, and since head colds were rampant in Washington now, she had provided "tooters" for everyone who had failed to bring their own.

Agnes announced that the cocaine was of such high quality, they would begin by snorting it. Later they might go on to free-basing, but that took precious time and they had been waiting impatiently ever since Agnes had called and said it was time to get off.

Like, in a sense, what was more fun than watching someone else take a hit while you anticipated taking your own? Right away with cocaine you were king and queen of the May, a Belgian chef, or whoever you wanted to be at the moment. Like Cinderella? Like Robert Redford? Everybody agreed that as soon as you took a hit, you wanted another. Cocaine is magic time, man. At twenty-five dollars a hit, it's all tingly.

Agnes and Sam and Harry and June and Dale and Gerry and Teresa and Max were all white college graduates who held medium-level jobs that paid well. They smoked marijuana when it pleased them, but the effects were beginning to pall and an opportunity for a free sleigh ride was not to be spurned. Even so, a few of those present wished Agnes would refrain from her goddamned pompous act and get on with it. Of course, she had possibly taken a few snorts already and was in no hurry.

Guy said that he had once tried heroin and didn't like it. The silence that followed his statement was lonely. None of these people would have anything to do with such junk—in fact they could not bear the mention of it and remain polite. Guy thought they either had not understood his reasonably fluent English or were hopelessly ignorant about life in France.

They sat on the floor in a circle and watched Agnes as she officiated at a low coffee table. To watch her in silence was a ritual; at most, any exchange of words was done in a hushed voice, as if some spiritual presence were about to be invoked.

Agnes placed a mirror on the table and took a brown plastic bottle from the pocket of her designer jacket. There was a faint gasp of appreciation at the size of the bottle—it had to contain at least two or three thousand dollars' worth of cocaine, but of course she wouldn't use it all tonight.

An invitation to join Agnes or any other host within the community was a proof of acceptability. People who did cocaine at this social level were rarely strangers. If not actually acquainted, they at least knew of each other through an intercommunication system that seemed to have no geographic limits. If you did drugs of any sort, you were a part of the society. If not, you were on the outside.

When Agnes took her first hit, she rejected Guy's offer of a glass tooter. Instead she used a rolled-up hundred-dollar bill and everyone agreed that she was being terribly chic. Conversation began to flow at an exciting pace, and after twenty minutes no one who had come to call at Agnes's house held any doubt that this was going to be a delightful evening.

At this same time in Montana, Lily Rogers retreated to the master bedroom to enjoy a rare hour of privacy. The chores about the ranch were seen to by Vernon Taylor, but there were always the barn cats to be fed, grain to the horses, and the car to be put away in the garage lest the aged machine fail to start in the morning. She thought the Chevrolet's age matched the outside temperature—twenty below zero. Hello, Montana in the winter. Then very soon she would have to do something about supper. Leftover baked ham again? The kids would mutiny.

Lily went to her little desk, which this very morning she had moved around until it faced the window. She took out her new journal, regarded it with trepidation for a moment, and then as the light began to fade outside she wrote carefully.

This is my second entry, as it's plain to see. Lee got off early this morning with a minimum of fuss. If my momentary breakdown into tears can be considered minimum. How I hate to see him go! My sense of abuse is self-created, of course, but it's there and I'm barely managing to shake it.

All the enormous pride I felt when Lee won the election and people started calling him "congressman" has just evaporated. Somehow. I don't know why I should be so uneasy about this dramatic change in our lives. Perhaps I'm aging prematurely, and am bound to view any change with suspicion. Here I am in a comfortable house, with plenty to eat and two fine youngsters to help me eat it, and yet I do have trouble keeping a stiff upper lip. Certainly this melancholy brooding can't be the opening chords of menopause!

But then why am I so . . . apprehensive? Nuts! Try for laughs. Fay said to me this afternoon, "Mom, how can I get some boobs?"

I asked her to clarify her question, although I knew damn well what she was talking about.

"Boobs. You know, Mom, like women used to have?"

I told her that I was not aware female breasts were now classified as historical.

"Cleavage is out," says she, "but boobs are in, and I don't want to be different."

"Then never the twain shall meet?" says I, before I could stop myself.

"What a neat way of putting it," she said solemnly.

Lily put down her pen, closed the journal, and sat staring at the scene beyond the window. The land stretched westward to the twilight horizon. There was not a human being in sight, nor would there be, she knew. Beyond the most distant hills lay Vernon Taylor's little spread, but he would long since have returned to his wood stove.

This Montana, she thought, was a dear land, somehow so vast and powerful that nothing could change it. Now it was still silent and frozen, stark and even dangerous. The same as it had been for millions of years.

The Indians, even those whose sensitivities had been dulled by college and computers, understood this land. Now Lily Rogers, born and raised in Montana, was beginning to wonder if the white man ever would.

Thinking about the modern Indians was at least healthier than fretting about her strange and most unwelcome apprehensions.

Oscar Brimmer thought that the soft Colombian night was at least tolerable for an unhealthy Anglo-Saxon. Better than the daytime, by God! At night a man could take a deep breath and feel the air go right down to his lungs—almost, but not quite, refreshing.

Brimmer plucked at the parched skin on his nose and thought about his last flight. The missions were becoming a piece of cake, he had decided. They melted into each other and it was hard to remember if his last flight had been last week or only a few nights ago.

Whenever it was, he had taken pains to time the unloading operation. Three minutes and twenty-seven seconds exactly from the time he heard the rear door clang open to the moment when a voice called out to him, *"Vaya con Dios!"* The door was slammed shut and according to custom he was free to get the hell out of there. He started the engines, which were still hot, and thirty seconds later took off from right where the old goat sat. No taxiing. Just up and away, as the air-force guys used to say a long time ago.

Now Brimmer found himself whistling "Wild Blue Yonder" as he drove his jeep through the steaming night. He was bound for the little cantina in the nearby village of Moros, where they kept a special brand of beer in stock for his sole consumption. It was so expensive the proprietor demanded payment in full before he would have it brought up the Magdalena River, and even then he placed a surcharge per case simply because Brimmer was so extraordinarily wealthy.

Brimmer always drank alone, a situation that still irked him, even if the only social prospects were a handful of Colombian farmers and petty clerks who spoke a language he barely understood. Nor could he communicate with the occasional Indian who sometimes came to the cantina to squat on the dirt floor and enjoy the novelty of urinating in a porcelain trough and smelling the powerful disinfectant. It made their eyes water, a reaction they found so pleasurable they often bent down to the trough and inhaled deeply. They also found the ammonia cleared their perpetual sinus congestion, which was brought on by the dampness of the forest. If there was no further excitement, they soon vanished. The proprietor had made it clear that Indians without money were unwelcome.

Once seated at his favorite table beneath the tattered awning, which offered more of a funnel to the rain showers than a protection, Brimmer was given to brooding on a variety of subjects until the pilsner closed down the machinery of his mind for the night. When he was barely able to walk or see, he would hoist himself into the jeep and negotiate the perilous trail back to his quarters at the camp. His passage home was rarely without incident, and his collisions with trees and shrubbery along the trail were numerous. He avoided major personal damage by driving very slowly, and sometimes when his foot slipped off the throttle, the jeep would come to a complete halt. Then he would nap for several minutes. Since there was never any other traffic, all the wounds inflicted on his jeep, including the one broken headlight, were the work of the terrain, and he was always surprised to discover new damage the following day.

Brimmer had always been information-hungry, and although his literary tastes were archaic, he enjoyed a remarkable ability to recall nearly every fact he had ever read or heard. He could quote the price of crude oil for the past ten years as easily as the names and flight records of the very early aviators.

There were occasions when Brimmer reflected on the nature of his job, but never morosely. He was making a living, and a very good one, wasn't he, and was therefore not a burden on his fellow man. Correct? He did his job probably better than any other pilot in the world. Correct? What difference did it make if the goddamned United States government was so stupid it failed to recognize that the country's oldest inhabitants had been swallowing red mescal beans ten thousand years ago? Didn't they know that carbon dating of rock shelters in New Mexico and Texas proved those ancient buffalo hunters were also using peyote? Those old farts had their own ways of enjoying life. Hell's bells, people had laughing-gas parties in the late 1800s, and legend had it that they didn't take the cocaine out of plain old Coca-Cola until 1914.

The goddamned American government, Brimmer concluded, was the most unreasonable and inefficient government on planet Earth. American bureaucrats were right down here in Colombia and in Peru and Bolivia trying to persuade the local governments to tear up all the coca fields, and poppy fields, and marijuana, and everything else they could find to destroy. We'll give you money to plant real crops, they told people. Big deal! Some poor peasant gets one hundred dollars a year to plant his hectares with soybeans or some such to eat, when he can grow marijuana and get a thousand for the same number of hectares? Even the Indians were not that fucking stupid.

And another thing. The locals in this part of the world had been chewing on coca leaves for three thousand years. Christ! It was their way of life. They would go to pieces without the stuff. What the hell business was it of the Americans to make the South American peasant's existence any more miserable than it already was? The thing to do was make those bureaucrats spend some time in a Bolivian mine at ten thousand feet, or make them work under the jungle sun like the locals. Pretty soon they'd be reaching for some leaves themselves.

There were times such as this evening when pure loneliness nearly overwhelmed Oscar Brimmer. Before his nightly expedition to the cantina, he would shower and shave carefully, and douse himself with cologne he called "froufrou"—as if he really intended to meet another human being with whom he might share a few words. He would arrive at the cantina, step from his jeep directly to his table, which stood within inches of the dirt road, and lower himself into a rickety cane chair. His pilsner would be brought to him automatically by a wide-eyed, wordless boy of ten or so, and that would be Brimmer's total contact with others of his species. They knew who he was and what he did, and so they didn't want to know. One day the FARC might become displeased with Oscar Brimmer and it was just as well not to be even slightly acquainted with the man.

This very afternoon Brimmer had experienced one of his rare direct contacts with his employers, Fuerzas Armadas Revolucionarios Colombians. He had been summoned to a meeting in the manager's tiny office. There a tall, gaunt, string-tight man, who said he should be called Leon, instructed him to take the chair by the window. Leon displayed a set of fanglike teeth and Brimmer saw his eyes were blood-sore, as if he had not slept in a long time. That smile, Brimmer thought, had the warmth of a bayonet, but at least his English was understandable. While the manager sat and sweated, Leon said, "You go to Barranquilla too often. For what purpose?"

"To screw the whores." Verily, Brimmer thought. For what other purpose would a man go to such a dismal town as Barranquilla?

"I do not believe you. You have too many years to fuck whores or others. You go there to gamble."

Brimmer sighed. "There are times, amigo, when I think you may be right. And then there are other times. . . ."

"You are paid too much money."

"If you want my job, you're welcome to it."

"I am not the air person."

"I am, and that's why I'm paid too much. Now, what's really on your mind?"

"We have information that some man is talking to the American DEA spies in Barranquilla, and they are here to—how you say?—to extradite certain persons who are fighting for the people."

It was an extraordinarily hot day and Brimmer was suffering from what he thought of as a thermonuclear hangover. Worse, he was suffering from one of his periodic bouts with malaria, and considered himself abandoned by God as well as by the human race. He was in no mood to account for what he considered his personal business. "Señor Leon, cut out the bullshit about what you're doing for the people and tell me what all this has to do with Oscar Quincy Brimmer?" He didn't know why he had said it. He had never in his life told anyone who didn't already know that his middle name was Quincy.

"If we see that you talk to persons in Barranquilla, we will have to kill you."

At the moment, Brimmer decided, it might be the easy way out. "Jesus! You guys really lay it on the line. Well, well . . . there are whores in Cartagena."

"Not for you. There are too many Americans there."

"How about Mompós?"

"No. Too many Colombians. You would be—how you say?—too conspicuous there."

"Then what about the other directions? How about Medellín? I could use some fresh air."

"No. For you it is the same."

"You're telling me I can't go anywhere?"

"It is the wish of Marco Fedles."

"Then tell him to send me a woman once in a while—for the good of the people."

"Perhaps. I will speak to him, but he will say only your mind is hungry. He likes your work, but you know too much."

Brimmer reviewed the conversation as he sat in the cantina, and he realized now that the manager had not said a word. Of course, the fat slob had been watching every move he made, and if a single report would gain favor for himself, he would rush to send the word. And so there was not even a fat slob with whom he might discuss the days' nonevents. Alone, alone . . . alone. Even memories of other times were nearly all gone.

Here, sitting alone in the cantina once more, there was a certain joy to be found in feeling sorry for Oscar Quincy Brimmer. A good cry, mixed properly with a few farts and belches, gave a man a certain cleansing. When ready, a guy could stagger to his feet and shake the hand of calamity.

Late that night the jungle was pummeled and bruised repeatedly by a vicious thunderstorm. Brimmer drove homeward through the wild commotion, the rain blinding him as much as the pilsner. As the lightning flashed and the artillery of thunder exploded all about him, he squeezed the wheel of the bouncing jeep, tilted his head back, and roared at the night with the full strength of his lungs. "Up your ass!" he yelled at the tumultuous night. "Ya-hoo! Who needs anybody? Meet my friend Oscar Quincy Brimmer! Mr. Brimmer, meet Mr. Brimmer! Yahoo!"

Brimmer's tirade was shut off when he collided with a fallen tree and removed a large area of freshly grown skin from his nose.

At almost the same hour, Mort Steiner was entertaining his friend Wilma in the Greek restaurant below his apartment. He had never known the slightest urge to socialize with Wilma outside the perimeters of his own bed; but this night, in a moment of unexplainable ennui, he had asked if she would like a bite to eat before they approached more serious action. He found that Wilma's behavior at such public recognition of her charms was touching. She was not such poor company as he had feared, and after a half-bottle of retsina, the sparkle in her eyes remained undiminished.

Wilma, he suddenly discovered, was proving to be a good listener, and if ever a man needed to share a few confidences, this evening was it. Wilma seemed to have sensed his distress. Reaching across the table, she placed her hand on his. "Poor boy," she said, "you're not yourself tonight. You're troubled. Can I help you?"

The sympathy in her voice was so genuine and compelling, Steiner found himself unburdening before he realized that for the first time in his life he was talking shop with someone who was not in the whimsical business of politics. "May this day never repeat itself," he said. "I've a sneaking hunch that I'm about to be mixed up with a crusader."

He saw that Wilma did not understand him, yet the sparkle in her eyes remained undimmed.

"Or perhaps Joan of Arc has been reincarnated—this time wearing a ten-gallon hat instead of a pretty helmet."

The sparkle, he saw, endured. He asked, "Have you ever watched a virgin who is about to be ravished?"

"Other than myself, no."

"Be advised that I stand back helpless before innocence in combat with the forces of evil. I just hope I can pick up the pieces before too much damage is done."

"You have the screwiest way of talking, Mort. Or I guess you sound screwy because we never tried this before." She hesitated and watched the window, which faced the street. "It's snowing so hard outside. Pretty soon we could build a snowman." She tried to laugh as she envisioned this prospect. He tried to join her, and between them they succeeded briefly.

"If my man melts soon enough, then I suppose he'll survive," Mort said.

"There you go again. Well, whoever he is, good luck to you," Wilma said, and she took a long swallow of retsina. Her attention shifted suddenly to the menu. "Can I have the moussaka?"

"Why not? Rome is burning and the fire alarms are clanging. We have no choice but to cling to the wreckage."

"Mort. Will you for Christ's sake talk English? With you I need a translator. You got so much education, it shows—know what I mean? Either I got to go up a level or you got to come down. There are some girls in the life who fake it—know what I mean? They pretend like they understand what their john is saying. I don't want to be that way with you. I don't know why, but I don't. You want to screw, that's one thing. You ask me to turn a trick with my brain, we both got a problem. Understand?"

The next morning just before eight, Lee Rogers's boots set up a reverberating echo as he marched down the long corridor toward his office. Despite the heavy clack of his boot heels, his step was both sprightly and youthful. Energy flowed from him; and for no reason that he could determine, he smiled at each doorway along his route. New Mexico . . . Minnesota . . . Nevada . . . Nebraska. He wondered why the doors were still closed on such an important day. Maybe it would be a good idea to have some bands playing to celebrate this date, and perhaps some sort of ceremony with the colors.

As he turned the corner and approached his doorway, he supposed the doors were still closed because the light snow had snarled Washington traffic. In Montana, he mused, they would have called the accumulation a "light dusting."

He had made his own way to the Longworth House via the subway and walked from the station. He found the chill air bracing; it swept away the sense of depression that had momentarily struck him in the club dining room. It had been a long time since he had taken breakfast alone. He missed Lily. Dammit. When it came to women, he had sure won the champion.

He found the door to his office closed and locked. He had forgotten to ask for a key, and no one had offered him one. He checked his watch. Where the hell was everybody? He stood contemplating the Great Seal of Montana for a moment, wondering what the people of the nation's capital would do if they had a real snowfall.

He paced the corridor, glowering at his watch impatiently. Where the hell were all the working people in this government?

Soon he found a broad windowsill just the right height for his long legs. He sat down, opened his briefcase, and surrendered himself to the pages of material that Lily had gathered for him. It was part of the same stuff that had been his bedtime reading for the past few weeks. Out of it he hoped to enhance the speech he intended to make before the House of Representatives. In his thoughts he had gone over the speech a thousand times, and he was still adding and subtracting. Just now he had decided to eliminate an attack on the Bonanno family and their pizza-parlor blinds . . . Tony Guiolamo . . . Frank Castronovo . . . Julio Zavala . . . Upstanding citizens all, who just happened to have an eye for the fast buck. The domestic Mafia no longer provided the kind of shock material he needed. So many of them had run afoul of the Drug Enforcement Administration or the FBI, they seemed to have wiggled out of current troublemaking or were already in jail.

One battle at a time would be acceptable, he thought, as long as the DEA and the FBI could be used like a scouting party of marines and didn't try to run the whole show. They knew the terrain. They could point the way, and then the heavy troops could come clattering in on target. The thing to do was get going. And it was already 8:24.

He flipped to another manila folder. *"Papaver somniferum* (opium poppy) pods and seeds have been unearthed in Neolithic sites all over Europe. . . . Aristotle mentions the poppy as 'hypnotic' (from Hypnos, the god of sleep). . . ."

Good God, Lily! Where did you find this stuff? "American kids do their drinking in cars because it gives them a choice of location and privacy. Smoking marijuana will cost them only $30 for an eighth." An eighth of what? An ounce? "It's easy to toot up $30 worth of cocaine in half an hour. . . ."

Damn it all! Why did so many people think the school drug problem was exaggerated or existed only in someone else's territory? Did kids ever tell their parents more than they needed to know?

He was deep into a confusing report on the legalization of drugs, and was muttering to himself that glasses of some kind would soon be absolutely essential, when he realized he was no longer alone. He looked up to see Steiner bundled up in a heavy muffler. The aide wiped at the end of his nose and attempted what Rogers thought was a very weak smile.

"Morning, sir. How do you fancy our blizzard? I'm considering buying a sled and dog team."

Rogers tried to identify what it was about Steiner that made him vaguely uncomfortable. Or was he just being unfair? Certainly the man had done everything he was obligated to do and more. As he watched Steiner unlock the door, he told himself not to be so damned critical. Sometimes there's too much of the leatherneck about you, Rogers. Keep your mind open and your mouth shut, as much as possible.

"I should have given you a key, sir. My apologies. You see we rarely open up until eight-thirty and your predecessor never arrived before ten. I don't think he ever had a key."

Rogers walked straight through the outer office with Steiner following him. "This is a very important day," Rogers said. "I guess everyone is pretty excited."

"I'm not quite sure what you mean, sir." Steiner whipped off his muffler, brought a starched white handkerchief from his breast pocket, and blew his nose delicately.

As they entered his office, Rogers said, "Opening day of the new Congress. To a hick like me, that's pretty impressive."

There was a long pause while Steiner blew his nose again and arranged the pencils on Rogers's desk. "Of course, sir. Quite a day it is." He hesitated, then added carelessly, "But I suspect most of your colleagues will use our blizzard as a perfect excuse not to show up."

"You've got to be kidding. This is the United States Congress!"

"Indeed it is, sir."

Again the silence. Rogers was puzzled. He sat down, pulled out a lower drawer of the desk, and crossed his legs over it. He studied Steiner's face for a moment. "What are you looking at?" he asked finally.

"Your boots, sir. They are really quite beautiful."

"For damn sure that's the first time anybody ever called them that!" There followed a long silence. Rogers found it embarrassing. Finally he said, "I wish you'd stop addressing me as 'sir.' I also wish you'd start leveling with me. There's something you're trying to tell me, and I'm not getting the message."

Again the silence. Rogers heard someone enter the outer office while he waited for his assistant to respond. "Come on, Mort. Get it off your chest. Have I done something wrong already?"

Steiner rested his weight on a corner of the desk and deliberately avoided meeting Rogers's eyes. "No, sir . . . you have not . . . as yet. Perhaps I'm a tad overzealous in protecting you against disappointment. This is a complicated world here in the capital, and people like you need a skillful white hunter to help you survive."

"In other words, you."

"Exactly. Although the rules say you may hire eighteen employees, only if you have the right executive assistant will the machinery work smoothly. You must now make a choice and confirm my appointment, or I shall have to start looking elsewhere."

Rogers made a face and pulled at his right earlobe. It was a personal gesture acquired in his youth and never lost, despite some joshing from Lily about his earlobes serving as a lever for the release of troublesome problems.

He squirmed now and recrossed his legs. If there was one thing that made him uneasy, it was being rushed. "Now see here," he said evenly. "We hardly know each other. Wouldn't it be better if we had a little time to make sure we could work in harmony?"

"I'm afraid that's not possible. I already have two other opportunities—Congressmen Ritter of Pennsylvania, and Wainwold of Ohio. They are both still without an executive assistant."

"Why do I have the feeling that you've been laughing at me?"

"Quite the contrary, sir. I wouldn't think of laughing at any man in your present position and it won't be long before you see why. I do confess to a certain tendency to patronize, but if you decide on my services, I'll try to rid myself of it."

Rogers deliberately kept his expression somber as he uncrossed his legs and stood up. He bent down until he could look directly into Mort Steiner's eyes. He smiled, "Okay, Mort. I like a man who sometimes shoots himself in the foot. I know I'm just a hardheaded country boy here, but if you're willing to teach, I sure can learn."

He saw Steiner shake his head and blow his nose again. And he saw that Steiner's eyes were moist and he wondered if Steiner might be catching a cold. For sure underneath his smart-ass exterior, this guy was a patsy. What a contrast to Edward Starbuck, who had made no effort whatever to establish a working relationship.

Just before noon, Steiner escorted his new boss to the underground train that ran between Longworth House and the Capitol. As they entered one of the cloakrooms adjacent to the House itself, Steiner halted before a large, shaggy man who wore an eye patch. He was drawing on a cigarette and blowing the smoke at the ceiling. Steiner introduced him as Gordon Hawkins, the most important man in Washington.

"Oh, now I wouldn't go quite so far as that," Hawkins chuckled. He attempted a yellow-toothed smile suggesting modesty, but Rogers wondered if he really meant it. He was further surprised when Hawkins waved away his offered hand. "No, indeed," he said jovially. "I don't shake hands in the city—not even if you were the president. Colds, you know. Everybody has a cold at this time of the year, and I'm the hypochondriac of the year. The Japanese now, they're smart with their little white face masks. Notice how they don't get colds like other people?"

"I really hadn't noticed," Rogers said. "We don't have too many Japanese out our way."

"No, of course not. But are the Indians still on the warpath?" Hawkins chuckled again and enveloped his mane of hair in a cloud of smoke. "Well, sir," he said after a fit of coughing, "welcome to the zoo." Hawkins scanned the room with his good eye, and then, as if he had found something precious in the distance, turned and walked away.

"Who the hell was that?" Rogers asked.

"You don't know? Gordon Hawkins has the power of the pen, and lots of it! An essayist and a columnist and a recognized bastard, if you will excuse my English. He can smell a story he's not supposed to tell at ten thousand yards. It's unlikely he'll give you any trouble, because freshmen are not his meat. He likes to knock the big and powerful off their pedestals. Best to stay out of his way."

"He could do with some manners."

"As you will soon discover, arrogance is part of his profession."

As they continued through the cloakroom, sometimes known as the "lobbying pit," Rogers decided the assembling congressmen reminded him of a herd of restless cattle. They seemed not in the least interested in the historic moment that would mark the official inauguration of the session. Steiner paused to introduce him to several of his colleagues: Baker of Pennsylvania, a Republican; Todd of New York, a Democrat; and Goldstein of New York, also a Democrat. Rogers also shook hands with Carlos Rivera of Arizona, and Ridgefield of Delaware, and he found it was always the same. A smile, a handshake, a few words of welcome, and then as if by some marvelous congressional legerdemain, each man suddenly vanished. Rogers would have liked to spend at least a little more time with a few— perhaps to ask their feelings about being a member of Congress, or (if an opening presented itself) to ask about the drug situation in their districts. The opportunity never came.

At last even Steiner's vast supply of introductory prospects thinned out and they stood uncomfortably amid the babble of reunions and greetings. Rogers found the uproar nearly deafening and difficult to tolerate. He instinctively retreated within himself and stood apart, marveling at all the backslapping and shouts of recognition. It seemed to him that his future colleagues were behaving like members of a promotional club, chamber of commerce friends hohoing and inquiring about families, children, and grandchildren, skiing in Colorado, sailing in Barbados, and the dire effects of Christmas on their golf game.

Steiner found a page to escort Rogers to his seat and excused himself. He was not permitted on the floor of the House. Because of the transition, there was much to do in the office, he explained: A schedule must be prepared for the rest of the week; there were some lunches to arrange and a bundle of letters to constituents to be written for Rogers's signature.

Rogers followed the pale-cheeked page to his assigned seat in the last row on the Republican side of the House. He eased himself into the big leather chair gingerly. After all, this was a historic moment for the Rogers family, too. His father and mother would be proud, he knew, and he assumed Lily and the kids would feel the same way.

He twisted in the chair experimentally, trying to assume a position he thought suitably dignified for a member of the Congress of the United States.

After a few minutes, he noticed that he was sitting in almost total isolation. He saw other congressmen wandering about, pausing for conversation with what looked like old friends and occasionally glancing up at the gallery, where the public was waiting for something to happen.

For a time he watched the podium, where the famous "Skip" Donovan, Speaker of the House, had already taken his place. The Speaker remained seated in his huge thronelike chair as a string of representatives came to shake his hand. He smiled benignly and laughed aloud as they brought him tribute in the form of quips and gossip, and Rogers thought it was a strange way to open the session.

Steiner had told him that he would be welcomed personally if he went to the podium and introduced himself, but he was reluctant to join the waiting line of representatives. It was already past noon, and no one seemed interested in getting down to business. Matters more important than socializing with the Speaker should be under way.

As Rogers surveyed the large room, he thought that right here historic speeches had been made by famous men. Here were held the debates on the Missouri Compromise, the Kansas-Nebraska Act, and the Compromise of 1850. Holy cow! It was unbelievable that a plain old cattle rancher should be sitting right here in the middle of things! Well, not exactly in the middle; more like on the fringes, he thought as he watched a casual parade of men and women enter and take their places along the two terraces directly below the Speaker's chair.

Skip Donovan continued to ignore what was taking place on the floor. He seemed uninterested in anything other than whom he was talking to at the moment.

Rogers wished he knew more about the people milling around on the terraces. They seemed to be clerks or secretaries. The fancy brochure on the Capitol that Alice Morgan had shown him before he left his office did not identify them or their duties.

He saw a man in suit and tie take a large silver mace out of a cabinet, examine it, then place it back in the cabinet again. That man had been mentioned in the brochure, he remembered. He must be the sergeant at arms. The mace represented the power and the authority of the House of Representatives.

Rogers shook his head unhappily. Suddenly he realized how little he knew about his new station in life, and he experienced an almost overwhelming desire to run back to the cloakroom, recover his hat, and hit the trail back to old Tango. It would all come clear tomorrow, he hoped, when he started in the school for freshman congressmen.

He saw an elderly man approaching him, bearing most of his weight on an ivory-headed cane. The man stopped at the aisle leading to Rogers's seat and smiled. His eyes were almost hidden in two tangled nests of wrinkled skin and his head shook ever so slightly as he said, "Well, by God, a freshman—and a prairie type at that. What's your name, where're you from, and why are you sitting here all alone? Didn't anybody look after you?"

"Which question do you want answered first? And I'm sorry, I missed your name."

"Wynne Barker—Michigan. There's nobody who's been in these halls longer than I have, except maybe Claude Pepper and Skip Donovan."

Rogers had risen as soon as Wynne Barker addressed him. Standing up for any stranger, young or old, had always been mandatory in the Rogers family. "I'm Lee Rogers, state of Montana," he said.

"Great country. Sheep or cattle?"

"Cattle."

"Good. I'm a meat eater. Vitamins. Protein. Keep you going forever. Difference between Republicans and Democrats is the Democrats don't eat the fat. Read too much. You bring your shootin' iron?" Congressman Barker winked one of his mischievous eyes, and Rogers found he liked the way the old man dispensed with all unnecessary words. He spoke in telegrams.

Rogers smiled. If Barker wanted to talk old-time western frontier, he had just met a man who knew how. "No, suh," he said. "I hardly thought I'd be needing a six-gun."

"Lots of congressmen will give you an argument on that. You don't sound like a rancher."

"Why not?"

"Don't drop your g's. Grammar's not bad either. You go east to school?"

"No. Did it all in Montana. I also have a wife who was once a schoolteacher. She's in charge of the family speech."

Congressman Barker turned away and surveyed the array of still half-empty seats skeptically. He seemed lost for a moment, as if seeing or hearing something long gone, then he said, "If you're goin' to make a speech, this here's the place to do it. Or used to be. Not that no one would pay you attention, but it's a good way to shake your old frustrations and acquire new ones." He sighed heavily and added, "House has changed a lot. So has the Senate. Hell, we haven't got a real orator still alive. The windbags today whisper and grunt softlike so they'll look sane and sensible on the television screen. Smart guys don't come here now except to vote—or, like today, just to be on record for the opening. Even so, I'll bet out of the four hundred and thirty-odd members, no more than two-fifty will show and they won't stay. Guys are too busy to sit around here. You on a committee yet?"

"No, I just arrived."

"You will be. Takes all your time, but that's where the real work is done."

Rogers said, "I thought the House was supposed to open at twelve o'clock."

"Never does. Not so long as Skip's running things. That clock above his head is a fake, says he. This here show runs on his time. They don't teach you that in the freshman's school."

"I'm starting it tomorrow."

"Good. Come to me if you need help."

The hammering of a gavel resounded through the House. Rogers saw Skip Donovan was now standing up, trying to focus attention on himself. He was not entirely successful. Those congressmen already lounging in their seats continued their conversations, and those still arriving in groups of two and three did the same. Rogers glanced up at a flock of children in the gallery and was sorry for them. This could hardly be the spectacle they had anticipated.

At last the hubbub diminished to an undertone and Skip Donovan ceased pounding his gavel. He continued standing and in a voice devoid of drama he said, "We will now post the colors."

Immediately the doors to the cloakroom were thrown back and four marines entered. They set two flags in place beside the Speaker and retreated.

Skip Donovan said, "I now declare the House of Representatives in session. The Reverend Harvey Chatsworth will give the invocation."

"We don't usually have marines," Wynne Barker said.

> Cindy Brunswick
> 124 Exeter Street
> Albion, Ohio

Hello, hello, hello to my friend Sandra on my new stationery! Screw the telephone, this is super-secret. I should really be writing in invisible ink.

If you send in to the H & S Pharmaceutical Company—how do you like that? I even got the spelling right because I copied it right out of the ad—you can get all kinds of stuff which is not too expensive. They are stimulator producers and their stuff is very good for dieting, or studying, whichever. You can get one hundred for five dollars, like Christmas Trees, which will knock you good, or number 29 and 30, which are mostly caffeine. They are six bucks. You can get Pink Hearts for five dollars and Black Beauties, which are, as you can guess, black. They even have Cross Tops, which will send you right to the moon! By sending away, you don't have to go to the drugstore, where they don't have them anyway.

When Mom found mine in my room where I keep my stash, I told her they were just vitamins that the school nurse said everybody should take. I was afraid she might try one herself, but she didn't.

Don't forget Wednesday. We will have a real party. It will be so neat to be fourteen. I hope somebody gives me a tape of Dr. Demento. You ever listen to him? Cool as can be, with all his funny dead puppy pies, and fish heads and geeks. But I would settle for either "The Whole World Is Jewish" or "The Ballad of Irving."

I am so bored, I am ready to screw off. All this rainy day I have been listening to "They're Coming to Take Me Away, Ha-Haa," by Napoleon XIV.

I am so bored, which is why I write you this letter, because this way I can say things that would not be so popular if I phoned you and Mom just happened to pick up the extension. Like how Sylvia Freeman, who has the locker right next to yours at school, met this other girl from Bremerton High who sold her some shit weed, and when she tried to sell it herself she got busted. I told Sylvia she should not mess with that stuff, but she was zoning, and I might as well be talking to some punk. Have you heard their records? Like "Kill the Poor" and "Nazi Punks Fuck Off." Both of them are on CDs, but I don't know if you can buy them on tape.

You can send for these from International Record Syndicate and I love to send for them because when things come it is like Christmas, depending on how much money you have to spend.

And, hey! Tell the troops. I found out about the place where we can get ID cards. They're just like for real and guaranteed. No telltale photo glued on. Just send your photo and six bucks to Eden Press, Box 248, Dept. ID, Monihan, TX. Give your age, like 16 or 18, sex, height, weight, hair color—you're brunet—eye color, and any birth date you want! Want to be a Scorpio instead of a Libra? I am sending my money now because think of all the things you can do if you are legal! I can't wait!

Hey! One more super secret! You know Gloria Swenburg? Well, her brother, Gary, who is 16, has a stash of Blue Hawaiian, which is grown on the island of Hawaii. Super-special! Gloria is going to swipe some of it if he won't give it to her, and bring it to the party! We'll get so high it will be like cooking for God!

Mort Steiner slipped down to the café that served the House of Representatives and he managed to take a quick lunch while the Congress was still in session. He was anticipating a busy day, and the thought of Lee Rogers on his own was a situation he was not sure he liked. It was, he decided as he polished off his dietary soup, dietary salad, and decaffeinated coffee, something like sending one's son away to school on his first day. Would the big boys beat him up or would he defy his teacher?

Westerners, Steiner concluded as he hurried back to his office, were difficult to understand. They were not exactly uncivilized, but there was an air about them that was almost impossible to categorize. Maybe it was too much fresh air. They always seemed so healthy and looked like they had enjoyed a good night's sleep.

Someday, he thought, he would make a trip out west, maybe visit Montana, which over the past fifteen years had occupied such a special place in his life. And then there was the West Coast . . . roses in bloom all year round if one could believe television, and hamburger drive-ins and people with lots of muscles everywhere. It would be quite an expedition and would require much preparation . . . might, come to think of it, benefit if a companion were involved— say like Wilma?

Once back at his desk, Steiner returned a series of telephone calls. Holly Semper, whom he knew vaguely as a public-relations flack, wanted new congressman Rogers to make a breakfast speech to the interns from Washington Center on Monday morning next. Piffle!

Sorry, Holly. Not important enough, and my man is not ready for that sort of thing yet.

Next a group of Shriners from Montana visiting the capital would like photos taken with Congressman Rogers. Contact one Sam Todd. Okay, Mr. Todd. Come by the Rayburn Building at ten tomorrow morning and if it's not too cold we'll take the photos outside on the steps. Rule One: Never ignore constituents.

Noon tomorrow. Invitation to luncheon Egyptian Embassy. Phone regrets. What in God's name can Egypt do for Montana, much less its newest representative?

Two o'clock tomorrow. Republican Study Committee. Annual meeting. Change bylaws, elect officers. A negative on that. Rogers was too new to be elected any sort of officer and the bylaws were not his concern. Besides, he had to attend school.

Better put a hold on the Reserve Officers' Association cocktails six to eight tomorrow night. Rogers might still be a gung-ho marine and want to go.

Steiner fretted and was almost surly when Senator Rheinhart's office called and offered an open lunch invitation for the new representative. A get-acquainted meeting. Later in the month maybe. Rheinhart was an old pro who was just to the right of Attila the Hun. Best not to become identified with him.

After some fifteen phone calls, Steiner sensed that the circus had begun. People were already trying to push Rogers, and he was not going to let him be pushed. Not yet. Give the man a chance to get off his horse.

A woman was on the telephone, calling from someplace in Montana named Parmalee? Said she had voted for Lee Rogers and knew he would help her. Madam, what is your problem?

"My son is in the army."

"Splendid. These days it's a promising career for a young man."

"Not for him. He slugged an officer . . . well, maybe it was a sergeant."

"That might be regarded as a mistake, shall we say . . . ?"

"I want him out of the army. Do something before they send him somewhere to break rocks."

Ernest K. Gann

With his fists? Steiner wondered. But he said, "Madam, if you will give me all the particulars, Congressman Rogers will look into it, but I must warn you his influence with the military is more or less limited by law."

"Whose law? He makes the law, don't he? At least he can cut the army's budget!"

Steiner throttled all the sarcasms his nimble brain formulated. Would Mother Dear like to have all the army generals court-martialed because her son slugged a sergeant? We have a Pentagon full of surplus generals here and it might not be a bad idea. Would she be satisfied if he was given the Medal of Honor for exposing and revenging the cruelty of sergeants? Would Mother Dear be satisfied if her son was transferred to the navy and made an admiral, of which we also have an overabundance in the Pentagon?

Steiner managed to restrain himself and wrote down the particulars. Another call was waiting for him. He raised an eyebrow when Connie Marcus informed him that the call was from Athens. A Mr. Andropolis was on the line. From Athens, Montana?

Steiner listened carefully to the unhappy high-pitched voice of Sergio Andropolis. He said that he had run a restaurant in the town of Percival, Montana, for years and then retired to his homeland. He went to the U.S. Embassy in Athens, and he went to the consulate, and they said it was not their business—can you imagine such jerks? They're all jerks in those places, he said, except for the marine guards, and you should tell the congressman Sergio Andropolis says the truth.

Steiner explained that there was now a new congressman who might not be familiar with either the town of Percival or the proprietor of what-was-the-name-of-that-restaurant? "Mr. Andropolis, if you will just state the facts succinctly, perhaps we can learn more of your problem and do something about it."

"Something happened. A terrible thing. I am in agony. My stomach hurts and my head hurts. My wife is very mad. Life is very bad."

"My regrets, sir, but what is it you want us to do?"

"My social security check did not come this month. This is very serious."

72

"Maybe the mails were delayed, Mr. Andropolis. Sometimes we must be patient."

"Maybe the ship sank or the airplane crashed. I don' care. I was born in Greece, but I American citizen. I want my check. The United States of America took my money away from me and now I want it back."

Steiner wanted to say that if Mr. Andropolis could afford to phone from Greece, then the United States of America must have allowed him to make a good living, but instead he said, "Now, if you will just give me your full name and address . . ."

It was days like this, Steiner thought, that were aging him prematurely.

When he had finished talking to Athens, he turned the mother-love problem over to Charles Jackson, who wanted to know why he was always stuck with such things; and he passed the Andropolis matter on to Randy Lewis with the advisory that he might get in touch with the social security people and see if, number one, Mr. Andropolis deserved a check and, number two, if it had been sent and, if so, when.

Just as he thought most irritations were subdued for the balance of the afternoon and he could get to work seriously on a schedule for Rogers through the rest of the week, his phone rang again. He was shocked to hear the unctuous voice of Gordon Hawkins.

"Hawkins here, Mort."

As if I didn't know, Steiner thought. Now, what the hell?

"How's tricks?" Hawkins asked.

"I'm giving up this work and hiring on to the Libyans as a spy. Or perhaps entering a monastery."

Hawkins laughed and went into a fit of coughing. Steiner wondered how much longer cigarettes would let him live. When at last his hacking subsided, Hawkins said, "This new boss of yours is quite a character."

"What do you mean by that, Gordon?" Dear God, don't let him prod the lions until after they've been fed!

"I mean he has a lot of dash. Guess what he did today—opening day."

"I couldn't possibly." Lie. Oh, God, *what?* He should never have been left off the leash.

"Skip Donovan nearly choked on his gavel." Hawkins's distant laugh, followed by a second explosion of coughs, was anything but reassuring. "Would you believe your man stood up and asked to be recognized? 'Who are you?' says Skip. 'Congressman Rogers, First District, Montana,' says your man.

" 'Welcome,' says Skip. 'Let us all welcome the gentleman from Montana.' Now, get this, Mort. That old fart McPherson from Maine is giving out with some kind of a problem his fishermen are having, and why they should be given emergency relief in the form of grants to match the farmers', and he pauses for a minute while he checks his papers for some figures. It's during the silence that your man jumps up and says he has a bill he wants to introduce—"

"A *House* bill?" Steiner found it difficult to believe what he was hearing.

"Right. Now you'll appreciate this. McPherson's pretty addled these days, and he can't find his numbers to prove his fishermen are starving, so Skip asks him if he'll yield to the gentleman from Montana. While he's still shuffling papers, he says yes, he'll yield, and there is your man right in there swinging. He asks if Skip wants him to read the bill, and Skip naturally asks him if it's been worked on in committee. Your dude says no, and Skip says put it in the hopper, that this is no time for learned debate, no matter what the bill is about. Your man says he is perfectly willing to go through committee, but his bill is so urgent that debate should start on it right here and now. About the time Skip is going to call out the sergeant at arms, old man Barker steps in and calms everybody down. Some fun, eh?"

"Please, Gordon. It's been a bad day. I'm not ready for this."

"You better be. Things are a little slow right now, and it occurs to me that your man might make an interesting piece. Maybe a magazine . . . I don't know whether to query the *New Republic* or *Cosmopolitan,* but since he's so damned handsome and simple, the gals who read *Cosmo* might go for him. I'd like you to set up an interview for tomorrow after the session is over."

"He can't. He has other appointments."

"Then the next afternoon."

"He's busy all that day, and into the night."

"Bullshit, Mort. I'm just being thoughtful and giving you a chance to get your act together. I'll be there day after tomorrow afternoon at five, and suggest you and your man have a dollop of Glenfiddich on hand to warm the heart of your fellow countryman. Pip-pip, until then, old boy."

Pip-pip, indeed, Steiner thought. Gordon Hawkins and his phony British accent. What was he telling people these days, that he got that bad eye when he was wounded in Vietnam? Hell, he never went near the front. Not when there was a reasonably comfortable hotel in Saigon.

Steiner went immediately to Rogers's office. He examined the papers on the desk with practiced ease. Here it was, dear God. A bill, all written out in the proper form. Everything except a number. "Be it resolved that a state of emergency exists . . . to authorize the attorney general of the United States to urge the president to make a declaration of war . . ."

Steiner moved quickly away from the desk. His ever-sensitive ears had heard Rogers enter the outer office, and greet Connie Marcus with a hearty, "Hi, there, Connie!"

Steiner inhaled deeply to ease his apprehensions. Dear, sweet Jesus, he thought, why me?

Now hey, amigo, here is me again. Businessman.

All right, you got four schools, understan'? No way in this whole goddamned world you gonna get so many to yourself—except from us, understan'? Jus' you behave and this here be your territory and nobody else come near, because if they do, you jus' tell us, y'know? We beat the shit outta 'em, that be that and they don' come back ever, right?

Now, we careful about everything, y'know? We cover the market, you might say. We got Mother-o'-Pearl cocaine—y'know there ain't nothin' like it. You sell it to your friends for two hundred a gram and to strangers for ten percent more. You pay us what? A stinking little one hundred.

You got this job because you got transport, and no bad record for violations. We know that from the local police who be wired to the whole country and he say you never been busted for nothin' whatever at all, y'know, not even no traffic

76

violations. So narcs are not itchin' to target on you, know what I mean? You don' have no fleas and they don' sniff no bad odor so they leave you be, okay, amigo? And we want to keep it so.

Now what we got here? All kinds of marijuana—Hawaiian, Acapulco Gold, Colombian Red Gold, and some Maui Wowee, y'know. Lot of ballplayers like it. You can tell your customers that. We also got somethin' different, y'know, like has never been used around here—in your territory, man. We got Thai stick, which you can push to the big boys because it's so special. Three dollars and thirty sticks a gram to you, amigo. You sell for six, maybe seven. It be even better than crack.

You ask me if we got PCP and my answer is no. We don' fuss with such stuff, because you get busted with some and, man, they put you away for a long time. Understan'? We be in business a long time. Like nobody give a shit about a little marijuana, y'know? It's like recreational and the narcs use it theyselves. But PCP? Everybody get real mad and tear up the whole fucking countryside, understan'? Know what I mean? The narcs and the police is real mad and they get together for a change and make misery everywhere.

You say to me your people don' want LSD no more? They don' know what's good for 'em. But don' get down, amigo. There will always be people around who lie about things, man, sayin' how bad this is and that is and all like that— y'know, people who don' know what they're talkin' about. Like what is really bad for you, man? You guess right. Like how about just plain ol' tobacco, which the United States government subsidize? Know what I mean? Hell, they *give* money to tobacco farmers just to keep 'em in business, and many, many people *die* every fucking day from using tobacco, man. How you explain dat? Know what I mean? You just go on with your schools the way you been, an' pay no attention to certain people who should have their mouths shut. Be a businessman.

Now, amigo, with four schools you got a variety of people

so you gotta have a variety of items for sale, know what I mean? You gotta have some uppers and downers and you should have some kif, which I can let you have at ten dollars a gram. Comes from Morocco. Know where is that? Christ, they don' teach nothin' these days! Even in Panama they tell us where Morocco is.

Okay, man, so you sell twenty grams at twenty. You got four schools. Easy, man. You rich in a hurry. You soon tool 'round in a new Mercedes!

Understan' we in business together, amigo? You goin' to be very much richer than you already are—jus' give yourself a little more time, know what I mean? Now take you yourself personally. I say to you, be more careful. I can see from your eyes you been takin' a hit for yourself now and then. Maybe? Okay—maybe too much, y'know? I give you some numbers. Jus' remember, twenty lungsful a marijuana equals jus' two of kif or hash. So if you wanna do drugs yourself, amigo, bear that in mind.

Steiner allowed a touch of bitterness to color his voice as he followed Lee Rogers into his office.

"Welcome home," he said. "I understand you opened the Congress with a bang."

Rogers managed a dry laugh. He was not at all sure of himself at the moment and he wished Mort Steiner would go away and let him think. "I seem to have caused a little commotion by opening my big mouth when I guess I was supposed to be listening. But what I have to say has trouble lying still while some committee spends a year or so discovering something everybody knows already."

Steiner emitted an "mmmm" because he could not find voice for real words.

"I only got started with what I wanted to say, but I have a feeling that I might as well have been talking to the pigeons on the roof. My new friend, Wynne Barker of Michigan, explained that I should have gone to something called the Select Committee on Narcotics Abuse and Control first. Hell's bells, I knew that. But why wait? Why should the chairman of a committee or anyone else present a bill that is mine to start with? Haven't I got just as much right to present a bill as any other congressman?"

"Yes," Steiner sighed, "you have. But the narcotics committee has been wrestling with the dope thing for years and the results have been discouraging."

"Maybe that's what's wrong. We don't have time for wrestling! We can't talk this thing away. Hell, the United Nations has tried it and the only countries that have put their money where their mouth is are England, Italy, and Saudi Arabia."

"You've done your homework, haven't you, sir?"

"My wife is still a schoolteacher at heart. She didn't want me coming to the final exam entirely unprepared."

Rogers grinned and looked out the window. Federal employees by the thousands were flowing out of every building exit he could see.

He was thoughtful for a moment. What would it be like to turn off your thinking every time the clock hands stood at five?

"Mort . . . ? One of the things my wife couldn't dig up much information about is our State Department. Could that outfit be one reason why this antidrug campaign has never really gotten off dead center? We get carloads of manure about our war on narcotics, but we keep advancing backward. It's like Vietnam. All the rules are protecting the bad guys."

Steiner held up his hands as if to fend off an invisible enemy. "Please, *please,* sir—don't start taking on the State Department. Congress thinks the sun rises and sets there because they have never understood what it does. If you take on State, they will eat you for breakfast."

"I'm not sure you understand why I'm here, Mort. Damn it all, I'm going to make this nation attack an enemy that's doing more harm than if they dropped a thousand bombs. I'm going to make us start fighting for our survival or there may not be any."

"I really haven't thought that much about it, sir, but I must direct your attention to more routine matters. Tomorrow after school you have an appointment with Amy Williams Smathers. I made it for five-thirty so you wouldn't be rushed."

Rogers frowned and groaned. "How did *she* get here?"

"I don't know what variety of transportation she used, but you should not forget that she's chairman of the Women's Political Caucus in your state, and she will have Henrietta Duncan, who is vice-chairman and a Garfield County representative, with her."

"Watch your language, Mort. Chairperson or chairwoman, please. What do they want to talk about? I want to start a real war and they want to talk women's rights? And by the way, where the hell is Edward Starbuck? He's in charge of public affairs. Why can't he handle the ladies?"

"Edward is at his dentist's. Edward is frequently at his dentist's."

Rogers cocked his head inquiringly. "You don't like Edward?"

"He does his best, sir."

"Not that I can see. Make sure he's here for a staff meeting tomorrow at eight."

"*Eight,* sir?"

"Right. And I don't smile at late arrivals."

"Very well, I'll pass the word. Now, sir, I've given the ladies an hour, and afterward you'll just have time to go to the club and wash up before you make an appearance at the Sierra Club reception. The Hay-Adams Hotel, which is right near you."

"I've got a pile of homework to do." Rogers recognized an incipient catch in his voice. Feeling sorry for himself? Already? What happened to the guy who arrived just yesterday and was so full of beans? "Is that all?" he asked.

"By no means. I haven't got everything set as yet, but a man who calls himself "Moose" Buckley called and said he's a close friend of yours. I said you had half an hour to spare at nine tomorrow morning."

"Thanks a lot. Moose Buckley runs an auto agency in Great Falls. He wears fancy cowboy outfits and doesn't know a horse from a cow. Not one of my favorite people."

"He's a laugher," Steiner said as if he'd suddenly bitten into a rotten persimmon. "I've no idea what was so amusing, but he laughed so loud I thought he'd break the phone. Still, when he said he contributed five hundred dollars to your campaign chest, I started listening. Thus his appointment."

Steiner paused deliberately. "You have a more delicate meeting the day after tomorrow, and I hope you'll listen to me carefully about it. It's with Gordon Hawkins."

"Humph. That should be interesting."

"Let's not make it too interesting."

"Can I have the weekend off?" Rogers smiled. Who the hell was he talking to, his keeper?

"Sure. You can look at houses to rent. Mary and Connie have been working on it and have three possibilities—two in Fairfax and one right in Bethesda. I'm told they are good areas for your children."

"You think of everything, Mort. Now, while you're making all those appointments, how about setting me up with the narcotics committee?"

Steiner hesitated. "That's a *select* committee—the big wheels in the House. You have Rodino of New Jersey . . . Stark of California . . . Ben Gilman . . . Mel Levine—"

"Mort, I don't give a damn whether they're select or what. I've got a lot to say to them and I want to do it as soon as possible. One way or another I'm going to be heard, and don't you or anyone else in this office forget it."

Gray, rainy days were the worst, Oscar Brimmer had decided. And there were many more of them in Colombia than a guy expected. Sunshine, okay. Things were more tolerable when the sun was shining. But when the breeze was gone, it was too damned hot here in the jungle to think about women. Who wanted to screw in a Turkish bath? Humid weather took the steam out of a man and put it in the atmosphere. Now gray days were some different. Usually. But here in the middle of nowhere, they were problems.

Leon, or somebody in the FARCs, had sent a woman named Maria to the camp. She arrived on a rainy day, which should have made things quite cozy because she was not too repulsive to look at. But what does she do after you're all undressed and standing there naked, like some old liverwurst left in the sun? She pulls out her kit and gives herself a hit—a speedball, no less, half cocaine and half heroin. Maria is a dedicated mainliner, with puncture marks all over her limbs.

That did it. There was no way in the world any self-respecting pecker could stand up under those conditions. Maria finally wound up exercising the fat manager's shrieking bedsprings. And good riddance.

The temptation to bail out of this awful place was very powerful, except when the consequences were given due consideration. Leon, with his snaggly teeth and billiard-ball eyes, summed up the situation in four concise words: "You know too much." Sure. Like just how and when and where—in that little field in Arkansas. Among other places. Even so, it was hard to believe they would terminate a guy who had done his job so well.

Hoo-hoo! They would erase a guy without taking a second breath. These people were reptiles. Their blood wasn't even warm.

Returning from the cantina that night, Brimmer's jeep collided with a small pig that had somehow found its way from a local farm to the jungle trail. The pig was dead when Brimmer finally stumbled around to see what he had hit. He spent some time mumbling his apologies to the pig and decided it deserved a decent burial.

After a considerable struggle, he managed to heave the prostrate animal into the jeep and drove off toward the camp. Obedient to an inspiration, which he later regretted, he heaved the pig through the paneless window of the manager's bedroom, where he supposed, along with Maria and her fat host, it would make a cozy trio.

Bryce Tuttle, a Bostonian who was following the tradition of his Massachusetts ancestors, had been at "State" for eleven years, and was by now accustomed to the "slings and arrows," as he called them, with which his department of the government was peppered from all sides. It had taken him some time to realize that no one loves an arbiter, even when the settlement of antagonisms pleases both sides. Which rarely happened. At State you were burdened with a sort of unmentionable inferiority complex that gathered with time like marine growth, and was resisted by undiplomatic rudeness or, worse, open defiance. The more astute employees of the State Department were aware that, like lawyers, they had been relegated to a dubious position in society; and like most groups in trouble, their loyalty to each other, and to whatever endeavor might be their assignment, was often touching.

Various secretaries of state had tried to change the image of their department and had mostly succeeded in temporarily destroying morale, a departmental affliction that survived until chaos was restored again. Certain personnel within the department were assigned to the narcotics situation in the country of their assignment, and almost invariably it was far from an easy burden, because they fought on two fronts—against the traffickers on their home ground, and against the Drug Enforcement Administration, which was most skillful in bureaucratic maneuvering. Working for the State Department was usually thankless and was becoming increasingly dangerous.

Many young people went to Georgetown University preparatory to a career in the department, but those who envisioned themselves at diplomatic receptions, covered with medals, while champagne flowed and string quartets played in the background were soon disillusioned. If they somehow avoided assignment to hardship posts like Pakistan, Romania, Poland, East Germany, or any of the third-world countries, they could find themselves in Mexico, Peru, Colombia, or even the Bahamas, where their personal safety depended on how far they could disassociate themselves from any campaign aimed at troubling the local narcotics traffickers.

Mexico was particularly fickle about eradication programs. The authorities had made notable seizures at some of the major cultivation camps for marijuana, but elsewhere throughout the land other *plantíos* produced two crops a year. As South American traffickers sought new routes to the United States, Mexico was being used ever more frequently as a transit country. Interdiction was extremely difficult. Most petty officials were accustomed to a lifetime of generous rewards for looking the other way. The "outside income" of Mexican policemen far exceeded their governmental pay.

While State employees, from the United States ambassador on down, were expected to do something about Mexican narcotics production, there was just so much a mere guest of the country could do. The cooperation of the Mexicans ranged from enthusiastic to indifferent and was sometimes even chilly. It was hard for a Mexican to tell another Mexican who was making the equivalent of twenty U.S. dollars a day that he was doing the wrong thing cultivating illegal plants when skilled silver miners made only ten dollars a day. It was difficult for any gringo to enter the complex family structure of Mexican life and accomplish much of anything except the arrest of a few minor traffickers. No matter how cautious the investigation or shocking the evidence, the hunt always collapsed before the whispered names of the most powerful people in Mexico.

The strain resulting from such activities created an unavoidable amount of antigringoism and on occasion had erupted into violence. Enrique Camarena Salazar, a special agent of the DEA known as "Kiki," and his Mexican pilot, Alfredo Zavala Avelar, were abducted and murdered, and a mass torture and murder of their own police had reminded everyone concerned that officials of both nations were not dealing with some good-natured amigos smiling beneath the brims of straw sombreros.

Despite the feeble efforts of the United Nations, the attitude of Mexican producers was often much the same as that held by traffickers in other countries. "It is your problem. You are the customers. Keep buying and we will keep producing. Meanwhile, don't try to tell us how to run our country."

State Department employees were accustomed to such rebuffs, and the Drug Enforcement people, who were usually sheltered under the same roof, were brave and learning. One of them was young Harvey Longfellow, a clean-cut young man from Virginia who had been with the DEA less than two years. He joined with Bryce Tuttle of the American Embassy in Bogotá, Colombia, in an attempt to locate more exactly one of the largest known cocaine camps in the country.

Bryce Tuttle, who had been in Colombia almost four years, was due to go home and be married. He had made many friends in Colombia, and on certain occasions had invited them to the embassy, and they had responded by inviting him to their homes.. On the surface it was a pleasant State Department assignment.

Eventually, through friends of friends, Tuttle and Longfellow learned of a man who was said to know where the camp they sought was located. They arranged to meet him in the Café Marigold on the day of the Saint Xavier fiesta at noon.

Neither Bryce Tuttle nor Harvey Longfellow were ever seen again by their own friends. The American ambassador enlisted the aid of the Colombian government in a national search for his former charges—without result.

One American who did see them was Oscar Brimmer. Their Colombian connection had indeed shown them the location of the camp. But they were quite dead when they arrived under an escort of FARC troopers. There was a single bullet hole in the forehead of each young man when their bodies were dragged deep into the jungle and buried.

Both the fat manager and Oscar Brimmer had witnessed the quiet event. They found it unnecessary to communicate with each other. The manager's miniature eyes displayed no change of expression, but Brimmer wondered how their families might take it when they were told their sons had sacrificed their lives for their country.

Far from such events, secluded in the hills near Bogotá, was the elaborate hacienda of Marco Fedles, a man who had already become legendary. He named the place Casa de Los Estranjeros (House of Strangers), although he never explained why. He had bought the original house from a descendant of a wealthy Spanish settler, and its graceful architecture still suggested the tranquil beauty of former times. The alterations engineered by Fedles left little doubt that times had changed. The house was now a fortress surrounded by high rolls of barbed wire, and the fields of fire in all directions were covered by heavily protected machine guns. Russian antitank rockets, together with all necessary launching equipment, had been promised but had yet to arrive. Fedles allowed his normal equanimity to be slightly ruffled when he thought about the rockets, although there was no question in his mind or anyone else's that if necessary he could repel an attack by the Colombian Army. At the very least there would be time to gather his reserve units of FARC, whose numbers were so great the Colombian government had so far been reluctant to challenge him.

Fedles, who had found himself doing more business with Fidel

Castro than he liked, thought the Cuban leader had stolen the rockets since they were supposedly transshipped through his country. He was as yet unready to accuse Castro of thieving from the people of Colombia—he wanted more confirmation from the Soviets before exposing his close neighbor. But any opinion from his Russian contacts took an interminable time. Meanwhile, Fedles quelled his Mediterranean temper and told himself he was impregnable with or without rockets. "The shield of the people," he was fond of saying, "is of the finest tempered steel. Once held in front of a gifted leader, no government dare attack."

Thus Marco Fedles was satisfied with his situation, and though the demands on his time were heavy, he still reserved hours for indulging in his favorite pastime—the quiet and artful seduction of very young girls.

Marco Fedles pursued his hobby with the same quiet dedication he offered his countless other projects. In all the major nations of the world, he maintained procurers whose sole responsibility was the discovery of suitable candidates and their transport to Colombia. Since Fedles had warned his agents to be sensitive to family relationships, and extremely careful concerning past moral records, the number arriving at Casa de Los Estranjeros was rarely more than one a month.

The volume suited Fedles because full enjoyment of his unique avocation required both time and skill. He wanted no part of sexual force and had been known to order the execution of his own men accused of rape; yet out of all the maidens who had come to Casa de Los Estranjeros, only two had actually been returned to their homes with their virginity, if not their innocence, still intact.

Fedles liked the intricacies of wooing and it took a very alert and determined youngster to refuse his cascade of gifts and blandishments when surrounded by the thrills of a fairy-tale environment.

Then, too, Fedles himself was far from unattractive. Although he was not a tall man, he gave the impression of being so, and his warm and ready smile was an astonishing denial of his cold-blooded reputation. His face was sharply cut as if by a master sculptor intent on revealing gentle masculinity, and his gray eyes were very nearly hypnotic when met for the first time. The combination of Maltese and "some Corsican," if his claim were to be believed, left him with a grace of movement seen only in the finest dancers, and this in itself had a way of intriguing the beholder.

Although the program was never rigid, Fedles restrained his approaches toward each young guest during her first week in residence. They shared occasional meals and watched films afterward. Nothing more. His preference for films portraying the more sophisticated environments was the result of a long-held desire to improve himself. His original manners had been those of a Mediterranean peasant, but after years of studying the behavior of various actors, he could easily pass as a formally educated European gentleman. It pleased him to play the roll of good-natured and cultivated uncle to the young females who came his way, and most of them soon found him captivating. A few convinced themselves they had found their white knight and were everlastingly in love.

Fedles wanted his imports to be at ease, have time to recover from jet lag and accustom themselves to his luxurious cuisine. Most of all he wanted them to become familiar in his presence and, through a long series of subtle suggestions and preliminary fondlings, induce them to accept his bed eagerly and with full enthusiasm. From the hour of their deflowering onward, he would tutor them in all varieties of sexual maneuverings and, depending on their natural talent, would keep them within easy summons until inevitably he grew bored. All his guests left several thousand dollars richer, and most of them departed in tearful adoration.

The people of Colombia were no more aware of Fedles' hobby than they were of his enormous wealth—which, thanks to ever-increasing shipments of narcotics, was multiplying beyond his wildest visions. At first, as he collected various currencies, he'd stuffed most European moneys into several Swiss banks. But he had ceased that practice when he found that the investment talents of Swiss bankers were far inferior to his own. While the Swiss accounts stumbled along through West German insurance companies and Italian supermarkets, investments he had made in American stocks such as Microsoft became very pleasing.

Fedles' daily receipts were almost entirely in cash, and placing such amounts was becoming awkward and sometimes dangerous.

One of his major dealers had been hit for over half a million U.S. dollars recently, and another for one hundred and fifty thousand. The hijacks had reportedly been carried out by "unknown parties," and five men were killed in the process. Their deaths did not trouble Fedles nearly as much as his conviction that the theft and violence had been successfully accomplished by members of the Mafia. The thought that "those dago apes" were intruding on this territory infuriated him. The families should stick to labor unions, prostitution, and gambling and stay off his sacred ground.

Fedles was only mildly annoyed when the United States government demanded that all U.S. banks furnish detailed records of every deposit over ten thousand dollars. Since he considered it folly to invest in anything Colombian, much less keep large amounts in Colombian banks, his solution was elementary. With his resources on deposit in Canada and several banks in Grand Cayman and the Bahamas, along with his real-estate holdings in Manhattan, Akron, Palm Springs, Atlanta, Denver, and Fort Worth, Fedles bought five American banks. Thus his deposits were divided. Although he assumed his collectors were skimming a little, each of them had been carefully chosen and trained to be acutely aware of their fate if their greed became noticeable.

Now there was so much money involved that Fedles had no intention of closing shop and settling down with a mere half-billion for his own use. He did everything in his power to generate even more income because of the ever-increasing demands of his private army, with which he intended one day to rule Colombia and very possibly Bolivia. Armies, he had reluctantly concluded, were man's ultimate toys and certainly the most expensive. While the Soviets were generous with their shipments of various munitions, they had lobbed a long series of *nyet*s when it came to the actual payroll of his troops.

As a consequence, Fedles was constantly displeased with the Russians and with Castro, who seemed to have the key to their hearts. He also held in contempt the Colombian government and their tolerance of Americans who had come to Colombia with the open intention of putting him out of business. He could not understand how the president of Colombia and the officials in Bogotá could give the invading Yankees such free entry. "The Americans are so stupid," he was fond of saying. "They are worse than the English. They think only of their ugly country with their wide streets, their overfurnished dull houses, and their incredibly dull wives. They have absolutely no imagination, so they miss innumerable opportunities for profit. They are a nation of fools who throw money in the ocean to see if it will float."

A telex machine kept Fedles advised of the latest street prices on every narcotic the world over, and he kept careful tab on trends that both his faithful and potential customers were inclined to follow. While heroin remained reasonably steady, the spectacular rise in cocaine consumption and its social acceptance were very heartening. Marijuana was becoming a crapshoot, as always, he thought. The competition was fierce and now many Americans were growing it in their basements or in blocked-off rooms, using halogen lamps to produce a superior product. Marijuana had now replaced both pineapples and sugar as the major product of the Hawaiian Islands. As if that were not enough, large areas of government land in the California mountains and elsewhere had been taken over by energetic bud growers who had the cheek to booby-trap their assumed territories and frequently demonstrated that they would shoot trespassers.

Fedles believed that the principals of his staff were among the best in the world. His demands on them were merciless, but he paid them handsomely and saw to it that praise fell where it was due. The chief instructors in his army were a tough trio of ex–British commandos; his comptroller was a former high officer in the World Bank; and the pilot of his personal intercontinental jet had flown as test pilot for the very company that manufactured it. Likewise his principal traffickers were former businessmen of some standing, far removed from the usual profile of operatives in their trade. His chefs, masseuses, political advisers, buyers and sellers, capital-management officers who had replaced the Swiss and financial analysts were all of outstanding quality.

Employing their combined talents, Fedles had parlayed both his and FARC's holdings into even greater sums. Barring untoward incidents, Fedles believed another year or two would see him in a position to challenge the present inept government and establish a "government of the people." He thought it unnecessary to mention who the leader might be.

Of all his departments, Fedles was proudest of his intelligence staff, which served under the direct command of an old crony from Marseilles. He was Louis Prevet, a former inspector of police in that city and a man whose appreciation of human foibles was invaluable. Prevet was well acquainted with Interpol and knew vulnerable officials in nearly every civilized and semicivilized country in the world. His alertness provided Fedles with an international picture of the worldwide narcotics situation every morning with his coffee.

It was Louis Prevet who also kept Fedles informed of any pertinent event that had taken place in Washington, D.C., and his shrewd assessments of their effect on any of Fedles' various enterprises were usually correct. They normally spoke in French, a language enjoyed by both men, and since both were given to patois, their morning conversation remained private regardless of servants or other personnel passing to and fro.

Prevet spent most of his day on the telephone, and this morning, more with intent to amuse than to alarm, he told Fedles of a new congressman who had offered a bill proposing that the United States declare war on all countries accused of shipping drugs to his country. Prevet's description of Lee Rogers addressing the chair, while not entirely accurate, did succeed in arousing Fedles' attention.

Fedles chewed thoughtfully on a slice of chilled papaya, and allowed his gray eyes to become fixed on Figaro, the captive monkey who at breakfast time was always hunched on the balustrade near the table. After a moment in which he appeared to be studying Figaro's pelt, he said thoughtfully, "I don't like the smell of it. Something is different here. Either this congressman is an utter fool, or he can cause trouble. I can't explain why I think so, but I feel we should keep a careful eye on him. Does he have a family?"

"I don't know." Louis Prevet kept his high position because Fedles knew he would answer truthfully and not just say what he wanted to hear.

"*Alors.* Find out. I want a full dossier on the man, just in case."

"Very well." Prevet sighed because he thought there was very little a single congressman could do to make real trouble for the Fedles organization. Yet Prevet was perhaps the only person in the world who knew of two emotional elements peculiar to his boss. The first was an almost uncanny sense of approaching threat. Again and again he had demonstrated his concern over minor matters that soon enough became very real problems. Prevet could easily recall at least a dozen occasions when Fedles had been slated for assassination, but each time some mysterious urge had compelled him to change his plans abruptly, and he escaped. When Fedles smelled danger, Prevet knew, it was time to look around and see how close it actually was.

Prevet had often thought his boss should have been an actor. For he loved the dramatic, sometimes much to the worry of his bodyguards. He seemed incapable of arriving at any hotel or other place of chosen rendezvous without a retinue of servants and assistants, and for such occasions he took great pains to appear in what he thought would be proper apparel. In London or New York, he wore a dinner jacket and black tie at night; or if it was a sporting locale, a jacket with the seal of Colombia embroidered on the pocket and an ascot around his neck. If his meeting was in Paris, he might appear in cloak and beret, a costume he augmented with a gold-headed cane.

Fedles' arrivals at his conferences were anything but discreet; it was as if the more attention he attracted, the happier he might be. Only last year he had insisted that a meeting with Turkish, Austrian, and Lebanese traffickers take place in the Parthenon. Although the great edifice was temporarily closed to the public, he bribed the officials into opening it for his little group and spent part of his time impressing his guests with quotations from Socrates and Plato.

Even Prevet's blood chilled when he thought of his superior's fascination with the melodramatic. Recently one of the FARC troopers had somehow managed to steal a few grams of cocaine from the factory complex he was supposed to be guarding. He then tried to sell it to a sewing-machine franchiser who had more sense than to buy it. Eventually the trooper approached several other possible buyers, and word soon reached Fedles. Instead of simply disposing of the young man with a bullet to his head, Fedles staged a grand execution in the courtyard at Los Estranjeros. He ordered the trooper's entire company to march by in full uniform, and then ordered them one by one to spit in the face of their comrade, who was chained to a wall. When that ceremony had been completed, Fedles himself wrapped a blindfold around the trooper's head, and he took his time about it. Every gesture he made suggested a grand finale, and as if enjoying a moment of supreme vindication, he joined the family of the victim before the actual shots were fired. When the trooper's body stopped quivering and lay in a bloody pool, Fedles allowed the family to take the corpse away for burial.

If it was possible for his boss to make a scene, Prevet thought, then certainly Marco Fedles would invariably seize the opportunity.

"Even if he is just blowing off steam," Fedles said on this morning, "I don't like this congressman's style. If he needs a gift to quiet him down, perhaps we might consider it. But if a kick in the ass will do the same, then that will be better."

Lily Rogers had rarely thought of her new journal in the morning; there was always too much going on around the place. But this morning, when spring had obviously decided to retreat forever, there was certainly no temptation to leave the house. The winds of February were sweeping down from the western mountains and picking up speed across the flatlands. Outside the kitchen window, where Lee had hung a thermometer so he could regard it with his breakfast, she saw the temperature standing at twenty below zero. She refused to think about the chill factor because both Robert and Fay had long ago caught the school bus, waiting for it in the wind as if such conditions were just a part of their daily routine. This was not a land, she thought, for soft schoolchildren.

While the old frame house trembled under the heavier gusts of wind, she left the kitchen, which was at least warm, thanks to the modern wood-burning heater Lee had insisted on installing several years back and had been notably unwilling to tend ever since. She smiled as she recalled how the chauvinist pig had a way in such matters: Whatever was new about the house was his responsibility until installations had been completed; then it was "once in, once out." Whether it was the wood heater, the dishwasher, the disposal, or the new stereo, Lee exempted himself from further association. Once in place and functional, it was up to some other member of the family to load it or unload it, clean it or repair it. Never let it be said that Lee Rogers failed to play man-about-the-house to the hilt.

As she mounted the stairs, Lily thought about the telephone call she had taken much earlier. It would be a shame to allow the wind or anything else to blow it away. Lee had called just before dawn and she was anxious to put his words in her journal, not because she expected to forget what he had said, but because it seemed appropriate. If she was going to be the wife of a congressman, then there should be some sort of history concerning his personal life as well as the political.

She sat down and began writing with more than her usual flourish.

. . . It was eight o'clock in Washington, he said, and apologized for calling so early. It was six here, which in winter is a tad on the early side unless you have dairy cattle. He said he wanted to call me before he went to his office because never in his life had he realized how much of his life I represented, and that was very nice to hear.

"I miss you! You are one marvelous woman!" he yelled, as if he had no faith in the power of electricity.

I allowed myself an overlong amount of self-preening.

Lily nibbled at the end of her pen, trying to recall as nearly as possible what he had said later in the conversation.

. . . So far I seem to have trouble getting people's attention on the subject of narcotics. There are so many other problems. It's much easier to argue over the appropriation for a dam, or space travel, or a tax change, because everybody here knows it'll go to a yea-or-nay vote. Finally the problem goes away all neatly wrapped up in a package for the president's signature, and everybody goes home that night feeling they've done something. I keep telling people I meet that there's a grizzly in the living room, but they don't listen!

She stared at the distant horizon a moment and armed herself to write down what Lee had said just before their conversation ended.

Don't worry, I'm not discouraged. I came here because of Jack and I'll hang in here until what happened to him can't happen to someone else's kid.

She put her hands over her eyes and breathed deeply. The merest mention of Jack was sometimes more than she could tolerate, if only because it always brought back a sense of guilt. The Rogers family had not had the faintest idea that there might be drugs in the school. In rural Montana? There were actually no signals that Jack might be a user before the incredible thing happened. That kind of tragedy happened to other people.

Here were the torment and the blame-laying all coming back again. Should Lee have realized something was wrong with their son? They had been so close to each other. Maybe she should have been more alert to possible changes in his behavior, rather than so confounded anxious to make sure he had enough to eat.

It was still almost impossible to realize that Jack was never coming back from the graduation party. His mischievous smile was still right here in the house . . . everywhere . . . in the parlor, where he used to stretch out on the floor after a football game; in his room, where he used to pump his iron; and even in the corral, where he spent weekends teaching dumb horses to do things they didn't want to do.

She focused unwillingly on the large manila envelope on top of her desk. An empty flowerpot held it in place. The envelope was full of letters from neighbors a hundred miles around who seemed determined to share the Rogerses' despair. ". . . Such a splendid young man . . . a real leader among his fellow students . . . his intelligence was always stimulating . . . never knew a student athlete who could be so gracious in victory . . ."

The plaudits went on and on, some sixty letters.

She closed her eyes and shook her head vigorously. The last thing Jack would want would be a blubbering mom.

She stood up quickly and slammed her journal shut. Then she

picked up the manila envelope and placed it carefully in the bottom drawer of her desk. Those letters would never again be reread.

Gordon Hawkins had long been convinced that during the normal course of his work he had met more fakes, liars, thieves, swindlers, and hypocrites than had any other human being. Yet he was neither bitter nor discontent with his work; the whole concept of political villainy fascinated him, and he was grateful that he could labor in such fertile gardens. He was also thankful that the majority of the politicians he knew were honest, hardworking people. They just didn't make very exciting copy.

Years of experience had given Hawkins a nose for bad human corkage as delicate as that of the most critical sommelier. Normally he would keep several rogues hanging in his private gallery, awarding them, male or female, one star or two stars or even five, depending upon the degree of irascibility or ineptness they had achieved. But in time they died, or retired to enjoy their riches, or were rendered untouchable by network talking heads whose stories were often based on only a hint of truth. He was always scouting for replacements; and presidential appointees, along with civil servants who followed the principle of protecting their backsides, were his favorite candidates. Yet Hawkins did not allow his cynicism to become a dagger poised at every victim he could discover. Instead he did his utmost to report on people and situations in a forthright manner.

As a consequence of his philosophy and frequent caustic scoldings, Hawkins was far from popular in Washington, a status he found stimulating rather than depressing. Once he said, "I do not give a damn what people think of me if at least in their condemnations they are experimenting with thinking at all. The average inhabitant who comes to my attention has so much power he has given up thinking lest he suddenly realize how helpless he really is against the tidal forces of events that are going to play themselves out regardless of his actions. Any reporter worth his salt must subscribe to the belief that the person he is interviewing is not about to reveal his true self. Everything he says is slanted his way in various degrees of subtlety. A man or a woman of even moderate power who tells things like they really are should be a candidate for the nearest lunatic asylum or sainthood, and as far as I know there haven't been any of those positions filled lately."

Hawkins was slightly uneasy with the trio who now waited upon his questions. There was Mort Steiner, whom he had never quite trusted, and Edward Starbuck, whom he considered a classic Washington hanger-on. And there was this new character from Montana, who, on the surface at least, seemed unorthodox.

The interview was not developing according to the usual freshman-congressman routine. Hawkins wondered if his nose had betrayed him. Or was leading him into muddlement? Where did this guy come from besides some obscure village in Montana?

Swallowing the scotch Mort Steiner had so thoughtfully provided was much easier, he thought, than swallowing some of the things Lee Rogers said. His statements smacked of sincerity and truth, which was enough to set off alarm bells in any Washingtonian. When asked if he owned a pair of spurs to go with his boots, he said, "Sure. Six pair, all rusting in the barn. We use horses that don't need a spur."

"What about that cowboy suit you're wearing? Are you trying to set up a Clint Eastwood image?"

"Clint Eastwood?"

"I take it you don't go to the movies."

"Not unless it's worth a sixty-mile drive."

"How about television? You watch it much?"

"Lily and I have thought about getting a set for the past ten years, but my neighbor says you can only get one station in our area."

"Your neighbor? Do you mean that plural or singular?"

"Singular. Vern Taylor is a very singular fellow."

"He lives next door?"

"Yes. It's only about ten miles from our door to his."

Hawkins took time to drain his glass, then offered it to Steiner for a refill. Who was this chap? Abraham Lincoln? Did he read by firelight? Or was Gordon Hawkins, who should know better, experiencing a royal leg-pulling?

"As seen through your eyes, Mr. Rogers, what is your impression of your fellow congressmen?"

Edward Starbuck fixed his attention on the ceiling and said lazily,

"Now that's a hell of a question to ask a man who's only been here a week."

Hawkins frowned at him. "I was unaware," he said crisply, "that this interview was with you."

He turned back to Rogers. "Well? You really haven't had time to make many enemies."

And now comes the bullshit full force, Hawkins thought. He glanced at Mort Steiner, who sat on the edge of the couch looking, Hawkins thought, not unlike a nervous wren perched on a telephone wire. Mort, of course, would also be worrying about what his man might say and he was obviously primed to make any necessary repairs.

"I've been scared stiff most of the time I've been here," Rogers answered, "but I hope to get the hang of it soon."

Lo and behold, the man has taken my question seriously, Hawkins marveled. He could have said things about being honored, dedicated, and determined.

Hawkins smiled, and washed his surprise away with another gulp of scotch. He made a slight adjustment to his eye patch and asked casually, "What is all this I hear about you wanting to declare war on the world and failing to include Libya, Cuba, or Syria? How do you think the third world will feel about that?"

Rogers smiled. "Deprived, perhaps?"

"I've heard conflicting rumors. There's even been some speculation that the good people of Montana might have inadvertently elected someone who happens to be just a little flamboyant?"

"If I remember correctly, similar things were said about Theodore Roosevelt."

"Are you comparing yourself to that man with the big stick?" The world was full of crazies, Hawkins reminded himself, and maybe he had uncovered a new specimen.

"Of course not. But I do think it's about time this country stopped paying every two-bit nation in the world to spit in our eye. It's time for our turn."

Hawkins smiled when he heard Steiner and Starbuck gasp simultaneously.

"You're pretty hard and fast with the solutions, Congressman Rogers. Is that attitude typical of cowboys from the West?"

"I don't know any eastern cowboys."

Hawkins was astonished to find himself laughing. "Oh, but I do, I do, I do!" he said. "And they usually don't wear a horse." Laughter was so foreign to him that he fell into a momentary fit of choking. Something might come of this interview after all.

"Let's go back to war," Hawkins said at last. "Are you serious about this?"

"Deadly."

"But with whom? You've got to identify the enemy if you're going to start a war worth going to."

"There are several nations involved, but actual damage to them would be only financial. We would advise them that we are not going to bomb their cities or direct any firepower whatever in the general direction of their honest citizens. We would not sink their ships if clean of narcotics or shoot down their airplanes if the same applied. We would blockade their ports until they could prove they're out of the drug business."

Rogers paused and met Hawkins's good eye. "We would shoot to kill all narcotics traffickers whether at sea or in the air. If we captured any alive, we would give their own governments the privilege of shooting them—here, on our own ground—and make the executions mandatory. Too many of these international bums have been getting away with murder for much too long."

Hawkins sighed. The scotch was good, but how in the hell was he going to handle this story without sounding like he had lost his own reason? "Pretty bloodthirsty, Mr. Congressman. There are various protective societies that might not approve. Most certainly the American Civil Liberties Union."

"We'll start a new society that does approve. The Society for the Protection of America's Immediate Present—SPAIP, if you want to be faddish and acronym it."

Hawkins made a note he knew he would actually use. This Rogers was something different. No wonder Steiner was squirming. He asked, "In your war—"

"It's not *my* war. We have to put the whole country behind it and stop fooling around with little skirmishes. I don't say we should forget about the Russians entirely, but if we don't win *this* war right soon, we won't have to worry about them anyway. Right now we're losing—and like any war, most of our casualties are young people. In my opinion, narcotics traffickers of every nationality deserve the same treatment as terrorists, and it is absolutely wrong to let them hide behind the flags of their various nations, who depend on our own laxity to keep them in business."

"Do I gather that you believe most of the traffickers are citizens of another country?"

"All of the really big boys are. And we have to go after them. They're not going to come to us."

Hawkins could see the headline now: CONGRESSMAN TAKEN AWAY IN STRAITJACKET. He said, "Since what you propose is unlikely to happen, what's the alternative?"

"We just have to make it happen. A declaration of war doesn't necessarily mean we have to launch a flock of bombers. We declare war so we can cut through red tape. Then we can use the military as needed—or at least almost as needed."

"How? What about the law of posse comitatus? As I understand it, the law says the military can't engage in any activity that might be considered a civilian matter."

"If you declare war, that's bypassed. It's no longer a purely civilian matter."

Edward Starbuck suddenly roused himself from an apparent trance and addressed Hawkins in his best Harvard diction. "If I may suggest, Gordon? Congressman Rogers's enormous enthusiasm for his project may have led him to leave out some of the preliminaries. In other words, only after strong efforts are made to solve matters through normal diplomatic channels would we appeal to the United Nations, and then, if all else fails—"

"Bullshit," Rogers said quietly. "That's not what I mean. And it's all been tried anyway—a thousand times. This war isn't going to be won by soft words."

During the silence that followed, Hawkins glanced at Mort

Steiner. The man is going to drown in his own bile, he thought. Any minute now he was going to make an extra squirm and explode.

Hawkins took a swallow of scotch and shook his mane of hair in approval. He pretended to make more notes while trying to restabilize his thinking. Christ! Could there be something to this mad scheme?

"I doubt if the Joint Chiefs of Staff would welcome your message, Mr. Rogers. They're always claiming they have too much to do now and must use all our resources just to keep the Russians at bay."

"The Joint Chiefs will just have to revise their thinking."

Oh? And is *that* ever past time! Hawkins thought. "Do you really mean that? Do you really think you can unlock those military minds from their orbit around a red star?"

Mort Steiner could no longer keep his peace. "Gordon, let's take a broad view of this. What Congressman Rogers is trying to suggest is that we should consider *temporarily* diverting some of our military efforts. Perhaps we could halt some of our exercises based on theoretical Soviet maneuvers and employ the same effort against the distribution of narcotics. *Temporarily,* mind you."

Spoken like a true wimp, Hawkins thought. The one thing he could not abide was double-talk.

Rogers said quickly, "Nuts. That's not at all what I mean. We have to go all out. You bring drugs even in the general direction of this country and you're dead. All economic aid to countries that fail to shut down all narcotics production within their borders will be cut off within thirty days. If we present it to them realistically and with our facts in hand, I don't think the American taxpayers will have too much trouble understanding such a war. At this time I can only guess that the extra costs of the war will about break even with the elimination of aid to the offending countries plus the immediate reduction in our own crime costs."

"There would be a lot of unhappy junkies in this country. They'd get their fixes somehow, I should think. After all, we once tried prohibition. You could be accused of trying to sell snake oil."

Hawkins knew he was baiting his man, but he could not resist. Here was a guy who believed wholeheartedly in what he was trying to do, and this he found infinitely refreshing.

"We can't fight this war the way we handled prohibition—with half a hand. If we go all out, the junkies will have a bad time for a while, but they'll survive. And our kids will be clean."

"Suppose for some reason this war of yours escalates. Other people get into the act. We make a mistake and shoot up a Russian airplane or boat."

"The Russians didn't hesitate to shoot down a 747 they only *thought* might be spying. Sure, it's a chance—maybe one in a thousand, if that. But it's nowhere near the chance we're taking with our future if we just stumble along like we are."

"Who was it said one death is a tragedy, but a thousand is only a statistic?" commented Hawkins.

"I guess I wouldn't know. I'm not very well read."

Hawkins made a few scribbles on his paper as he finished off his scotch.

"You don't drink, Congressman?" he asked without looking up from his pencil.

"Not when I'm talking to reporters."

"Aha! Has Mort here infected you with disdain for the press?"

"Don't be silly," Steiner said quickly. "Congressman Rogers has the highest regard for the press."

"Not always, Mort," Rogers said crisply. "I've met some sonsabitches . . . and then there're some good ones."

Gordon Hawkins stood up and Rogers rose with him. "I remember you don't like to shake hands, Mr. Hawkins."

"Right you are. Well . . ." Hawkins retreated a step. "Pip-pip."

"So long."

Hawkins reached the door and turned back suddenly. A mischievous smile crossed his face. "One thing more, Congressman. Haven't you neglected to take something into account? How about the human element? Won't you agree that as long as there is something humans are not supposed to do, they'll find a way to do it?"

Lee Rogers hesitated only a moment. "The knowing will, but the innocent won't if it's not handed to them on a silver platter. And they're the ones we really care about."

* * *

After Hawkins departed, Lee Rogers closed the door. He turned back then and stood in front of Edward Starbuck. "I think," he said quietly, "that you and I are going to have trouble understanding each other."

"Look, Mr. Rogers. You're the new boy on the block, and the Congress is ruled by a relatively small band of elders. Maybe after you've been around a few years, they'll listen to you—as long as you don't mention the word *war*. It makes them extremely nervous. Your proposal would be viewed by them as rash, inconsistent, impossible, and probably outrageous. We do a great deal of trade with Colombia—coffee alone is a most profitable import. The same goes for Mexico and Bolivia. Congress won't stand by and see that sort of trade wrecked just to rescue a few junkies."

"Okay. Mr. Starbuck, you're fired."

Steiner protested quickly, "Now just a minute, sir—"

"I respect your opinion, Starbuck, but I can't go into a battle like this and win unless my team backs me all the way."

Starbuck pushed himself to his feet very slowly. He looked at Rogers and shook his head unhappily. "The days of the big stick are gone forever, Mr. Rogers. Thank God there are cooler heads in the Congress. When you come to your senses and realize we are a bit more civilized than we were a century ago, you might ask Mort to give me a ring. Yes-men are easy to find in this town. The other kind are not. So long, Mr. Rogers. It will be interesting to see how long you last."

Starbuck went out the door and closed it gently behind him. He did not look back.

Steiner pursed his lips. "Well! I suppose that was inevitable. I did see it coming."

"He won—for the moment, Mort. And he feels better because he told me off. There's a difference between a no-man and a negative thinker. Now you go out and find us a press guy who believes we stand a chance."

Gordon Hawkins lived with his sister, Rebecca, a comely widow of striking beauty who had managed to retain her exquisite figure and poise into her fiftieth year. She was not only a lady of considerable charm, but a graduate naval architect who worked presently in an experimental laboratory north of the city.

Since Rebecca led an active social life in the capital, her brother rarely saw her except on Sunday mornings, when they shared a pile of Sunday papers over breakfast. Their relationship was serene and amicable, which allowed them to enjoy a rather larger apartment than if each had lived alone. Occasionally, when both found themselves at home for the evening, they would mix up a batch of martinis and exchange personal confidences of the most private nature. Such was their easy accord that many people thought them to be man and wife, a supposition the two Hawkinses did nothing to erase. They sought and found amusement in the occasional company of their acquaintances and for friendship they were content with each other.

Hawkins wrote in a small book-lined room off the living room. After many years he had developed what he called "thrombosis of the typewriter," a condition that allowed him to walk right past the machine without even seeing it. It was there, but it was not there, and he supposed it would be the same with a word processor. When he did apply himself, Hawkins wrote in staccato literary leaps and bounds. His style was lithe and muscular in comparison to most of those journalists with whom he played pinochle at the Washington Press Club. There he usually lunched on what he identified as "muffed peasant chowder."

"My compliments to the chef," he would say with a smile to the bewildered waiter. "Please be so good as to tell him he missed again."

Hawkins was unusually slow in getting to the story of Lee Rogers. He dawdled with a few approaches and he talked about it frequently. "Believe it or not, I've met a very interesting congressman," he would say to his pinochle cronies. Yet in his thoughts the complete story of the cowboy politician needed some credibility anchor. Every time he started to write about Rogers, he seemed to be creating the outline of an old Walt Disney movie.

Finally to his sister, Rebecca, he said, "Do you think it would be a violation of the building code if we invited a freshman congressman to dinner some night? I gather the poor man is living on combat rations at the Army and Navy Club."

"Why isn't his little wife home slaving over a hot stove? And since when have you developed a social tolerance for politicians?"

"I gather his little wife is geographically unavailable. Somewhere in Siberia. And he is no standard politician."

"Why is he so special—to you of all people?"

"I don't know." Hawkins ran his hands through his mane as if he might find the answer among the thickets of hair. "I've been fussing for two weeks with a piece on him and I still can't quite nail him down. He speaks madness and yet he makes sense."

"You know very well that a person who makes sense can't survive here."

"I do. That's what worries me. I think this chap might either get himself killed or disgrace the nation."

"Then for heaven's sake bring him around. We'll invite a few others and light the best candles. If you can't see through him on your home territory, then maybe I can."

"He's quite handsome if you like the rugged type. The boots-and-saddles sort. I suspect he's not in the market for a quick affair."

"What a pity. You'd just raised my hopes."

"You're looking hungry. Maybe you'd better go back up to Stowe and settle in with one of your ski instructors."

"They're getting younger by the minute. The last one, Philipe, kept calling me 'ma'am.' I could have killed him."

"You do the honors, but call the congressman at the club. If Mort Steiner gets wind of the invitation, he may find a way to cancel it."

"You haven't told me his name."

"Lee Rogers, congressman from the great state of Montana—wherever that is."

Hawkins was uncertain whether it was by accident or by some hidden genius of timing that he had delayed so long in devoting his whole column to Congressman Rogers. Editors who published him were grateful to him. For it was a time of nothingness in the news—one of those periodic gaps in events when absolutely nothing newsworthy happens anywhere in the world. Editors found the situation alarmingly sterile and began scraping up old flying-saucer stories, a new cure for mumps, and recent percentages on AIDS. A band concert in Oslo would have made copy. Even the mayor of New York failed to provide a headline.

So the Hawkins story on Congressman Rogers exploded. *Newsweek* printed its own follow-up story, and the next week *Time* sent its troops to develop an even fuller portrait of "The High Noon Kid." Lee Rogers's piercing eyes challenged several million readers from *Time*'s cover. United Press found another angle by suddenly discovering that meat was not poison for consumers, and *Parade* canceled its long-lead-time story with a special on "The Cowpoke Who Would Challenge the World." The television news networks, dragging through swamps of relatively ancient events, seized upon Lee Rogers and pursued him everywhere. The "Today" show, "Good Morning America," and all the midday shows across the country were on the telephone begging for even a few minutes with the man described as

"Honest Lee," "Mr. Good Guy," "The Fearless Cowboy," "Don't-Tread-on-Me Rogers," and "A Breath of Fresh Air in a Sea of Indecision."

Everything Lee Rogers did or said was recorded, photographed, and often altered to further enhance his stature. He had trouble finding isolation enough for a trip to the bathroom. Other guests at the Army and Navy Club, all of whom had previously ignored him, now stopped at his table in the dining room offering encouragement and advice. Within a week his face had become as familiar as any film star's and he was obliged to stop riding the subway. The back-pounding and handshaking were as overwhelming as the oohs and aahs of young females. He considered buying a cap to conceal his identity. And tennis shoes.

Again and again he repeated the message, "We've got to stop pretending we're getting anywhere with the drug problem and start a real war on this special breed of terrorist. No more pussyfooting and no more apologies. These are our young people who are being destroyed as surely as if a bomb exploded among them. We have a perfect right to defend the future of our country, no matter who is involved."

Again and again the media ran with the theme, interviewing representatives and senators whose cautious responses only made Lee Rogers look more the man who knew what he was talking about. Soon the tenor of the public became obvious. More and more congressmen were openly willing to admit that the present antidrug efforts were insufficient, and each day more had sympathetic statements to make on what had become known as "the shame of a national defeat."

Congressman Wynne Barker, revitalized by the notoriety of his prodigy, buttonholed any colleague within reach to sing the praises of "the most promising representative we've had in forty years! A Sir Galahad, by God!"

It seemed Lee Rogers could do no wrong.

He was even invited to attend a meeting of the Select Committee on Narcotics Abuse and Control.

The president smiled wryly when Lee Rogers's name was mentioned in the White House, and said he wished he could enjoy the same unanimously benevolent press. Then he went back to worrying about the Russians.

One national organization appeared to be dead set against Congressman Rogers. The National Rifle Association flexed its enormous lobbying muscles and said that this cowhand smelled of manure. Their Washington spokesman refused to give the reason or comment further.

As the tide of Rogers's reputation flooded higher every day, Mort Steiner found himself whimpering under the load. There was as yet no replacement for Edward Starbuck. Steiner hired two extra persons to answer the constantly ringing telephones and did his best to filter all requests for "just a few minutes" of Rogers's time through a most rigid set of values. A major magazine, yes. A network interview, sometimes. A newspaper other than the *New York Times* or *Washington Post,* regrets. Foreign publications that had suddenly rediscovered the romance of the American cowboy, by Rogers's own request, yes.

There was also the regular business of a representative, and there were times when Steiner nearly wept at his inability to include things he thought deserved more time. For this day so far there was the Montana State Hospital Association, which wanted to discuss health issues; the Great Falls Housing Authority, which wanted to discuss money; a Madam Sophie Herzhorn from the Israeli Embassy, whose wants were impossible to ascertain because of her heavy accent; a congratulatory reception for Congressman Tony Duval of Vermont; the National Federation of the Blind, which wanted a meeting; and Common Cause, which wanted to ask Rogers his views on campaign financing. Two warehousemen's union officials from Montana wanted an hour with Rogers, which they were not going to have, and the Navy League was honoring the Joint Chiefs of Staff in the Caucus Room. Not more than fifteen minutes there either. How, Steiner thought, would his favorite cowboy handle all that glittering display of medals and gold braid when he was now known to be stirring up trouble for them?

The lists went on and on: reception for Congressman Worth,

Capitol Hill Club; a delegation of Baha'is to present him with *Book of Peace;* Council for a Livable World to discuss nuclear test ban; invitation to Subcommittee on Coast Guard and Navigation. Wonder why? National Association of State Agencies for Surplus Property, 6:00–7:30. Dear God, at a time like this?

There were many more requests for Rogers's attention, an unheard-of phenomenon for a freshman congressman. Steiner was proud, and pleased at the way his man handled newfound fame. Difficult as all of this was for Steiner, he found it inspiring to watch Rogers stick to his guns. War on narcotics was his constant and almost only concern. "I think it would be advisable, sir," Steiner had said more than a week ago, "if you paused long enough to get a haircut."

Rogers regarded him with little enthusiasm. "How many times have I told you not to call me 'sir'?"

"About one thousand, sir." Steiner smiled. They had by now begun to trust one another and even an occasional riposte seemed in order. This day, as Steiner faced his boss, he had a list of further appointments he wanted confirmed. "At eleven this morning you're meeting with the River County Housing and Community Development people. Alice will sit in and take notes if you like. Eleven-thirty you're with the Montana State Mortgage Bankers Association. Charlie Jackson has it all in hand and will introduce them. Twelve o'clock you're due in the House to vote on HR 715. Twelve-thirty you're lunching with the dentist, only you don't get anything to eat unless you can manage with his paws in your mouth. It is the only time he can take you, and just remember, most dentists think they are more important than congressmen."

"Maybe they are."

Steiner offered a tolerant smile. "Two o'clock you have a full hour with the Semiconductor Industry Association. They want your views on locating new factories in Montana."

"I don't know beans about semiconductors."

"Don't tell them that. They propose to bring money to your state. I've canceled all appointments for the rest of the day because you said you wanted to work on revisions to your bill. But I think you should drop by the Monet Room at the L'Enfant Plaza and spend some time with the National Association of Letter Carriers. Cheryl is the flack in charge. She'll meet you at six-thirty."

"Where did you say?"

"L'Enfant Plaza."

"What the hell is that?"

"A hotel."

"No dice. I've been invited elsewhere. Sorry."

"Since you are hardly the social butterfly of the nation's capital, may I be so bold as to ask where?"

"Gordon Hawkins's sister invited me."

Steiner caught at his breath. *"Hawkins?* You're going there alone? That, sir, is *very* peculiar company."

"Why? What's wrong with it?"

"I do not relish the thought of the nation's new white knight dining amid what is reported to be an incestuous relationship."

Rogers tipped far back in his leather chair and laughed heartily. "I love this town!" he said. "Everybody, with the possible exception of the president, is supposed to be up to something. Well, I'm going."

"Please remember your good wife and children, sir." Steiner sighed and turned away.

That evening Steiner left the office early and went directly to his flat. Once there he disrobed and, groaning unhappily, lowered himself into a hot bath with a martini close at hand. He did not wash himself but only stewed, sipping occasionally at the martini, and frowning at the ceiling.

When the martini was gone, he emerged from the bath and went, still dripping, to the telephone.

"Wilma. I have need of you."

"Now? At this hour? It's only seven o'clock. You gonna take me to supper again?"

"I'll consider it. Mostly I want you within arm's reach."

"But I can't screw. It's my period."

"Come anyway. I am suddenly . . . unbearably depressed."

"Okay. Twenty minutes?"

"Beautiful." He hung up the telephone, returned to the bathroom, and dried himself. Here was Lee Rogers come to the capital barely one month ago, and already the world was his to devour.

It was absurd.

It was nothing short of miraculous. What did this booted, simpleminded cowboy have that others of his ilk lacked? In some ways it was frightening because fast-track fame had a way of collapsing overnight. Unforeseeable reasons.

Steiner shivered in spite of his vigorous drying. Where the hell was a crystal ball? Where was the trip wire? Maybe it was just the hot bath plus the martini, but now all of his old Washington instincts were aroused. "Beware," he whispered to himself. "Beware."

As he dressed, he wondered why the fact that his charge had accepted a social engagement without his help bothered him.

There was so much else to worry about.

A special meeting of the Select Committee on Narcotics Abuse and Control was still in session when Lee Rogers hailed a taxi for the only social evening he had known since leaving Montana. He hated to admit that he had accepted the invitation to the Hawkinses' because he was "just plumb lonely." Montana and all it represented now seemed like an episode in another man's life—something he had read maybe in a paperback about the West, which before he became a crusader had been his favorite reading. Now he thought he understood why so many crusaders died young and unsung.

While his taxi plowed slowly through the early-evening traffic, he tried to recall what he had said in the large mahogany chamber with the big brass chandeliers. Although he had been received most courteously, he was not at all sure the committee was pleased with his testimony or agreed with any of his recommendations. They were obviously sincere men, but as he watched and listened to them, they seemed to be disheartened and drifting.

After he had spoken, it was Gratio of Illinois who said, "Mr. Chairman, I would like to remind us all that Section 481 of the Foreign Assistance Act gives the responsibility to the president, who in turn assigns it to the secretary of state, who ultimately delegates the responsibility to the assistant secretary of state for international narcotics matters. That's the foundation for day-to-day operations."

The chairman grunted and responded dourly, "No wonder we can't accomplish much, with a chain of command like that. And if we add the bureaucracy to go with it, we have the speed and agility of an oxcart."

Tracy of Maryland said, "When we talk about diplomatic efforts to kill the drug problem, what we're really trying to do is force the cooperation of other countries without the use of force. I strongly disagree with Congressman Rogers because he is recommending we abandon the traditional tactics of a civilized people."

The chairman glanced up at the mahogany-paneled ceiling and allowed a soft whistle to escape his lips. "I'm beginning to wonder how much we're handicapped by the War Powers Act. And by the way, I'm also concerned that members of this committee continue to use their good judgment and not be in any way influenced by the abnormal amount of press that Congressman Rogers seems to have created. Let me take this moment to thank Mr. Rogers for appearing here. I think we must now all be agreed he is a cowboy with considerable class."

There was a gentle ripple of approving laughter among the members. Then Watson of Pennsylvania said, "Maybe Congressman Rogers has something more than an understandably pugnacious attitude toward the problem. Maybe we've had more than enough diplomacy. We must be dealing the wrong cards, because we don't produce any hard drugs ourselves and those nations who do produce them go right on doing it and selling to us. As if that isn't enough insult, we're continuing heavy economic and military aid to the offending countries, not to mention technical assistance of all kinds. And yet each of those nations is in violation of an international treaty."

"As I understand it, that's part of our cowboy's beef," quipped Gratio of Illinois.

There were groans from the majority of members, and Rogers wished he were invisible.

"I apologize," Gratio said quickly. "I couldn't resist."

Watson of Pennsylvania was an extraordinarily impressive man. He had only to raise a long, bony finger for attention.

"What I want to know is, if this all has such a high priority, when do the American people hear about it from us and not only from some stalwart individual who just came in off the range? After all, we've been working for years on this problem—"

"Maybe that's the real problem."

"Mr. Chairman, I suggest the members of this committee forsake levity for a more appropriate reaction. I suggest this is not the place to flash our wit or play upon our senses of humor."

There was subdued applause as Watson continued. "Now, it wasn't so long ago that the president was talking about all these people belonging to a family of nations who should be concerned about the survival of the world. I can only suppose that when the leaders of those countries visit the White House, the subject of narcotics is included in the matters of discussion. The same goes for the participation of the vice president and the secretary of state when he visits their countries. Unfortunately, none of those gentle exchanges seems to work. The traffickers in narcotics are prospering beyond imagination. Figures range from one billion a year in dollars to as high as a trillion.

"Regardless of the accuracy of such numbers, it is true that when Congressman Rogers says we are trying to combat a billion-dollar industry with a few million, he's absolutely on target. We can't even get ten million together from the international community, and most of the major countries contribute zero."

Gratio of Illinois responded quickly. "We can't expect to stop production in the offending countries with a snap of our fingers. It takes long-range planning—"

Watson responded instantly. "I suggest we've had more than enough long-range planning. We've been at it for years and accomplished very little. I'm with Congressman Rogers in believing that this country has got to get tough."

"The urge to *do* something is quite natural, sir, but the penalty for haste is often terrible," the chairman said.

"Indeed. So, might I add, is our narcotics situation. We are supposed to come up with a solution and have failed. Why? I don't know all the reasons, but it's obvious something happens to people when they collide with the State Department. State is so concerned about another nation's sovereignty they forget who they're supposed to be.

The sugar instead of the big stick doesn't always work. Remember when Nixon was president and he wanted to use paraquat to spray the poppy and marijuana fields in Mexico? The Mexicans said no, that Mexican soil was the soul of the nation. Then Nixon closed the borders and they took another look at eradicating heroin. The same went for Turkey when we cut off military assistance. They banned opium completely."

Stark of California interrupted. "Mr. Chairman, I've recently visited several of the countries in question and I met with our ambassadors to those countries. There were times when I gathered the distinct impression that our own staff people in those countries considered the members of our group a bunch of do-gooders who were taking up their time and pulling them away from more important work. I think that's a sorry state of affairs."

Watson of Pennsylvania said, "I agree with the gentleman from California. Let me get my oar in here again for a moment. One approach is passive and the other is active. I don't want to serve on this committee any longer if I feel my government—and that includes the State Department—is not behind us. We are all tangled up in jurisdictional turf. The people locally, the states, counties, and our various government agencies are all exercising their perogatives, and rarely in harmony. There's no adequate funding and no overall strategy."

Watson paused and looked directly at Rogers. His heavy gray eyebrows rose as if sensing challenge and then resettled themselves over his piercing eyes. "Congressman Rogers . . . let me ask you something. If we somehow managed to reorganize ourselves and our policy and placed the whole problem under the command of one person, have you possibly visualized yourself as the czar of such an operation?"

"Absolutely not," he had replied quickly. "Once this job is done, I want to get on back where I belong."

"Would you say that under oath?"

"Of course."

"Thank you. That's very reassuring."

Rogers sighed as he realized the taxi was progressing slower than he could have walked the same distance. How could all these people stand living so close together year after year? Then he wondered if he had bungled his testimony. Maybe he had been too dogmatic and punitive? But dammit, they were just sitting around and bouncing words off the mahogany wall, and that would not sink the enemy. Iran, Mexico, Burma, Thailand, Bolivia, Peru, and too many others were in the business. And their very best customer was . . .

When Wilma arrived at Steiner's flat, she was breathless. A fine rain persisted outside and the light from Steiner's reading lamp caused a mist to appear about her hair, which he thought quite remarkable. The moisture also accented her high cheekbones, delicate nose, and broad mouth. Looking at her, it struck Steiner that if she could not be considered beautiful, she was at least not unattractive. Or was it, he warned himself, in the eye of the beholder?

"Jeepers, I never answered such a fire alarm! You see anything funny about me?"

"I can't say I do."

"I didn't even take time to put on my wig!"

"I think you look better without it."

"But my hair's so fucking unruly!" She paused a moment and wiped the moisture from her cheeks. Then she looked at him cautiously and asked, "You sick?"

"No, I'm not sick, but for the first time in my life I feel the need of reassurance."

"Is that something *I* can give you? I'll tell you right now I'm no headshrinker and I've had enough crazies in my life to last me forever. So don't give me the confused bit."

"I won't. Just sit down and make yourself comfortable."

Wilma circled a chair warily and finally seated herself.

Steiner plopped into his large leather reading chair. He said kindly, "While I wish to avoid further conversation about your period, if it will help I'll make you a drink."

She seemed not to have heard him. She spoke softly, her eyes roaming about the room. "You realize this is the first time I ever sat down in your place?"

"It had not occurred to me."

"I like it. . . . I like it," she whispered. "It's sort of homey."

A silence fell between them.

"Do you have any pain?" he asked. "Sure you don't want a drink?"

"No. I just like everything the way it is right at this very moment. There's no way it could be improved."

"I'm pleased you seem to be so enthralled."

Steiner finished the last of his martini.

"What does that mean?" she asked after a moment.

"Enchanted. That's how you look right at this moment."

"Yeah! You got it! I am . . . I am." She looked at him steadily for a moment. Then she said very simply, "Sometimes . . . sometimes, Mort, I wonder about you. I mean, do you screw a lot of other women?"

"No. Just you."

"Why? Can't you afford it? Can't you get your share of freebies? Jesus, Washington is loaded."

"Probably yes to both questions. I'm just not interested."

"You go for guys in between? Don't tell me you're a switch-hitter. You only see me once a week at most."

"That seems to be all that's necessary. And I did not ask you here to discuss my libido."

"I mean, it's like you're special, understand? You are the only man I know of who makes me feel like I'm something more than a hunk of meat. Do I hear you wrong? Does that scare you?"

Mort Steiner rose and went into the kitchen, where he hastily made another martini. He tested it, then shook his head in disapproval. It was as if the drink failed to match his wild thoughts. Out of control—almost totally out of control! Mort Steiner, of all people, rendered speechless by a Washington hooker! Lee Rogers, you've done this to me, and goddamn you for it. I don't know my left hand from my right anymore.

He returned to his leather chair and sat down in silence. He saw that she was watching his every move and he squirmed uncomfortably. "My common sense tells me," he said at last, "that I should tell you . . . to go back where you came from and never return."

"Why, Mort? You don't have to pay no attention to what I say. You don't even have to take it seriously. But I know one thing. I don't like to take money from you, just for doing it, know what I mean?"

"No, I do *not* know what you mean, and I wish you would stop using that appendage to every sentence. I am fluent in English and if I take what you say at face value, then I automatically translate and at least get the gist of what you have on your mind."

"I'm sorry, Mort." She hung her head and he thought she was like a very little girl who had made last place in a spelling bee. She took a handkerchief from her bag and blew her nose.

"Don't weep, for God's sake. I didn't ask you to come here to cry. I can't stand the sight of tears." A common male frailty, he thought, and hated himself for having so obviously hurt her. "Do I gather that you might actually visit me for free?"

"I've sure thought about it."

"I'm touched. I'm flabbergasted."

"What's that mean, Mort? Sometimes you say things I don't relate to at all."

"That's because you didn't have a middle-western mother."

"We never discussed your family before."

"We are not discussing my family now and will not be. The various Steiner ghosts are best left in the closet forever."

"How can you talk like that about family? You had a real mother and father, and you should respect them."

"Now you're telling me how to treat my family. What is this?"

"I guess if we can't screw, we have to talk about something. Of course I could just sit here for days . . . just sort of soaking in your company—know what I mean?"

"There you go again. Yes, I do know what you mean. Let's think about dinner." Steiner polished off his second martini with a flourish. He was suddenly elated and simultaneously dismayed at the power of alcohol. Or was it something else? Even a gulped martini would hardly create such a sense of well-being in a few minutes.

"You mean you're going to take me to a restaurant again?"

"That's precisely what I mean. I propose taking you to Henri's, where we will engage in further discussions on everything except a certain Mr. Rogers and/or narcotics."

Wilma was visibly shocked. She recoiled slightly in her chair. "Mort . . . you don't do dope. Tell me you don't."

"No, Wilma. I absolutely guarantee that."

"Oh, thank God," she sighed. "You never did have that look about you. I seen it in so many of the girls. They don't know no better, understand, and they get hooked early, know what I mean?"

He stood up quickly and stepped across the room with new vigor. "Please, Wilma." He bent down and took her cheeks in the palms of his hands. Then he kissed her gently on the top of her head. "Wilma," he said softly, "what am I going to do with you?"

"Just . . . well, just maybe love me a tiny bit, know what I mean?"

Rebecca Hawkins had a well-deserved reputation for staging impeccable parties. She had a wide acquaintanceship among all sectors of Washington society, and she not only chose her guests with care but made a special effort to ensure they would be compatible. Even so, she was somewhat dubious about this night's collection of personages and she worried that she might have trusted too much in her instincts rather than cold appraisal. She thought it unfortunate that she had never actually met Lee Rogers, who her brother insisted must be the guest of honor.

According to local custom, the dinner was catered by Berkly & Sons, whose expertise left any hostess with very little to do except keep her guests genial. The initial seating at table was simple, Rebecca thought. Lee Rogers would be on her right, and next to him would be Tracy Delano, a glamour puss if there ever was one, not to mention a jet-setter with the grace and looks of a queen. She was also whispered to be a nymphomaniac, but with her money and talents, why not? Rebecca was not sure why she had invited her except that she spoke fluent French, which should make it more comfortable for the man next to her, a Guy Amonte, who Agnes said was in the French Embassy. What did Monsieur Amonte do? Agnes had not explained, other than to say he was precious, a sure indication that she was once again in love.

Agnes, a friend since Vassar days, had problems and had been in and out of more institutions than she could remember. Bit of a dingbat and quite sticky about her marijuana devotion, but otherwise keen of mind. She would be sitting across the table from her new paramour.

Brother Gordon would be at the far end of the table, flanked by Gloria Strickland and Bonnie Mae Birnbaum, both of whom he liked. Gloria was rather dull sometimes and had no sense of humor whatsoever, which made one wonder why Gordon liked her. Perhaps it was her face, which should be used only for launching ships. Her many marriages—was it three, or four?—had left her with a few million; among other items, she owned the building in which this very party was taking place.

Bonnie Mae Birnbaum was on the plump side and always a jolly soul. She would be next to George Strickland, who owned the world. Perhaps not all of it, but the firm he inherited and then built into a colossus was the largest manufacturer of medical supplies in the world, and people everywhere were always getting sick or being injured. Just to cover the spectrum, he also owned most of two huge insurance companies.

Bonnie Mae would be good for George, and on his other side would be Agnes, who just might tease him about his wealth. Reminder: Tell her to stick to big game hunting, which George Strickland adored—or his sprawling place in Virginia, where he was master of foxhounds of one of the best hunts.

Next would be dear David Birnbaum, who was an exquisite man, utterly brilliant, and newly attached to the White House staff . . . doing something, but what? Whatever people there did besides cut each other's throat. He also wrote erudite essays for the *Nation,* and added warmth and dignity to any gathering.

All for one lone cowboy? Gordon must be mellowing.

When Lee Rogers arrived at the Hawkins apartment, he heard himself introduced as a man who needed no introduction. He tried to remember the names of the other guests and found his score was almost zero. He apologized for being late. He had failed to tell the taxi driver that he wanted a northwest address rather than a southeast, and they had spent time milling about in the rain and fog trying to find the place. Gordon Hawkins escorted him through the babble of voices and said there was just time for a quick drink, which Rogers must need.

"Thanks, I'll just skip it tonight," Lee said. He tried not to stare at Gloria Strickland, whom Rebecca had described as looking positively ravishing this evening. He certainly agreed. The dark brunette who reached for his hand and introduced herself was also very easy on the eyes. Tracy something? Hey, Lily! You should see your husband now! Nothing like this in Montana. Of course, this was not what he had come to Washington for, but he might as well enjoy it.

Rebecca Hawkins came to him and asked, with a lilting laugh he found fascinating, "What in the world have you done to my poor brother? I've never seen him so enthusiastic about any individual. He's usually pouring salt in wounds, not doing any praising. I think he's starting some kind of Rogers cult."

"He's sure done a lot for the program. I guess not so many people would have heard about it without him sort of launching things."

She introduced him to David Birnbaum, who studied Rogers's face a moment and then smiled warmly. "Bless me if you don't look just like your pictures. That rarely happens. My pleasure, sir."

Rogers was still trying to adjust himself to the realization that all these stimulating people were making an effort to talk with him when Rebecca announced that they should move into the dining room. After the relative barrenness of his room at the Army and Navy Club, he found the Hawkins apartment almost overwhelmingly plush, and yet it was comfortable. This was very good living indeed. And the other guests! He admitted to himself that he was a bit dazzled; he was answering questions with a laconic yes or no for fear he would say something inappropriate. He smiled privately, remembering the old saw about taking the country out of the boy, whenever he was approached by one of the women. All of them seemed to sparkle so. A bit too much makeup, maybe, but holy cow, they sure were interesting. Now, Lily, he thought suddenly, there was no harm in *looking!*

He found his hand straying to his western string tie, which sure wasn't much compared to what the other men were wearing, and he thought that maybe he should have stopped by the club and given his boots an extra polish.

David Birnbaum, who stood barely as high as Rogers's tie, looked up at him through the biggest pair of glasses he had ever seen. Smiling genially Birnbaum said, "We get a lot of celebrities here in Washington, but if what I read is anywhere near accurate, you represent a real breath of fresh air."

Rogers found he was at a loss for an answer. He stumbled over a few words. "Well, see . . . it never occurred to me things might turn out this way. . . ."

"Timing, Mr. Rogers. Everything is timing. The trouble is, you can't predict it. Had you arrived here six months ago, or even the day after tomorrow, the timing might have been all wrong, in which case—blah. Has that occurred to you?"

"Not exactly. No, I never gave it a thought."

"You might enjoy doing so, now that your success is after the fact. Your timing was masterful. All great people have an instinct for what I call the 'law of election.' Every week there are thousands of events. Perhaps only one will leave an impact on society—for a few hard-to-identify reasons. It occurred at just the right time, or it might have gone down in history unnoticed. It is the same with people. . . ."

Rogers wondered where he could go to hide. Holy cow, this kind of person was too much for him. A man needed time to get his sights adjusted. He hadn't heard the word *acre,* or *breed,* or *market* since he arrived. It was absolutely amazing how many people took their meat for granted. Why in Montana, at least in the First District, people wouldn't be together five minutes before they'd start talking cattle, or feed, or the range, or how the Bureau of Land Management was making life difficult, or what they saw for sale behind the Safeway meat counter when they went down to Billings or over to Great Falls to buy parts for their machinery or see a doctor. Here, everybody talked at the same time, which made a guy wonder who was listening. And in Montana everybody sort of gravitated to the kitchen before they actually sat down to eat. Well . . . different worlds.

Rebecca Hawkins took him by the arm and eased him toward the dining room. He thought the way all the guests moved along together was something like pushing a bunch of feeders into a chute. If you could get the first of the herd started in the right direction, the rest would follow.

By the time the soup bowls had been taken away, Rogers was more at ease, although he now realized that he was poised unnaturally on the edge of his chair. It semed a guy almost had to be if he was going to keep up with the conversation. Or just keep track of what came next. The swell-looking woman on his right kept patting his hand every time he put it on the table, and she would state some strange opinions—like how a horse was the noblest of creatures in her estimation, and how poorly she usually did in dressage, whatever that was. If she thought a horse was a noble animal, she should see some of the critters on some of the poorly run operations in Montana.

After the soup, they fell into a discussion of Appaloosas, which failed to terminate happily because the woman—Tracy was her name—had never seen one and he didn't think much of them. Appaloosas? Hell, they were for Indians.

"I suppose you ride a western saddle, Mr. Rogers?"

"Lee. The name is Lee, and, yes, I do."

"I tried one once, and found it horribly uncomfortable."

"I guess it's what you're used to. But I wouldn't care to rope a calf from an English saddle."

"Do you actually do that? I mean lassoo? Just like in the movies?"

"Sure."

Rebecca interrupted. "You be careful, Mr. Rogers. That gorgeous woman on your right may lure you down to Virginia and have you riding to the hounds before you know what's happened."

"The name's Lee, please." When was this "Mr." business going to stop?

"You would love it!" Tracy Delano insisted. "There's nothing more exciting than a smashing good hunt."

"I'll second that," George Strickland said from across the table. "If you'd care to join us in Orange County next Sunday, I'll be pleased to mount you."

Rogers tried to laugh. "I'm afraid I'd kill myself." No way, he thought. Over those stone walls? People had to be crazy to ride like that. On a horse the size of an elephant and no horn on the saddle? "Maybe another time," he finished lamely.

The main course proved to be ducklings poached in a light sauce and surrounded by what Rebecca identified as wild-grain dumplings. It was backed by a burgundy that Rogers found so tasty he nearly emptied his glass before the others had so much as taken a sip. He dispatched the duckling almost as fast. The poor little thing was no bigger than a quail, he thought. He drained another glass and wondered what had happened to the salad. They sure as hell ought to have some salad to precede a fancy meal like this. Maybe the cook forgot?

Maybe it was he who was confused? Now the woman named Tracy was talking in French to the young man who sat on her other side, and then the woman who sat on the opposite side of the table would chime in, also speaking French. It sounded like some kind of debate. As if this were not enough, David Birnbaum was in heavy argument with Gordon Hawkins way down at the far end of the table, and Rebecca was alternately bouncing questions off George Strickland and the woman she kept addressing as Bonnie Mae, who always answered with a laugh. Rogers decided that as far as he was concerned, they all might as well be speaking French.

Suddenly the woman he could not identify as Agnes called across the table to him. "All right. Why don't we take an opinion from the honorable Mr. Rogers? Maybe he knows a lot more than we do."

"I doubt that," Rogers said defensively. Was he beginning to slur his words? Holy cow, Gordon Hawkins had left his chair at the head of the table and was now pouring white wine for his guests. Well, why not sample some?

"I'd like to ask you a question, Mr. Rogers," Agnes said, unsmiling. "If I may?"

"Sure. Shoot." Hey, that white wine was smooth!

"What do you think about legalizing drugs?"

The vision of Lily and her research books suddenly passed through his thoughts and then disappeared. "We tried it—long time ago. It didn't work. They've tried it in England, and it's not been successful. It did work temporarily in Japan, but that's a disciplined society."

"Don't you think it's silly to make marijuana smoking a crime? Good American citizens are thrown in jail just for having a few joints around. What happened to our freedom?"

"Machine guns are also illegal, unless you have a license."

"Come now, Mr. Rogers. You know very well there's no comparison."

Agnes must be a little tipsy, he thought. She was not smiling and her eyes were hostile. All conversation along the table had ceased and all the exuberance was gone—missing like the salad, he thought.

Rebecca cautioned, "Now, Agnes, don't be so serious," but Agnes seemed not to hear her.

Her voice cut very clearly through the unnatural stillness. "If we legalized drugs, wouldn't we cut down tremendously on crime? People could just go to the drugstore, or, say, a doctor's office, and buy what they needed at a very cheap price because those wretched smugglers and pushers would be out of business."

"It wouldn't work," David Birnbaum said. "Look, the congressman is trying to enjoy his evening—"

"I didn't ask you, David. I want to know what the congressman thinks."

Rogers took another gulp of wine. Why the change from red to white? he wondered. Something special must be about to happen. He made a face and wiped his lips. Then he realized that the whole table was waiting to hear what he might say. It took a moment before he could resurrect her question.

He saw her frowning at him and he became increasingly uncomfortable. That's right, he remembered. A congressman was supposed to be an authority on everything. And there was no way to escape.

Agnes was insistent. "Marijuana is a lot less harmful than rum, whiskey, nicotine, and glue, and they're all legal."

David Birnbaum said, "Maybe the cigarette companies could be authorized to sell mild marijuana cigarettes—highly taxed, of course. At least that would be a few more billions in the Treasury every year."

Agnes squared off at him. "Marijuana smokers don't want mild stuff! They want the strongest, stickiest bud they can buy and they like to smoke it through a bong to get the true flavor."

"What's a bong?" Gloria Strickland asked from behind the mask of her stunning beauty.

"A water pipe. It's the only way to fly."

"You should know," Tracy Delano said crisply.

"Meow," Gordon Hawkins sounded from the end of the table.

Agnes's voice was rising ever higher. "Would you all shut up for a second and let the congressman answer my original question? I think every individual has a right to decide what enters his body. Congressman?"

Lee Rogers sighed. Why was it so difficult to gather his thoughts all of a sudden? During the past few weeks, he had been asked the same question at least a hundred times and he'd always had the answer, but now . . .

"Well, it's complicated," he began. "I don't think we want to send a message to our young people that drugs are okay, and it's pretty well proven that availability is a very important factor in usage. The more . . . the more. The easier, the more. And then it's wrong to say drug trafficking is a victimless crime. It's like a machine gun that never runs out of ammunition. It hurts the individual, and it hurts our society. Sometimes you have to balance human rights against the public good." *There,* he thought, he had gone and blown it now.

He was astonished when Gordon Hawkins applauded from the end of the table and he heard comments of approval from the others.

His renewed confidence was cracked almost immediately by the arrival of the salad. At the end of the meal? They sure had strange ways in the East. He must remember to tell Lily how maybe the salad had been forgotten earlier and had been dragged in at the last minute. Never mind. It sure went fine with the white wine.

Rogers was grateful that the focus of conversation had drifted away from him and onto a scattering of other subjects. It was as if the arrival of the chilled salad plates with some kind of French saying on them signaled his own dismissal. He was ignored, except by Tracy Delano, who said she had heard it was rude to ask a rancher how many head of cattle he had. He told her it was like asking someone how much money they had in the bank. But horses? She could ask that, couldn't she? When she was told ten or twelve, she gasped and said that must represent quite an investment.

"Oh, we don't pay much for them. Usually we raise our own. If we have to buy . . . maybe three or four hundred per animal."

"Do you know what a good hunter costs, Lee?"

"I suppose being so big, and trained as they are and all . . . no, I couldn't even guess."

"Fifty thousand for the best. Ten might just keep you up with the hunt, if you're lucky."

"Wow!"

"I like the way you say wow, Lee. It's so . . . different."

He looked at her and smiled. It was very easy to smile at this woman. You might say there was a lot of mischief in her eyes, and she had a sort of saucy way of tilting her head. He had never seen a woman quite like Tracy. It seemed strange that she didn't appear to have a husband—at least handy. He found himself looking at her hand. There was no wedding ring. Humph! What a waste!

He took a long pull at his wineglass, which certainly held the best liquid he had ever tasted in his life, and he was surprised to find himself saying to Tracy Delano, "I guess when I see a lady like you, I'm compelled to say wow more often than usual."

"Wow yourself, Mr. Rogers. You're quite an orator. I always thought big strong men from the West were limited to grunts. Or a few yahoos?"

"Only when the Indians are attacking."

"Does that happen often?"

"Every day in my country. Big powwows after."

They laughed together, and their eyes met and held upon each other long enough to say a great deal more. "I like you, Lee Rogers," she said at last. "I like you very much." And he decided that this was certainly a lot better than sitting all evening in the library at the club trying to get smart.

Later there was a cream-puff dessert and coffee, and Agnes and her friend, Guy Amonte, asked to be forgiven their immediate departure since he had an odd-hour shift at the French Embassy. Rebecca Hawkins knew this was nonsense and so did Tracy Delano. They knew the pair were off for a few snorts of cocaine or a bong of marijuana. At least they had the grace not to indulge themselves while they were part of the present company.

It was before the first brandy had been offered that the Stricklands departed, with repeated wishes for Rogers to visit them in Virginia. Soon the Birnbaums said they must go. The White House knew no hours, you know. "Working on the international clock is a distinct social handicap," David Birnbaum said. Bonnie Mae Birnbaum chuckled and added that she kept herself on North Pole time so she could be ready for anything.

Eventually Tracy Delano said she would be happy to drop Lee Rogers at his club. To Rebecca's amusement, they left together. After all had departed, she eyed her brother mischievously when he said he thought the evening had gone very well, except for the cheese, which he had found disappointing.

"I'm afraid you're in for another disappointment," she said evenly. "Your vaunted cowboy—savior of America's ideals, champion of righteousness, and defender of the American family—is human."

Tracy Delano drove slowly along the wet streets. Her car was a small Mercedes, and Rogers thought she must have the heater on full blast. Yet the warmth seemed to emphasize the exotic scent of her perfume.

Here was *some* woman, he decided while he studied her profile. Lots of pride there. The way she held her head said so, and she seemed to have a built-in smile—not a big grin, but a play of amusement about her mouth as if she might be laughing at herself. Or would it be at him?

"Have you ever tried growing orchids in here?" he asked.

She reached for the heater control and moved it slightly. "It is a bit warm, isn't it. Sorry."

"Oh, I'm not complaining—at these prices."

"You have earned some complaint time. That dreadful Agnes was trying to heckle you. She's a little balmy at times."

"She has a point. There are some things to be said for legalization.

On the surface it even makes sense. But I'm finally convinced it would only compound the problem."

There was a pause. It was remarkable, he thought, how much more everyone seemed to know about him than he could discover about them. Apparently no one had to ask why he had gotten into this crusade; they seemed to know all about Jack's death, and thanks to more stories about himself than he cared to read, they knew everything else. It was a strange feeling. Fame had some strange side effects. There was a sense of isolation from others that was not very pleasant. Suddenly it occurred to him that Mort Steiner, the first person in Washington he had met only a month ago, was the individual he'd known the longest. And one month didn't build much history. Back in Montana he had known most people all of his life, and in comparison all of these would be strangers for a long time.

Still, there were people like Tracy here who made things look a bit different.

"What are you looking at?" she asked suddenly.

"Your profile. And I just noticed you have dimples."

"My nose turns up and my cheeks are beginning to sag."

"You look to me . . . well, what can I say?"

"Anything you wish. My feelings have been hurt by experts."

"Hurt? I was just trying to find a way to tell you I've never been driven around by such a pretty taxi driver."

"Thank you, Congressman Rogers. Such flattery deserves a free ride anytime!"

Their eyes met for a moment, then went back to watching the windshield wipers. Finally she said, "My place isn't far from your club. Would you like to stop by for a nightcap?"

Their eyes met again and they both smiled. An instant passed, then Rogers shook his head.

She said, as her smile faded, "Okay. I didn't think you would."

When she pulled up in front of the club and stopped, Rogers waited uncertainly. Did he shake her hand to say thanks, or just get out and say thanks? Good Lord, it must be years since he had been alone with another woman, and now how should he end it? Maybe he should give her a peck on that smooth cheek. Near a dimple. Or since it would be coming from a relative stranger, maybe she would resent it?

"Well, I sure thank you," he said.

"Sometime, Congressman, you must tell me more about the cowboys and Indians. My number is easy to remember. The same prefix as your club's, and add the date of the Spanish armada."

"Fifteen eighty-eight?"

"As every school kid knows. In case you've forgotten, the name is Tracy Delano. The accent is on the second syllable."

He climbed out of the car. Just before he shut the door, he said, "I'm sort of lousy at names, but I don't think I'll forget yours. Good-night."

It pleased him that as he stood back and flipped her a little salute, she responded by blowing him a kiss. It pleased him very much, he thought. Hey, Lily! Better come here to Washington and make sure your man stays on track.

Even as Rogers mounted the steps to the club entrance, Guy Amonte departed from the French Embassy. He had not wanted to be seen there, certainly not at this hour of the night, when he probably smelled of that heavy Colombian Red Block, which Agnes provided in such generous amounts. But meeting the ambassador or any of the higher functionaries at this hour was extremely unlikely. It was worth the risk, he thought, to get his message off tonight, and—*merde!*—he had left the necessary telephone number in his desk.

He walked the two blocks to his tiny apartment at a fast pace, grumbling at the rain and soothing his fears with the admonition that no sensible mugger would be out plying his trade in such abominable weather. Of course on this frontier of civilization—another Senegal except the climate was worse—no one could predict what might happen.

He checked his watch once more. He should not have lingered so long at Agnes's place. One party a night should be enough. Still, if he hurried, there was time enough to make the connection he desired. Louis Prevet should still be awake . . . or was it possible that he never slept? Prevet the owl, he was once known as in Marseilles. Things were different then. Prevet had fought against the Algerians during the trouble in Africa, and he had come to the attention of the Foreign Service because he gave warning of a plot to blow up the consulate and had not asked for reward. This untypical attitude so impressed the officials that they began using him in other ways and never to their regret. Then one day he vanished with all the currency in the building. He had always been, Guy Amonte considered, a very enterprising man.

They had first met in Paraguay, Amonte remembered. Prevet had prospered mysteriously, but he was generous with his money, and in the social life of that blighted country there was not much choice of company. They had enjoyed each other's companionship until they had both been transferred. They maintained contact, faithfully doing small favors for each other on request, and now Prevet's number was in his shirt pocket.

Standing at his telephone, still dripping from the rain, Amonte dialed the number and received a series of loud squeals for his trouble. What could anyone expect from an American company that kept urging its customers to dial direct overseas and only charged a pittance?

He hung up, pressed the Operator button, and heard her lazy voice. "Can I hai-up you?"

"Overseas. Colombia."

"What city?"

"No city, but it's near Bogotá. Here's the number."

Amonte wiped the droplets of rain from his face. Seconds later he heard Prevet's unmistakable voice. *"Buenas noches?"*

"No, Prevet, *bonne nuit.* About your inquiry of last week. I have managed to be with the man you asked about. There can be no mistake. He's a bit of a fool."

"Is he being taken seriously by the Americans?"

"It's difficult to be sure. But he has definitely started some people thinking. And just now the crazy Americans need any kind of a hero. They are like little children, as you know."

"What is he after? What's in it for him?"

"I think he's too much of a boob to know. Certainly he's not being paid off by anyone."

"No one? You are sure?"

"Reasonably so. There is no unified group to do it."

"Are you telling me he's making all this noise because he believes it?"

"Yes. Incredible. But then, one must not expect common sense from an American."

There was a long pause on the other end of the line, and for a moment Amonte thought he had lost the connection. Then Prevet came on with a fast series of questions and he knew neither his evening nor his call had been wasted.

At last Amonte said, *"Mais oui!* But that can be done. It is quite possible."

He listened again and warned himself to avoid overconfidence. "But of course! All you have to do is give me a few days' notice and I will try my best. One hundred thousand francs will be quite acceptable. *Merci.* Yes, of course, my account at the Banque de Marseilles. I'm hoping to be transferred home soon. You may reach me here or at the embassy. It is only necessary to say what you wish and in a few hours I can make arrangements. *À bientôt!"*

Rogers regarded the mirror in the tiny bathroom with dismay. Who was this pie-faced idiot staring back at him, mouth slack, dull eyes half-closed and apparently loose in their sockets?

He had come into the bathroom to brush his teeth before going to bed and had made the mistake of glancing up and there was a mirror in the way. There he was. Plain as the nose on the dumb face—smashed. Not falling-down drunk. Just drunk enough to know he was not at the party, whichever party was in session at the moment.

Two brandies and about four or five glasses of wine—not much, but too much. Where the hell were his faculties? Scattered all over the bathroom. Hanging in shreds from the shower curtains. Cylinders missing.

When he was with the marines, he had been drunk several times. But that was a long time ago. And there seemed to have been at least some kind of a reason then. And now? Have another look, dumb-ass, because what you see right there in front of you is the way you look to the rest of the world. And you are the guy who looks down your long nose at people who deliberately change themselves, or get away from themselves, through drugs. What's the difference? You don't say "Let's bring back Prohibition."

So? Booze is all right, but drugs are a strict no-no? You there, in the mirror, attention! Are you the same guy who came from Montana?

Why you pompous jerk. What's wrong with getting a little buzz on now and then? You wanna take all the joy out of life?

He looked away from the mirror and resumed brushing his teeth. Some people you had to keep corralled all the time. Let 'em out one night on the town and they get derailed.

He tried to remember what he had said to Tracy . . . whatever her name was. Piano? No . . . Tango? No, that's the name of your horse!

He poured water into his mouth and spat out the residue of toothpaste. *Soprano?* No. Well, never mind. You have a brilliant mind, Rogers. As the market goes, you might be able to sell it for a dollar ninety-nine. Big deal. The windbag cowboy everybody is writing about might just as well have smoked a few joints or snorted cocaine. You could go to jail for that.

Some people were always trying to take the fun out of life.

Lily, you would not be proud of your husband tonight. At least he hadn't tried to climb into the sack with Tracy what's-her-name, but the idea was sure there . . . sure, sure, sure, sure. Nice lady.

He told himself that it must be the brandy squeezing his brain. Slow motion. Queasy. What the hell was he doing going to bed with his socks on? Now *there* was some character exchange for you, folks. Lee Rogers too far gone to get out of bed and take his socks off. Gone fishin'? Gone, gone? Which way did they go, all those people at the party?

A man should drink regularly. Every night. Then he might get used to what happens and think it was all just dandy. The life of the party. He could be a hero to his own self.

He reached up and fumbled for the light switch. Good-night, folks. Show's over. Congressman Rogers is off to the big nod.

Delano! *Right!* Accent on the second syllable. . . .

The following morning, Rogers studied a series of reports Steiner had been able to find for him. Except for his head, which he decided had been cast in cement, he saw that everything was satisfactory in the world.

"... During the last fiscal year the Drug Enforcement Administration played a crucial role in this administration's campaign against organized crime and drug trafficking. We have taken tremendous strides in effecting a unified sustained assault against illicit drug traffic both domestically and abroad. . . .

"The Federal Bureau of Investigation is satisfied it has done its best. . . .

"The U.S. Customs Service is satisfied it has done its best. . . .

"The Coast Guard is satisfied it has done its best. . . .

"The navy and air force are satisfied they have done their best. . . .

"The Bureau of Alcohol, Tobacco, and Firearms is satisfied it has done its best. . . .

"The Internal Revenue Service is satisfied it has done its best. . . .

"The Immigration and Naturalization Service is satisfied it has done its best. . . .

"All six NNBIS [National Narcotics Border Interdiction System] regional centers are satisfied they have done their best, and the OCDETF [Organized Crime Drug Enforcement Task Force] is satisfied it has done its best."

Anagrams, anyone? Tracy Delano would be good at this game. Now why the hell was he thinking of her and even remembering her name?

"Along with all these combined efforts, the importation and use of cocaine in particular has doubled over what it was five years ago. Deaths increased 77 percent last year. . . ."

Very satisfactory.

Tail chasing of the highest class.

How about the bright side?

A kilogram of cocaine in New York City has fallen to twenty-five thousand dollars. And the Swiss government has frozen more than one hundred million in drug-related assets—which to no one's surprise will undoubtedly be forfeited to the Swiss government, which might or might not channel some of it through the United Nations' drug program and at least earn a small star on its report card.

At the party, Tracy Delano had said she went skiing in Switzerland every year. Out of my aching head, woman! There were more important things to think about. Or were there?

Rogers sat back in his chair and reviewed some new facts he intended to include in an address to the House. He read his notes over and over again, trying to clarify what he had scribbled down only yesterday. Now, sifted through his concrete brain, it sounded like so much compromising. Very soon, perhaps even next week, he must be ready, and right now he needed friends, not enemies. Skip the sarcasm. Try to find some dignity so people will take you seriously.

He looked up from his notepad and saw Mort Steiner standing near the end of his desk. He had been unaware of Steiner's entrance and he knew it was not just concentration. He was not alert to much of anything. He glanced at the clipboard in Steiner's hand and asked what was on his mind.

Steiner flipped through the papers on his clipboard. "Various appointments. The wheels of government must keep turning."

"Why?"

"That's a surprising remark from you, sir. Are you quite all right?"

"No. I have a hangover."

"Pity. I was afraid of that." Steiner clutched the clipboard piously, as if he were reading from a religious testament. "I need some answers. You're due at a meeting of the Association for Equality and Excellency in Education. Budget problems. The Rayburn Room, nine forty-five."

Rogers groaned and wiped his eyes. One of these days he was certainly going to have to buy a pair of glasses. Out on the range, who needed them? But here with all this stuff? Better buy a harness for your featherbrain.

"There's a concert by the Music Educators National Conference at twelve-fifteen. Constitution Hall. Buffet lunch to follow in the C Street Lobby. You're saying a few words about the need for action."

"At the concert? Who set that up, for God's sake?"

"Don't be irritable, please. Your wisdom need not flow until the luncheon. Now, you've got to be back here at three for a meeting with the Service Station Dealers of Montana. They want to assure themselves of your future support."

"I don't even know any service-station dealers—except Matt Lewis down at Clayburn, and I think he's selling out."

"You will. Now at three-thirty there's a screening at the JFK Center you should not miss—*The Liberation of Auschwitz*. And at four you're due back here to talk with an Arab male whose name we still haven't got straight. He wants to discuss arms sales to the Saudis. He wants your vote when it comes before the House, of course."

"I don't know anything about selling arms to the Saudis."

"You will. That's what he's paid for. Now for the good news."

"It's about time." Rogers leaned far back in his chair and began to massage his eyes. He thought about Lily. What a sight for sore eyes she would be right now! By golly, he would call her tonight and suggest she come to Washington for a week or so. . . . Wait a minute! Lincoln's birthday was in the offing and the whole government would be closed down for three or four days. Maybe he should go home and see how those new heifers were doing in the hands of Vernon Taylor?

"The good news," Mort Steiner was saying, "is that things are really snowballing. I can hardly believe my eyes and ears. The Select Committee is about to ask you for a full proposal. You're on their agenda again next week although we haven't been officially notified. Win that one and you've about won them all. My spies tell me your performance yesterday was a definite success and a few of the members are already convinced that yours is the only way to go. Approval there can mean that everyone will listen when you address the House and your bill will come up for vote shortly afterward."

"That's sure encouraging."

"There's more. Two senators—Harrington of Maryland, and Dutton of North Carolina—have *volunteered,* if you can imagine it, to lobby for you in the Senate. They say it looks like the majority of Republicans are already on your side, and while the Democrats are still wishy-washy because they didn't think of it themselves, they'll probably come along once the whole package is presented."

Rogers patted the notepad. "This package grows by the minute. I never would have guessed that just declaring war would be so complicated."

"I have a friend in the White House who is privy to a variety of matters and she tells me the president is showing a new interest in the whole narcotics mishmash. Those are her exact words, which is pure White House-ese, but that's the way they talk over there. And more. Both *Time* and *Newsweek* are planning a special issue on your war—"

"It is not my war." Rogers sighed. "How many times do I have to say that?"

"It's going to be *your* war no matter how many times you deny

137

it. There isn't a publication in this country that hasn't been on our back about more stories. The BBC is sending a special crew over here for a TV interview with you—tentatively set for Monday next."

"What's the BBC?"

"British Broadcasting Company. They're inclined to be a bit caustic, but I think you'll handle them. I just wish you hadn't been in such a hurry to fire Edward. He could have handled a lot of this."

"Are you feeling overworked? Find another press rep."

"I've tried. Most of them make Edward look like a ball of fire."

Rogers massaged his temples. He told himself he was just not in the mood for office problems this day.

"Mort. A question. Are you married?"

"No. I'm allergic to Mendelssohn." As if the matter had never been mentioned, Steiner went on with his appointment list. After some twenty had been confirmed or canceled, he hesitated. "All is not entirely perfect, but I'm more curious than worried about the few parties who seem to have taken the opposite tack insofar as you and your war are concerned. First, what did you ever do to the National Rifle Association?"

"During my campaign I said I was against handguns because they're no damn good for anything except killing people. They didn't like that."

"I understand. What about the Women's League Against Narcotics?"

"I haven't the faintest idea why they should be mad at me."

Steiner consulted his clipboard again. "And the Teamsters? What did you do to them?"

"I think I once let my personal views get in the way and told some ranchers I thought something was cockeyed when a guy who drove a heated truck full of cattle to market made more money than the man who had spent a year of his life fighting the weather to raise them."

Steiner frowned and chewed thoughtfully on the end of his pencil for a moment. "I wonder . . . It's strange. Very strange. All three of these organizations have received unusually large contributions to their general funds within the last month. . . . I wonder . . ."

"How do you learn such things?"

Steiner assumed his most patronizing air. "Congressman Rogers"—he made a significant pause and rocked back and forth on his heels—"I have circulated through the bowels of Washington for more than twenty years. When I see a potential threat on the horizon, I make it my business immediately to find out why it might become troublesome, or promise to be. I'm not always successful, because sometimes my contacts clam up and other times they just don't know.

"For example, why should the United Churches Association have printed a pamphlet in which you are labeled a dangerous warmonger, a bellicose bully who will get us into another Vietnam? I can't find out if they've received any extra money recently, and in none of the others have I been able to identify the source. What I can deduce from all this is that some people with a great deal of money to spend are definitely against you."

"I didn't expect a free ride."

"There are several senators and some representatives beholden to those organizations and they have already vowed to shoot down your bill. Because of so much popular support, they're being very quiet about it as yet, but let's not discount their intention or their power."

"Why? Why are they against such obvious need?"

"I don't know. Some are fearful of any more foreign adventures, as they call it—some on religious grounds, some for reasons they won't divulge to anyone. They are the ones I worry about."

"You sure know a lot for a guy who spends most of his time in an office."

Steiner smiled. "Sir, Alexander Graham Bell was the savior of my kind."

Three nights later Rogers returned to the Army and Navy Club weary from the apparently ceaseless demands on his time. There seemed to be no end to it. If it wasn't a meeting of the Budget Strategy and General Update Group, which he attended because he hoped it would further his congressional education, it was the U.S. Council for World Freedom, or a reception for the Soviet ambassador, or the National Association for Home Care, or another briefing on Nicaragua. Add a few items—a meeting with representatives of

Ernest K. Gann

the Montana Professional Insurance Agents and a breakfast with the Committee for Teenage Mothers—and there was a long day.

He dined alone as usual and went directly to his room. He intended to watch television for as long as he could stand it, which was normally about twenty minutes, and then go to bed.

As he entered his room and switched on the lights, his phone rang. Certain it must be Lily, he quickened his pace to the phone. "Hi there!" he said with unrestrained enthusiasm. This was just what he needed. "I'm sure glad you called!"

"So am I." It was not Lily's voice, and his shoulders slumped. "I'm Rosalie Bennet and I have very good news for you. I hope I'm not disturbing you?"

Rogers was confused. The woman's voice was cultured and even had a curiously inviting tone, but he was damned if he could remember ever meeting a woman named Rosalie. He wondered if there was some kind of night course he could take in name remembrance.

"I've read a lot about you in the magazines and papers. Then I saw you on television and decided you're my kind of man. I have an interesting offer for you."

Steiner or Alice Morgan usually screened the nut calls, but this one had found out where he lived . . . or, wait, he had heard about Washington call girls, but it had been his impression that the customer called _them_. "I'm not interested," he said lamely, and started to hang up.

"Oh, but you will be. How would you like to find an envelope in your box downstairs tomorrow morning with fifty one-thousand-dollar bills in it?"

This had to be someone's idea of a practical joke.

"Who are you, the tooth fairy?"

"You might say so. And two weeks from now, you could find the same amount in the same place. You can't make that kind of money in the cattle business, and if your farm is like most of them, you need a new tractor and maybe a new barn."

"Did you say your name was Rosalie?" Dammit, how could he find another phone and try to have this call traced?

"Yes. And I have looks as well as money, but you don't really need to see little old me. Just be sure to pick up the envelope."

140

He was becoming desperate for ways to stall. Somehow she didn't sound like a nut. He tried to laugh. "Don't tell me I'm so much your type that you can't resist burying me in thousand-dollar bills!"

"That's the way it is, Congressman Rogers. And if you want to party, I'll be on my way."

"You stay right where you are. I don't think the Army and Navy Club would approve. What's the catch?"

"All you have to do is take a more reasonable attitude on drugs. It's going to go on no matter what you do, and I don't like to see such a smart man wearing himself out for nothing. Say you just quietly dropped your campaign—say you felt you needed a rest and took off for a well-deserved vacation in Spain or somewhere until things calmed down. All expenses for you and your wife would be paid and all first-class, of course."

"Sounds very interesting. Let me think about it and I'll call you back." His next call would be to the police, for sure, and he was willing to bet there was a tape recorder running right along with Rosalie's pitch.

"No, my friend. This is a take-it-or-leave-it proposition. Time is important to my sponsor."

Rogers slammed down the phone and regretted it instantly. He picked it up again, hoping Rosalie was still available, but there was only the dial tone. His mind, he thought, was running on one cylinder. If he had been more alert, he might have been able to milk more information out of the woman—something that might give the police a clue. Or the FBI? It was very awkward, he thought, that he simply did not know whom to call when someone tried to bribe a congressman.

He found Mort Steiner's number on his Washington call list, which was all too short. Delano, Tracy, 1588; Hawkins, Rebecca, 4970. That plus Mort was the entire list.

Mort was not impressed with the story of Rosalie. "If that's the first time you've been approached, I'm rather surprised. Forget about it. I'll handle it."

Five minutes later Rogers found his spirits rose remarkably when daughter Fay answered the phone and whooped with joy at the sound of his voice.

Ernest K. Gann

* * *

No one knew better than Tracy Delano that Washington was one of the smallest cities in the world and was divided into segments in which everyone knew or at least tried to know each other's business as well as their romantic affairs. In many ways it was like a large circus with various rings in which the performers were dependent upon each other for gossip, hard news, rumor, and the exchange of other information that would enable them to survive socially and keep their jobs, or, as very occasionally happened, move to the big center ring—the White House.

Tracy Delano occupied a permanent ring just off the center. Her fellow performers were diplomats of the higher ranks, among them a few ambassadors. Also included were several senators who had been long on the Washington scene and had established reputations for themselves or gained leadership in powerful committees. Only a few representatives had ever been invited to join. For reasons no one could explain, members of the lower house failed to jell easily with the multimillionaires who had a fancy for dancing along the fringes of politics or had somehow persuaded themselves they might actually influence the ponderous mechanisms of the government. A very few journalists were included in this ring, among them Gordon Hawkins, whose territorial rights were established sometime during the Eisenhower presidency. There were also drifters, mostly from foreign embassies, who were invited to functions as long as their assignments to the United States lasted or their hands did not linger overlong on a dinner partner's thigh.

A few single females performing in the same ring with Tracy Delano often found life unjust and difficult. Eligible male partners who could be trusted not to fall into the punch bowl, or label people Communists in an audible voice, or eat meat with their salad fork, were very few and far between. It was a pity that so many promising newcomers to the Washington scene had, God forbid, developed an unforgivable tendency to bring their wives.

Thus while Tracy Delano held no serious designs on Congressman Rogers, she saw little reason to let him roost quietly in the somber halls of the Army and Navy Club. "All those portraits of old generals

142

and admirals," she said to him, "all of them looking like toy soldiers with unbearable gas pains . . . how do you stand it?"

Rogers said that he had never noticed, but would.

The first time it was up to her to break the barrier, as she had known from the beginning she must. She called him at his office and was put through with misgivings by Alice Morgan. "If you're never going to call up the Spanish armada, then the fleet will have to come to you. How would you like to play escort this evening at the Kennedy Center? I hear the new Neil Simon is very much fun."

"Who's Neil Simon?"

"That's why you'd better take me. I have two tickets. You might learn a few things that could come in handy."

There was a long silence on the other end, and Tracy knew he was struggling with propriety. She had her fix ready. "Oh, two other people will be sitting with us—Claude Roper and his wife. He's a senior vice-president of the World Bank, and a man who might be helpful in your campaign. We would go on to their place for a late supper afterward."

It began so easily, and during the next two weeks Tracy Delano managed to make Rogers believe it was his idea they attend the Pavarotti concert ("He sure can warble" was Rogers's comment), a performance by a troop of Nigerian dancers ("Just plain old New Orleans"), and the opening of a fashionable new restaurant known as the Druids. Rogers said he thought the food was adequate but the prices must have been reckoned by someone in the Department of Defense.

One night she persuaded him to attend a reception at the French Embassy, where he renewed his acquaintance with Guy Amonte. Later he told her that he had enjoyed himself because Guy spoke such good English. They had talked about the influence of Charolais cattle on the American market.

To Tracy's regret, that evening was the last she expected to see of her newfound escort. After he had explained that he was taking off for Montana in a few days to see his wife and children, she went to the mirror a number of times. There she made faces at her image for some time while she tried to discover what was wrong except for a little age. Four evenings they had spent together, in one environment or another, and not once had Congressman Rogers made a pass at her—not even a hint, a suggestion, or any other indication he might be reacting to the forces of nature combined with loneliness. What was it with this new world? It was like having a date with your big brother, she thought. A puzzling, frustrating waste of time.

At least the gossipers were having a field day, and some of the speculation had come back to her. Had Tracy Delano at last found her right man? How did she get so lucky? She had tall-bright-and-handsome just waiting for the next flip of her finger. All of which was nonsense, of course. Lee Rogers was not about to obey a flip of anyone's finger unless he wanted to, and, much more inconvenient, there was a wife in Montana. Was she fat with an apron and pink elbows? Tracy wondered. Sagging all over? Maybe a slight moustache? Maybe a huge rump from sitting by the stove all day . . . hair cranked up tight by a dresser every Saturday night? It was much easier to visualize Lee's wife as a frump—much easier.

Recently the Rogers children had encountered a sense of separation from other students. It puzzled them. "R.R." Rogers (the genius) had always been the kind of boy who preferred to back away from an argument if given a chance. Now, very suddenly, R.R. found that victory was not at all like he thought it would be. During his time in grade school, there had been other fights, but they had always been mere tussles and the winner never certain. They normally ended in good humor or were forgotten soon afterward. Now, looking at his bloody hand, R.R. realized it was possible to have real enemies. And he decided it was very unpleasant.

Fay Rogers was in the high school, which shared the same building in Clayburn with the lower grades. She had been alternately embarrassed by and proud of her father's increasing fame, although most of her classmates were unaware of his specific activities in Washington. All of them knew there had been occasional drug use in the school, but the majority chose to look the other way. There were so many other things to yak about. And Fay, like her classmates, flexing their recent sense of independence, decided the less said about her parents the better.

Fay was popular with both sexes, and although she had yet to choose a "steady," she had more than her share of applicants. But ever since there had been so much stuff on TV about her dad, it seemed as if everyone had decided she must be different. She had been very careful never to say a word about her brother Jack, or what she thought of those who did drugs, but she noticed she was no longer invited to Saturday night parties. Even if she did live out in the boondocks, if her friends would only invite her, she could at least say she couldn't come because she had pneumonia, or her horse was sick, or *something.* Couldn't she? It was easy to see how everyone tiptoed around the whole subject in her presence. It was hard to realize that Jack had become some sort of a folk hero, and that this certainly isolated her from just being one of the gang. She was Fay Rogers, the girl whose father was senator or something and probably even knew the president.

Fay decided it was not all fun being a congressman's daughter.

Undersheriff Norm Swift sat in his patrol car with the engine idling and the heater on high. He was a big man, a former rodeo performer with a multitude of wounds, all of which pained him by this time of the afternoon. He was, he thought, getting too old for Montana winters and he often dreamed of retiring to southern California. Now, as he frequently did, he was parked near the main entrance to the Clayburn School, just behind the school bus that would take many of the students to their homes.

Undersheriff Swift's presence was as familiar to the students as they were to him. He was just there, and they accepted it as an area to be avoided if they were worried about any petty infringements of the law that they might have committed during the past week. It was understood that all students who drove their own cars to school would depart the area at a reasonable speed—thereby, Swift reasoned, saving countless slayings of grade-schoolers who made their way home on foot.

It was also understood that as soon as the student drivers were well away from the school, many of them would use the broad, relatively traffic-free Montana roads to test the power they had been able to tweak into the engines of their vehicles. Accidents were frequent and sometimes deadly, but Swift had long ago decided there was not much he could do about it. He was reasonably content if he could just keep mayhem away from his territory.

As he watched the students emerging from the entrance, Swift sighed involuntarily at the sight of so much physical exuberance. If he did not know every student in the school, he at least knew most of their families and where they lived. Most were ranch or farm kids, and it was hard for him to believe that before going away to the rodeos, he had been one of them. Glory days.

Now he sat on his fat butt, with a pot that barely cleared the steering wheel, no hair, and perpetual indigestion. Sad days.

Swift reached over and rolled down the window and immediately his glasses steamed over. Nice and balmy today. Only five below zero. He removed his glasses and wiped away the mist with his handkerchief, which he realized unhappily was none too clean. He squinted at the entrance, trying to spot Fay Rogers, a girl he had always liked. What could anybody expect with a father like Lee and a mother like Lily? They could all read manure, which was one of the first things real cattle people knew. That's how you followed the health of your animals and coincidentally the health of your bank account. Real good people.

He saw Fay just as she emerged from a group of students and turned toward the bus. Her kid brother, he had noted, was already aboard.

He beeped his horn gently, caught her attention, and beckoned to her. She came to him smiling. That Fay now, he thought, she was most of the time smiling, and he was pleased to see that she displayed no sign of nervousness. Although he knew that his presence was merely tolerated by the students, he had only rarely faced any open resentment. These days, he thought, that was something to jack up a peace officer's pride.

Fay bent down until her face was level with the open window. "Hi, Uncle Norm!" she said. Her greeting floated away in small clouds of vapor. "What's doin'?" She laughed and said, "You're going to die of heat suffocation in there!"

"Fay, let me have your bag a minute, please."

Her smile faded. She glanced at the satchel in which she carried her books; her peanut-butter sandwich, which was her usual lunch; a pack of Kleenex; and her little purse for just-in-case. She had not checked it lately, but she remembered it contained about two dollars and fifty cents.

Undersheriff Swift watched her face carefully as she handed him the bag. He saw only question and he was deeply gratified.

He opened the satchel, poked about for a moment, and brought out two sticks of marijuana. He pretended to be surprised as he held them up to her. "What are you doin' with these, Fay?"

She shook her head in bewilderment, and Undersheriff Swift, who took such pride in knowing his locals, was completely satisfied. If he ever saw innocent eyes, he thought, he was looking into them.

"I don't know . . ." he heard her say, and he saw she was about to break into tears. "I don't even smoke!"

"Now, now, never mind, Fay. I don't think you use these things—"

"I *don't!* I don't understand. . . ."

"Someone doesn't like you. Bessie down at the office had a call this morning. She said it sounded like some kid's voice. He told her we should have a look at Fay Rogers's satchel. Well, I have."

Swift took an envelope from the glove compartment and carefully placed the sticks inside. "But I didn't find anything unusual—did I, Fay?" He put the envelope back in the glove compartment and slammed it shut.

Fay wiped away a tear, and Swift smiled at her. "Don't twist your pretty face around so, Fay. I don't need a Seeing Eye dog to tell me somebody put those sticks in your bag. So just be kind of careful in the future. Now that your dad's so famous, a few people are bound to resent it. They can't help it. They're just that way."

It was then that Undersheriff Swift had something happen that he thought overpaid him for all the years he had kept his patience with the kids at the Clayburn School. For Fay reached inside and took his big hand and brought it to her cool lips and said her thanks in a way he was certain he would never forget. She kissed his hand.

Dammit, his glasses were steaming up again. "We just didn't see anything, did we, Fay? And we're the only ones who should know. Now beat it before the bus goes without you."

Fay hesitated, then most of her smile returned. As she turned away
and ran for the bus, Swift was convinced he had a sound analysis for
his discovery in Fay's bag. A few days back there had been some kind
of a scrap between her kid brother and the youngest Spalding kid.
He had an older brother who was real nasty. They came from a
family down in the Hollow Creek area—people who were still complaining about Indians getting too much education at white men's
expense. Garbage people.

And if he guessed right, the Spalding kids had tried their own idea
of vengeance.

A week later Lily Rogers waited at the Great Falls airport so full of
excited expectation that she could barely refrain from trying to jump
up and click her heels in the air. Dear Lord, she thought, she had
never really known how much she loved her husband. Somehow
when he was away in the marines, it had seemed different. There was
a more tangible reason for their separation then, and maybe age had
something to do with it. It was quite surprising, she thought, that in
time married people became more dependent on each other—unless
genuine hatred had festered over the years, to the point where two
otherwise nice people maintained almost continuous silence between
themselves. Such as the pair she was watching in the airport restaurant. Observed over the rim of her coffee cup, they seemed to ignore
each other's existence. Or did they communicate by some private
means? Or just endure? Watching them was like waiting for the
moon to turn pink, which was about as patience-straining as waiting
for Lee.

At least Lee would have plenty to talk about when he arrived—if
his doggone plane would just please hurry up and get here. And she
had a few thousand things to say to *him,* beginning with I love you.

It helped to pass the time just reviewing a few of those things. Like
here's the facts, man. Did you know that Mongol warriors like
Kublai Khan were heavy drinkers and used opium and marijuana
constantly? And how about a gent named Dioscorides, who traveled
with the emperor Nero and wrote a book describing the effects of
marijuana, opium, henbane, hemlock, and juniper?

After some digging she could now testify that priests of the Inquisition considered the coca plant the devil's weed, although they never hesitated to feed it to conquered Incas so they would work harder in the mines. . . . Well, love, a woman had to spend her spare time doing *some*thing!

One subject, she had already decided, was taboo. She was not going to ruin this brief and glorious reunion moaning about superficial worries and the just ordinary things that went wrong on every ranch. Thank God they weren't calving—yet. Troubles at the ranch must remain a secret between Vernon Taylor and herself—unless Lee stumbled into what had gone wrong instead of what went right. His homecoming (only two days, he had said) must be as near perfect as she could make it. No mention of the broken gate in the woods back of Ginger Creek, or the ten yards of fence broken along the mountain. The damned hunters were the usual villians; they had no concern whatsoever for property rights. As long as no one was looking, knock it down. Drive over it or through it. I'm a mighty hunter. It would be very satisfying to see a bighorn ram butt one of them off a high cliff. One of those heroes, aiming at what his bleary eyes told him was a buck deer and his mate, shot two of the heifers. It happened to every Montana rancher sooner or later.

Or *hadn't* it been just another hunter? Vern said it looked like both the gates and the fence had been deliberately knocked down.

It was a chinook day and what little snow there was at the airport was disappearing fast. The visibility was pure Montana, she thought, not considered quite perfect until you could see forever. A perfect day for the boss man to come home. Phooey on the women's liberation bit. What good did it do if you didn't have a dominant man to be liberated from?

She checked her watch for what she thought must be the tenth time in the last ten minutes. Then at last she saw a plane approaching. She ran all the way to the arrival gate.

"Well!" she said, and slipped into his open arms.

"Well . . ." he muttered against the side of her neck.

They stood holding each other as if they were very young partners in a new love. When they separated she said, "How can a plane be so late when it's on time? I was beginning to wonder if I'd lost you."

"No chance. You look mighty fine to me. I don't think I'm de-

149

signed for the Washington ways. Those are different people back there. They speak the same language, more or less, but you're never quite sure if they mean what they say."

They walked out to the mud-smeared pickup standing in the sun. It would be a two-hour drive to the ranch, which would be just fine, she thought. Coming into Great Falls it had been a lonely ride, but this little time together would give Lee a chance to ease back into his former life.

"How are the kids?"

"R.R. is communicating with Mars via his personal satellite, which he fired off the front porch. And guess what Fay is doing?"

"I don't dare."

"She came home from school one day with a cornet. She can now play *La Traviata* and will whether you ask or not. She hopes to make the school band. You may be sorry you came back."

They laughed together and he started the pickup. While he allowed the engine to warm a moment, he put his hand on her leg. She smiled and said, "Your place or mine?"

"I'll settle for a certain big old bedroom over a kitchen."

As he put the truck in gear and drove away, Lily Rogers concluded that in all their married years she had never been so proud and happy. With the ribbon of highway stretching to infinity before them, she wondered if she should risk telling him about the two men who had come to the ranch. At the time, she had decided their visit should be one of her postponed worries. She didn't have to go running for help on every little problem just because Lee was away.

And maybe it wasn't really anything to fret about. Maybe it would just go away. Things always seemed so much worse when you were a few thousand miles away and on the phone. And then if things like what happened were not told just right, they could so easily be misunderstood. Somehow since Jack died, Lee seemed to take even unimportant things seriously, and he certainly didn't need more worries than he already had. Anyway, maybe the whole thing was just some kind of a hallucination. Doggone it, she decided, she was absolutely not going to let events like the recent arrival of two rather peculiar men at the ranch ruin their precious few days together.

She said, "For sure, I never thought I'd be married to a famous person. Everybody in Montana knows about you by now."

He frowned. "I don't know how things got so out of hand, but the press gets on to something and they don't let go until they've torn it to pieces. I keep telling myself it's good for accomplishing what we set out to do, but sometimes I'm not so sure."

"I can't see much change in you—except maybe you look a little tired, and a bit more handsome."

"Same old Lee, here. Two strangers on the plane came up to me and said they recognized me and to keep up the good work. That was sort of satisfying. And if I'm to believe what I'm told, we just may get this whole thing going this year."

"I liked the story in *Parade*. Whoever wrote it seemed to understand what kind of a man you are. Do you blush much these days?"

"You bet. Especially when a lot of the stuff they write would be better spread on those open fields over there."

"The kids are basking in reflected glory. They say it's better than having a movie star for a father."

"I trust you've disillusioned them."

"I'm not sure I should. Right now anything you say will be like Moses hath spoken. Maybe we'll acquire a little willing discipline around the place."

"At least for a few minutes."

They were quiet for a time and she thought it was because they were so content with each other. Perhaps it had been the same with those dour people in the airport restaurant? Maybe they had a different system of signaling to each other—a different way of saying I love you.

The highway still stretched endlessly beyond the windshield, as all highways in Montana seemed to do. Which was probably why the accident rate was so shocking considering the population. People drove too fast, or fell asleep because they just sat there and swallowed the river of concrete rather than the beauty surrounding them. There was not enough traffic to keep them alert—praise be.

She tried to concentrate on the bronzed beauty of a distant mesa, but she could not keep her thoughts from drifting back to the men who had come to the ranch. There were still a few traditions left in Montana, leftovers from pioneer times, and so after a moment's hesitation she had invited them into the house. They were both very pleasant and well groomed, and they drove up in what was obviously a rental car. They apologized for their intrusion and explained they just wanted to talk about Lee.

The largest of the two, a bald-headed man with a merry little chuckle, said that although he had never had the privilege of meeting Lee Rogers, he was certainly looking forward to it. "Has it ever occurred to you, Mrs. Rogers, that one day you might become this nation's first lady?"

After that opening shocker the only answer was, of course, a hearty "Go away!" Now, it was all too easy to reconstruct at least some parts of the conversation.

"Mrs. Rogers," the big man went on, "we are what you might call scouts. As you may be aware, the Republican party is having trouble focusing on a candidate for the next presidency—and the vice-presidency as well. We just don't seem to have the material this time and it's our duty to come up with some really solid candidates. *Masculine strength* are the key words these days—and from what we know about your husband, he sure seems to qualify. During these trying times the people of this country need a hero badly, and we're bound to provide one. That's why we wanted to see how you and your husband lived. What's the old saying? You can't make a silk purse out of a pig's ear? Something like that. I'm sure you'll understand that if the party really starts campaigning for a man, we don't want to find out later that he beats his children or has three wives, or is a member of some weirdo East Indian religious sect."

While serving them coffee and yesterday's brownies, for which they were most appreciative, she had said she understood that might be a problem.

They remained in the house for almost an hour, and it was not until they announced they must leave that the large man began to frown as if something were troubling him. "I'm very glad we came," he said solemnly, "and certainly we can make some positive recommendations to the committee. However . . . there's just one thing your husband would have to adjust. I assume you communicate with him frequently?"

"Not frequently enough. I'm not at all sure I like this political-widow business, but the two houses Lee has looked at so far in Washington can only be afforded by Arabian oil barons."

"Yes, indeed," the big man said. "Things do seem to be more expensive back east." He hummed for a moment, as if mulling over a decision. Then he said, "Perhaps we might be able to help with that problem if your husband can just ease off a bit on some things. What disturbs us is this war your husband is involving himself in. We're afraid it may backfire if we eventually persuade him to announce his candidacy. We don't like to spend a lot of money on the preliminaries if there's much of a chance we might lose the main bout, you understand? And we're talking millions."

It was a golden opportunity to make a pretty little speech, like "I only want my husband to be happy—whatever he wants to do is fine with me."

Congratulations, Lily. At least you refrained from that sort of melodrama.

The big man was not quite finished. Was it deliberate or an accident that he saved it for last? "Unfortunately, there are a lot of people opposed to your husband's ideas. When those kinds of people get unhappy, they are inclined to play rough. It could even be that if your husband insists on his present campaign for a narcotics war, those people would try in various ways to stop him. They could do some ugly things. Mind you, I'm not saying it would actually happen, but I'm sure you'll recognize that scandal is a powerful weapon."

"What do you mean by that, sir?" She added the "sir" because she had suddenly taken a strong dislike to both men.

"Suppose they circulated the rumor that your husband was involved with another woman? I'm sure that would not be pleasant for you, and it would definitely jeopardize his chances for the nomination. And then, who knows, they might even attempt some physical violence."

She had pressed her lips together tightly as she fought to keep her temper. She said with a new brittleness in her voice, "Well, sir! I don't know why *they* might, but I have a busy day and I think it's time for you to get on your way to wherever you're going."

It was not until they were on the front porch that the smaller of the two spoke for the first time. He surveyed the landscape and shook his head unhappily. "You sure have a nice place here, Mrs. Rogers. Thanks for your hospitality. It would be just a shame if anything ever happened to such a peaceful place . . . or to you . . . or even to your children. . . . Forgive me—we certainly have no intention of frightening you."

Now, stirring through her memory, the departure of the two men sounded more sinister than it really had been. Or had she just been so angry she underestimated them? They were so genial, so at ease, so genuinely appreciative of the view and apparently so anxious to leave a good impression. They each handed her their cards with the usual "If there's anything we can do." Lawrence Cornell and Charles Butterworth. Republican National Committee. Along the bottom of each card were listed the partners in their law firm.

For sure, those same men could not have had anything to do with the dead heifers Vernon Taylor found near the west corral. Pure coincidence, Mrs. Worry Wart. Pure happenstance. Even if it happened to have happened the very next day.

"Lee," she asked, trying not to sound like she might be prying, "do you think you might want to make a career of this political business?"

"Hell, no! As soon as my term is up, I'm bailing out. By that time we ought to be winning the war."

"Are there lots of people who are against you?"

"You have to expect some people will have different opinions. It's their right."

"If somebody asked you to run for president or vice president, what would you say?"

"I'd say they'd better go see their psychiatrist. I haven't got any more qualifications for one of those jobs than an Angus bull."

"We've had haberdashers, army officers, and actors. What's wrong with a rancher?"

"What's bugging you?" He looked at her steadily a moment and laughed. "You of all people should know that anyone who's in the ranching business doesn't have enough common sense to run a country."

"Do you know a Mr. Cornell or a Mr. Butterworth?"

"Maybe. You know how I am about names."

She was about to tell him about her visitors, then suddenly changed her mind again. No! Don't ruin these magic hours. Tell him later.

He took a deep breath and waved his hand at the vastness ahead of them. "By all that's holy, this is some place! God's country! A man can expand here. He can live. I wouldn't live in Washington permanently for *any* job—not even if the vote was unanimous. I just feel plumb sorry for those people back there."

She was over it now. The temptation to spill imaginary troubles was gone. Lee knew what he was doing and there was no sense parading a few female fears just to grab attention. If Cornell, Butterworth, and partners wanted to do a little exploring, that was their business. Their warnings should be taken as an honest expression of their concern—under the circumstances, quite understandable.

No. Not now at least, she thought. Don't go running for a rifle just because some stranger thought he saw a bear on the back steps.

Enjoy.

He wore a checkered coat that was several sizes too large for him, and beneath it a hang-out white shirt of matching size. He wore three rings on the fingers of his left hand, a metal bracelet and a wristwatch on his right wrist, and braces on his teeth. His pants were wrinkled, clean white, and voluminous. His high-top tennis shoes were dirty and worn, and the laces were not tied, indicating he was a teenager who knew how to dress. His hair was cut medium-long, and a part of it was carefully brushed across his forehead.

Except when they were in class, she clung to him until they were as close as Siamese twins, never out of physical touch with each other; a hand, a leg, the body, the rump, were intertwined as much as possible, as close as possible. She ate him and he ate her, or so they said, not laughing. In fact they rarely had time to eat or laugh. There were so many other things to do together.

Her hair was a time consumer and she wished they could find some way to have their hair done together. Hers was "electrified" to match her "New Wave" rig, of which she had two. One was an overlarge white shirt, properly rumpled. Beneath it she wore a pair of black leotards, and white tennis shoes. There was nothing but herself under the shirt, which horrified her parents but pleased him. Rig number two was another white shirt and a pair of harem-style black pants.

They felt of each other constantly.

They often made plans to grow their own weed, but finding a place was a problem. It became impossible when they were strung out, and they forgot it.

Long ago when they were both fourteen, before they had established their present communion, they had both begun on Pink Hearts and Black Beauties. Now, such easy little pills were for children. Her mother, who always shot up in the privacy of her bathroom, disapproved of many things her daughter did. But then, everyone said it was wrong to stifle a child's ego. She did warn her daughter about acid and all the hallucinogens, and the girl did stay away from them. Besides, they were sort of not in.

Cocaine was in, and you could get all you wanted at school if you could come up with the cash. Wild. Just one-eighth ounce maybe two hundred dollars? Just enough for four people to party. But then crack was getting cheaper. And it was definitely in. Most guys saved up for Friday or Saturday night, but during the week there were usually several guys smoking pot in the school cans. A few were even doing crack right in the very next shit booth!

There were some students who would never touch a thing, but they weren't at all cool. They were the brains, or a few of the jocks, and maybe a few girls who were afraid of their parents. But not many. Those who looked away soon discovered what it was like to be different. Like being cast away on an island, can you believe?

Her grades in school were very good, but she was not in one of the popular cliques. Because she was far from beautiful.

He was not a jock. His breath smelled of beer most of the time, but he was careful not to drink too much. Alcohol was not really in anyway. Especially since the police began to be so unreasonable about drinking and driving. Who was nuts enough to risk losing his driver's license. Nothing in this life was so awesome. You could lose your whole identity. Even if you got busted doing a drug, it wasn't awesome. Some older person shot his mouth off for an hour or so, you made a bunch of promises to be good, and that was it.

They both agreed that "A Diamond Hidden in the Mouth of a Corpse" was ultracool. It provided a nice background for the four S's: smoking, snorting, shooting, and screwing.

These were things you did together.

He said he'd been told that next year he would be old enough to be a businessman.

Oscar Brimmer had draped himself around his favorite chair, a dilapidated contraption of wood and canvas that he kept on the shady side of his cement-block cabin. He had spent many months in the chair, reading from his small but treasured collection of books. There was nothing else to do in the camp during the day-time but read and sleep, or watch the lizards climb the walls. At least a man could carry on a reasonable conversation with the liz-ards, which was more than could be said for the local Indians and *pisadores* or the fat manager. Lack of more normal companionship left Brimmer with friends bound between the covers of books, and he admitted to himself that his choices were anachronistic. In Brimmer's opinion, very little worth his eyesight had been written during the present century. He read Thackeray, Tennyson, Kip-ling, Goldsmith, Wordsworth and Poe, Washington Irving, Steven-son, Shaw, Macaulay, Bulwer-Lytton, and Dickens. He could quote at length from many of these friends and often did when liquor loosened his tongue.

Brimmer regarded his book collection as his salvation. Some-times when he was sprawled in his chair, which like everything else he owned was rotten with the jungle dampness, he would close his red-rimmed eyes and pretend he was on the rambling porch of a southern mansion waiting for old Sam to bring his mint julep. When his thoughts were properly adjusted to a purely Confederate environment, he could even hear his children playing on the front lawn and his lovely wife at the piano in the drawing room. It was at such times that he wondered what the hell he was doing in a Colombian jungle.

On this, his third day on "standby," he wondered even more about his apparent inability to extricate himself from his present career, and his temper became frayed to the danger point. For three days—to be exact, sixty hours—not a drop of alcohol had crossed his corrugated lips, and the various rumples of his face had fallen into a hound-dog position. The workers in the camp avoided his eyes; and the fat manager, who had never forgiven him for the episode of the flying pig, smiled at the torment he knew Brimmer must be enduring and deliberately drained a beer while standing in front of him.

"Standby," the fat manager knew, meant Brimmer's psychic return to his airline-pilot days, when it would have been unthinkable for him to have a drink and fly. Now, prepared to leave at any moment, a mixture of habit and dedication kept him baleful but sober.

Never on this job, Brimmer mused, had he waited so long, nor had there been so little evidence of a cargo being assembled for him and his trusty flying machine. Something was cooking. And it was not only cocaine, he finally decided. This time his notification had come directly from La Casa de Los Estranjeros, or so the manager claimed.

Just before noon on the fourth day, when Brimmer was seriously considering a visit to the cantina if no orders came through by sunset, the manager's radio crackled his instructions. Brimmer was to proceed at once to Havana, there to await further orders. The manager waddled over to Brimmer's cabin, a visitation he rarely attempted.

"Amigo," he said through his sweat-drenched lips, "all of these months we have not been good friends, no? Now that will change because you fly away forever. You go to Cuba, where all the sonsofbitches we want to be rid of go sooner or later. Our marvelous leader, Marco Fedles, has said so."

Brimmer regarded the manager from beneath the tattered brim of a straw hat he wore even in the shade. It was drawn far down to protect his volcanic nose. "What's the cargo, fatso?" he asked.

"*Nada.*"

"You're bullshitting me."

"No. *Nada.* You go empty. You never come back, I hope."

Brimmer unraveled himself from the chair and rose very slowly. "I'm going to miss you, fatso," he said evenly. "I've rarely met a man of whom I thought so little."

"Look who talks the gentleman. I pray for the day when you and your airplane fall in the ocean or you get the bust and are put in jail forever."

Brimmer allowed a slight smile to play around his mouth. He scratched thoughtfully at the stubble of beard he had allowed to grow since he had forbidden himself a visit to the cantina, and he said, "You know something, fatso? I'll almost be glad when it happens."

The sun was a garish scarlet when Lee Rogers brought Tango to a halt in the glade high on the mountain. From here he could see nearly all of his place, and since the distances were considerable, the defects melted into the landscape. Far below in the twilight, nestled like little boxes against a rumple in the land, was his house, the barn, and the outbuildings. They looked very small from this elevation, and as always when he had reached this special promontory he was reminded of his own insignificance.

Lily had offered to ride with him, but he had said he preferred to be alone this afternoon and he said the same thing to Vernon Taylor, who was anxious to complain about the usual ranch problems.

Lily understood his wanting to be alone, but Vernon Taylor did not. He was a relic of the older Montana, where thinking was normally a by-product of discussion.

Rogers wanted to be alone for a time on this early winter evening because his room at the Army and Navy Club had seemed too small to rehearse what he had to say. The House of Representatives was a room of huge dimensions, and here on the side of the mountain was something to match it. From where he sat on Tango, it was almost two miles to the house, and the hills rose on both sides to make a long and gentle valley now dappled with the blobs of fading maroon. So here, he thought, was a place to make all the mistakes a man could make without anyone hearing.

Or was he not so alone? Somehow Jack seemed to be here in this same glade where the black bull had gone on a rampage. And there was a bald eagle in that tree to the north who might as well serve as the Speaker of the House. Not so visible but just as certainly present would be rabbits, chipmunks, and perhaps a brown bear or two, probably a tribe of raccoons, a fox maybe, and coyotes for sure. They would be listening and he hoped they would not be prejudiced against him simply because he was human. It was sort of inspiring to think that maybe Jack was listening, too.

Still at ease in his saddle, he took a few deep breaths and watched the vapor of his exhalations curl upward. Here at home, he thought, it was so quiet that the silence itself became a sound. Then when something moved, or screeched or squawked, or mewed, or the warm chinook wind caressed the tree branches, each sound became an alarm or an opinion. Here before a tolerant audience, he could yammer on as long as he pleased without somebody throwing things at him.

He turned slightly in his saddle, which caused Tango to snort violently in anticipation of going back down to the barn. Rogers looked up at the eagle, whose bald head was now pink in the sun, and he raised his voice to the pitch he intended to use when the big day came.

"Mr. Speaker!" he called out to the eagle. "I would like to address the House on behalf of H.R. Bill 623, sponsored by myself along with Representatives Dum-tee-dum, Dum-tee-dum, Swayback, Punchbowl, Dum-tee-dum, Airhead, Grumpy, Shylock, Posterior, Rednose, Swifty, Dum-tee-dum, and Chipmunk. This bill has been referred jointly to the Committees on the Judiciary and Energy and Commerce, Health and Human Services, Drug Enforcement, et cetera, et cetera. . . . It will authorize the attorney general of the United States on instructions of the president of the United States to declare war on the following countries—Colombia, Peru, Bolivia, Mexico— with warnings of possible additional declarations of war upon the following—Venezuela, Panama, Burma, Jamaica, and Pakistan."

He paused and searched the horizon nearly eighty miles away, as if there on that hard, thin line he might find the names of nations he had forgotten. He turned to look behind him and saw the vertical expanse of rock that caused his voice to echo so pompously. Holy cow, was he becoming one of *them?*

"Fellow members of this House," he continued, raising his voice so every resident of the mountain might hear him, "Bill 623 will instruct—excuse me, *advise* the president that this House authorizes him to declare war is officially begun after a thorough advisory to those nations already specified."

Clumsy, but right. No shooting from the hip.

Remember, he warned himself, try to bring about a change of attitude. Congress and the administration must stop viewing the narcotics problem as just another problem.

"My fellow colleagues . . ." Oh, no! Not those two words together. "My fellow . . .

"Members of this House, please hear me. We are being invaded as surely as if foreign troops arrived and were shooting American citizens at random. While I do not suggest that the Russians had any fist whatever in this attack, we must appreciate that if they wished to destroy our society the easy way, suffering an absolute minimum of loss to themselves, they would choose to attack our physical and mental capabilities. Now, right now, that is happening as surely as I stand addressing this House. About twenty-five million Americans have tried cocaine and about six million use it regularly. . . ."

There were still so many steps to be taken, he wondered if his patience would hold until the final day when he would actually deliver this speech. Hearings, hearings in committees, marking up the bill, then finally out of committee. Then the House leadership would decide where it went next. Then a batch of "Dear Colleague" letters to mobilize support. Then the House Rules Committee to decide the rules—a closed session or an open one? Then debate and somewhere in there this speech, which had to be just right. Somehow all this rigmarole had to be bypassed, because the war was being lost right now while Tango was snuffling at the grass.

". . . We must and will make sure that certain conditions will prevail. We will advise those nations that we will not bomb their cities and villages or place their honest citizens in jeopardy. Any damage that may occur through our military actions will be compensated for after peace is won. We will urge the maintenance of their embassies and their staffs in Washington, and their freedoms will not be restricted, because this must be an open war and there must be no secrets about our methods or intentions. We will say to these temporary enemies in the clearest terms, "Clean up your act!" And we will inaugurate the following measures until, in our opinion, they do."

A bit wordy there, he decided. Sounds too much like a politician. Was he catching the disease? For God's sake, Rogers, keep it simple. This had to be a complicated war, but the rules must be elementary: You play our way, or you lose.

He was damned if the eagle was not looking down at him! "Hey there, Mr. Speaker, listen carefully. . . . We will blockade your harbors. We will sink your ships, large and small, if they are carrying narcotics in our direction or even look like they're thinking about it. We will shoot down any aircraft departing from your land if we even suspect it might be carrying narcotics although we will except airliners. They will be confiscated upon arrival at any port of entry within the United States and will never be returned."

He paused to clear his throat. God Almighty. On a silent afternoon like this, they could probably hear him even down at the house. Hold it down, Rogers.

"Your attention, please, ladies and gentlemen of the House, because this is a very important part of our declaration. Pursuant to the 1985 amendment to the Foreign Assistance Act of 1961, Section 1003(a) and 481(a), we will cut off *all* aid to these countries, both civil and military, until we are satisfied they are clean. Not one penny of the American taxpayer's money will be allocated to any country designated an enemy because of drug production and trafficking in any form whatsoever."

Now, once again, he debated a minor insertion that Mort Steiner had thought much too bloodthirsty. "Any prisoners of this war taken by U.S. forces will be tried in the United States and if found guilty— shot." No, better turn them back to their own officials with the strong suggestion they do the shooting if they want aid back to normal.

He looked up at the eagle, who was now ignoring him. And he thought of Jack as he watched the light change the distant snows to purple, and finally a vague gray. He hoped it was not just vengeance that drove him. Jack would not approve. Jack had lacked the urge to anger. Always had. He liked this kind of place, where there was such great peace. They had reined their horses here many times and just sat, spellbound. This was not where people lived or wars had to be fought.

The slightest touch on the reins told Tango it was time to leave, and he moved out instantly along the face of the mountain. The sound of his hooves was almost inaudible when there were patches of snow to traverse, yet the friction of Rogers's chaps against the saddle became almost raucous in the stillness of the evening.

By the time he dismounted at the barn, it was dark, and the stars were glittering boldly against the cold sky—as they did above no other place he had ever seen, he thought. It was fine to have such stars handy, and it was pleasant to give a good horse an extra massage along his withers when he had given a good ride. Here was contentment enough for any man, he decided as he started toward the house. The rest of the world could have their luncheons, their receptions, their cocktail parties, and even their Tracy Delanos. Here you had Mars and Jupiter nudging each other in the night sky.

Lily stood waiting to greet him at the door. He laughed and was about to tell her she must be part witch to know of his approach when he saw that her eyes were troubled. "What's the matter with you? I know I'm holding up supper, but it was so pretty on the mountain I just couldn't pry myself away."

She took his hand and led him through the door, saying, "I must talk with you, alone."

She led him into the living room, which they rarely used, and pushed him gently into the big chair that had been in her father's house. She eased herself down to the arm of the chair and took his hand again. "Lee . . . something happened this afternoon. I'm not sure . . ." She bent her head and shook her shoulders as if trying to rid herself of a heavy burden. "Today, after school—"

"By the way, where are the kids?"

"They're up in their rooms and I don't want to bring them into this. I don't want to make any more of it than can be helped, because I don't want to alarm them—and really, the decision to do something about it should be one we make together."

"Would you mind telling me what you're driving at?"

She looked over her shoulder at the staircase as if expecting an interruption, then lowered her voice. "You know Louise Baker who drives the school bus?"

"Sure."

"What you might not know is that it takes the bus quite a while to get out here because it has so many stops along the way and we're at the end of the line."

"There's not much we can do about that."

"Louise was waiting for the kids to come out of school, as usual, when a nicely dressed man came up to her and introduced himself. He said he was a friend of ours and that we had asked him to pick up R.R. and Fay and bring them home right away and would Louise please point them out when they came out of the school. Well, she did, and they said the man was very nice so they got into his car—"

"I don't like the sound of this," he said.

She could feel him stiffen and she found herself instinctively looking over her shoulder again.

"Anyway, they got into his car—all three of them in the front seat—and the man couldn't have been nicer, according to Fay. She also thought him quite handsome. Then a strange thing happened. As they passed that garbage dump just outside of town, the man slowed down and drove very slowly.

" 'What's the matter?' R.R. asked him. 'Is there something wrong with your car?'

" 'No,' the man said. 'I was just looking at that dump and thinking what a swell place that would be to hide a body.' He claimed he had heard it was an old Indian burial ground and no one would ever know the difference after a few years.

"Fay said she gulped until she nearly choked. She was scared stiff until she saw the man was laughing, and she decided it was just his way of making a joke. He was a talker-down to kids, she said. R.R. told him the bulldozer would sure cover everything up."

Rogers tried to smile and failed. "Then what happened?"

"The man drove them right to the front gate and let them out. On the way he asked them how they would feel about living in the White House someday, and a lot of other stuff they couldn't remember. But one thing they did recall because he was careful about it. He wanted them to be sure they knew a Mr. Charles Butterworth brought them home."

"Maybe I'd better call the sheriff."

"No, wait. His name is important because I think maybe somebody is trying to tell us something, and maybe we'd better listen. There was a Mr. Charles Butterworth here with another man last week. Remember I asked you if you knew a man by that name when we were driving in from the airport?"

"I really wasn't paying attention. I was so happy just being here."

She told him then about the visitors who had said they were with the Republican Committee. She repeated parts of their conversation, as well as she could remember it.

When she finished he cocked his head to one side and stared at the ceiling. They could hear Robert and Fay now, engaged in some kind of an argument. "I suppose," he said slowly, "the man might show up again."

"I don't think so now. He's made his point. I questioned the kids as casually as I could because I didn't want them any more uncomfortable than they already were. They both insisted the man was very thin—almost like a scarecrow, R.R. said. But the Charles Butterworth who was here last week was a big, heavy man. How many Charles Butterworths are there wandering around this part of Montana?"

Lee doubled his fists and then slowly relaxed his fingers. Not since his marine days had he realized he was capable of killing.

Lily shook her head. "I think that this so-called Mr. Butterworth is trying to make very sure we understand how vulnerable the children are. I don't believe he has any relationship at all with the Republican National Committee."

Lee glanced at the ceiling again. The upstairs argument was in full swing now—something about leaving the tube of toothpaste in the bathroom with the cap off and making a mess.

He said, "To hell with our budget. I think it would be better for everyone if you packed your gear tonight and we all went back to Washington together."

"I'm already packed. And I also think the less we make of this in front of the kids, the better."

She kissed him on the forehead and said that her appetite had suddenly returned because the man she loved had soothed her fears. In thirty minutes, she promised, she would have a feast for the Rogers tribe.

Wilma Thorne was reviewing her account with Merrill Lynch when the telephone rang. She allowed it to warble several times before she bothered to pick it up, because she was reluctant to dismiss the cozy feeling she knew every time she saw that her balance was more than eighty thousand dollars. At ten percent on her investments, she could squeak by, she told herself with a smile. Her very own retirement fund, and if that amount of money had been squeezed out of her clients over the past ten years without her spending a dime for foolishness, then she deserved a rest.

Why did she go on in the life? Because she had damn well seen what happened to the girls who opted out. Little Wilma was going to keep on giving johns their money's worth as long as they wanted to deposit a hundred dollars plus cab fare, and usually a tip in her hot little hand, *before* they got their jollies.

"Wilma here," she said in her professional soft voice. The general opinion among most girls in the life was that the first greeting on the telephone was all-important.

She listened, then said, "If you know Winifred, it's fine with me. . . . One hundred plus cab fare . . . about twenty, twenty-five minutes. Okay, room 612, the Mayflower."

She switched the phone over to her answering service and took her black dress out of the closet. Why did men always like black? Mort didn't. Mort didn't seem to care what she had on as long as it was nothing.

She laughed on her way out the door and wondered if she would ever in her whole life get up the nerve to call Mort Steiner straight up—just like a friend.

As Wilma passed through the lobby of the Mayflower, she was once again impressed with the competition. Jesus, in addition to the three women she knew were hookers on their way to or from the elevators, there was just as much amateur fluff floating around. It was getting tougher and tougher to nail a john, because the available talent was multiplying so fast. Even so, more and more men were alone in town and they needed something to do with their evenings. It was said to be the same in San Francisco, but the percentage of kooks was much higher.

Exactly thirty minutes from the time she entered the lobby, Wilma was putting on her black dress again. The john was a powerful guy who paid without even trying to bargain, which she thought wouldn't have done him any good anyway. And he laughed easily. It was the johns who didn't laugh who had to be watched. If they got rough, what could you do? Call the cops? Which was why only dumb girls worked the streets or the bars. Born losers and ninety-five percent of them hooked on something. All their money going to the pimp who got them hooked in the first place.

It was strange the way this particular trick worked out, she thought. Quirks of the business. When he opened the door to the room, he sort of apologized and said he was on the phone to South America. He told her to sit on the end of the bed and wait. Time was money, but she complied because there certainly wouldn't be too much time wasted if he was talking all the way to South America.

While he was talking, she reached to pick up a copy of *Time* magazine that was on the bed. Hey, now. What was this? The whole inside of the magazine was missing. There was just the cover. That cowboy congressman was on the front, the guy Mort had something to do with, although he never explained what exactly.

When the john was finished with his call, she held up the cover and asked him if he knew the cowboy. "I don't, but I will," he said. Sort of a mind-your-own-business type, she thought.

That was the end of it, even after she had commented that the cowboy was a pretty good-looking guy. The john wanted action as soon as he peeled off a hundred note from a roll of same. He did come through with the ten dollars for the taxi, and twenty for a tip, which was not too bad for half an hour's work, except that if you'd known he was so loaded, you would have asked for two hundred. That dumb Winifred should have cued you.

As she descended in the elevator, she was, as always, relieved that it had all gone as per routine. No freak requests and no complaints. He seemed to be a normal john who started fretting about how maybe he would catch the clap after he was satisfied. But why did he have that cowboy's picture? What for did he have just *that* picture on his bed—like maybe he was queer for cowboys or something? Jesus, you never knew these days!

While she waited for a taxi—didn't it ever stop raining in Washington?—she was glad she was wearing her wig, because the dampness raised holy hell with curly hair. Bound for the Carlton Hotel, where another trick awaited her, she thought about what the john had been saying on the telephone when she was in his room. Maybe it didn't mean nothing, but there was something fishy about the way he said, "No, I'm not goin' to try handling this alone. Too risky." A long pause. Then he asked, "Will you authorize my bringing in some help? If there're four of us, he'll have to behave himself."

What was he talking about? A poker game? The cowboy? What gives here?

For a moment she considered calling Mort and telling him what happened and how strange it made her feel. But to do that, she would have to let Mort know that she was with a john, and that was sort of a no-no. It was not like a marriage between herself and Mort or anything like that, or even a steady relationship, like if Mort was paying her bills. Naturally Mort understood how she made a living, but he would sure like to pretend he was the one and only. Sometimes if a person gets hit right in the face with a fact they don't want to recognize as a fact, they become very antagonistic and just run away.

She was not anxious to cause such a thing to happen in the case of Mort Steiner. Not when they were just kind of sliding sideways, you might say, into a very special relationship.

"Mr. Chairman, the abuse potential of marijuana is seven times greater than that of alcohol. The abuse potential for cocaine and heroin runs fourteen times higher. All young brains are in the process of development and the pleasure centers are still dominant. They signal 'Give' first, and 'Give me pleasure' next. Training and discipline cover the born brain with a neocortex that enables an individual to wait for a reward. With narcotics, this restriction is short-circuited. . . ."

Dr. Neil Hathaway, director of the Family Institute for Drug Education, was testifying before the House Select Committee on Narcotics Abuse. He was a young man obviously devoted to his subject and his enthusiasm was carried on a pronounced southern accent that echoed melodiously about the hearing room. His most intent listener was a man he recognized as the "cowboy from Montana," and because the doctor knew the value of endorsement by a famous individual, he addressed a large portion of his remarks directly to him.

Lee Rogers was obviously embarrassed. This was his first invitation to join in a committee hearing, and he was certainly the greenest horn ever. The chairman had thought it might be educational to have him fill in for Congressman Barker, who was ill and could not attend. Rogers was not at all sure that having so much attention paid to him in preference to others, not to mention the chairman, was a good omen.

"Mr. Chairman," the doctor went on, "the Asian democracies have partially succeeded in reducing their epidemics of narcotics abuse. We can't seem to do it, because we continue to hold that there are no bad drugs, just bad users. We also overestimate man's ability to overcome his dependence on drugs, and we even have people who go so far as to claim sugar and cocaine are a similar evil because they are both white crystalline powders and addictive. In fact, two professors of psychiatry wrote in the *Scientific American* of April 1983 that cocaine is no more addictive than peanuts or potato chips. . . ."

Rogers found himself only half listening. So many things were competing for his attention. He had almost forgotten what it was like to have nothing but cattle worries; now there were countless details and facts to be assembled before he could hope to persuade anyone to do anything so daring as to declare war. Then there was the safety and comfort of Lily and the kids. Right now it was not too difficult for her because the abundance of museums in Washington kept all three of them busy most of the day, and the little two-bedroom furnished apartment Lily had found in Alexandria was at least adequate. But it was far from being a home; there was the big question of the kids' future schooling, and certainly things could not last as is.

At least he had been somewhat reassured about their safety. At his request, the FBI had sent an agent to his office when he returned. After hearing him out, the agent said, "I doubt very much if this is a Mafia approach, Mr. Rogers. Those we haven't put behind bars are lying very low these days, and while they're up to their usual tricks, they seem to be discouraged with drug trafficking on any large scale. It's too risky, especially when they weigh it against their more profitable ventures—their unions and various gambling operations, which, if they're smart enough to pay their taxes, offer relatively little risk. So I'd say the chances of Mafia involvement are very slight. They're all rotten eggs, but they do seem to have a taboo on molesting families of people who annoy them. They might break your knees, or worse, but if possible they would avoid hurting your children. It's just not their style."

The agent had also been a marine and they talked about the Corps for a while. Before he left, the agent said, "If anything more happens that you consider even slightly suspicious, let us know. Meanwhile we'll see what we can find out about our friend Butterworth. And from now on, if I were you, I'd sort of keep my back to the wall."

Rogers tried very hard to concentrate on what Dr. Hathaway was saying. ". . . Of course, in this country we believe that the rights of an individual are sovereign—an individual should be able to treat his body as he pleases. The question is, will reason prevail over the yearning for pleasure?"

The man made sense, Rogers thought, but he knew he had not heard all the doctor had said. Intrusions on his mind were too constant. What to do about Guy Amonte's party, for example? Tracy Delano had called to say Amonte was being transferred to Spain and a small party was being given before his plane departed. He would be most honored and deeply touched if Rogers would attend.

"Are you going?"

"Of course," she said. "I understand perfectly that you're not as free as you were, but it would give Guy such a lift if you could drop by for just a few minutes. You could be on your way home by six."

There was no use asking why Guy Amonte had not called him directly. Their acquaintance had been very brief and hardly the kind that might develop into friendship. Was Amonte aware that if Tracy called, the chances of a refusal were almost nil? It was so easy to rationalize. Go with a purpose. Here was an opportunity to tell Tracy that Lily could not be expected to endorse their friendship, no matter how innocent . . . and good-bye. Which was baloney. The honest answer was that it would be exciting to see Tracy just one more time.

He glanced at his watch and fingered the paper in his shirt pocket with Guy's address on it. He still had an hour and a half and he was beginning to wonder if he would be obliged to spend all of it listening to Dr. Hathaway.

". . . Gentlemen of the Committee, we have to understand that those drugs commonly imported to this country cause neuropsychotoxicity—which is quite a mouthful. It means that individuals so affected lose their ability to view the outside world as it really is. Their psychological and psychomotor performance is impaired—"

The chairman interrupted. "What about nicotine, caffeine, and alcohol? Don't they produce that neuropsychotox—I can't even say it!"

Rogers joined in the general laughter.

"Yes, to a much lesser extent, they do. Which is why we try to control tobacco and alcohol by law. It works—to a certain extent. Sully Ledermann, the French mathematician, proved that the more consumers of alcohol in a society, the more alcoholics. If we want to reduce car accidents among our eighteen-year-olds, then raising the legal drinking age to twenty is actually effective."

"May we assume such a theory would apply to drugs?"

"Yes. Right now about eighteen percent of our high-school seniors use marijuana daily. Surveys made in Jamaica, where the drug is much easier to buy, indicate that sixty-four percent of the villagers smoke some ten joints a day and are intoxicated as a result."

Rogers glanced at his watch again. He had to tackle his mind and keep it from wandering. Forget Amonte. Forget Tracy Delano. You're with the big boys today. If the war is ever going to get off the ground, these are the men who will launch it. Without their support, the whole thing could die in committee.

When a Mr. Arnold Sigornich began to testify, he recaptured Rogers's attention. He identified himself as a former trafficker who had seen the light.

"Mr. Sigornich," the chairman addressed him, "would you mind telling us why you quit the so-called business? We can only assume it was lucrative."

"I married the wrong kind of woman. I brought her over from the old country because I liked her old-fashioned ideas about how a husband and wife should live together. She said quit or else." He shrugged his powerful shoulders and added, "I was in love with her and I still am."

The chairman smiled, as did most of the other members of the committee. "We understand the cause of your defection, Mr. Sigornich. Please continue."

Rogers was impressed with Sigornich's enthusiasm.

"The gross revenue from drug sales in this country last year was more than ten billion. And it costs another one hundred million every year in lost productivity and law enforcement. That's some bundle of money."

Rogers was certain that his kind of war would cost considerably less.

"I can give you numbers that won't quit, but instead I give you

174

Manuel Espinosa. He makes like he's going to college, only he don't spend much time in class. He's in the business, see? He's got everything you want and he gives fair weight. If it's buds you want, he'll sell you a Baggie that maybe runs closer to three point six or seven than light. He gets all his stuff in Miami and makes frequent trips to resupply. Now this is a bright young man who comes from a nice family and wouldn't hurt a flea. Last month he arrives in Miami with sixty thousand dollars to buy from the people who come from Jamaica. He makes this big deal and they say thanks and see you around."

Sigornich paused and surveyed the committee members one by one. "They were nice enough to send his body back to his mother and father, complete with flowers and twenty-six stab wounds in his throat and chest. I tell you this because I want to make it very clear to every one of you that you're not dealing with Boy Scouts."

Amen to that, Rogers thought.

Later, Rogers was amused at what Tracy Delano had said would be a "small" party. The hearing had lasted longer than he had expected and it was after six when he arrived. Once inside the door of Guy Amonte's little apartment, he was greeted instantly by total strangers. "The cowboy! . . . Here's the cowboy!" rose again and again from the babble.

He was becoming heartily sick of the "cowboy" label, and for a moment thought to turn and leave. This noisy clutter of bodies jammed into such a tiny space was not for him. He tried to smile, but he found the air was close to suffocating and the noise overwhelming. Through a momentary separation of bodies on the other side of the room, he saw the woman he knew as Agnes and the sight of her capped his decision to retreat.

He had already accomplished his exit when Guy Amonte suddenly appeared in the hallway and held out a glass of champagne. "*Mister* Lee Rogers! How very kind of you to come. There is no way I can thank you enough. You have made this a big day for me!"

He placed the glass in Rogers's hand and seized his arm. "Come with me please, sir," he said. "Many people wish to meet you, but one is very special."

Rogers did not like the faint suggestion of a leer in his host's dark eyes.

Amonte twisted expertly through the huddles and emerged in a small pantry, where Tracy was waiting. "At last," she said, holding her glass toward him. "The real refreshment has arrived."

Rogers decided she looked nothing short of spectacular in a black knit dress that discreetly emphasized the few curves of her slim figure. "Did I ever tell you I've never known any other man who made me feel like I've just taken a huge breath of fresh air?"

Rogers did his best to cover his embarrassment by looking at the floor. Why in the hell did people talk so funny back here?

"I've missed you," Tracy said. "How goes the war?"

"Inch by inch. One thing I've learned about this town. Nothing happens in a hurry."

"They say it's the quality of the light." She lost her smile and hesitated. Then she asked, "Did you find a good place for your family?"

"It'll do." Rogers discovered that he was trying desperately to avoid meeting her eyes, but having little success. He should not have come. Now, damned if he wasn't struck with a sense of guilt. Holy cow, was it wrong to just say hello to a woman other than Lily? Of course Tracy might be considered a little different.

"Congressman Rogers," she said with what he decided was one of the world's warmest smiles, "I promised you would be on your way home by six and it's already half past. I've had enough of Guy's lovely party and I suspect you have too. You've done your duty and it was sweet of you, because Guy doesn't know any celebrities and, like it or not, you are one. Just your showing up will be enough to keep these people talking for days. So how about walking me home?"

It was a mild evening and they took their time, sauntering more than walking with purpose. They exchanged a series of unrelated statements guaranteed to bring safe and easy responses. Although his uncomfortable sense of guilt still lingered, Rogers realized how much he was enjoying himself and he regretted that it was hardly more than a few blocks to Tracy's apartment. Then what? He would take her to the door . . . and say good-bye? And thanks. For what? For just being. How wrong was that?

They were only a few steps from the entrance to her building when she halted and said, "There's something I've been wanting to tell you, but you've been . . . unavailable."

He noticed that her tone of voice had changed markedly. Now, almost for the first time since he had been with her, the saucy smile was gone and she was utterly serious.

"Maybe it doesn't mean much, but then it could. I've debated even telling you, and yet I worry about you. I don't suppose there's any chance of persuading you to modify your campaign for a war?"

"Sure there is. I'm open-minded. If someone would just come up with a plan that would accomplish the same thing, I'd buy it. But something has to be done. Now."

"I just hate to see you out there fighting alone. Davids don't win very often against the Goliaths. You could get a bloody nose."

"Very possibly."

"I wonder if you're aware of certain other dangers, some of which have been brought on because you've so captured the public's eye. Stepping on a few toes as a freshman congressman would ordinarily go unnoticed, but publicity has given you power and you're kicking some very powerful people in the shins. They don't like it."

"If anybody is for our drug situation, they're sick or crazy, or a traitor, or all three."

"It's not a question of being for or against drugs. You're threatening to upset a lot of money carts. It troubles me to hear you called a rabble-rouser who will do anything to forward his career, even if it means getting us into a war."

"Where did you hear that nonsense?"

"My former husband."

"Ouch! I gather he doesn't approve of our . . . friendship?"

"He doesn't even know we've met. Have you ever heard of Randall's Delicious Coffee?"

"Who hasn't?"

"My ex works for the man who owns it and a good chunk of the rest of the world. His boss is obsessed with you and your plan, because among other titles he's also very high in the World Coffee

Ernest K. Gann

Association and will probably be the next chairman. If the supply of Colombian coffee is cut off, he and his friends will be badly hurt."

"Too bad. Maybe he's got enough clout to make the Colombian government knock out the narcotics production in their country. Then he won't have anything to worry about."

She took his hand. "Lee, please listen to me. I know the man and the people he associates with. Their coffee cartel is important to them. They're all very rich and very powerful and they think alike. They don't like strangers playing in their private court. They are determined to stop you and they won't be nice about it. It would be easy for them to start some sort of scandal—about you and me, for example. I don't want to see you hurt, or your wife and family. They won't give a damn what happens to you—in fact, they'll probably toast your downfall with an extra martini. Try to see it from their point of view, Lee, and remember that the press is just as eager to knock you down as build you up."

"Your ex-husband's boss can get in line with the rest of the people who are mad at me. I'll take them on one at a time."

"They don't fight that way." Her voice was pleading now and he found the change in her so complete it was as if he had never met her before.

"Dear man, listen! Listen to little old Tracy, who knows her way around this life. You come from a nice world where the majority of people are pleasant to one another. It's different here, because the power has been here for generations. If you tag along like a good soldier, you can accomplish a lot, but if you cross the wrong lines and antagonize the big boys, they'll run right over you.

"They're not the movie version of a bunch of mobsters, but they are a gang. They dress and talk well. They vote Republican. They wear ties even on weekends, and they play tennis with their families. They all went to the same schools and so did their fathers. You would like them personally, but don't underestimate them. They don't carry guns or knives, but don't think they can't ruin your life if you attack them."

Rogers reached for her arm and urged her gently toward the lighted entryway. Suddenly he wanted to be at home. He wanted to sit down and look at Lily and renew his resolve.

178

"I suppose," he said, "that if this thing goes I'll have all the coffee drinkers in the country on my neck. And I'll never be reelected. Your ex and his boss and his boss's friends should know that I don't want to be."

She hesitated a moment while she reached out and brushed a piece of lint from the shoulder of his coat. "All right, Congressman. I admire your guts if not your common sense." She rose on the tips of her toes and added, "The doorman is watching and he would be terribly disappointed if I failed to receive even a farewell kiss. Would you please convince him that the world is still on its correct axis?"

He bent down and kissed her. He held her briefly, then stepped back, "So long, Tracy. Thank you."

"So long, cowboy. Please be careful."

He saw what he thought was the approach of tears in her eyes, and he vowed to kick himself all the way to Alexandria for starting something he could not finish. He turned away quickly and heard her call out, "The doorman will call you a taxi!"

He told himself he had not really heard her and kept walking.

A car that had kept pace with them as they walked the last few blocks continued after him.

At midnight Mort Steiner's nose was nestled comfortably in the soft hollow between Wilma's shoulder and her neck. He had never before even considered sleeping with her, but this time he had asked if she would care to spend the night, and somewhat to his surprise she answered, "That would be very nice."

Nice? Sleeping with a known harlot? Steiner assured himself that he must be out of his mind. And yet, here she was, apparently content as a kitten. It was very difficult to think how much money she might be losing while she slept so peacefully. He refused to think about it, and yet nasty visions of other men enjoying her exciting body returned so frequently that he could not sleep. "Woe," he thought, allowing his cynicism full play, "woe is the lot of the bachelor who would raffle off his couch and include an overnight ticket."

Somehow he must restore his peace of mind. Had he impulsively offered an overnight stay because he was secretly in love with Wilma Thorne? Why else would he have considered such a breach of wisdom? Now he was trapped. One could not awaken a sleeping maiden and order her to get dressed and out into the elements. And what were the elements?

He studied the open window that faced the back of an adjacent building and the higher branches of an old tree. There was always enough reflected light from the street to define the branches, and if they were dripping moisture, he at least knew if it was raining or snowing. A city man, he reasoned, rarely knew what the heavens promised unless some electronic device told him. And the forefathers who chose this dank swamp for a capital must have been meteorological masochists. Now, without so much as a hint of an approaching storm, he was vaguely disappointed. How could he play his role as a protector without a suitable tempest? Now Wilma was in his cave; he would bring her food when necessary and protect her against passing savages, but even more elementary threats would be stimulating.

The faint light from the window revealed Wilma's wig hanging on the bedpost. There was a homey touch, he thought. He would ask her not to wear the damn thing in the future, at least when she came here. It smacked of the vulgar somehow, of deception—and anyway, her natural hair was very pleasant to contemplate.

Watching her now, he thought she seemed utterly at peace and he found it intriguing to anticipate what it would be like when she awakened in the morning. Would she prove to be one of those cat-women whom daylight offended? How would he know, since he had never spent an entire night with a woman? Suppose she was cheerful and bright of speech. One might say then that if the same occurred at the start of each day, then the quality of a bachelor's life was grossly exaggerated. And yet how could he judge Wilma, whose hours, like the rest of the world's, were based on her profession? While others were rising, she must be going to bed. *No,* he corrected himself angrily—to sleep! God knows how many times she might have gone to bed before dawn.

To his astonishment, the telephone rang. Certainly a wrong number. No one ever called him at this hour. He lay still in the darkness, wondering if he should bother to answer. As he reached for the phone, he decided against turning on the light. Why wake sleeping beauty?

He said hello and heard a woman's voice he could not identify. "Mr. Steiner? This is Lily Rogers. . . ."

Mrs. Rogers? He had met her very briefly on the day she arrived in Washington and he had been impressed with her poise, if not her beauty. The "plain" type, he thought. Needed stylish hair and dress. He remembered thinking she would look very much at home driving a wagon train or shooting hostile Indians. "Yes, Mrs. Rogers?"

"I'm extremely sorry to call you at this hour, but I'm worried about Lee. Do you know where he is?"

Steiner glanced at the still-sleeping figure beside him. Remarkable. Neither the phone, the light, nor the sound of his voice had troubled her. Something was out of kilter here. It was only the innocent who were supposed to sleep so soundly.

"Did you call the office, Mrs. Rogers? Sometimes he works late."

"Of course. There's no answer."

She sounded a bit peevish, he decided; but then, men who got themselves married could expect trouble if they failed to show when expected. Still, with all of his frailties—and who knew them better than Mort Steiner?—Congressman Rogers was not the type to disappear with some dolly in the middle of the night.

"I'm considering calling the police," she said.

Steiner sat upright immediately. Was this the whammy he had anticipated—the thing that had been lurking on the doorstep of Longworth House ever since Rogers moved in? The *police?* One never knew what the police would do with any kind of story. Politicians and police were an unpredictable and highly dangerous mix. "Perhaps," he said lamely, "he ran into an old friend."

"You know better, Mr. Steiner. He would have called. It's after midnight and he was due here six hours ago."

"He usually takes the bus home, doesn't he?"

"Not always. Sometimes if he's late he takes a taxi. I'm sure something must be very wrong."

Steiner told himself that he did not believe the information he was still trying to digest. Here he was, cozy as a man could be, tucked in with a luscious and most agreeable woman, and Lee Rogers chose this time to desert his family. He envisioned a long night's work ahead of him.

"Mrs. Rogers, please don't call the police just yet. Let me make some inquiries and see what I can find out. I'll call you back within the hour."

She sounded content for the moment and said she would wait to hear from him. Inquiries? Where to start? Certainly not directly with the police. He flipped through a rotary file beside the telephone; then, cupping the phone in the same place on his own body where he had rested his chin on the soundest sleeper ever born, he quickly punched in the date of the Spanish armada. If Congressman Rogers was naïve enough to believe he was concealing anything from his administrator, he would now learn a lesson.

The ringing repeated itself many times before he smiled at the sound of a throaty, sleepy voice. No question the woman had class and a certain seductive tone. "Miss Delano? Mort Steiner here. With apologies for disturbing you. We're rather in a quandary here at the office. By any chance have you seen Congressman Rogers recently?"

He listened and saw to his amazement that Wilma slept on. Maybe she was on some kind of pills? "And when he left you, he was *walking?*"

"Yes, yes. The doorman could have called a taxi for him, but he just kept on going. What's wrong?" she asked apprehensively.

La Delano, he thought, was very concerned. "Nothing really. We had expected him at a late meeting here at the office, but he hasn't shown up. Did he say anything to you about where he was going?"

"No. I assumed he was bound for home."

"Had he been drinking?" Give her the benefit of the doubt, anyway. This was becoming less and less amusing.

"He had a glass of champagne and I don't think he even finished it. You've got to tell me what's happened."

"One of the reasons I called you is to find out, Miss Delano. I'll see to it that you know soon after we do. Thank you, and please forgive the lateness of my call. Some government workers do work late, you know."

He said good-night as cheerfully as he could manage, and pressed the cut-off switch. He punched in another number immediately, one he knew by heart. It was a very long shot, he thought, and he must be very careful of his approach, but it just might pay off. In a moment he heard Gordon Hawkins's voice. Hawkins was indeed still up, enjoying, he said, that rarest of privileges, a good book.

They discussed the frustrations of book lovers for a moment, and then Steiner sailed gently into his query. "Gordon, we've worked together for many years, and if I may say so, we are obligated to each other. I hope that mutual trust will continue."

"I don't see why it shouldn't, but that's not why you're calling me at this hour. You're a conniving bastard, Mort. You always have been. But I'll go along with you as long as it doesn't inconvenience me. What's up?"

"May I say that you're quite as charming and gracious at this hour as you are at any other? As a matter of fact, I would never call you unless information that you might have could be useful to me. You get around more than I do. You see a different brand of people, and after all, it's you who was initially responsible for the well-deserved recognition of my boss."

"How *is* that noble individual?"

"Splendid. He continues to amaze me. And yet I'm troubled, which is why I'm working so late. Do you know of any individuals or even organizations who might not share our enthusiasm for Lee Rogers?"

"How many do you want? There are probably hundreds—maybe thousands."

"Let us confine ourselves to local threats."

"Why? What's wrong. Goddammit, quit waffling and tell me what's wrong."

"Nothing. It's been very dull around here lately—"

"Are you trying to tell me you're still at the office?"

Steiner hesitated. The rat smells a rat, he thought. Hawkins would be the sort to call the office just to make sure he was hearing the truth. "No. I just got home and was ruffling through some papers. We think it might be wise to assemble some kind of a list. . . . By the way, have you seen our good man since his return from Montana?"

"No, I have not. And if I had, I'm sure you'd know about it. Now, tell me, little bird, and stop squirming around in circles. What's happened? You tell me first and I give you my word I'll not use anything until you say go."

Steiner hesitated a long time. He had opened a can of beans and they were spilling all over the floor. Better to tell Hawkins before his imagination started working. He would damn soon find out anyway. At last he said, "Our man was due home at six. He's not arrived there yet."

Silence, as he knew there would be. He heard Hawkins whisper, "Shit."

Had he notified the police?

"First I wanted to know if you had any leads."

"You might try Tracy Delano. They were quite taken with each other, or so my dear sister tells me."

"I have. She hasn't a clue. And our man is not the sort to fail calling home if he's delayed. Now, the Delano woman. Apparently she was the last to see him. Do you trust her?"

"With what?"

"With the welfare of our man."

"Yes, and no."

"Just what do you mean by that?"

"She's a single woman on the prowl and I think she spends more than her alimony. That's a volatile combination. But physical harm? I'd say no. Tracy is a romantic. She's interested in landing a man rather than throwing him away."

"Thanks so much. You finally told me one of the things I need to know. Sweet dreams. Avoid diseases and you'll live forever."

He replaced the receiver and looked at Wilma. Could she be dead? No, her lovely bosom was rising and falling with marvelous regularity. Was she pretending? He called her name softly, but there was not the slightest reaction. God, what a healthy animal! Did she know she was going to live forever?

He called the police and inquired about accidents between six and midnight. There'd been three. One in the northwest district and two in the southeast. One injury. A female. Taken to Bethesda Hospital. How about muggings? None in the northwest district. Very quiet night. Alexandria? Not our responsibility.

He was damned if he would call the morgue. They wouldn't answer at this hour anyway. He turned to Wilma and was suddenly acutely aware of the warmth of her body. But the pleasure of her flesh was gone suddenly. She was a nuisance now, and she would have to shift for herself. He was going to have to get up and grapple with this problem until it could be solved.

As he rose from the bed, a sense of dread nearly overwhelmed him. There might not be any thunderstorms outside, but there was one in his belly and he knew why. For the first time in his professional life, a situation had developed for which he was totally unprepared.

He dressed, although he was still unsure why. What could he do at this hour? Charging around the deserted Washington streets would accomplish nothing except possibly a mugging, starring himself, and yet he certainly could not remain in bed thinking of all the gruesome possibilities. He put on a sweater and an old pair of tennis shoes he had not worn for years.

He went into the kitchenette and made a cup of coffee. He sipped unhappily for some time while he tried desperately to outline exactly what he intended to do. Supposing the Delano woman had lied? Supposing Lee Rogers was right there beside her, smiling at their little deception? . . ."

No, not Lee Rogers. Unless he was the greatest actor in the world, it was just not in him. God, the flag, and family—that was more the real Rogers. But maybe he hated his wife. Maybe he was unhappy about her being in Washington and this was a way of telling her to go back to the boondocks and stay there. Maybe he was enjoying a taste of freedom he had never known. Maybe fame had gone to his head.

Ridiculous! All unproductive reasoning. There was not a disloyal bone in Rogers's handsome physique—which, incidentally, was the way Mort Steiner was going to look in his next life. Hey, man, tall in the saddle!

His nerves, he decided, were going to jump right out of his sweater.

He went suddenly to the kitchenette phone and again punched in Tracy's number. "Mort Steiner here once more, Miss Delano. My most humble apologies for troubling you again. Far be it from me to pry, but perhaps you would tell me what you and Congressman Rogers did before he departed. It might be very helpful."

She did not reply immediately. The phone was dead. Was there some kind of a pill in his medicine cabinet that would calm him? This was how loonies were made.

Had she covered the mouthpiece while she turned on her side and asked the man in her bed what she should say? No, no! Get off that tack. It's a blind alley.

"How do I know I'm talking to Mort Steiner?" she asked finally.

Good question. On the other end of this telephone, there was a wise and wary Washington woman. "You don't. But I'm only asking for a sequence of events, not the results. I'm only interested in your travel itinerary from the time you met on this one evening. I know where he was before that event, and the time you separated, which you've already told me. Please. If you'll help me, it will undoubtedly help him. I'm not asking you to be indiscreet, and please don't tell me to mind my own business, because Lee Rogers is my business and I've lost him."

Again there was such a long pause that he thought she must have hung up. But there had been no click and he thought he could hear her breathing. Somewhere in the distance he heard the wail of a police siren. Did they have to do that now? Old jangled nerves did not need that sort of sound track just now.

"Well," she said at last, "we met by chance at a friend's farewell party. . . ."

He listened carefully and scribbled notes as she spoke. Guy Amonte . . . transfer to Spain . . . 1166 Connecticut Avenue . . . apartment 126 . . . Phone? Didn't know. French Embassy. Left about 6:30 . . . walked four blocks . . .

He jumped involuntarily as he realized he was not alone. Wilma was standing in the doorway. Her yellow slip complimented the subtle curves of her body and for an instant he thought she looked like a very small girl just awakened. But she had come at the wrong time. He held a finger to his lips to silence her. Even so, she came to him and while he still held the phone she caressed the top of his head and pressed against him.

When he finally put down the phone, she kissed his forehead. Stepping back she said, "Mort, there's something I got to tell you."

He folded his notes and placed them in his pocket. His damned hands were shaking. What next? Should he reconnoiter Amonte's place? Something was cuckoo there. A French diplomat and Lee Rogers? "Wilma, dear, I've got a lot on my mind. Can you keep what's on yours for a while?"

"No. I can't any longer. Promise me, Mort . . . oh, please understand. Promise it won't make any difference between us, because tonight has been one of the happiest times of my life and I'm scared stiff I'll louse it up."

She appeared to be in agony, and he thought, well, here we go. The minute a man lets his guard down with a woman, there are all the emotional entanglements falling like a net over his head. Wilma was a professional. She should know better.

"Yes?" he said. He must try not to sound impatient. "What's eating you?"

"Us. I don't want nothing to separate us."

Why the hell was she bringing this up at almost three in the morning—or whatever time it was. That face and those totally honest eyes—one couldn't just say, "Beat it, kid."

"All right, Wilma. Nothing will change my opinion that you're one of God's better creatures. What's on your unique little mind? And while you're at it, tell me how you can sleep like a mummy with the whole world coming down around our ears."

She clutched his hands tightly, almost as if she were certain a physical separation was imminent.

She told him then about the man in the Mayflower Hotel, and how he had the empty *Time* magazine on the bed and how he was talking to South America on the telephone and how he had answered when asked if he knew the cowboy, "No, but I will."

"You mean you've not been asleep all this time?"

"No, Mort. I was too happy to sleep even before the phone rung. And now I want to be real close to you if you're in some kind of trouble."

He took her in his arms and held her for a moment. Then he pressed her tightly against him and kissed her lips, her eyes, and the tip of her nose. "Wilma," he said before he could stop himself, "I sure like you."

14

When Mort Steiner decided a personal patrol of the streets was useless, he also resolved to wait until dawn before contacting his friends in the FBI. He knew Rogers had a tight list of appointments in the morning; at 8:30 a meeting of the Human Resources Committee; at 9:00 the Asian and Pacific Affairs Subcommittee; at 9:30 a meeting with Montana State Housing officials. If he failed to show for all of these—and it now seemed reasonable to suppose he would—then the fat would really be in the fire.

He pondered the idea of calling a press conference before anyone had a chance to sensationalize the strange absence of Congressman Rogers. Where, oh, where, was Edward Starbuck? Steiner contemplated the possibility of manufacturing some story about Rogers going to Burma to check on the narcotics situation. No good. They would want to know why his mission was so secret. The hunt would be on, and Mort Steiner's neck would be twisted liverwurst.

Steiner felt his pulse with the expertise of a born hypochondriac. He was disappointed to find it quite regular.

While Mort Steiner was counting the rhythm of his pulse, others, far away, felt theirs quickening and then halting forever. In the chapare region of Bolivia, where many of the drugs were produced for export, eleven peasants were shot for refusing to "cooperate." Raoul Diego and Sebastian Cassavantes, who performed the executions on the orders of their employers, were also instructed to take postexecution photos of the carnage and see to it that the international edition of *Time* magazine, complete with the cover portrait of the Washington Cowboy, was prominently displayed near the bodies.

A few hours later, in the upper Huallaga Valley of Peru, the mayor of Tingo María was murdered and six policemen who responded to his cries for help were bound and tortured and then slain for their past interference with narcotics trafficking. The perpetrators were quick to inform the press that the dead had been accomplices of the Yankee cowboy.

Night in Burma was a perilous time for ordinary inhabitants in the rugged areas. They had learned to stay home when the sun went down. The so-called insurgents, whose activities were financed mainly through the export of narcotics to Thailand and wherever else there was a buyer, were ruthless in their conscription when they needed produce and labor.

The government was almost helpless to curtail the production, transport, and sale of heroin, or prevent the insurgents from forcing local farmers to raise poppy crops. Even among the most remote bands, whose politics ranged from pseudo-Marxism to pure brigandage, the Yankee cowboy was becoming known and his name reviled.

And in the Soviet Union there were now two translators whose sole occupation was to furnish their government with all that was printed about Congressman Rogers. They were also charged with a continuous assessment of his possible success along with daily reports on his activities.

* * *

They waited until the last guest had been shoved out the door, and then they fell gratefully into each other's arms. They pretended exhaustion although Guy Amonte was far from weary, nor was his friend Agnes. She had brought her "outfit" with her and they were both charged with anticipation. For now, at last, among the scattered remnants of a cocktail party that had outgrown itself, they could join each other in free-basing, and the rest of the world be damned.

There was just nothing like the impact of free-basing. Amonte had done cocaine many times in the past, but not until he came to the United States was he offered the opportunity to free-base. Agnes, bless her generous heart, had introduced him to the joys of doing things right, and the almost instant reaction created a wild desire for another hit as soon as possible.

They sat on the floor beside the coffee table, which was convenient to the all-important ritual. Guy had selected some Chopin for a musical background and he watched with solemn concentration as Agnes placed her outfit on the table and removed the contents. No hurry. As with sexual encounters, anticipation was half the delight.

"Let's go for a quarter of a gram to start," she said, bringing from her tooled leather bag a glass pipe, a small mirror, an eyedropper, a razor blade, a flask of water, a small vial, three small plastic bottles, and a box of kitchen matches. "You get off first and I'll be right behind you."

As he watched, she poured water into the vial until it was three-quarters full. "Distilled water," she intoned. "Nothing but the best for us, love."

She opened a plastic envelope and very carefully shook a pinch of cocaine into the vial. She closed the envelope, then placed her finger over the mouth of the vial and shook it gently. The cocaine dissolved quickly.

Using the eyedropper, she took two drops of ammonium hydroxide from a small bottle and squirted them into the vial.

The water turned cloudy as she continued to rotate the vial.

"You're a superb cook," he said, laughing.

When she was satisfied the mix was complete, she opened a small bottle of ether and poured almost an ounce into the vial. She shook it a few times, then let the vial sit while she ran her fingers through Amonte's heavy black hair.

"Dear boy. What am I going to do if you're not in Washington? I can't be running away to Spain when we get the urge to free-base. If you get caught with all this over there, they shoot you—or so I'm told."

"It's not quite so bad as that, but I'm not going to Spain anyway."

"Really? Then what was this party all about?"

"I'm going away for just a few weeks. It gave the party more zest if it seemed official. When I return, it will all be forgotten."

The champagne Agnes had consumed was still with her and she seemed to find his reasoning uproariously funny. "And your ambassador? Your boss doesn't mind if you just take off when you feel like it?"

"I've made certain arrangements. Our ambassador is a true Frenchman. He understands the value of money." He eyed the mixture on the table and saw the ether absorb the cocaine and rise with it to the surface of the liquid. "I can hardly wait," he said.

She smiled and carefully inserted the eyedropper into the vial. She drew off the top layer of liquid and squeezed it onto the mirror. The ether evaporated almost instantly, leaving a white film.

She picked up the razor and scraped the film into the glass pipe. She handed it to him and rechecked the bottle of ether. The cap was secure. She handed the matches to him, and he held the flame just above the pipe bowl. His intent was to melt the cocaine base within the pipe but not scorch it. As smoke rose from the bowl, he sucked in deeply.

He sighed with satisfaction. She took a special joy in watching the hit transform him. Ecstasy. She began immediately to prepare a hit for herself. This was good medicine for the soul. "Where are you going?" she asked.

"I don't know yet." He was already deep into his hit. She could be sure of it because of his eyes. Watching others take a hit was half the fun.

"Take me with you," she said. "I can pay my own way."

"That won't be necessary."

She filled the pipe and held a match to the bowl. "This is the best part of your party," she said.

"What time is it?"

"Half past."

"Negative or positive?"

"Either."

"Good."

They sat smiling at each other, untroubled by the coming of light outside the windows.

At 2:00 A.M., eastern time, Seaman First Class Elwood Keim of the U.S. Naval Base shoreside radar installation at Key West removed himself from the glittering face of his radar screen and went to the opposite end of the building, where the "head" was located. The little journey took a total of three minutes, including the time required for a cursory wash of his hands. He then went to the automatic dispenser at the end of the hallway, drew a cup of coffee, and placed a quarter in the machine for an overlarge ginger cookie. When he returned to his scope, he noted that he had been gone a total of six and one-half minutes. Even so, Harry Black, who shared the same screen, asked where the hell he had been.

Keim responded with a grunt and the advice that Black did not urinate frequently enough. It was necessary that a man drain his system regularly; otherwise fistula of the bubo could be expected. In fact, he already saw evidence of that disease in Black, along with symptoms of poleaxe and probably some spooning of the clavicles.

Black said that his duty-mate was more full of shit than usual, and what did he make of the odd target that had appeared on the screen while he was gone, and was it worth reporting to the officer of the deck, Ensign Childers? There was nothing on the computer that matched with the presence of such a target. No flight plan—nothing.

Elwood Keim watched the small green dot that seemed to glow and vanish with every sweep of the antenna line. He chuckled and took a bite of his cookie. Whatever it was moved very slowly—in fact, it was difficult to be sure it was moving at all. "Hell, man, you want to go tell Mr. Childers you got a fucking pelican as your target for tonight? You wanna see if you can make him laugh? There is no ensign in the United States Navy knows how to laugh, and I suggest you don't try to teach Mr. Childers how."

Since Keim was infinitely superior in seniority to Black, and was technically in charge of their particular screen, the conversation ceased abruptly. Soon afterward the target, whatever it was, passed off the boundary of the screen.

"You happen to get a pelican that's close," Keim said, "and you can easy mistake him for something else."

"I wonder if the radar rays kill the pelicans like they sure would a human being if you're just standing in the way."

"Whoever the hell told you that? Radar won't harm you no more than a microwave oven."

"My wife has one of those and she sure ain't dead yet."

They both laughed, and waited easier for their relief.

Soon afterward the helium-filled captive blimp at Ocean Station Six, west of Marathon, recorded an unidentified target (slow-moving) passing almost directly overhead on a course of 332 degrees, speed 150 knots.

Those who observed the target were puzzled because it originated in Havana, was then lost for a while, and finally reappeared overhead. While it was probably a drug runner's aircraft and worth reporting, there were several other, similar targets flying more normal courses and they were chosen for further observation. The target, which presumably departed Havana, was lost almost immediately after it crossed the coast of Louisiana.

Since the radar unit at Marathon was one of several new experimental installations designed to give better coverage of the Caribbean and Gulf areas, no one as yet quite trusted it. The target was fuzzy and its behavior eccentric. When it vanished altogether, the brief debate concerning its worth ended. With so many other birds asking for evaluation, why bother with one that had already gone to nest—if indeed it had actually existed?

At 4:00 A.M. Lester Riding, the only person on duty at the Texarkana flight station, received a strange telephone call from some nut he thought must have been swallowing too much of the local whiskey.

The man said, "Is this the FAA? Are you the guys I talk to about airplane crashes? Well, what I seen a while ago was not what you might call a real gory crash, but it didn't have no business bein' where it was. See what I mean? I drive a truck for the Arkansas Milkers and I pass this field all the time and it belongs to Barney Romano, who is over in Little Rock getting his prostate cut out. Well, this here airplane is an old one—Christ knows how old it is, but I seen photos of what they call a DC-3 and this sure looked like one—and there it set right in this field with nobody around, I guess, because I didn't stop to investigate. But it sure as hell don't belong in that field, if you know what I mean. I mean, this was like seeing a carbuncle on a monkey's ass, if you follow me. It wasn't there when I went to the creamery in Kitstown at midnight, but when I come back homeside, there it was. . . ."

At the time of the call, Lester Riding was so busy he only half listened. He had the weather at Texarkana to get on the goddamned computer network—four thousand overcast, fifteen miles on the visibility, and a good spread on dew point and temperature. No problems. But meanwhile some ying-yang in a Cessna kept calling in for weather all over the southeast part of the United States. What was he doing in the air at this hour of the early morning—troubling people because he was probably just lonesome?

As an FAA employee, it was Lester Riding's duty to give the Cessna all the information the pilot wanted, but it would have been a much easier night if these ying-yangs had stayed in bed.

All right. So there was a DC-3 in a field over by Kitstown. Why not? DC-3s were not quite yet extinct. He should have asked the kook who called if it was standing on its gear or lying on its belly, but the guy had hung up before he got around to it. Anyway, nobody else had called in, and Little Rock Air-Traffic Control didn't have any emergency alarms, so unless something new came in, best let it stew. Old government employee maxim: Never do less than your assigned job, and never do more. Only with careful respect for the last three words of that rule can one's ass remain covered.

At 6:00 A.M. Washington time, Lily Rogers called Mort Steiner again. She had been unable to sleep and was aware of her irritation, but certainly there was cause for it. "Mr. Steiner, I haven't heard from you."

"I know. I've been waiting on some information, which unfortunately hasn't been of any help. However, I'm hopeful that very shortly . . . as soon as the rest of the world wakes up, maybe . . ."

"Mr. Steiner, I don't care what you think at this point. My husband is a missing person and I do not expect him to show up on the doorstep via some magic carpet. I'm going to call the police right now and I think you should do the same and tell them everything you know. Do I make myself clear, Mr. Steiner?"

"Very."

"Furthermore, I'm coming down to your office, which we'll use as a headquarters until my husband is found. I'll be there by eight and I'll expect to see you there also. Any questions?"

"None. Absolutely none."

Lily slammed down the phone a little harder than she had intended, but, dear God, something had to break somewhere. Whatever happened to those ranching days when the most worrisome item of the day was a fence break? Oh, Lee, she thought, where are you!

Lee Rogers could not remember when he had ever known such a sense of humiliation. He had walked two blocks along H Street toward the Army and Navy Club, where he knew he would stand a reasonable chance of finding a taxi at this busy hour. He brooded about leaving Tracy Delano so unceremoniously, but, dammit, that relationship was headed for sure trouble unless someone ended it.

He gradually became aware that a car was keeping pace with him. Suddenly it pulled ahead and stopped. A large man stepped out of the car and blocked his way. "Good evening, Mr. Rogers," he said. Almost simultaneously Rogers sensed someone behind him. He attempted to turn, but his wrists were seized and he heard the snick of cuffs closing. "Now just take it easy, Mr. Rogers," the man said.

A couple followed by a single man passed them. All three kept their heads down, not wanting to see what they could hardly avoid seeing. "Hey!" Rogers called to them. "Hey! Call the police!"

The man behind him laughed and called out, "We *are* the police!"

On a major street with plenty of light. In the nation's capital.

Passersby. No one lifted a finger. No one dared inquire. What the hell kind of a country was this turning out to be?

"Hey! What's this all about?" Rogers struggled, but the men were powerful and expert. Almost before he understood what was happening, he was sitting between them in the back of the car. A third man in the front drove the car away from the curb and was almost immediately halted by a stoplight. He waited patiently for it to change.

The man on Rogers's left, who had first accosted him, said, "Keep your mouth shut and we won't have to gag you. You're going away for a while. We have a job to do and we want to make it as easy on everybody as we can. That means you do exactly what we tell you."

"Who the hell are you?" Rogers demanded. He found it difficult to believe that he had been so unwary, but here he was. Too many other things had been on his mind or he would have noticed the car following him and made a run for it.

The man smiled. "We just do a job on a contract basis. We don't like to hurt nobody, but be advised we never fail to deliver."

"Where are we going?"

"Far away."

"You know what the penalty for kidnapping is?"

"Yeah. But my buddy and myself need a new yacht and some polo ponies. Besides, we don't like that word you just used. We asked you to join us, and once you found out what wonderful guys we were, we couldn't get rid of you."

The man brought a black kerchief from his coat pocket and tied it around Rogers's head. His fingers smelled of tobacco. He yanked the kerchief down until it covered Rogers's eyes. "It's silk," he said. "We go first-class. If it's too tight, say so. Otherwise why don't you settle down and get some sleep. You may need it."

Rogers was seething with an anger that gradually melted into self-condemnation. Why hadn't he asked for a Treasury agent to stand by as bodyguard or maybe someone from the FBI? Or wouldn't they do that for a mere congressman, unless he could prove a threat? There was too much about the federal government he didn't know.

They were in the car for a long time and it seemed to Rogers that during most of the journey they drove at high speed. Finally he was pulled from the back seat, led across concrete, and helped into what he supposed was an airplane. He hit his head against the door opening and he heard the man say, "Oops, sorry about that. I told you to keep your goddamned head down."

He was guided to a comfortable leather seat and someone strapped a seat belt around him. His hands were numb from their confinement, but he was damned if he would ask for relief.

Relief? Maybe he could get rid of the cuffs for a few minutes. Maybe he would find a half-decent chance for escape. "I've got to take a leak," he said.

"Oh, no, man, can't you hold it?"

"No."

The other man, who had a thin, high voice, said, "Then piss in your pants. I'm not going to hold your tallywacker for ya unless I get a bonus by certified check and a pair of rubber gloves. Guys like you spread AIDS."

He laughed at his own humor, and Rogers resolved that if his hands were ever free again, they would first close on the man's neck.

Once the engines were started, Rogers knew he was seated in a small business jet and he tried as best he could to estimate the time they were in the air. Somewhere, he thought, between one and two hours, although sitting for so long with his arms behind him seemed closer to an eternity.

When they landed, he was hustled into another car. Wherever it was, the temperature was much warmer, and after trying to visualize the time lapse, he decided they must have landed in Florida, Georgia, or Alabama.

The second car ride was much the same as the first, except that the sounds were different. He was sure the road was gravel, and at least the air was better. He could not identify many of the various odors, but they were country smells, among them hay and manure.

"How about telling me where we are?" he said to the air in front of him. It was strange being a blind man—all the other senses came rushing to the brain's aid, but there was no urge to turn the head toward the conversation.

"Close your mouth, Mr. Rogers." It was the man with the high voice again. Against the whirring sounds of the moving car, it sounded almost falsetto.

"How about telling me what time it is?" he asked.

"It's early."

Early what? He tried some simple arithmetic. He had left Tracy Delano about seven, maybe ten minutes before seven. They must have picked him up about seven. He could only guess at the length of the first car ride. An hour? Make it eight o'clock by the time they were in the jet. Then they must have taken off from someplace other than Washington or Dulles. There had been no sounds of other aircraft in the vicinity.

They'd been in the air for two hours, say . . . at five hundred miles an hour, give or take a few.

Hard as he tried, he could not visualize the southern states vividly enough to choose a possible landing site, but it must have been ten o'clock by the time they were actually loaded into this car.

Early? Ten o'clock was late in his language, but it could be later and maybe his escort considered it early.

"I'm guessing it's about eleven-thirty," he said, hoping to annoy his captors.

"You keep that mouth goin' and we'll plug it." There was that high voice again. The other man was more formal.

For some unknown reason, Rogers found, he was not frightened. His captors were almost clinical in their attitude. They apparently had no urge to do him any physical harm as long as he obeyed. He believed Formal Voice's story about being a contract courier, so there was no use in fighting back—yet. Best keep his strength until he knew what was happening. He was obviously not going to be told by his present company.

"What do you guys do in real life?" he asked. Not afraid, but worried. Lily and the kids would be having a fit by this time.

There was silence for a moment; then he heard one of them sigh, and he heard Formal Voice's answer. "I'll tell you one thing, Mr. Rogers. I wouldn't mind having myself a nice little setup like yours in Montana. But that climate would affect me real bad because I got asthma. I suppose if you were all tucked in with a nice lady for company, it wouldn't be impossible—"

"That lady is my wife and I don't want anything to happen to her."

"We won't have to bother her no more, so relax," said Falsetto.

"What do I have to do to find out where we're going and why you kidnapped me?"

"Nothin'. The first is not your business, and the second we don't know. We have a contract to deliver your body—preferably still breathing."

"I like that last part. Who gave you the contract?"

"The Bell Telephone Company. Now, shut up. We got just so much patience."

Oscar Brimmer lay on the floor of his DC-3 and wished he were elsewhere. These old tail draggers were not meant for sleeping unless they were in the air, because the floor of the fuselage slanted and the blood ran to a guy's head or away from it, depending on which direction you sacked out. Unbelievable. Here he was, stretched out like some old Spam sausage left over from World War II.

Because this was not exactly a major airport, and the less commotion the better, lights were out of the question. So much for passing the time reading. After three days waiting in beautiful downtown Havana—an unbelievable place where the whores had all gone so far underground nobody even remembered how to find them, or they had all died of old age—plus all that time waiting with a dry throat for a signal, a man needed rest. To say nothing of some recreation.

Enough! Enough of the People's Revolution was too much. They should post a reward in Havana for smiling. Nobody smiled but Castro's oversize portraits, which were everywhere and proclaimed that he was not a smiler at heart. They should award one red star per smiler and a glass of Soviet vodka if you smiled twice. Castro should consult with Oscar Brimmer if he wanted to know how to run his government.

Now here he was, former captain Oscar Quincy Brimmer, trying to snooze in this old bucket that he had planted so nicely in the same old Arkansas turnip field. There were times in every man's life when a guy just had to suspect he was a born loser.

Be there waiting at twenty-one hundred hours, the signal said.

Okay. Where was the action? No cargo from Colombia to Havana. Empty from Havana to Arkansas. The guys had been on hand with their car lights, but they disappeared immediately after touchdown. They must have been informed there was nothing to remove from the DC-3, but they also knew they had better be on hand to greet it. Okay, sports fans, what next?

Lying in this aluminum can, he thought, was not only uncomfortable but dangerous. Normally he would not be on the ground here for more than five minutes. Now it was—what? Almost two hours? Sooner or later somebody passing along that road in the distance was going to get curious. "Hi there, stranger! How come you picked this turnip field for your old bunch of tin and rivets when there's a nice airport only ten miles away?"

There was more. The signal said, "Return direct Bogotá."

Bogotá? Colombian Customs might be delighted to greet Oscar Brimmer and a payload of dope, but you didn't take stuff to Colombia, you brought it out.

He decided it was safe to assume he would be met—but by what? A firing squad? Miss Cocaine of the year, maybe, or just one of those jerks in a black beret who believed Marco Fedles was a man of the people?

What transpired here? Fedles was supposed to hate Castro, and vice versa. Maybe those two yokels had decided on a honeymoon somewheres and were going to fly away in a humble people's-style DC-3. And with Oscar Quincy Brimmer as their pilot? In a pig's ass. Those two Carioca characters had long ago forgotten that humility was a wise man's middle name.

Brimmer sat up and looked at the stars through a badly glazed window just above him. Maybe he should set fire to the old bird right here and now. Give her a Viking funeral and hightail it through the bushes until he came to a tolerable town. Get a job as a dishwasher, handyman, janitor, door-to-door salesman—one of those jobs where they weren't too concerned about a guy's past. Yeah! Stay in the good old U.S. of A. Fix it so the fat manager would never have a chance to put a bomb in the world's best little ol' flying machine. At least, he thought, his reception in Havana had been polite, right down to free fuel. Castro was being big these days. Even the exit formalities were easy. There had to be a joint project in the works, and with crooks like Fedles and Castro, this was probably not the best place for Oscar Brimmer.

The longer he looked at the stars, the more troubled he became. What kind of a Mickey Mouse flying circus was this? The Colombian government was supposed to be trying to hang Fedles up by the thumbs and he sends one of his flying machines to plunk down right in their lap. And he has at least four fields of his own where nobody would know what goes on.

Brimmer became extremely restless, a by-product, he thought, of alcohol denial. What was it now—four, no, six days with nothing to moisten the lips? Terrible trauma for the system. All kind of diseases could be acquired when in this mode. Insanity for one. Every cuckoo bird whose habitat was the desert began to hear the tinkle of ice in a martini. And lo! He who hath spent his time in dry solitude might never be liberated. Where was a match? Set fire to the old girl right now and make a beeline for the nearest cantina.

Brimmer squirmed about in the darkness and finally rose to his feet. Lord God Almighty, deliver me on wings of aluminum to the nearest oasis!

He was still searching through his pockets for a match when he saw a car swerve off the road. The lights of the car splayed along the fuselage, blinding him for a moment. Then they were turned off.

Against the deep gray of the field in the starlight, he could see the black shape of the approaching car. The driver obviously knew exactly what he was doing.

Brimmer sighed and walked stiffly down to open the door.

Marco Fedles had dined later than was his custom and was watching a movie with eighteen-year-old Annette of Florence, Italy, when the phone beside his chair rang. It was Prevet reporting from the communications center, which now occupied space at Los Estranjeros formerly used as a servants' bathhouse and laundry.

Fedles was nervous this night, an unusual condition for him. Annette, a recent import, had thus far proved a disappointment. She was extremely lethargic and not at all impressed with what she saw in Los Estranjeros. Worse, her face had broken out in a childish rash and she exuded a peculiar odor, which Fedles could not identify. He had already decided this was to be her last evening as his guest and she was welcome to take her virginity with her—if indeed she had brought it.

A new guest, Gretchen something-or-other, was already en route from Germany. Fedles rarely knew or cared about the last names of his female imports since there was never any cause to introduce them. Only his close aides ever laid eyes on them, and then only briefly, for if there was business to be discussed, he sent the girl away.

Tonight at dinner he had found the breast of partridge overdone, the rice greasy, and the flan mediocre. It had not helped that Annette agreed with him. (The punk should eat so well in the much over-praised Florence she kept ranting about.) The chef was called to table and reprimanded, which made Fedles feel somewhat better but caused a great cloud of disapproval to spread across Annette's pimpled face. And the movie, an Italian production ordered before Annette's arrival, was impossibly dull.

Prevet said, "They took off one hour ago. Bogotá arrival estimate is about five this morning."

"Very good. And the welcoming party?"

"Someone from the American Embassy or the consulate will be there long enough to see him. I must tell you again, Marco, that I think this whole thing is a mistake."

"How can you say that when we already have the man?"

"That's just it. I still don't believe the Americans are going to take this lightly."

"What can they do? He is a dangerous man. I can smell him from this distance. And he must be silenced. By the time the stupid Americans get around to filing one of their silly diplomatic protests, the problem will be eliminated."

"I urge you to use the utmost caution, Marco. This could backfire on us and we should anticipate trouble."

"I always anticipate trouble. What about our own people at the airport? Is everybody standing by?"

"All clearances are in order. Paying off was rather high. Ten thousand."

"Bloody thieves! But it must be. It is important that he be seen so there can be no doubt."

"Of course. After Bogotá? Do you want him taken directly to the camp or brought here first?"

"Directly to the camp. The manager is prepared?"

"If he's not, I'll barbecue the fat bastard."

"Good. He may taste better than my dinner."

As Fedles replaced the phone, he accidentally brushed his hand along Annette's breast. She recoiled, saying, "Don't touch me!"

Fedles thought of slapping her, then changed his mind. "Rather would I caress a leper," he said, standing up. He left her with her Italian movie.

At 7:30, while he was having his morning coffee, the president of the
United States noted a short item in his morning advisory. Happenings of the night before were recorded for his information, which
saved him from digging through newspapers, a chore he abhorred.
Later, during the day, important information would be passed on to
him in bold type on blue paper bound in an embossed leather holder.
For some items, there were option boxes that he could use to express
his wishes or preferences. He had merely to tick off one of the boxes
and it became a presidential decision—something like having to pick
a good potato out of hundreds, he was fond of saying. This morning
there were three boxes applicable to tonight's dinner music for the
Canadian prime minister. String quartet? Piano soloist? Harpist?
Since it was a small and intimate dinner, no great musical assembly
was offered. Check one.

On another blue page. The Oval Office ceremony for presentation
of the new "Arts" trophy. Should awards be made entirely by

. . . First lady? President of society? Mixed? And in what order? Literary number one? Music number? Graphic-arts number?

Below these requests was an item that had given him pause in his box-checking. It was the sort of thing carefully selected by his staff to prevent the president from looking hopelessly bewildered when various events of the day were mentioned, an attempt to give him at least a glimpse of the real world.

Washington police have been advised that Congressman Lee Rogers of Montana is listed as a missing person. He failed to return home last night after attending a meeting of the Select Committee on Narcotics.

The president read the note twice before it occurred to him that the item referred to the "cowboy" who had gained so much notoriety in such a short time.

The president scribbled across the note, "Find out more and keep me advised." Then he went back to his options.

Oscar Brimmer bent forward over the control yoke of the DC-3 trying to see something of the weather ahead. He was not happy; in fact, he could not recall when he had ever been so uneasy. Goddam-mit, it was one thing to be a smuggler, but a damned terrorist was a nut of another flavor.

Who the hell was trying to kid Oscar Brimmer? The guy in the back with the two goons was the "cowboy" whose face had been all over the cover of *Time* not so long ago. And it did not take any great mental strain to understand what was happening. Obviously the cowboy was not making this journey exactly of his own free will, although they had taken the blindfold off once they were in the air. As it was, no one could see anything anyway—including Oscar Brimmer, the general manager of this accumulation of airplane parts flying in loose formation. And the management of this here aeronautical enterprise was having his problems.

Almost twenty thousand hours flying in all kinds of situations had given Brimmer a sort of ghost mind that he employed only when aloft. Then, because of past experience he saw things and thought of things that he knew his original mind might not have noticed. He had long ago developed an instinct for "flying ahead" of his airplane. Thus he had almost always been able to avoid a situation known as "snowballing," the accumulation of many small things occurring in sequence and finally arriving in one big, unmanageable package. He had learned the hard way how easy it was to run out of fuel, altitude, and brains all at the same time. Now it seemed quite possible that such a conjunction of events might soon be at hand unless his aeronautical cunning could ease him and his battered ship to safety.

At the moment and for some time now, the total extent of his vision was the two-foot airspace between his mutilated nose and the forward cockpit window. Given an ordinary flight with a legitimate beginning and end, he would have thought nothing of flying like this for hours. But this was different—man, this was more like roulette than five-card stud, and there was no indication that things were going to get better.

Maybe he should try for a sneak end run? Around the east end of Jamaica.

He shook his head vigorously. Where the hell did a nutsy idea like that originate? Maybe it came to him because he had not had any real sleep since the night before, and it was now three o'clock in the morning.

It was all just fucking lovely. Here he was, somewhere over the Gulf of Mexico, with absolutely no idea what sort of weather he was getting into. All lightning flashes were hostile. Soon after he had left land behind, he had noticed bunches of fire flickering along the horizon. Okay, that might be expected over the Gulf at this time of the year, but this same body of water had a nasty habit of developing water spouts or "white squalls" that could conceal winds of more than one hundred fifty miles per hour. That was very unhealthy. Aircraft had been set on their backs and a few presumably torn to pieces by these local storms. Fortunately they were small and most of the time easily avoided. *If* a man could see. You want adventure? Learn to fly. You want to live forever? Put your faith in gravity.

"Aye," Brimmer echoed one of his favorite authors, "there's the rub!" He was at two hundred feet. The sky was black and the sea was black. Rain hissed against the forward windows and the outside temperature had dropped until he was shivering in his own sweat.

"Aye!" Brimmer sighed while he wiped at the dumpling mounds and crevasses in his face. "What in Christ's name am I doing here?"

He took no comfort in the knowledge that he was at an altitude of two hundred feet, although his immediate other choices were even less inviting. If he climbed even a hundred feet, he would be in the solid cloud layer and have no visibility at all. Then, if his navigation was off very much, he would stand a fair chance of drilling a hole in the island of Jamaica. He would also lose all choice about sticking the DC-3's nose—or his own, for that matter—into either a water-spout or a thunderstorm or both. If he climbed high enough to avoid hitting Jamaica, he just might collide with other aircraft, of which there were far more over the water at this ungodly hour, he thought, than there need be. And for damn sure at least one of the American radars would pick him up and "Good evening to you, fighter-inter-ceptor." Finally, an approach to the coast of Colombia solely on instruments was too much like Russian roulette. The clouds in Colombia were packed with stones, and once they swallowed him, there would be no coming down unless he could communicate with the ground and get a descent clearance. As for alternative landing fields, they were not going to hang out a welcome sign for a guy carrying his kind of cargo.

He became aware that he was not alone and looked around to his right. One of the goons was leaning against the bulkhead. Brimmer raised his voice above the rumbling of the old round engines and asked, "What can I do for you?"

"Tell me when we're going to get wherever we're going. This bouncing around is bad for my asthma."

"I did not pave this road," Brimmer grumbled, and thought, There, by God, was passenger service for you. "You mean to say you don't know where you and your buddies're bound for?"

"No."

"You got a lotta faith in somebody."

"Oh, yeah? How come I don't see no lights anywhere?"

"They got turned off. We didn't pay our electric bill."

A flash of lightning illuminated the cockpit, and Saint Elmo's fire began to form huge halos around the spinning propellers.

"I'm scared shitless," the man said.

"So am I." Brimmer smiled inwardly. In all aggravations there was a touch of the satisfying.

"I never have liked to fly."

"Neither have I." Especially, Brimmer thought, on nights like this.

"Are we gonna be all right?" the bulky figure asked.

"I'm not a swami, so I don't know. If you want me to guarantee you'll arrive in one piece, forget it. Why should you care? If you die tonight, you avoid old age, which is full of bad backs, false teeth, and disappointments. If you die now, you don't have to worry about getting your pecker up in the future."

"You're some help, fella. A real smart-ass."

"We only want to please. Now get the hell back where you belong. When I want to chat, I'll send for you."

A moment later Brimmer was alone again. And in spite of his displeasure with the night, he was momentarily pleased with himself. He was, he thought, probably one of the two men in the world who could tell a gorilla like that to fuck off and live to remember it.

The other man, he reflected, would be Marco Fedles.

Mort Steiner was in his office by seven. The wildness was gone from his eyes and he was freshly shaven and groomed. He sat down to his telephone, notched it between his cheek and shoulder, and began a long session of punching buttons. He made strictly formal calls to the FBI and the Washington police. He found one of his many CIA friends at breakfast and got him to promise to initiate a worldwide search and inquiry on Rogers. His friend also offered the standard CIA homeric—that he did not like the look of things. All through the third world and in some parts of the second world, there were increasing reports of opposition to "the Yankee cowboy" and his war. Steiner was somewhat surprised at the general reaction among his early-morning contacts. While a few seemed genuinely distressed, the majority were cynical and seemed to say Rogers had been asking for trouble. There were even a few who sounded relieved. "We can junk all this talk about a shooting war," one said.

For a short time Steiner was bewildered. Was his boss just a

Roman candle that fizzled out at apogee? Would he just become lost in new events, remembered once a year in summations as the man who had tried to start his own war and failed?

Steiner's thoughts became increasingly gloomy as the tempo of ringing telephones compounded rapidly.

He called the operations desk at the State Department and talked to one of the narcs on duty. All embassies and consulates would be alerted to watch for Rogers's possible reappearance.

He called Gordon Hawkins and told him he was free to print what he liked. "He's your hero. You made him. Now find him."

Hawkins said he would play the story as an international outrage, and please give him an hour before notifying any others of the press. Steiner agreed to do so in exchange for Guy Amonte's number.

A drowsy female voice answered, "He's asleep."

"Wake him up."

"I can't do that. He's so weary, the poor boy—"

"This is an emergency."

"What kind?"

"The French government has been overthrown. Now wake him up or you'll regret it."

While he was listening to a rustling in the telephone, Lily Rogers strode into the office. Her two children were with her. A mere glance at her eyes convinced Steiner that she was not going to tolerate any halfway measures. Good. He could use her because the telephones were going wild. He waved Lily into a chair, nodded to Fay and Robert, and spoke into the telephone. "You don't sound very alert, Mr. Amonte. I'm sorry to wake you, but I must know if you saw Congressman Rogers last night?"

Why the hesitation? Steiner listened carefully until at last Guy Amonte said, "Yes."

"Was he, as far as you could see, in good health?"

Another hesitation. "Yes."

"When he left, did he leave alone?"

"I can't remember. There were many people here."

"Could he have left with a Miss Delano?" Christ! He had completely forgotten that Lily Rogers was sitting just opposite him. And was not missing anything. He immediately provided his own answer. "He did not? Very good. Thank you, Mr. Amonte, and good luck on your transfer."

He hung up and saw a new fire in Lily Rogers's eyes, but decided to ignore it. Before she could ask what a certain Miss Delano might have to do with all this, he flipped quickly through his card file and dialed the French Embassy. He contacted a sleepy-voiced attendant whose English was very limited. He declared an emergency and asked Lily if she would help out by answering any one of the ringing telephones in the outer office. "Take your pick," he said. "Record the call and say we'll get back to them."

Finally a man who identified himself as the French ambassador's deputy came through on Steiner's telephone. "This is Congressman Rogers's office. Mr. Rogers wants to express his gratitude for being invited to Monsieur Amonte's farewall party last night and would like to choose an appropriate remembrance. A new umbrella would hardly do if he were being transferred to the Sahara, if you know what I mean."

"He's not being transferred anywhere. He has at least another year to go here."

"Really? There seems to be a misunderstanding. We thought it might be Spain."

"No. I do believe he's going to take a week's holiday, but I know nothing about any Spanish assignment."

"Thank you veddy much." Steiner used his best clipped accent and hung up.

He sat thoughtfully for a moment, ignoring the continuous jangling and chirping of every telephone in the office. Was it just his imagination or did he detect the aroma of French self-interest here?

He heard the staff arriving in the outer office amid the dissonance of telephones. Alice Morgan and Connie Marcus and the new hirees must be briefed before they all started answering with their own stories.

"I heard on the radio driving in . . ." Alice said, nearly breathless with apprehension.

He eased her back to the outer office, where the rest of the staff waited with what he thought were suitably long faces. "Now here is what we know, and what you can tell any of the media. Congressman Rogers has disappeared. We are using every resource to locate him. That's all. Don't say anything more. Do not venture any opinions, no matter how hard they press you. Be polite and uninformative. Do not mention that Mrs. Rogers is here, or . . ." he added as he noticed that Robert and Fay were concentrating on his every word, "or mention the children. Their safety may depend on what you do not say. Okay, start answering."

The ringing din was continuous as he returned to his own desk. He was grateful to his staff for being properly subdued. This was sure to be a trying day and he did not need any further distractions.

He found his thoughts drifting back to Wilma as if they were meant to bend in her direction. He found a phone that was not ringing and called his own number. He heard Wilma's drowsy voice.

"What the hell are you doing answering my phone?"

"There's nobody else here."

"That does not entitle you to answer. Why don't you go home where you belong?"

"I like it here. I'm still in bed and the sheets smell of you."

Steiner was pleased in spite of himself. He took a moment to visualize Wilma between his sheets.

"Supposing my mother called and you answered, what would she think?"

"Who cares? Maybe she would get the message that we like togetherness."

"Don't talk like that. My apartment is my private affair. Suppose some other woman called . . ."

"I'd tell her you were dyin' and I was your nurse."

"Go home! But first, that man you were with at the Mayflower? Did he have an accent?"

"Well, sort of. You know, like he was from Long Island someplace, or maybe Jersey, know what I mean?"

"Yes, dammit, I know what you mean. Stop *saying* that! Then you would not take him for a foreigner?"

"No."

"Okay. Go back to sleep."

He clicked off the phone. For reasons he could not explain, he knew a momentary sense of elation.

The sensation was short-lived. Moments after Steiner had finished talking with Wilma, three youngish men wearing almost identical topcoats entered the outer office, displayed their badges, and announced they were from the FBI. Steiner was impressed with their air of righteousness if not their diplomacy. They stated that they wanted to examine all of Congressman Rogers's files—now.

"I can't let you do that. Those files are his personal papers."

"Are you going to give us the invasion-of-privacy bit at this hour of the morning?" It was the oldest man who spoke, a heavy, square man with a rumbling voice. "Look," he said, "if we have to, we can get a court order, but that takes time. We want to find the congressman, and the more information we have, the sooner we can do it."

Steiner blocked the way as they started toward Rogers's office.

"You can't go in there."

"Why not? Look, Mr. Steiner, we're here to help." The spokesman sighed as if to signal his patience was strained.

"Mrs. Rogers and her children are in there."

"Fine. We need to talk with them. And you, later."

Steiner backed up until he blocked the open doorway. Why was he being so obstructive? he wondered. Lily Rogers was upset, but she certainly could handle three visitors who were presumably on her side. Am I losing my marbles? he questioned. The phones were destroying his nerves. And beyond the three men, just entering the outer office he saw two more male visitors. One he recognized as a "spook" from the CIA.

"The files are all out here," he said. "How about starting with them?"

"Whatever. You got any ideas where your boss could be?"

"I wish." Steiner beckoned to Alice Morgan and asked her to open the files for their guests. She explained that there was really very little to examine since the congressman had been in office such a short time.

Steiner closed the door to Rogers's office and went to greet the men from the CIA. All in disorder, he thought. Everything is out of place and time. This was an insane asylum overcrowded with patients! Any moment now some hidden speaker would blare, "Paging Dr. Steiner!" How he hated this! Things awry. Everything at sixes and sevens and the devil in charge. Now, from God only knew where, came strange visitors. Washington street people had found their way to the entrance. They were standing, blank-faced, bundled up in their rags for the weather outside. Waiting for something to happen. Or were they just warming their bones?

It was all the media's fault, Steiner decided. If not for the damned media, this chaos would never have been born.

Later, when Steiner had calmed himself, he introduced the FBI trio to Lily Rogers. And from one of them he learned that the machinery of the media had not been caught sleeping despite the early hour of discovery. Brief episodes concerning Rogers's disappearance made the tail end of the "Today" and "Good Morning America" shows. The theme "Missing Cowboy" was embraced by both, and clips of Rogers's past activities were aired willy-nilly. One network alternated between the weather report and an interview with a distant relative of a man who had once been kidnapped, while on another channel an eastern dairy farmer offered his opinion on what had happened to Congressman Rogers. Both authorities were overly willing to share their expertise and were cut off in midsentence. A third network ignored the story entirely except to say that "according to a congressional spokesman, Congressman Rogers was presumed to be on some secret mission relating to narcotics." They obviously considered the whole thing a publicity gimmick and, according to Alice Morgan, who took the calls, they hinted as much on the telephone.

By ten in the morning, Lily Rogers was convinced everything that could be done was being done. She was impressed by a call from Warner Grange, the president's top aide, who said his boss wished to convey his genuine concern about Congressman Rogers. He also wished to invite Lily and the children to the White House for dinner that night if she felt up to it. Lily declined.

More and more of the media sensed a prolonged suspense story as the morning wore on and they were obviously determined to make the most of it. Steiner had managed to resume command of his nerves as well as the office. He gave crisp, direct answers to a continuous series of questions and wound his way through the overcrowded offices as if conditions had always been uncomfortable. He even offered coffee to the street people. Why not, as long as they drank from paper cups? He took a call from *Newsweek* magazine, which was preparing a major story on the cowboy's disappearance. The *Washington Post* called to confirm some facts for a story to be headlined, PRISONER IN THE CAUSE OF THE NATION'S YOUNG.

Steiner said he thought the lead was corny, but he stopped worrying about media interest. For the moment.

The networks dug in their files for film of cattle and cowboys to back the talking heads who would employ their most solemn manner on the evening news, and Steiner learned that a search was already under way for interviews with Lily and the children. Obviously Rogers's disappearance had made him the number one story in the world. Steiner prayed that the intense interest would help rather than hinder.

Soon after the FBI and the CIA visitors had left (vaguely dissatisfied, Steiner noticed), he took a call from Paul Hagenberger on the Central American desk at the State Department.

"Mort. Something's come through that might interest you. Be advised I'm not really making this call. It never happened. Colombia is not even my territory, but sometimes these little items get lost in the bureaucracy and maybe this one shouldn't. Bear in mind it's secondhand—or I guess thirdhand by now. Anyway, one of our staff in Bogotá got a rather puzzling summons last night. He was requested by an unidentified party to go to the airport and witness an important surprise. He thought it must be some freak calling, especially since he was asked to be there at five this morning. He decided not to trouble himself, and then changed his mind—it might be a military coup. The surprise, he claims, was your cowboy escorted by two big men."

"He was sure?" Steiner asked, trying to conceal his anxiety.

"Yep. He claims he recognized him immediately."

"Was he okay?"

"He didn't say otherwise. You have to remember it couldn't have been anyone else, because our guy said he'd seen at least fifty pictures of him."

"Are you suggesting the Colombian government might be involved?"

"What else? There they were, right in government Customs."

"But that's kidnapping a congressman! It just isn't done!" A bad time for that kind of humor, Steiner thought. You keep your sleepy tongue in your head.

"How do you know he's been kidnapped? Did it occur to you that maybe Rogers had this all planned, and that he has made an agreement to talk directly to the Colombian government about cutting down their narc trafficking?"

Steiner went into momentary shock. No! For some reason it had not occurred to him that Rogers might take things into his own hands. Steiner bounced his fist off the side of his head. Could it be? Could Rogers have figured that by such devious means he would get even more press attention for his war? No, he decided. That sort of thing was not Lee Rogers.

After he had thanked his friend in State and offered to reciprocate on request, he wondered if he should tell Lily Rogers what he had just heard. Suppose the report was fake? The disappointment would be devastating. There were always rumors started by people who wanted to be identified with an international incident. No, he would wait a few hours and see what the afternoon brought.

At noon Steiner set up a rotation system with Alice Morgan so at least one person would be on telephone-answering duty during the lunch hour. Then, heavy with misgivings, he invited Lily, Robert, and Fay to join him for lunch in the House restaurant. Dear God! What was he doing? Lunching with children? Absolutely incredible, this wild transformation of Mort Steiner. At least, he hoped, the underground train would distract the little monsters.

He opened his eyes and saw two lizards plastered against the cement-block wall and he saw they were looking directly at him. "Hello," he said to the lizards. "I'm Lee Rogers . . . I think."

Patches of sunlight shimmered on the wall and somewhere outside he heard a raucous chorus of birds cawing. He was covered with perspiration. My God, it was hot!

He rolled out of his cot and put his feet on the cement floor. He sat dazed for a moment—then it all came back to him, in an ugly lump. Sometime this morning—he supposed this was still the same day—the DC-3 had landed on a jungle strip. A squad of young soldiers in tennis shoes had escorted him to this room. One of them had removed his handcuffs, said something in Spanish, and departed.

There was no door in the entryway, but now two uniformed boys wearing black berets and nurturing submachine guns stood on either side. Rogers guessed they were no more than fifteen, and he thought they did not look particularly menacing. He tried to make an exit and changed his mind immediately. One of the boys had jammed the muzzle of his gun between Rogers's ribs and shoved him backward. There was no question that he was just hoping for an excuse to pull the trigger.

Soon afterward Rogers approached the doorway warily. Somehow he had to make his guards understand that he had to take a leak— badly. He was astounded to see that the guards were gone. He stepped outside and stood for a moment looking at the view, which was not inspiring. Enormous trees completely enclosed the area, which contained five buildings, all built of cement blocks. All had thatchlike roofs and were without doors or window frames. He could see a DC-3 parked at the end of a dirt runway, and some men were moving in and out of a building at the far end of the complex.

He ventured a few steps beyond the entryway, and even though it was obviously afternoon, the sun seemed to pound on his head. He realized suddenly that he was still wearing the same shirt, pants, and socks he had worn to Guy Amonte's party. He sniffed at his armpit and confirmed his suspicions. Humph! He hadn't smelled as ripe since the last roundup.

He saw a bush a short distance to one side of his building and walked toward it carefully. The bush should offer at least some privacy.

He stood urinating, listening to the cawing of the birds in the dark forest. He surveyed his surroundings in all directions. Nothing. What was to keep him from just heading for the woods?

He heard a voice call out to him, "Hey! You don't have to piss there. We're civilized."

He turned and blinked at the deep shadows along the side of the cement-block house. A man rose out of a torn old canvas chair and walked slowly toward him. He thought the man looked like the chair he had just left, fit only for the junk heap.

The man said, "There's a can complete with magazines over there." He nodded toward the nearest trees. "As a matter of fact, there's one magazine over there with your picture on the cover." He chuckled gently. "It isn't every day a man can find his portrait in a strange can."

"Who are you?"

"Oscar Brimmer. And, no, I'm not one of those German South Americans. I'm a Yank just like you. Well . . . in some ways."

"What are you doing here?"

"Funny, I was about to ask you the same question."

"I'm not even sure where I am."

"Colombia. Garden spot of the universe. I'm the guy who flew you here. Welcome to the land of Nod."

Rogers took a moment to appraise this stranger with the forlorn eyes. He watched Brimmer light a cigarette and saw that his hand trembled as he held the lighter. And he saw that although Brimmer was half a head shorter, somehow his drooping bulk gave the impression they stood eye to eye.

"I've been reading about you," Brimmer said. "You got yourself in some deep shit."

Rogers hesitated. The sun was in his eyes and he was not sure whether this man who said he was a pilot was sympathetic or otherwise. He saw him reach to peel a bit of dead skin from his nose, and he thought there was something about him that he liked. If they were standing in Montana, he thought, here was the kind of stranger he would invite to stop by the house for coffee. "If I'm a prisoner—and I guess that's what I am—what happened to those cute little Boy Scouts with the guns?"

"Oh, they're around—probably down in their barracks shooting pool. There's plenty more where they came from. Don't cross 'em."

"I don't get it. One minute I'm in handcuffs and guarded. Now I can wander around."

"Sure. But where you gonna go?"

Rogers surveyed the forest and saw a sad smile cross Brimmer's mouth. "Forget it," Brimmer said. "I know what you're thinking, but let me give you the picture. There is one village about eight miles from here, and one road. That's the only village for a hundred miles, and no one there would dare help you even if they wanted to. If you take off through the woods, you have just committed suicide, which is what nobody would care about if you did. It'd save them ammunition. Not even the Indians can survive what's back in there. You might be able to get along with the animals, but the bugs, poison plants, reptiles, and diseases you and I never heard of are all waiting for you, along with a few squadrons of Colombian buzzards to finish off the job. On the other hand, you might drink the local water. You'll die right away. Letting one of the Boy Scouts shoot you would be a much easier way out of your misery. Do you hear me?"

"I do."

"Tell you what. Looks to me like you could use a little liquid in your system. Dehydration is a very bad thing, you know? Kill you fast. Follow me." Brimmer turned and walked slowly back to the shade of the building and then around to his own quarters on the opposite side. "This here is the Presidential Suite," he said as he entered.

Rogers took a frayed canvas chair and sat down in obedience to Brimmer's command. He watched as his host opened a small refrigerator and took out two bottles of beer and a length of what looked like salami. "German beer," Brimmer said bitterly, "is very hard to come by in these parts. It's not very cold because the fridge is electric and the sonofabitch who manages this place won't turn on the generator until nightfall."

Brimmer removed the bottle caps expertly and handed a bottle to Rogers. "To your good health," he said without changing his tone. "May it not last long enough for us to get too well acquainted." He tipped back his head and took a long pull at his bottle. Then he picked up the salami and waved it at Rogers. "You hungry?"

"I could do with some food."

"This here is a old communist horse cock, but I don't think it'll kill you. I bought it in Havana and so maybe it's a little better than awful, which is better than the food you'll get come nightfall. I assume you'll eat with the manager of this establishment, the captain of the Boy Scouts, and me. Our table manners are a match for the food—disgusting."

Brimmer tinkered with the skin of his nose a moment and then asked quietly, "Mr. Rogers, how did you ever get yourself in such a tough situation? Guys like you with a wife and family should stay home and enjoy life. You got a nice ranch, I read. Why should you mix up with this bunch of misfits?"

"I sure didn't come here of my own accord." The beer, Rogers thought, was without doubt the finest he had ever tasted. It was also too potent on an empty stomach. He glanced at the sausage.

Brimmer took a jackknife out of his pants pocket and neatly cut off a slice. He offered it, still on the knife. "If you don't die right away, I'll try some," he said solemnly.

Understan', amigo, these days on the street things are some stiffer than when people smoked leaf. A while ago if you was willin' to piss off a customer, maybe you could sell him or she a kind of dilution—say grind up some oregano or basil with the leaf and say it come from some foreign country. You say that there, wherever it be, you say there it be the thing. You share a secret, understan'? Amigo, there is no way you make a friend like share secret, understan'? You is *intimate,* understan'? You know what nobody else know.

Now any male or female who has done pot at all knows better. They smoke bud, and if you handed a person a loaded bong with something or other besides bud in it, then the taste be like unreal, understan'? You know, people are suspicious and most of them can find even a little impurity, even if it's in the very bottom of a Baggie. You know, the better the bud be, the more crystally, which they can see whitish on top of the green, understan'? The crystals are sort of a resin, sticky and sweet-smellin', and you can see them crystals on the tiny leaves which grow with the buds, understan'?

Now you take an inferior bud. Maybe it looks good, but it won't give you no high—just burns you out or gives you a headache. Maybe. Some dealers will sell such shit for maybe twenty-five dollars or even twenty dollars an eighth instead of a fair market price like thirty. But nobody wants it because for one thing we got haloid-light production now and so the quality is way up, understan'?

You got to trust yourself. You don't want no arguments about weight. If you're a businessman, you don't want arguments about nothin', you know, so always have your product weighed out right in front of you on one a them little triple beam scales. Most good dealers got 'em. I sell you one, amigo, when you got more business.

We don' talk about bigger deals, understan'? Say a quarter-pound at six hundred dollars or a whole pound say two thousand, you know? That be for people who been on the streets for a long time. They is surrounded by experience and they be prepared to speak words the other dealers will recognize.

Just don' be foolish sometime and front for some jerk who can't pay. People have to understan' they can be hurt real bad if they don' pay. It's like some seesaw, understan'? Maybe you up. Maybe you down. You gotta all the time think of the net. Understan'?

16

Steiner was appalled at what he was doing. Mort Steiner, the old Washington hand, the cynic, the political sophisticate, the durable government employee who knew that every man and woman working for the same organization was far from what they should or might be; Mort Steiner, the disillusioned and blasé, was at this very instant transformed—or was it transmogrified?

For reasons beyond his comprehension, he had decided to take the Rogers family to the Rotunda before going to the restaurant. And here he was, incredibly, standing before them and pointing out the friezes that encircled the interior of the great dome, pontificating like a capital guide! He was astonished at the sincerity in his own voice.

"Notice," he said, pointing upward at the friezes around the dome. How satisfying to watch R.R.'s and Fay's eyes follow his command. "See what a lot of trouble people went to so they could create a nation!"

Steiner found himself regarding the friezes as if he had never seen them before—which, he thought, was more fact than fancy. He had passed beneath them a thousand times without so much as a glance. Now he stared at the figures chopping wood, raising beams, suffering torture by the Indians, charging and being charged at by a potpourri of Hessians, surrendering and being surrendered to, worshiping and claiming and discovering and finishing off rather sedately with the Wright brothers airborne.

My God, he thought, if anyone played the "Star-Spangled Banner" at this moment, he would burst into song and tears at the same time! Maybe it was his almost total lack of sleep last night. Maybe it was sudden old age, or he was in love with Wilma. Or was the Danish he'd eaten for breakfast disagreeing with him? Something certainly was out of phase when Mort Steiner could stand here, the mentor of two young Americans, not to mention their mother, stand right here in the monstrous old Capitol and almost feel the whole country pounding upward right beneath his feet.

It was embarrassing. Steiner waving the flag? Mort Steiner saying right out loud so he was sure to be heard, "I don't see how anyone could stand here and not feel proud to be an American. This old building is where it's at. The president in his White House can pretend he's running the country, but the real doers are here—for bad or good. And I have to say that on the whole they haven't done too badly."

Mort Steiner, he warned himself, a witch is going to come along any minute and cut your tongue out. "So far not one of the presidents nor anyone else has managed to take our freedoms away."

My gawd, Steiner! These pearls from *your* lips? The men in white will be coming for you. Do you request a fife-and-drum corps for your recital or the whole Marine Band?

A totally new thrill ran through him as he looked down into Fay's expectant eyes. "Your father is a big part of this, even though he's one of many. I am, too, and so are you. It's controlled insanity, but it works."

He fell silent as he saw Lily Rogers looking at him quizzically. "Something wrong, Mrs. Rogers?" he asked finally.

A thin smile touched her eyes, the first he had seen this day. "No. Nothing's wrong. I'm afraid that somehow I'm quite surprised. I gathered the impression that you were not—how can I say it?—such a patriot."

"Mrs. Rogers . . ." Steiner dipped his head ever so slightly and he thought that he could hardly be criticized for giving such an Academy Award performance. Music cue, now, please. "Mrs. Rogers. I am touched."

The House restaurant, which served representatives, was located in a lower level of the Capitol and was reached via a series of labyrinthian hallways so modified over the years that now only experts like Mort Steiner could find their way unerringly.

Lily and her children followed him blindly, impressed by the frequent greetings that came his way. Steiner recognized a hollow sound to the salutations and he knew why they were set to an unusual tone. There were discreet messages being conveyed; the greeters were bound to have heard of Rogers's disappearance and they wanted to find out more from the man who should know, but hesitated to approach while Lily and the children were in tow.

Steiner's opinion was reinforced when they entered the restaurant. The noontime chatter was at its peak. It diminished simultaneously with their entrance and people seemed to become very absorbed in whatever was on their plates.

After they had ordered, Steiner did his best to point out the local celebrities. "The white-haired gentleman over there is Jack Kendall of New Jersey. He's chairman of the House Immigration Committee. . . . Then there's Bernard Hertz, who's our expert on organized crime. . . . Jack Wombatch over there at the corner table is from New York—he's on the Narcotics Select Committee, and—"

"Who are all these others? Are they all Congresspeople?" Fay wanted to know.

"No. You're looking at a mixed bag here at lunchtime. Staff members like myself, friends of congressmen, friends of friends, lobbyists, and—"

"And all these people get paid to eat here? I mean"—she giggled—"they get paid to work here and then eat here? Do they have to pay to eat here? There's so many! Why does it take so many people to run the government?"

"This is only a handful. Remember, there's a Senate and an administration. It's a big country. And, yes, they pay just like we do."

"Right out of their own pockets?" R.R. asked. "This is not all paid by taxes?"

"Right." R.R., Steiner thought, was going to wind up in the IRS someday.

R.R. was obviously not satisfied. "Then why don't they just pass a law that says they can eat for free?"

Lily saw the approach of panic in Steiner's eyes and hastened to relieve him. "Fay and Robert do a lot of reading, Mr. Steiner, and it does seem that their opinion of government employees is somewhat influenced by what they read in the press. In real life they're not at all bitter."

"I'm afraid I don't know much about young people."

"Lee tells me you've never quite gotten around to marriage."

Before Steiner could think of a reply, even before he had time to be uncomfortable, a strange transformation came over the restaurant. Conversations languished and suddenly all the congressmen present rose and left their tables. They seemed to share a common expression of gravity and they looked straight ahead as they marched almost in unison out of the restaurant. R.R. said softly to himself that he knew all along that congressmen would be able to leave without paying, but Steiner was not listening. He knew that only one summons could have such an effect. Every member of Congress carried a beeper to warn him when a bill was about to come up for vote in the House. They were usually given fifteen minutes to leave wherever they were and reach the House and Senate floors. Once their votes were cast, they could return to their regular business. But now?

This was different, Steiner knew. This could only be an emergency summons, and judging from their expressions, they had been warned it could happen.

Steiner stood up and tried to smile at Lily. "I'm very sorry. I shall have to abandon you. Ask any one of the guards to show you the way back to the train and the office. I'll meet you there as soon as I can."

"What's happening?"

"I don't know, but I'd better find out. Excuse me."

Marco Fedles was having his gray hair trimmed by his personal barber and his nails manicured and polished by his physical therapist, who kept him on a rigid exercise program. He was treated on the shady side of the porch at Los Estranjeros and until the arrival of Prevet with his latest report, he had been talking to his pet mynah bird, Estrellita. The bird had been a gift from Hsu Shui, the legendary Chinese whose worldwide drug-smuggling enterprise from the Golden Triangle was even bigger than Fedles' operation.

The difference between them, Fedles thought, was that Lu Hsu Shui, along with the handful of other real big-timers, had failed to adopt a political creed. In his own case, the value of identifying his operation as a manifestation of "the people," and the usual gilding of the underdog that went with it, was incalculable. Three cheers for the hammer and sickle—if and when it was convenient.

Fedles often said that Estrellita's nostrils were as sensitive as his own to the approach of either victory or defeat; the bird would cock her head in a certain way and whine or cry out with a peculiar cadence that had almost convinced Fedles she might have been his soul in another life. Having once visited Egypt, where he had seen a bird similar to the mynah painted on the ancient walls, Fedles assumed he might once have been a pharaoh. Any lesser role, he was fond of explaining, would be unthinkable for a Fedles. The fancy amused him all the more when he reminded himself of his true origins, a stinking little street in Valetta where the Fedles family was regarded with open disdain by all solid citizens.

Now when Prevet came to him smiling, Fedles was pleased. It seemed Estrellita agreed with his conviction that a triumph was at hand.

"*Alors . . . ?*"

They spoke as always in thick Mediterranean French to keep their confidences from others.

"The situation is exactly as you foresaw," Prevet said. "There's confusion, which you said was the best initial attack. It was a good idea to bring Rogers through Bogotá and have him seen by at least one of his own people. The Yankees will not know if the Colombian government is involved until too late. But, Marco, I'm still nervous. As the Americans say, we have bitten off a big chew."

"Why do you still doubt me after so many years? The Americans are so afraid of another Vietnam, they'll only make loud noises, they won't really do anything. Remember Iran and Lebanon? Most of the countries in the U.N., they sit right in New York and tell the Americans to kiss their ass. What happens? Nothing. Trust me, dear Prevet."

"I keep thinking about Libya."

"Don't. This is quite different. If the American government protests to the Colombian government, all the better. Even further confusion will create distrust among them, which is what we're after. How have you handled the message?"

"As you suggested—delicately. The Speaker of the House and the vice president both received the same notes."

"By what means of delivery?"

"We must avoid any appearance of unreliability. I was afraid your notice might be classified along with the hundreds of crank letters and lunatic proposals that are bound to come in every day. So I selected the most prestigious law firm in Washington—Peebles, Kraft, Monroy, and Bachman. They refused to deal with us until I came to the matter of finance—"

"And they changed their minds for how much?"

"Two million dollars, U.S."

Fedles blinked at Estrellita. His calculating mind hummed. He twisted his lips and took a deep breath. "Mother of God! Did you have to pay that much?"

"Lawyers," Prevet said simply. He shrugged. "We bargained for an hour. They wanted five. We're paying for their name."

"How about the cowboy? He's in safekeeping?"

"There's hardly a more secure place than Camp Four. He'll be shot whenever you give the word."

A frown crossed Fedles' handsome profile. He studied the busy hands of the manicurist, and without looking up he said very slowly, "You're right about one thing. We must be cautious—very careful not to make the cowboy a martyr. But we certainly can't afford to have him around in the future if he's the kind of man I think he is."

"Would you like to meet him?"

"Not yet." Fedles squinted at the sunlight on the distant trees and seemed for a silent time to have forgotten Prevet's presence. Then, as if talking to himself, he said, "If we shoot him, then he will be a martyr, although how much that would actually influence the U.S. government is problematic. Their martyrs don't last very long. Perhaps, when the time comes, we should arrange his escape? Wouldn't that handle the problem if it was at Camp Four?"

"Yes and no. There's always a chance his body might be found. Or, worse, by some miracle he might survive. He's tough, I'm told. I would prefer the helicopter. It's foolproof. The ocean receives, but it rarely pays back." Prevet made an attempt to smile, then abandoned the effort.

Fedles was silent for a long time. "Yes," he said at last. "Perhaps that's better."

World events once more lapsed into a period of doldrums, and editors everywhere had trouble finding good copy. The Russians had not released a single insult to the world's intelligence, and American political rhetoric reached an all-time low for credibility. No Soviet submarines had run aground and claimed they were not really there; no one had climbed a Himalayan peak; and not a terrorist bomb had exploded anywhere in more than a week.

As a consequence the Lee Rogers story, manufactured of genuine parts, was restructured until it dominated the news. Editors thought it had everything going for it: a *cowboy,* always a romantic figure; *courage* against bad guys; *love* for his impeccable family; *patriotism,* conjuring bugles everywhere; and *suspense.* No one could even guess how long this story would continue developing. No editor could ignore it.

Only a very few news analysts thought the whole story might be a hoax.

A gathering army of political activists were preparing for a march on Washington. They were painting their signs: SAVE THE COWBOY! LISTEN TO ROGERS!

Prayers for Rogers's survival were said in cathedrals and synagogues and churches throughout the United States. The Mormon Tabernacle Choir composed and sang special prayer-poems for his deliverance.

Urgent advisories and alerts were circulated through all Coast Guard units as well as the army and navy.

Special bulletins were issued by the FBI and CIA.

Television networks competed fiercely for the few scraps of information available.

Chambers of commerce, Rotarians, Kiwanis, Veterans of Foreign Wars, the American Legion, the Daughters of the American Revolution, the National Organization for Women, the American Bankers Association, the ILGWU, and the American Civil Liberties Union all joined in various resolutions supporting the search for and rescue of the "Cowboy Congressman."

Police phones everywhere were deluged with reports of Rogers' having been seen everywhere from Alaska to Florida and back through Texas. The Soviets found it necessary to deny that he was in their custody.

The president of the United States called a cabinet meeting to discuss strategies, and conversation in Washington's National Press Club became almost entirely devoted to the subject.

Through it all, Lily Rogers continued to keep her journal.

    . . . It is night again, and Lee is still not home. We are besieged. I have never in my life felt so helpless, frustrated, and angry. I keep racking my brain, trying to think of something useful I can do besides give the FBI yet another description of Mr. Butterworth, who, it seems, they have had dealings with in the past.

I was quite miffed when a Miss Delano called this afternoon and instantly clouded my thinking with a fit of jealousy. It seems Miss Delano and Lee had what she called a "friendship" going, and while I took that with a large shakerful of salt when she started, I gradually mellowed out (as Fay would describe the reaction). Miss Delano seemed very forthright and after some hemming and hawing (a chicken scratching the dust while thinking things over), I decided we were desperate enough to take a chance. She invited us to stay with a friend of hers in Virginia, an Alice Mills, where she says we will have perfect privacy and protection.

So, R.R. and Fay and I are leaving first thing in the morning. Something had to be done before all three of us go mad—or worse. There has been an army of press people surrounding the apartment house day and night, and the phone never stops ringing. Our neighbors are furious, and I can't blame them. R.R. made a slingshot, but thank heaven I confiscated it before he used it on the reporters, which he vowed he would do.

I never realized what a terrible thing notoriety can be, and I find the merciless attitude of the press people absolutely incomprehensible. I know they have to make a living, but they have no right to so ruthlessly invade the privacy of individuals. We are holed up here as if in a fortress and will be very glad to get some fresh air, even if provided by strangers. Miss Delano says not to worry, Alice Mills is a superb hostess and is honestly concerned about Lee, as God knows I am.

I feel so sorry for the children, who are in a strange town among strangers. Except for Mort Steiner, who is an unusual sort of man, to say the least, and Miss Delano, whom I've never met, it's all a foreign land to me, too. I keep telling myself that this will all turn out all right, but as the hours pass, it becomes increasingly difficult. Oh, God, *please* bring him home safely!

Lily Rogers had just closed the cover of her journal when, on the opposite side of Capitol Hill, Skip Donovan banged his gavel for attention. He was surprised at the immediate response. For the first time within his long term in Congress, the floor of the House fell silent in seconds. He was impressed, particularly when he saw that the attendance was very nearly complete and the galleries were empty. This would be the first closed session of the House in a very long time.

Donovan's political antenna now exerted a powerful influence on his usual jovial demeanor. This was not the time, he knew, for rhetoric or personal reflections or any other expression of anger if he could avoid it. He had called the House to order and they had obeyed. He would keep it simple and see what happened. He stood up and rotated his head slowly, his eyes surveying the packed House.

"Ladies and gentlemen," he said into a hushed silence he had never heard before, "this body has received a message from a prestigious Washington law firm with which many of you may be acquainted." He held up a sheet of paper. "This paper bears the letterhead of Peebles, Kraft, Monroy, and Bachman, and I have checked with that office to confirm the signatures of the senior partners and the contents of the message, which is as follows."

Donovan took a deep breath and slipped on his half-glasses. He read slowly and distinctly. " 'To the House of Representatives of the United States Congress concerning a certain proposal for war against people hitherto friendly to your country. Your imperialistic activities are unacceptable to the people of Colombia and we will defend our freedom with all that is available to us.' "

Donovan paused to clear his throat and to reassure himself that he had his listeners' full attention. Then he read, more slowly, " 'As a token of our resolve, we hold your congressman Lee Rogers. You have four days to call off all efforts and all thoughts of war against this country. If at the end of that time you have not abandoned your outrageous policies, Congressman Rogers will be executed as an enemy of the people.' "

Donovan allowed the paper to drop from his fingers. He looked out thoughtfully toward the faces below him. Then he removed his glasses and frowned. "There is no signature on the message itself, but after consulting with the aforementioned firm, whose senior partners I've known for years, I can only conclude it is genuine and means exactly what it says."

Donovan sat down and waited for the turmoil he knew must come.

* * *

By the end of the first day, the original atmosphere of chaos within various branches of the government took on some semblance of order. Pressure was put on the firm of Peebles, Kraft, Monroy, and Bachman to reveal the source of the communiqué. The attorneys claimed total ignorance of their client's identity but saw no reason not to cash the certified check that had come via a courier, who subsequently vanished.

At last, after the president expressed doubts about the character of the transaction, it became necessary for senior partner Peebles to explain that the message had been translated from Spanish. Peebles denied knowing the name of the client, and insisted his honorable associates had had nothing whatsoever to do with the composition of the original text.

As Peebles further declared, in a tone that the president found both patronizing and offensive, the receipt of two million dollars obviously removed the message from the hoax category. Peebles and his partners saw no need to elaborate further on the matter.

The president immediately queried the FBI and the attorney general, without result. The Senate, having studied and railed and vowed action, was still in session as twilight came to Washington. The House, furious that "uncivilized bandits are holding one of our own hostage," alternated between calls for some kind of military action and pleas for patience. The consensus seemed to be that a Libyan-type retaliation was not only wrong but impossible.

"We're hoisted by our own petard," the president said, although very few people understood him.

The president called in the Colombian ambassador, who professed to know nothing of the message, much less of the presence of Congressman Rogers in his country. The ambassador's telephone call to the president of Colombia directly from the White House was met with similar surprise and passionate regrets.

Privately the ambassador suggested that his government was in no position to take immediate action. If Marco Fedles held Rogers captive, then obtaining his release would be extremely difficult and dangerous. They had long known that Fedles had been waiting for some kind of confrontation; too hard a line on the release of an individual he had personally identified as an enemy of the people might provoke the full mobilization of his FARC troops. There were presently some very real doubts as to who would win if Señor Fedles attempted a coup.

Bribery was also impractical since there was unquestionably more money in Fedles' banks than in the legitimate government treasury. Most disturbing of all was a CIA report indicating that a good proportion of the Colombian people were persuaded to Fedles' thinking.

The Colombian ambassador took pains to explain that since the formal note was anonymous, it might even be possible that Señor Fedles was not involved. Comparing Fedles' operation to a hornet's nest, he advised that it would be unwise to stir up such a formidable opponent until more absolute proof was at hand.

Later, the staff meeting in the Colombian Embassy revolved around three words, "What to do?" And a similarly unproductive meeting was held by the president of Colombia and his cabinet in Bogotá.

The Organization of American States was called for advice and went into emergency session.

The president of Uruguay delivered a violently anti-American speech calling the whole affair a dangerous Yankee gamble intended to subvert and eventually dictate to all the governments of South America. The leaders of Ecuador, Bolivia, Peru, Chile, and Panama discovered the same plot and sent off stinging rebukes to the United Nations in New York about the ruthless behavior of the American president, his cabinet, the Congress, and the CIA. Americans wintering in Mexico considered packing their bags.

By the end of the first day, no conclusions had been reached anywhere. Hoping to give the impression that something was being done, the president of the United States addressed the nation with a confidence he found difficult to maintain.

"This day, in the person of Congressman Lee Rogers, the United States of America is being held hostage by terrorists of a new breed— narco-terrorists. This insult to our country, to you as citizens, and to me as your president cannot be allowed to continue. We have three days left if we can believe what the brigands who hold Congressman

Rogers say. It is my hope that they will come to their senses before that time expires. I have directed our State Department to pass on our sentiments through the proper channels. We expect the return of Congressman Rogers in good health and spirits within that time. Otherwise . . ." The president paused significantly and focused his eyes directly on the television camera. "Otherwise, it will be my regrettable duty to inform the government of Colombia that we are coming to get him."

Even as the president was conveying his sentiments to countless millions in the United States, Oscar Brimmer was well into his fourth beer. He leaned against the wall with one foot on his locker and pummeled his face and waggled his eyebrows and twisted continuously, as if the thoughts he wished to express must be uncoiled from some inner basket.

"I'll tell you something, Rogers. You're the kind of guy I always wanted to be. I don't like what I'm doing here, but it's the only flying job I can get these days. It's a strange thing, talking to you. I figure I can say anything and it won't go no further. You probably aren't going to live long enough to tell anybody anything much—at least anybody outside this camp."

Rogers, who was still nursing his second beer, wished he could brush his teeth and shave and convince himself that what was happening was real.

He kept telling himself that he must be suffering from some sort of hallucination. Maybe he had been struck by a car after leaving Tracy Delano and he would wake up any moment in a nice clean hospital.

As for Oscar Brimmer, whose hospitality was better than none, the man was obviously mad. And yet there was a strange quality about him, an impression of former integrity that belied both his appearance and much of what he said.

"I know I'm a no good sonofabitch," he was repeating. "An' I talk too much right now—I guess because I don' have anybody to talk to down here. I don' have anybody at all in my whole goddamned life. Can you imagine what that's like? Years now it's been going on. And on and on. Sometimes I just know I'd be better off dead. Maybe

I'd meet up with a few ghosts or, for God's sake, somebody to pass the time of day with.

"Once I had a wife. Once I had some parents. Once I had at least a few friends. Now, what've I got? The manager of this place hates me and the feeling is mutual. You can't imagine what it's like to be in solitary for every day of your life. You can do as you please, all right. Nobody gives a shit what you do. My beat-up old flying machine is closer to me than any human being. Tin and rivets with soul, my friend. That ol' girl lives and breathes."

He paused and pulled a flake of skin from his nose. "You got hope. I don't even hope anymore. But I started out much better than this. University of Nebraska—graduated pretty high on the list and was never arrested. I got into flying through the back door, taking lessons in a little field and then crop-dusting and some barnstorming and instruction, and finally got on with TWA. Made captain in three years. You care about hearing all this shit, or are you bored with hearing how sorry I am for myself?"

"As the old saying goes, you have a captive audience."

"You're a punner, for God's sake! The manager is a punner. When they shoot you, I'll be glad because if there's one thing in the world I don't need it's one more punner."

Brimmer finished his fourth beer and opened another. Rogers noticed he was wobbling a bit more now and his face had fallen into hundreds of rumpled drapes. His diction slurred occasionally, but his eyes were sparkling with his message.

"I'll tell you what, Rogers. I'd like to tell you how I came to this, but I've never told anybody and I won't start with you. I could put myself in a pretty good light and say, 'Well, how could I help it if I was so handsome, women couldn't leave me alone and they drove me to drink?' or something nice and understandable like that. You understand what I'm saying, Rogers? There's many a man been ruined by rotten women, right? Well, Oscar Brimmer is not one of them. No, sir."

"Did I understand you to say there might be something to eat in this place? It's getting dark fast."

"Have another beer. Eating is for real people who live in the regular world."

"I always thought it helped a person stay alive."

"What are you, some kind of Hitler? One of those strength-through-joy fellas? What you get to eat here is not meant for humans. No wonder the Indians ate each other now and then. I tell you there have been times around here when I would have been more satisfied to chew on some old bag's collarbone."

Rogers said, "I'm sorry. I didn't get your name. I'm terrible about names."

"Oscar. Oscar Brimmer. The best goddamned aviator in South America—which isn't saying much. But flying is the only thing I have. Can you understand that? If I was a kid and had somebody take my picture with tears in my eyes, for sure I'd be adopted. But nobody—and I mean *nobody*—wants to take on a sixty-four-year-old alcoholic who works for the worst bastards in the world."

"How about the people you work for? Who are they, and what are they going to do to me?"

The sound of a generator starting reverberated through the forest, and the lights in Brimmer's room came on. "Well, well," he said. "It must be coming up dinner hour. And damned near dark. Old fatso, old pig eyes, won't start the generator until the last minute so he saves two drops of diesel. Gets a red star on his report card or something. Now our beer will chill down—"

"I asked you a question." Talking with Brimmer, Rogers thought, was like trying to rope a yearling colt. He was all over the range.

"Yeah, I heard you the first time." Brimmer sighed heavily and said that he had kidney trouble, or maybe it was his liver, which was probably in an advanced state of cirrhosis, and nobody cared about that either, including himself. "The head mother is a gent named Marco Fedles. He's a Turk or an Armenian or something like that. I've never met him and don't expect to. This much I can guarantee you. If he says you're dead, you're dead."

"Thanks a lot."

Brimmer moved directly in front of Rogers and eyed him carefully. He shook his head unhappily. "You seem like a nice guy. Why couldn't you just mind your own business? What did Fedles ever do to you?"

"He killed my son, or someone like him did. And I don't like what he's doing to my country—which, in case you've forgotten, is also your country."

Brimmer's eyebrows arched, but he gave no other sign that he might have heard what his guest had said. He turned away from him suddenly and went to stand in the doorway, his ravaged figure silhouetted like a scarecrow against the last of the twilight. He stood for some time, taking nervous little sips from his beer bottle and shaking his jowls as if some deep and loathsome misery longed to escape from him. He rubbed at his tortured eyes and he made a series of little moaning sounds like a hound that had been beaten.

At last he turned to stand in front of Rogers again. He stuck a finger in one ear and waggled it fiercely as if to drill out some dreadful evil from his brain.

"You know what, Rogers? You give me that patriotic crap and I almost fell for it. It gives me shivers. I got a lot of trouble realizin' how sour a guy gets. I read all about you being an ex-cowboy and all and I said to myself several times I can remember, Now there is one smart sonofabitch. He makes a lot of noise, which he knows won't amount to beans in the end, and he waits until the right time to sell out. And he lives rich and happy ever afterward." He paused and his eyes appeared devastated as he tried without success to smile. "Jesus Christ, Rogers, I'm so fuckin' sour I been thinkin' all along you must be one of them."

Brimmer held his beer bottle out before him a moment and regarded it with open displeasure. Suddenly he turned and hurled the bottle through the open window. "I think I'll have myself a puke," he said, wiping at his mouth.

He backed away from his guest, as if Rogers represented something he could not bear to face longer, and for some time afterward Rogers heard him retching in the darkness beyond the doorway.

Evening at Los Estranjeros was always a busy time and it was often nearly midnight before Marco Fedles could free himself from his obligations long enough to take his dinner. During this period his officers reported on the training and morale of his FARC troops. At this same time of the evening, the mood of the working people in every region of Colombia was transmitted through lieutenants or civil representatives, some of whom had waited for days to present their views. Prevet also screened a constant parade of petitioners, most of whom were after financial aid or had suffered what they thought had been some injustice on the part of the federal govern- ment and were convinced the great man at Los Estranjeros was their salvation. Fedles' genius permitted him to maintain that illusion with very little sacrifice to himself.

At this time reports came to the communications center concern- ing the trafficking in substances that most of the world had declared harmful and illegal. There was the very important dealer market in Amsterdam to be considered, there was the poppy market in Burma to be reviewed, and the recent loss of considerable hectares devoted to the same crop in Thailand. Pakistan was reporting a constant battle with the authorities, who seemed less and less inclined to accept bribes for looking the other way. The Middle Eastern re- presentatives claimed they needed much more funding to cover re- cent losses, and several of Fedles' best men were already languishing in Turkish prisons.

Fedles was neither pleased nor distressed. He had long ago written off the Middle East in his thoughts. What was left of the Sicilian Mafia was welcome to it. Instead, he intended to increase his traffick- ing in the low countries and Scandinavia, with special efforts in West Germany. His whole European campaign, thanks to the recent harassment of his rivals by the Italian government, was prospering well beyond his original calculations. All of this was reported from Luxembourg, seat of his European operations.

Yet the whole picture varied from day to day.

The seizure of ships and fast boats bound for the United States was on the rise, although Fedles expressed only minor irritation at their occasional interception. At times he even smiled when a certain vessel and crew were apprehended. Little did they realize that the information leading to their arrest had originated at Los Estranjeros; it was good to throw an occasional bone to the Yankee narcs so they would have something to brag about in the newspapers. It kept them from becoming overly curious about much larger and more lucrative shipments. Usually the men involved were people Fedles wished to be rid of anyway. "What a pity," he would say to Prevet as if he meant it, and indirectly he would manage to convey his profound sympathies to their families.

There were countless other matters brought to Fedles' attention during these hours. The Colombian government was becoming a nuisance, lately flexing its muscles and making rash statements about "driving the men of evil from our beloved land." A series of new judges had been appointed to replace those who had been killed, and a few were allowing their zeal to overcome their common sense. It would be necessary to see to their elimination, one by one. Their deaths must not be even vaguely connected with Los Estranjeros, of course, but it must be done. Only then could the onetime tranquillity of the country return. His tolerance, Fedles mused, was like his time. Limited.

During these hours, darkness concealed what the surrounding forest did not; there were often clandestine meetings at Los Estranjeros, and the names of the principals involved would have shocked the higher castes in Bogotá. Fedles saw to it that those he courted and won over to his benefit never knew about the others. Their original bountiful rewards were followed afterward by gentle hints of exposure that guaranteed their silence. Within this group of occasional visitors were several officers in the air force, a handful of colonels in the army, and two generals. There was also a bundle of assorted bureaucrats, each in his way capable of performing some service for the Fedles organization.

It was not until the following noon that Fedles was able to view a tape of the president's stern address to the people of the United States. Fedles smiled throughout and shook his head in wonder. To Prevet he said, "Do you suppose that silly man really believes what he is telling his voters? 'Coming to get Rogers'? He must think Colombia is about the size of Liechtenstein! If he landed fifty thousand marines this morning, they'd be lost in the jungle by teatime."

Fedles took a moment to make a face at Estrellita and then very gently smoothed her feathers. "Say something, little bird," he murmured. "Say that the time has come at last. Tell our poor, unimaginative, overly cautious Prevet that opportunity is here and we must take advantage of it. All of the elements are falling into place. We have a so-called government that is very distracted. We have in our hands an enemy of the Colombian people. A spy, perhaps. Perhaps the leader of an invasion by American armed forces. Don't you see, dear Prevet? The CIA plot is so obvious. This fellow Rogers is only a capitalist tool sent here as an excuse to stage a heroic rescue by the Americans."

Fedles sat back and closed his eyes as if savoring a sweet and very private vision.

Prevet asked, "Did this idea just come to you, or have you thought it all out?"

"Foresight, dear Prevet. Foresight is a combination of instinct and daring. We may never have another chance like this. It is our duty to protect the people—"

"Are you being serious?" Prevet made no attempt to hide his disapproval.

"Absolutely. We have the men and equipment to be the saviors of our adopted country. A coup is inevitable. As of tomorrow morning, you will place all FARC units on ready alert. I will see that our special friends in the government understand the urgency of the situation and the need of a strong man to save us all from disaster."

Prevet studied his employer suspiciously. "Marco," he said, "you're forgetting we have a big and profitable enterprise that demands a lot of attention. You don't have time to play power politics."

"As I see it, there won't be any need for politicians in the new government. The people will rule, and I will be their guide."

Prevet noticed that Fedles' voice had changed. He seemed to be speaking as in a dream. His eyes were closed, and yet he continued to smile. "It will be inspiring to see our FARC boys go to the rescue of the government. And afterward the Yankee marines. I will be generous with the American president and accept a mere fifty million in damage claims. And you, dear friend. I can see you now talking with our own ex-president and persuading him to take a helicopter ride for his safety. Can you imagine his agony of choice? The poor idiot's wondering where he can hide."

Skip Donovan ordered the bell-and-light system activated, although he realized that at this moment it was only a convenient formality. The system brought order to the House of Representatives; one long ring followed by a pause and then three rings and three lights served notice of a quorum call for the "Committee of the Whole," which would be vacated if one hundred members were on the floor.

Surveying the crowd below him, Donovan turned back and forth in his great leather chair counting noses, and was gratified to find that nearly every member of the House was present. They all wanted their votes to be counted, for despite their constant bickering and differences, a member in trouble was a family matter.

The resolution said in part, "The members of the United States House of Representatives are resolved to reject and deny any negotiations whatsoever with the captors of their colleague, Congressman Lee Rogers of Montana. While we hold the courage and dedication of Congressman Rogers in the highest regard, we represent the people of the United States and we cannot sacrifice the integrity of this institution to spare the life of an individual any more than we could surrender in battle to save the life of a single soldier."

The three lights on the left were extinguished and there was one long ring, indicating the quorum call had been vacated.

Next there were two lights on the left, followed by two rings. A recorded vote yea or nay was in order.

Donovan watched as the representatives lined up and inserted their ID cards in the electronic vote stations scattered throughout selected chairs in the chamber. Each member then pressed the appropriate button to record his vote.

Later, Donovan was not surprised to learn that the Senate had seen the wisdom of echoing the vote in his House. The proposal set forth in the memorandum presented to Congress by Peebles, Kraft, Monroy, and Bachman was overwhelmingly rejected.

Lee Rogers lay flat on the cement-block shelf that served as his bunk and stared at the roof. It was woven of some sort of long leaf that he had been unable to identify. There were cobwebs high in the leaves, and he thought there were also too many cobwebs in his mind. If what Oscar Brimmer said was true, then for the first time in his life, he realized, he was helpless.

It was inconceivable. After being surrounded by what seemed like hundreds of people for so long, with Lily to love and the kids to worry about, now suddenly there was nothing. Washington and Montana were like two planets as distant as Uranus and Pluto, if indeed they still existed. Since he had walked Tracy Delano to her apartment and continued along on a city street, light-years had passed, sweeping those minor events to the limits of the universe. Not even visible through a telescope, he mused.

If Brimmer was telling the truth about the jungle, that way of escape had to be canceled. And it must really be impossible, because last night and well into this steaming morning no one had paid the slightest attention to him. The FARC guards were apparently considered unnecessary, and the few laborers he had seen looked right through him. But since when did Lee Rogers accept anything as impossible? Getting old?

When Oscar Brimmer had escorted him to the "dining saloon" the night before, the fat manager had glanced up from the gruesome-looking mess on his plate and stopped chewing. He'd fixed his tiny eyes on Rogers for several seconds—then, without the slightest sign of greeting, he'd gone back to his gobbling. Rogers could not decide whether he was trying to get his meal down before it walked off and left him, or before it dissolved in the rain of sweat that dribbled from his chops.

The fat manager had not been visible when the coffee and bread was offered at breakfast. Nor was Oscar Brimmer present when the day began. The sound of his heavy snoring was still audible through the open window of his quarters.

Rogers tried to find little encouragements in the ocean of negatives where he seemed barely afloat. He had been provided with a mosquito net, for one thing, and the result had been a tolerable night's sleep considering the circumstances. Did that mean he was expected to live, or was he just being preserved for a more convenient moment?

It was a sobering thought. Lee Rogers come to the end of his rope in a Colombian jungle? There was one hell of a big decision to be made, because it was reasonable to suppose, if Brimmer was to be believed, that he was not going to just be left to rot in this place. He asked himself if he was willing to die just because he was against drug trafficking. The answer was easy. Definitely not. Then, he thought, you were campaigning for a war that might kill other people, but not you.

How about a compromise? Would even a thousand kids be saved from drugs if he refused to give in? Who was going to tell the kids and make them believe some nut would die just because he didn't like the smell of marijuana and objected to a little coke? A good number of narcotics agents from one agency or another had been shot in the course of their daily work, but they'd had no choice. Their life work involved betting on the chance they would not be standing in the wrong place at the wrong time.

Now, the only answer seemed to be a retreat. Wasn't it a sad fact that people who died for a principle often just died? Maybe the solution was to survive somehow, then come back later and win. Maybe. Jack would approve. Or was even trying to imagine what Jack might think just another excuse for a coward to save his skin?

Maybe Oscar Brimmer was the key. There was something very peculiar about the man and it wasn't all alcohol that twisted him so out of shape.

He thought about Oscar Brimmer, whose snoring suddenly reached a crescendo. He had said before they parted last night, "You're a kook, one of those idealists, Rogers, and guys like you always wind up either getting their ass burned or making a lot of trouble for other people. So let's get something very straight right now. When they come for you, I'll say so long and that's all. Just because we both happen to be Americans does not impress me. I have my life on the line enough on this operation without borrowing trouble. And even if I wanted to, there's not one damn thing I can do. But no hard feelings, cowboy. Tomorrow, if you're still alive, come by my place and we'll drink some more beer."

Had Oscar meant every word he said just because he kept repeating himself? How drunk was he, and was there any help he could give even if he suddenly became more willing? Where was the key to Oscar Brimmer?

He was trying to capture some possibilities, no matter how wild, when he heard the whine of a jet helicopter approaching. He spun off the shelf and went to the doorway. He saw the helicopter descend on the side of the airstrip and he saw that it was surrounded immediately by young FARCs with their weapons held at present arms. Then a slim, well-groomed man in a white suit stepped out and greeted the fat manager. Another man descended from the helicopter and followed them toward the long building with the corrugated-metal roof, which Brimmer had identified as the "works."

Rogers saw the party disappear inside, then emerge shortly afterward. They were coming in his direction. Halfway, the man in the white suit halted and said something to the others. They remained in place while he continued toward Rogers's quarters.

Rogers stood waiting, his thumbs locked in his belt, his back straight. By God, he was going to look defiant even if he had to fake it. For he knew the man approaching him had to be Marco Fedles.

"So, you're the cowboy," the trim man in the white suit said. "I wanted to have a look at a man who has such strong opinions. Wrong opinions."

Rogers met his cold gray eyes and was instantly reminded of a Montana snowfield. He had never seen eyes so open and interested and yet so devoid of warmth. There was no longer any question, he thought. This man was lethal.

Rogers decided a bold approach would be as good as any other. "Who the hell are you?" he asked, as if he were both annoyed and surprised.

He saw that Fedles was momentarily puzzled. He had not expected such a greeting. The man is a mountain of ego, Rogers decided, and at least he had pricked him. He saw a half-smile twist Fedles' lips and he forced himself to seem unconcerned.

"I'm your future," Fedles said quietly. He lit a cigarette and blew the smoke at Rogers's face. "Providing you have any future." He turned to look down the hill, where the squad of young FARC troopers stood waiting. "My troops need target practice. They prefer Yankees who won't mind their own business. You people seem to have a national bad habit of running all over the world telling other people how they should live. Why do you think you're here?"

"I demand to be returned to Washington immediately."

"You demand? So you're arrogant as well as stupid. This is not your country. Here you are only a nuisance."

Fedles paused and surveyed Rogers's tall frame, his eyes roving up and down as if measuring the cowboy's physical strength. He sighed. "You're a young man. Why are you so anxious to die?"

Rogers looked at the doorsill beneath his shoes. He remained leaning against the doorframe, trying to maintain an air of indifference. These few moments, he was certain, were vital to his survival. Now looking into those gray eyes, he knew that if he displayed the slightest evidence of cringing, Fedles would shrug and have him shot. He knew he was fighting for the seconds remaining in his life and he had better treat each one of them as precious. "You seem to be an intelligent man," he said slowly, and he hoped his deliberate drawl was convincing. "What would you gain by shooting me?"

"Suppose I let you go back to Washington and you say to the Congress that you have made a special survey and found that the people of Colombia are your friends? You say that you have learned there have always been drugs and always will be. Suppose you say that all this talk about a war is something from the CIA, who always makes trouble around the world? Suppose you receive every month for the next year an agreeable sum in cash—enough to guarantee the future for your two children and, of course, your wife? I have considered your future carefully. Big things are about to happen in Colombia and I might find some value in your name."

Fedles paused and brushed at a wisp of hair that a rare breeze had lifted out of place. He shrugged, and Rogers thought his attempt to smile was like a cornered wolf baring its fangs.

"I'm a businessman," Fedles continued, "and so I understand your need to consider my proposal. You have until this time tomorrow." Fedles sighed deeply, then added, "Be sensible." He turned his back and walked casually toward his helicopter.

Rogers glanced at his watch. Twenty minutes until eleven. He wondered if Fedles was also aware of the exact time, and decided it would not make the slightest difference. The man in the white suit obviously kept his own time. As he listened to the whine of the helicopter spooling up, he blinked at the hard sun, and the phrase "Be sensible" rang in his ears.

The Senate vote was almost unanimous and the House vote was unanimous. When the vote was official, the president called what all White House correspondents thought would be a superfluous press conference.

"Drug traffickers are terrorists," the president said, as a few of the correspondents failed to suppress a yawn. "And this government does not do business with terrorists. One of our representatives has been kidnapped and may lose his life. We cannot lie down and allow this vicious crime to succeed."

The president made a significant pause while a small clique of reporters, bemused and arrogant as ever in their grubbies, waited for a chance to hurl questions and perhaps become the focus of a television camera. Suddenly even their jaded eyes displayed surprise.

"We believe the Colombian government is primarily responsible for the behavior of its citizens. Therefore I have advised the Colombian ambassador as well as the president of Colombia that if Congressman Rogers is not delivered to our embassy in Bogotá in sound health by tomorrow morning, certain units of our armed forces will come for him. These units are already standing by."

A woman correspondent was on her feet immediately. "Mr. President! Doesn't this mean that we're declaring war on Colombia? Isn't that exactly what Congressman Rogers has been proposing?"

The president hesitated. "At this time I am not recommending any official declaration of war—"

"Does the president of Colombia understand that?"

"Yes. He also understands that our objective is an individual and that our presence will be confined to certain areas."

Another reporter—this one from such a prestigious news service that he wore a coat and tie—was recognized. "Mr. President, do you know exactly where Congressman Rogers is being held?"

"Yes." The president smiled sourly and added, "Colombia."

"Are you saying that we are going to invade the whole country?"

"No. Only those sections we believe necessary."

"Aren't we then committing ourselves to a war?"

"We've been so committed for some time. Colombia and all the other nations who permit the manufacture of drugs for sale to us are at war with our society and particularly our youth. So far our efforts to stop any of these operations have made very little real progress. It's past time we corrected this situation."

Another correspondent was recognized. "Mr. President, what will be our policy if this invasion escalates? If it becomes another Nicaragua, another Honduras, another El Salvador—perhaps even another Vietnam? Even Congressman Rogers admitted such possibilities."

"I hope and believe your fears are very much exaggerated."

A very young reporter found the president's eye and asked, "Will the Colombian government join our troops in this exercise?"

"At this moment I don't know. I'm not even sure we want them."

The president ran a finger down his nose as a signal to his aides that he had run out of patience. Even before he turned away from the microphones, the Secret Service had surrounded him. He was on his way through the exit doors before more questions could be launched.

Marco Fedles listened thoughtfully as Prevet made a final attempt to dissuade him from an action in which Prevet could find little merit. They were sitting in the smallest of the patios at Los Estranjeros and Fedles was feeding macadamia nuts to Figaro. He seemed more interested in the monkey's slow mastication than in what his chief deputy was saying. And Prevet sensed his disapproval. Something had happened to Marco's attitude ever since the cowboy affair had surfaced. He was becoming increasingly irrational and there was a dangerous light in his eyes. Figaro, he had said once, had more intelligence than anyone in the organization.

All of this, Prevet thought, was the fault of the cowboy. Once Marco Fedles discovered that he could make the United States Congress and the president jump to attention, he wanted to crack the whip. He was reveling in his new power.

"My dear Prevet," Fedles said in a cutting tone, "whatever is eating at you? Are you becoming an old woman before my eyes? You know as well as I do that one cannot win without some risk. One must expect and prepare for it. But we cannot spend our time worrying about every little thing that may not be entirely to our satisfaction."

Prevet shook his head unhappily. "This is no longer a little thing. Two hours ago the American president announced he would send troops to take Rogers back. He delivered an ultimatum to Bogotá and they are in a quandary about what to do."

Fedles made a face and seemed to concentrate entirely on Figaro's chewing. "Poof! Of course! Bogotá? What can they do, except run around in circles and cry for help? The people will come to their rescue. There will be much confusion. Then I'll arrive to solidify a totally new government."

"What about the cowboy?"

"No one knows where Rogers is. By the time they find out, he'll be cheering for us or he'll be dead."

"Is it your impression that he will come over to us?"

"Of course he will, my dear Prevet. What has become of your education? You know as well as I do that every man has his price, and at this moment I'm quite sure Rogers is calculating his. It would be stupid of him to decide otherwise, and he is not a stupid man."

"One hour ago I talked to my friend Amonte in Washington. He says the Americans are not just making noise this time. They really mean to use their military strength, and I hope you're not under the delusion that if they do, our ragtag troopers could fight them off."

Fedles appeared to be deeply offended. "Please. We must never lose faith in the people's army."

Prevet caught a twinkle in his employer's eye and said in English, "Bullshit. They wouldn't last five minutes and those who were left alive would take to the hills."

"Probably. What do we care? By then we will be the government. If the Americans come to us, we say, 'Rogers? Rogers who? We know nothing of such a man.'"

Fedles shrugged, and flipped another macadamia nut into the air. Figaro caught it expertly. "Señor Rogers? He does not exist as far as we are concerned. In the unlikely event that he is too stubborn for his own good, you must make the necessary arrangements."

"Marco! You've suddenly stopped listening to me. You are forgetting how many people know Rogers is in our hands. Eventually the Americans will put so much pressure on the law firm in Washington, they'll track down the origin of their payment."

"Eventually is a long time away. The world may come to an end if you don't stop fretting."

"There are couriers and car drivers who knew who he was, and there's Brimmer, our pilot, who brought him to Camp Four. Remember, he's an American too. Then there is the manager and the FARC troopers who went to the camp with you, and several of those stationed there. I suppose some of the Indians and other workers might have seen him. How can we say we don't know anything about him?"

Fedles linked his hands behind his head and studied the evening sky. He closed his eyes for a moment and kept them closed as he spoke. "While I regret wasting my time with negative thoughts, I see you must be satisfied or you'll worry yourself into doing something wrong."

Fedles hesitated, then went on more slowly. "If it becomes necessary, which I doubt, then you will send Brimmer on a mission with a sufficient amount of plastique to blow his airplane out of the sky one hour after takeoff. Rogers will be a passenger—and while you're at it, you will find reason to include the camp manager, too. You will employ the FARC troopers to burn the camp down and move all our materials to that place we chose two or three years ago. How time passes! I've been thinking about that place. It is less convenient than Camp Four, but the security is greater.

"If you have any more questions, be so good as to keep them until morning. While I've never been enthusiastic about females from the Argentine, one is due to arrive before dark. She comes with the highest recommendations, particularly the development of her bosom at such a young age. Drop by early if you care to inspect her."

"No, *merci.* I have very much to do tonight."

Prevet tried unsuccessfully to smile and took his leave. He left the patio via a side entrance and walked along a twisting path to the communications center. Now, he thought dismally, Marco Fedles has finally gone mad, or at least is standing on the fringe of lunacy. Power, too much power. It had finally got to him as it did to all men. Now, he thought, he must do things entirely on his own, even if it should conflict with Marco's whims. There was real trouble brewing and it would be foolish to depend on the determination, or lack of it, some American cowboy might display. Nor could anyone depend on more than two people remaining silent. The whole operation, at least in Colombia, was definitely at hazard. If it was to be saved, then it was up to him alone.

He checked his watch. Almost noon. Too late. Tomorrow at first light he would helicopter direct to Camp Four. He would take two plastiques, one for each wheel well of the DC-3. He would set one to explode in an hour; the other in one and one-half hours, just in case of a failure.

He would also take along the video camera Marco used occasionally to film his girls. He would film the departure of the DC-3, making sure that not so much as a frown crossed anyone's face—just in case a later story for the Americans or even Bogotá needed proof. Rogers, Brimmer, and the camp manager would be seen willingly departing for . . . why not Jamaica? He would send a telex now to the American Embassy in Kingston, advising of Rogers's arrival. In Jamaica he could transfer to a jet for Washington. All according to his own choice, of course.

Explanations would be easy. Rogers had come of his own free will on a fact-finding mission. He had found little to support his previously antagonistic claims. And he departed according to his own time and in good humor—see film.

The Caribbean was very big and very deep. A truly regrettable accident.

Oscar Brimmer sat on the edge of his cot and held his head in his hands for a long time before he blinked at the daylight. If the normal human head weighed fifteen pounds or so, then what kind of a humanoid was this with a thirty-pounder? Drinking beer with cowboys was injurious to the health, and when the outside temperature was in the nineties, as it must be now, the whole purpose of mankind became questionable.

Brimmer lit a cigarette, coughed resoundingly, and stumbled to his refrigerator. He opened the door, found it at least cool within, and brought out a bottle of beer. He removed the cap and swallowed rapidly for several seconds. When he put the bottle down on the wooden table next to a copy of Hawthorne's *Scarlet Letter,* it was nearly half-empty. He belched once, farted twice, and very nearly fell on his ravaged face when he bent over to slip on his sandals. Glory hallelujah, what a morning. Or was it afternoon?

He was not addicted to anything, he told himself, but this was certainly the time to recoup his energy by enjoying a touch of the local bounty. He opened the fridge again, reached far back, and brought out a small plastic vial. He saw that his fingers were trembling as he dribbled a minute pile of white powder on the back of his hand. He sniffed at the powder and inhaled deeply. One thing could be said for Camp Four: They turned out a first-class product. Even so, he rarely used it, because the damn stuff was tricky. It provided a lift for a while, but it released emotions all over the place—which was why, he reminded himself, it was to be avoided by people like himself. Except in emergencies.

He squinted at the window and judged the extent and intensity of the shadows. It must be about noon. Where the hell was his watch in all this confusion? Then he remembered. A week ago—maybe it was ten days—he had resolved to do away with his watch. It was out in the jungle somewhere, as far as he had been able to throw it. Time was a tangible enemy and it was possible to reach out and choke it. Why had he never recognized that before? Time not only marked his aging, it measured his distance from a world that had once been his, a separation ever increasing.

Once upon a time there was Tessie. As wives go, she was tolerable, although too much given to pampering son Willie. The kid needed more masculine exposure, but his father was always away on some damn flight. So by the time Willie was seventeen, he was no damn good for much. He was interested in baking and in playing seventeenth-century music on his flute. A pain in the ass.

The light hurt Brimmer's eyes. He squinted to see into the shadows and searched about until he found his wrinkled pants. He pulled them on as he had a thousand times before. Left leg first? Right leg first? What the hell difference did it make? Nothing had made any difference for too many years.

Too many long-agos, my friend. High on the seniority list at TWA. Nice house near the lake in Chicago. Not a worry except for Willie.

Brimmer pulled a T-shirt over his head and yanked it down to his waist. He went to the table and finished off the bottle of beer in one long series of swallows. A man came to a point in life when maybe he had lived too long. He began to hurt in his body, in his brain, and, worst of all, in his heart. Matters that had once seemed so important were no longer so, and all but the most animal desires were dead. The last whore he had been with chided him for his flabbiness. What the hell did they expect from an old pelican?

What to do today? Sometime in his slumbers he had thought he'd heard the arrival and departure of a helicopter, but it was probably a dream. Life here was a dream. A bad one. A fucking nightmare when a guy came right down to it.

Tessie got sick and went for a long swim in the lake. Suicide.

Coroner said she had cancer of the stomach. God knows why. She ate like a canary bird. End of home. Beginning of end.

Suddenly Brimmer became aware that he was not alone. He turned to see a stranger standing in the doorway. He blinked his inflamed eyes and, after a puzzled moment, recognized him. "Hello, cowboy. I see you're still alive."

He studied Rogers a moment. Then an inspiration struck him. "Hey, cowboy! I've got an idea. If they don't shoot you before dark, how about coming to the cantina with me?" The vision of actually having a companion at his little table in the village was so exotic he forgot that Rogers was not the most scintillating company he had ever known. The guy didn't drink much and he didn't say much, but hell, times were tough. Just another body sitting in that vacant chair would be an improvement. "We'll go in my jeep," he said. "I'll work all afternoon to make sure the damn thing will start."

Rogers cocked his head. "Are you telling me that we can just pick up and go to town when we feel like it? I've been watching those kids with their Uzis and I do believe one thing Fedles told me: They would sure like some live targets."

"Going to the village here is not the same as going to town back in God's country. This village has a cantina, seven houses, a stinking hide-and-tallow works, and a canned-goods store. That's it. It's cut right out of the jungle alongside a river full of piranha—which, in case you don't know, are nice little fish that'll eat you down to the bone in five minutes. There's probably a crocodile or two and a current that runs about six knots. I wouldn't recommend it for swimming." Brimmer paused and eyed Rogers skeptically. "So you've met Fedles? God himself. No doubt he mentioned your future."

"He did."

"He always does to anyone who works for him. He's clever. He has you by the balls and he lets you know he knows it. You're going to give in, I hope. Doing things his way is better than not doing anything at all."

"He gave me until tomorrow morning to make up my mind."

"Jesus, he's going soft. How long does it take a guy to decide between—"

255

"I've already decided."

"Don't tell me something silly. I'm not in the mood for it today."

"I've decided you're going to help me get out of here."

Although he saw that Rogers was smiling, Brimmer jerked backward as if he had just stepped on a scorpion. "Whoa! Whoa, cowboy! Not me. You come to the wrong man. Forget the cantina. I don't want any part of you. You go your way and I'll go mine. If Uncle Fedles has plans for you, I don't even want to hear about it."

Brimmer shook his head and regretted it instantly. He moved backward until he collided with the wall. "I've seen what those sonsabitches do. They go by the one prime rule in this nasty business, and that is if too many people know too much, get rid of the whole bunch. Now go away and leave me alone before I have a seizure. I have them at times like now, when I have a hangover and get scared. I beat my head against this wall, I foam at the mouth. Go away. You're talkin' to a born coward." Brimmer reached for his upper chest and massaged it vigorously. "I could have a heart attack any minute now."

Rogers held his smile. "Your heart," he said, "is down there."

"Please. Will you go the hell away?" Brimmer's voice took on a pleading tone. This cowboy, he thought, was already driving him crazy. Why should he give a shit about what happened to the man? Marco Fedles would have a real seizure if he was denied his piece of meat, and that was all the cowboy represented. Just like Oscar Brimmer, who at least had sense enough to keep a great distance between the great man and himself; far enough away to avoid being within range when one of his snits took hold.

Brimmer avoided Rogers's accusing eyes. He began to tremble slightly. He clenched his teeth and growled, "You got no idea how nasty these people can be. You'll be lucky if they just shoot you. So go away. Go away, for Christ's sake. I don't even know you."

Suddenly Brimmer began to perspire and his hound-dog face twisted and contorted as if he were suffering severe physical pain. "I don't know what to do," he groaned. "I can't help you. Nobody can." This is awful, he thought. Rogers standing there cool as a beer bottle when he must know he doesn't have a prayer of going home with a tight skin. There he was, standing there all guts and hope like

Brimmer himself had once been. It was like waking up and looking at a ghost, a once-upon-a-time guy who had run out of guts. Goddamn the cowboy! Just standing there without saying a fucking word brought a whole life tumbling back. There he was just looking and not saying anything except with his eyes, which were saying plenty.

His eyes were saying, "We're inspecting a pile of ruins with a jerk slumped in the middle of it. We're looking for a guy who killed himself that awful day and never came back to life. And that's too bad because once there was a lot there. Any life left now in the corpse?"

"Why don't you say something?" Brimmer asked apprehensively.

Rogers kept his silence.

"What is this? You intend to stand there all day not saying anything? Speak out, cowboy. For Christ's sake, say something! If you knew about Tessie and Willie . . ."

"You told me about your wife and son last night."

"Forget it. It's none of your goddamned business! I was making up a fairy tale. Always do after a few beers. What do I have to do to get you out of my sight?"

"Help me."

"Screw off, cowboy! I'm not helping anybody! I've got a few more years of life I want to live."

"You call this a life? You're a murderer. You're the man who delivers the package that wrecks lives. Lots of young lives. And you kill quite a few. You wake up in the morning and feel good about that?" Rogers shook his head. "Somehow I didn't figure you for that kind of man. I should have guessed when you told me about your wife and son. Willie, you said his name was? Momma's boy? Didn't want to fly and you made him and that was the end of him? I can understand your grief, but not what you did with it. Too bad. I did come to the wrong man."

Brimmer blinked his eyes slowly and saw that his visitor had departed. He covered his eyes with his hands and to his astonishment began a soft sobbing. What the hell was this? One beer and a snort of cocaine was not enough to start him hallucinating. Or was it? Had the damn cowboy been real or an illusion?

* * *

257

Sometimes Wilma Thorne wondered why she should be uncomfortable about spending so much money on taxis. It was a necessary business expense because the better hotel doormen knew the drivers and shared a tiny portion of their tips. If Wilma arrived on foot, chances were that the nosy doorman would give her a hard time—and that could be a waste of time. Now, en route to the Ritz-Carlton to turn a late matinee trick, her taxi passed a cathedral. She ordered her driver to wait while she went inside and uttered a brief prayer for the life of Congressman Rogers. "I hope it works," she murmured as she emerged from the cathedral. For a non-Catholic who hadn't been inside a church since childhood, she had done very well, she decided. God would understand that amateurs used a different set of words.

At this same twilight hour in Washington, Gordon Hawkins called Mort Steiner. "What's new?"

"You probably know more than I do."

"Thanks for nothing. Where are his wife and kids?"

"Do you really think I'd tell you?"

"No."

"Then why bother me?"

"Because I heard a rumor I find hard to believe. But one never knows, does one, old boy? Someone has started a rumor that this whole thing has gotten out of control—a big to-do that never should have been started."

"Clue me, maestro."

"The word is that the DEA, not to mention the CIA, has been working all along with the Colombian government and was about ready to spring their big trap and Rogers was supposed to do the final negotiating."

"Insanity."

"I'm only telling you. There's no question that both the CIA and the DEA are involved in this somewhere, but is this kidnap business just a setup to justify their future actions to the public? In other words, Rogers went of his own free will and is not in any real danger. Never has been—at least on this expedition."

There was a long pause, then Steiner said he would be curious to know the source of such unrefined manure.

"I don't know for sure myself," Hawkins answered. "But I was tipped by a reasonably reliable source who had heard from another source that it started at the law firm that delivered the original threat to Congress. Odd, isn't it?"

"*Preposterous* is a better word. Call again when you have something worth listening to. And pip-pip yourself." Steiner slammed down the phone, picked it up again, and dialed the Mills home in Virginia. A familiar voice answered. He decided to take a chance. "Are you Tracy Delano?"

"Yes. How did you know?"

"Easy. This is Mort Steiner and I want to talk with Mrs. Rogers."

"She's not taking any calls, Mr. Steiner. That's why I'm here."

"I have to ask her an important question."

"Hold on just a moment." Shortly afterward he heard Lily Rogers's voice. She sounded weary.

"Mrs. Rogers, before your husband was elected, did he ever have anything to do with the CIA or the DEA?"

"No."

"Did he after he came to Washington?"

"I don't think so."

"Would he have told you if in fact he did have? It is my impression that you two are very close."

"I suppose he would have."

"Thank you. Sorry to trouble you."

Steiner inquired after R.R. and Fay, and said that if all kids were like them, he might even consider midlife marriage should a rich widow come so equipped.

He hoped he had put a least a trace of a smile on Lily Rogers's face. Then he sat back in his chair and thought that Shakespeare was right about lawyers.

The president of the United States was grateful to National Security Decision Directive Number 138, which was intended to free his hand in combating terrorists. He could see no reason why the liberation of Congressman Rogers should not be covered by that directive. Furthermore, as this was not to be a covert operation, he assumed his orders to the Pentagon would not be shackled by the Hughes-Ryan Act, which required close consultation with Congress before the enormous bureaucracy of the military could be activated.

Despite the urgency of the president's orders, it was more than three hours before the Second Airborne was on full alert, ready to load men and matériel. It would be eight hours before the aircraft carrier *Constellation,* diverted from a training exercise in the Caribbean, would be standing off the coast of Colombia.

The chief of combined operations, Admiral Sweeney, called the White House at 7:00 P.M., Washington time, and told the president that because of cloud conditions over Colombia during the morning hours, it would be advisable to postpone the actual operation until noon the next day.

The president reluctantly agreed.

It was nearly midnight, Bogotá time, when Prevet finished his duties. He had been on the phone twice to Guy Amonte, who claimed to know nothing new. He had talked with two wholesalers, one in Amsterdam and one in Miami, both of whom complained of a declining market for cocaine. Miami, $23,500 per kilogram. The thieves were crying and refused to pay more. He sent a coded telex to Montreal advising of a Fedles ship even now entering the St. Lawrence River. The ordered consignment of one hundred kilograms was aboard, but funds to cover same had not been received.

He called Camp Four on their discreet radio frequency and told the manager to have the pilot and aircraft ready for departure at 9:00. Another special mission.

Later in the evening he was the unwilling host to a surprise visitor. Actually not so surprising, after he had thought about it. Colonel Felipe Barretta of the Colombian Army, a man who had hitherto been considered as one of Fedles' regulars (at a monthly fee), arrived by car for an urgent interview. When it was explained that Fedles himself was unavailable, he refused to get out of his car but agreed to convey his message to Prevet.

Colonel Barretta bore discomforting news. The Americans, may the good God bring syphilis to them all, had put so much pressure on the Colombian government that some kind of military show was imminent. Idealism was sweeping the capital and there was no stopping the change of sentiment, even though there was silent agreement among the more realistic leaders that the threatening inconvenience to Fedles and a few others would be temporary. Meanwhile, because Fedles' FARC troops might be tempted to use their Uzis, requiring a response in kind from the federal troops, which was bound to leave someone hurt, Colonel Barretta had come to warn Fedles of an impending attack. It was all because of that cowboy, he lamented. He also wanted to assure Fedles that if and when such an intrusion occurred, his old friend Barretta would not be involved. Through the most opportune intervention of his cousin Alberto, who stood high in the government, he had been appointed Colombian military attaché to Paraguay and was leaving in the morning.

After assuring Prevet that the situation would soon return to normal, Colonel Barretta stated that he would be most appreciative if his final month's honorarium were forwarded to the embassy in Asunción.

Prevet agreed to see what he could do. As he returned to the communications center, he told himself that he was too tired and frustrated to argue with the man. This was all most unsatisfying. Fedles should be on deck like a proper captain when a storm was approaching. Instead, he was diddling around with some Argentine child while his empire caught fire. Worse than Nero.

Prevet knew better than to disturb his boss when he was so preoccupied. Any intrusion upon his sexual symphonies was absolutely forbidden.

After Prevet had taken sufficient plastique from the armory and found a triggering mechanism that worked reliably, he set aside the film and video camera for use in the morning. Then he called the helicopter pilot and told him to be ready for takeoff at dawn. Nearly exhausted from such a long and trying day, he went to his little house within the compound, swallowed a Valium, and tried to sleep. For a time he remained restless, his mind churning with the difficulties he foresaw. Should he tell Marco of his plans? A change of mind? Negative. Wait until noon at least and judge how the whims of an

Argentine girl affected the mood of her middle-aged host. He thought of the camp. It would be wise to have a squad of FARCs nearby in case the plastique was discovered before the DC-3 took off. Handy, yet concealed. He must not forget that the video tape portraying all those present as being in good humor would be excellent insurance against what now appeared to be a dubious future.

Fedles, who was always mentioning the future, seemed to think of everyone's but his own.

Rogers was still very much awake when he heard movement outside his open doorway. Man or animal? He lay in the darkness visualizing a Colombian youth prowling the camp with a yearning to fire his Uzi at a live target. Holy cow. Since when, he wondered, was he a downbeat thinker? Especially now. Something had to be done, and quick. All right. The hell with that sorry guy, Brimmer. A long chance was better than none. Make a run for the jungle and try to keep going northeast toward Venezuela, which was God-only-knew how far. He could survive. He could make it. There wasn't a damn snake, bug, or animal that could stop a Rogers.

He had been staring at a patch of stars framed in the upper third of the doorway. Now suddenly they were obscured. He instinctively started to rise when he was thrown back and a hand closed firmly over his mouth. Another seized his throat. Rogers smelled beer.

A hoarse whisper came out of the darkness. "Quiet! It's me. Brimmer."

Rogers mumbled through the hand on his mouth, "What the—"

"Shut up and listen. I'm crazy. So I changed my mind. I'm gonna try to get you out of here."

Brimmer removed his hands and Rogers sat up. Brimmer whispered, "Sorry to be so rough, but I was afraid you might be asleep and make some noise when I came in. The FARC are asleep, but they wake easy, and the fat bastard never sleeps. You willing to take a long string of risks? We may not make it—in fact, for one reason or another, we probably won't."

"Other than kids with Uzis, what's the problem?"

"For one thing, I'm drunk. Too much cantina. I've never flown an airplane drunk—or even with a single drink in me. Not recommended for your health."

"What about yours?"

"I don't give a shit anymore. While I was sitting in the cantina, I was thinkin' about what you said. You're right. All I can do is get your ass out of here."

"Let's go." Rogers put his feet on the floor and hoped he was not dreaming.

"Not so fast," Brimmer whispered. "Listen carefully. We can't just walk down to the airstrip, because the FARC barracks are on the left and Fatso lives by the plant on the right. His light is still on. So we have to go the back way, through the jungle."

Brimmer found Rogers's hand. "Here's an old pair of boots I had. I think they'll fit, but wear them even if they don't. You'll need 'em. The monkeys and all the other people who live in the woods will set up a hell of a racket when we pass through, so we got to make our circle far away from the camp. It's gonna be a long hike and we can't even use a flashlight. You wanna beer?"

"No, I don't want a beer. Let's get going."

Brimmer's speech became a grumbled slur. "A man could get dehydrated being around you."

A few minutes later they were walking along the trail that led eventually to the village. Occasionally, as the stars shone through the overhanging tree branches, Rogers had a moment to appraise his guide, who had insisted on bringing a bottle of beer along with him. He weaved now and then and stumbled to his knees once, but he kept going. His speech was more slurred than ever, yet he somehow managed to make sense. Rogers hoped that by the time they reached the airplane, his physical coordination would improve.

"Pretty soon," Brimmer said, "we gotta leave the trail and cut back through the trees. Then we go a long ways till we come out on the airstrip. Trouble is, we got to keep changin' direction—like in a big half-circle. We probably won't be able to see any stars. Lucky it isn' rainin' . . . every fuckin' night it usually does."

"How do we know our direction without the stars?"

"Inshtink. Remember, cowboy, you're with the old pelican."

Soon they turned into the forest and began to fight their way through a tenacious assembly of underbrush, grasping vines, and spearlike plants. Brimmer emptied his beer bottle and threw it away. Rogers could hear his heavy breathing as he thrashed along just ahead. Time passed as if forever had arrived, Rogers thought, and he remembered the same discouraging notion had struck him a few times during his service with the marines. By comparison, those days had been easy. Here he was floundering blindly through a jungle behind a drunk who proposed to take him for an airplane ride if they didn't get shot en route.

At last Brimmer came to a halt and said, "We should be just about even with the end of the strip now. We gotta move fast when we get there, and I'll need your help. We get to the airplane and I open the tail door and climb in. There are two wooden slabs on the elevators. Gust locks. You pull 'em off. The same for the main wheels. Pull them away. They gotta rope on 'em. Just yank. Stay away from the props because I'll be starting the engines. Run back and pull the wooden slabs off the ailerons, then jump in and close the door. We should have three or four minutes before they start shooting."

Rogers wiped the perspiration from his eyes. He was considerably relieved. "You sound sober."

"If I was I'd turn back right now."

"You really give a guy confidence."

The steady and monotonous exhaust sound of the generator had always annoyed the manager of Camp Four. It was located in a wooden shelter with a tin roof, and the sound reverberated off the metal like an endless series of cannon shots.

The manager rarely heard anything except the generator at night, which was one of the reasons he hated to run it in the daytime. A day keeping an eye on a crowd of *pisadores* was enough aggravation.

The manager usually eased his nightly frustration by listening to Radio Havana, which came in much more powerfully than Bogotá. And the communist bullshit sent out by the Cubans was always more amusing than Bogotá radio. Even the music was better.

This night the manager was listening to Cuban calypso and was drumming his fingers on his fat belly in time with the beat. Even as the music reached its peak, he realized that he was hearing a third sound intermixed with the generator exhaust. He recognized it as a commotion in the jungle. Hundreds of creatures were sounding a warning.

He ignored the sound for a moment, then decided it was very unusual. Were some of the *pisadores* trying to run away?

He sighed unhappily. Were his duties never done? He heaved his bulk out of his cane chair and waddled to the screen door. He listened carefully. The door squeaked as he opened it. He stepped out on the tiny porch that adorned his cement-block house. Definitely, definitely . . . something was going on down by the airstrip.

He heard the cranking of an airplane engine and shook his jowls in disbelief. Then he heard a backfire and an engine starting. That scoundrel Brimmer. Running off with a load on his own. It was bound to happen sooner or later.

He moved quickly for such a fat man. He rang the alarm bell that hung beside his door, and ran inside. He emerged almost immediately, armed with his own Uzi, and fired a burst over the FARC barracks. A light went on in the barracks. When he saw figures rushing out, he stopped ringing the alarm and aimed his Uzi toward the airstrip. He fired several bursts at an area where he knew the DC-3 had been tied down. Then, shouting at the FARCs, he started a fast waddle toward the airstrip.

As Rogers hoisted himself into the doorway of the DC-3, he heard gunfire and the whine of bullets overhead. He slammed the door and ran up the inclined deck to the cockpit. He heard Brimmer swearing at the top of his lungs. Both of his hands were busy reaching in the dark for switches, mixture controls, and the right throttle. "The fucking right engine won't start! I flooded it!" He pushed the throttle full forward and pulled off the mixture. He continued to hold down the starter switch while the right propeller revolved slowly. "Catch fire, you sonofabitch!"

Rogers thought the clanking and groaning from the engine sounded like one of the old gas combines back in Montana. Looking past Brimmer's head he saw the bright twinkle of automatic gunfire. "They're coming," he said as calmly as he could manage. "Even with an empty airplane I don't suppose there's a prayer we could get off with one engine?"

"I'm not that drunk. Start, you miserable bastard!"

Suddenly there was an explosion of flame outside the right window as the engine caught. The vibration shook the whole airplane vigorously. Brimmer eased back the throttle and opened the mixture. "Hallelujah!" Brimmer yelled. "Hold on to your balls, cowboy!"

Rogers almost lost his balance as Brimmer shoved the throttles forward without hesitation. The DC-3 began to move through the darkness and soon Brimmer pushed the stick forward. The tail came up and he yelled like a wild man. "She's gonna fly, cowboy! On cold engines! She's gonna fly right now!"

Rogers held his breath. Time was forever again. The DC-3 bounced through the darkness, weaving left and right as Brimmer tried to keep it on the strip.

"Giddyap, old girl! This is your last chance!"

Rogers heard a series of thuds just behind him and then a loud hissing. "We've been hit!"

Brimmer eased back on the stick and fed in a half-turn of elevator trim. Suddenly Rogers knew they were flying.

Moving instinctively in the dark cockpit, Brimmer reached down with his right hand, released the safety latch, and pulled up on the landing-gear handle. Over the roar of the big Pratt and Whitney engines and the wailing and whining of the hydraulic system as it retracted the landing gear, Brimmer yelled, "You say you're hit?"

"No. The airplane. There are holes behind me."

"Good for ventilation! Can you see anything?"

Rogers bent down so he could see forward. "It looks like there are trees coming up!"

Brimmer pulled back on the stick. The old DC-3 hesitated, shuddered as if with a chill, and in a moment Rogers called out with new enthusiasm in his voice, "I see stars!"

"Good! I can't see much of anything!"

"Why not?"

"I forgot my fucking glasses! Can't see too much without 'em!"

Brimmer laughed uproariously. He reached back and grabbed Rogers's arm. "We're flyin', man! Sit down and enjoy the ride!" He shoved Rogers into the right seat. "You be my eyes!"

Minutes later when Brimmer reduced power and there was much less noise in the cockpit, Rogers leaned toward him. "Where are we going?"

"Now that's a fair question." Brimmer reached above his head. He turned a rheostat and the cockpit lights glowed. He played with the light until the intensity was apparently as he wanted it. He leaned toward Rogers and the multiple folds of his face draped themselves into a smile. "Cowboy? I got a big investment in you. Would you settle for Washington, D.C.?"

Hours later, Rogers realized he must have been dozing. For it had all been black outside the cockpit windows, and now, very suddenly he saw a gray sea almost at eye level. Listening to the steady drumming of the DC-3's engines, he watched the ocean develop features; what had been an ill-defined mass gradually became large, roiling waves streaked with white foam. Their size made the DC-3 seem very small.

He looked at Brimmer, who sat motionless except for his hangdog jowls, which twitched occasionally. The crinkles, bags, pouches, crevasses, and knobs of his face were all assembled in what Rogers thought was total resignation. Brimmer's right eyelid drooped frequently to cover his pupil. From Rogers's position in the right seat, he could not see Brimmer's left eye. But they were flying so straight and level, he assumed Brimmer was not asleep. When no words passed between them for the better part of an hour, Rogers could no longer contain himself. "Where are we?" he asked.

Brimmer leaned slightly forward and squinted at the ocean as if he might find the answer placarded on the waves. He pressed his lips tightly together and snatched at the loose skin on his nose. "I dunno," he said finally. He glanced at the compass and reached to reset the gyro. "I dunno where we are, but I do know we have a problem. One of the little things I didn't tell you about. No sense in the two of us worryin'."

Rogers waited. Maybe Brimmer was just teasing; he seemed to be that sort of man. Yet now when he turned his head, his eyes were serious. He waggled a finger toward the left cockpit window. "Over there somewheres is the United States of America. Kind of hard to miss such a big hunk of land. Over there is the coast—maybe Georgia, maybe the Carolinas, or maybe even Virginia. I just don't know how far we are offshore."

"Can't we just turn that way and find out?"

"Not unless you want to tangle with hills, trees, television towers, and God knows what else. We have almost a one-hundred-foot ceiling out here and not too much rain. Hell, we can see for a mile or so between squalls. But inland? I have to bet it'll be right down on the ground."

Brimmer sighed heavily and, to Rogers's amazement, pushed himself up from his seat. He reached out and placed Rogers's hands on the controls. "You fly—it's past my bedtime," he said. "I'm going to take a leak and a nap. In that order."

"Hey! Hold on! I don't know how to fly an airplane!" The man is insane, Rogers thought as he instinctively squeezed the stick. "I'll kill us both!"

"No you won't. The old self-preservation instinct will take charge. Relax. Just remember when the waves get bigger, you pull back. When the waves get smaller, you push forward. Just a little bit each way. You'll catch on to it. And see that *N* on the compass? Keep it looking at you."

"It's bouncing around!"

"We all do when we have that much alcohol in us. Good luck." Brimmer stepped back toward the cabin, then returned. "We have one other problem you may want to share. Can you swim?"

"Yes."

"You may get the chance. Usually I top off the fuel tanks when departing north. This time refueling was sort of unhandy."

"Are you telling me we don't have enough?"

"Cowboy, you heard about a fart's chance in a windstorm? We stay down here where we don't have much head wind and maybe we make it. Up higher? No way." Brimmer smiled and disappeared into the cabin.

The drowsiness that had nearly overwhelmed Rogers vanished. He

268

was suddenly very wide awake. He smacked his dry lips and wiped the sweat from his palms. Keep your wits, man. And be gentle with an old mare.

He breathed deeply, trying to ease the tension that threatened to lock his muscles. "Ride herd on this thing," he whispered to himself. "Don't let it throw you now."

After a moment he tried to smile. How quickly he had forgotten that Brimmer was his benefactor! Sure, the man was nuts, but he had shown no signs of being suicidal.

Soon he found a wisp of confidence left in himself. The horizon rose and fell several times, but gradually the degree of inclination became less and less. Under any other circumstances he thought he might enjoy this. Keeping the compass N in place was difficult, but not impossible. By holding the course at right angles to the waves, he found the N stayed in place. Most of the time. God Almighty! Brimmer wasn't really going to take a nap—or was he?

He was so preoccupied with the controls, he had no idea how long Brimmer was absent. The seat beside him, he thought, was the emptiest area he had ever seen. Worn, torn, and abused leather, he thought, like Brimmer himself. A relic of another time.

Now there was much more intensity in the light reflected from the surging seas. Rogers was cheered, until his eyes found the fuel gauges. He had forgotten Brimmer's warning. Now he found it almost impossible to ignore the gauges. The damned things were hypnotizing.

Rain hissed against the forward windows and he tried to concentrate on the thousands of rivulets sliding across the glass and on what he could see of the fuzzy horizon beyond. Yet always his eyes came back to the gauges, and each time the movement of the indicators seemed accelerated.

He leaned to his left and shouted at the dark and noisy passageway to the cabin. "Brimmer! Hey, Brimmer!"

He waited. There was no response. Then he almost panicked. In turning to look back, he had inadvertently put the airplane in a climb. Suddenly he was in solid cloud.

"Brimmer!"

No answer.

He pushed down on the stick and there was the ocean again.

His attention focused on the two red levers he knew were the throttles. During the night he had watched Brimmer fiddling with them until he was satisfied that the power on the two engines was as he wanted it.

Rogers took a deep breath. Unless Brimmer was dead, there was one way to rouse him. He reached for the right red knob and pulled the lever backward. He was appalled at the resulting commotion. The smooth roar of the engines was replaced by a wild, unsynchronized beat. The airplane slewed to the right. The horizon was cocked at an angle. The compass spun. The *N* disappeared.

He was just reaching to push the red knob back into place beside the other when Brimmer knocked his hand away and made the adjustment himself. Almost immediately all was as it had been. Brimmer appeared more incensed than frightened. "Hey, cowboy! Did I tell you to tinker with the machinery? You wanna give me a coronary?"

"I want you up here where you damn well belong. Do those fuel gauges mean what they say?"

"Yup."

"Then we don't have very long?"

"Nope." Brimmer glanced at his watch and frowned. "About thirty minutes, I'd say. Maybe thirty-five."

"Then what?"

"We go for a swim. Unless . . ." Brimmer leaned forward until his ravaged nose was almost against the forward cockpit windows. He squinted at the rain-swept horizon. There was no audible sound to compete with the engines, but Rogers saw that his lips were pursed as if he were whistling. "Unless," he said at last, "this here is Chesapeake Bay. I kind of like the color of the water."

"I don't see any land."

Brimmer checked his watch again. He eased himself into the left seat and twisted knuckles into his weary eyes. "Of course I could be wrong. Easy. Easy to be wrong in this business when you don't have a chart of the area."

Brimmer paused and checked his watch again. He appeared to be deep in thought and made no attempt to take the controls.

Rogers listened to the constant whirring sound as the slipstream passed over the bullet holes behind Brimmer's seat. He longed for Brimmer to take over the controls, but he was damned if he would ask him.

He found the *N* and managed to keep it reasonably steady. And he thought that if he survived this new day, he would never forget a man named Brimmer.

He glanced at Brimmer just long enough to catch him yawning, which he found somehow reassuring. Then he heard him say in his hound-dog voice, "Cowboy? One of the things you learn quick in the smugglin' profession is never trust anyone or anything. Now this old pelican did some serious calculatin' a while ago when he shoulda been sleepin', and we may pass a miracle. . . ."

Brimmer paused and looked down at the sea. "Yessir. I sure like the color of the water. If this isn't Lake Michigan, it's got to be Chesapeake Bay. All we have to do is wait a little while to find out which one it is."

Although Mort Steiner knew almost nothing about the military mission to Colombia, his usual informants had cued him on certain possibilities. And from where he stood in the state of Montana's congressional office, he knew there was going to have to be some gigantic unraveling of plans. For several moments he had been so exhilarated he found it impossible to think clearly.

The boss was waiting for a taxi at the old College Park Airport in Maryland. It had been his voice on the telephone, no question. The same easygoing quality. The same lack of strain—sounding as if he had just finished breakfast with his family and would be a few minutes late arriving at the office.

"I only have eight dollars, so would you please meet me down in front of the building and help me pay off the driver?"

Dear God, what a man! Steiner shook his head in wonder and shouted the news to his staff even as he was calling the White House. His friend there put him through to the president's military aide, whose tone was suspicious. "Sir, are you certain it was Congressman Rogers?"

"I guarantee you no other man would be thinking about taxi fare."

"If it's really him, I'm sure the president would want to send a car—"

"Too late. He's already on his way."

"What was your name again, sir?"

"Steiner, goddammit. And I have a strong feeling the president would like to hear about this immediately."

"If you'll give me your number, someone in this office will get back to you, sir, if necessary."

Steiner gave him the number, chided himself for loss of patience, and hung up the phone. He dialed the number he had for the Mills estate in Virginia. He could hardly wait to hear Lily Rogers's voice.

It rained in Washington on the twenty-fourth of March, but the meteorological gloom that blanketed the capital seemed to have little effect on the members of Congress who attended a combined session of the House and Senate.

It was Skip Donovan's idea, and in a rare gesture of cooperation he had gained the hearty approval of both the vice president and the president. "We have a perfect catalyst in the cowboy and I believe we should take advantage of it," he argued. "I've discussed it with him. He will not make a formal address, but he'll say a few words and I'm convinced that will be enough to inspire the whole of Congress. For once we can all get together and get something done about our drug problem. I believe everybody will stop shilly-shallying and put some real force behind those DEA people who've been fighting their own Alamo for years."

As Donovan looked down upon the joint session of Congress from his seat beside the vice president, his political nose caught the mood of the rows of faces. The applause when Lee Rogers strode to the podium was just as Donovan had hoped and prayed it would be— long and thunderous. Now, Donovan knew, was the time to seize upon such unity and substitute action for talk.

Lee Rogers waited for the applause to subside. His embarrassment at such a wild tribute caused his cheeks to turn crimson. He tried not to notice that every person in the room was standing, including those in the balcony directly opposite. There in the front

row were Lily and Fay and R.R., all smiling. And beside them
Mort Steiner, Alice Morgan, and the rest of the office staff. He
wanted to yell up at them and ask who was minding the store.
Nearby he saw Tracy Delano smiling and applauding with Rebecca
Hawkins. For a moment he thought about Jack. The one face that
should be present was missing.

When the applause finally subsided and all had seated themselves,
there followed the usual throat clearings and soft exchanges of conversation. Then there was an expectant silence, broken only by a
feeble squawking as Rogers brought his hand to his face and inadvertently struck the microphone. He took a deep breath and said, "I
am honored. And I am proud. I don't know how to make speeches
and when my term is done I'll go home and stay there, so you won't
have to listen to me again. I am here and happily rejoined with my
wife and children because of one man's courage. He is pilot Oscar
Brimmer, whose flying skill is unique. I had hoped to present him
to you, but he is indisposed. . . ."

Rogers tried to drive away the vision of Brimmer as he had last
seen him only an hour ago. Brimmer had also been invited to stay
at the Mills place in Virginia until things calmed down. Unfortunately, on this very morning he had found his way to the Millses'
extensive cellar and immediately launched his own wine festival. He
was roaring drunk by the time they were due to leave for the capital.
"Me?" he yelled at the sopping Virginia landscape, "associate with
a bunch of politicians? I got better shense!"

His resolution was compounded when he saw the marine helicopter sent by the president to ferry the party. "Me? Get in one of those
whirligigs? Never!"

Regretfully, they were obliged to leave without him.

Rogers took a moment to gather his breath. All the statistics on
the narcotics situation worldwide were easily available, he told his
colleagues. "What is not so easily apparent is the cruelty and agony
and grief endured by this country for much too long a time. Yes, I
am a warmonger. And I am firmly convinced that if we really do go
to war against this problem, it will be the only war with a true
reward. If we win, the rest of the world may even thank us for a

change, because their children are also at high risk. So let's go to it, all together and all out."

Rogers glanced up at the balcony and smiled. He looked back at the assembly of faces before him and said, "Thank you, ladies and gentlemen of the Congress."

How you doin' there, businessman? I hear you got busted las' week. Shit. Forget it. You be back on the job soon. Me, Panama boy. I got memories, amigo. Take in the sixties. Oh, they was rough then. Put you away a long time. We almos' outta business.

But not to worry. Because you got rights, understan'? What the man calls the Levi Guidelines. Like say they wanna raid some rock house—say some Puerto Ricans in business here in this safe house, understan'? They gotta prove you doin' it before they go in, understan'? The man say, Hey, amigo, you wanna spy on Americans? No, no, amigo. You can't fuck with civil liberty, understan'? The man gotta be very careful about it, so you just go about your business an' don' forget it, like this time. Next time you be more careful than they be and don' spit in their eye when they pass by, understan'? Be cool.

Now's not bad at all. You be back on the street soon. Maybe you think about Oregon where they be maybe twenny, maybe thirty thousand marijuana growers and only about twenny narcs. I mean, they got no chance, understan'?

They organized out there. They take a little Forest Service land and put punji sticks around, understan'? Then they grow and grow and who gets in the way gets blown away, understan'? But that not our business. We got much better for you, amigo. You young. They don' do too much to you. Afraid, man. Afraid you be locked up with bad influence, understan'?

You hear big numbers on sinsemilla. Two thousand bucks per plant, say the big mouths. Fuck 'um. Growers got risk, understan'? We move. We circulate. We wheel and deal. Businessmen, understan'? We don' have to poke around and find out if da plant be male or female so we can grow the right product, understan'? We got it from start-up, amigo. Like you take oil comes from the earth, you gotta refine and fuck around with it before you can put it inna car. Jerks do that. You sell, man. Nobody from da feds come put paraquat on your product and ruin your hard work. No problems. You get out from the joint, you a businessman. Same as before. I'm your angel, man.

Same as it always be.